Second
Chances

SCEPTRE

Second Chances

ZITA ADAMSON

SCEPTRE

Copyright © 1997 Zita Adamson

First published in 1997 by Hodder and Stoughton
A division of Hodder Headline PLC
A Sceptre book

10 9 8 7 6 5 4 3 2 1

A CIP catalogue record for this book is available
from the British Library

ISBN 0 340 68941 2

Typeset by Palimpsest Book Production Limited,
Polmont, Stirlingshire
Printed and bound in Great Britain by
Mackays of Chatham PLC, Chatham, Kent

Hodder and Stoughton
A division of Hodder Headline PLC
338 Euston Road
London NW1 3BH

For Aunty Hilda

An old woman and a young girl were sitting outside. It was hot but where they were sitting, under the shade of the copper beech tree at the end of the garden, it was cool. They had been playing cards but now they were doing nothing; just sitting, just the two of them while the leaves above made patterns on their faces.

'Tell me again, Gran. Tell me again how it happened. How you became famous. Why they made a statue of you.'

The old woman looked sideways at her granddaughter – at the lips stained red with strawberry juice, the sunburnt cheeks, the bright, hopeful, expectant eyes.

'Please! I won't fidget. I'll sit very still.'

The old woman smiled.

'All right then. Pour me another glass of lemonade, though, before I start. It's a long story. I don't want to get hoarse.'

The young girl stood up, lifted the jug with the swirly green glaze and poured her grandmother a drink, carefully, letting the ice out one by one so that it clunk clunked against the bottom of the glass.

'There you are.'

'Thank you.'

The old woman took a sip of the drink then put the glass on the table and leant back in her chair.

'It all started a long time ago when I was a young girl . . .'

'As young as me?'

'No, not quite. I was about twenty.'

'But that's old,' protested the young girl.

'Well, maybe. Anyhow, young or old, there I was. It was summertime – about the same time as it is now. I had just left

1 •

university and I didn't know what to do with my life. So, while I made up my mind, I found a job in an old people's home. I met a woman there, an old woman – you'd probably call her a very old woman – and we became friends. She told me about her life and it made a big impression on me. That's how it started. I didn't realise at the time. But later, looking back, I saw that none of it would have happened without her, that she was the turning point, the catalyst . . .

Another, younger, woman appeared at the top of the garden and began calling.

'It's your teatime, darling,' said the old woman. 'Go on, don't let it get cold.'

'But I want to listen to your story.'

'The story will wait,' said the old woman. 'So will I. We'll both wait.'

'And besides, it's only sausages and beans,' muttered the young girl as she rose and began to walk towards the house. 'I don't even like them very much.'

The old woman leant back in her chair again and looked up – at the branches, moving now in a small breeze, the dark almost purplish-black leaves, and beyond them, the sky, the clear blue endlessness of it.

She closed her eyes and thought of another summer afternoon, more than fifty years ago now, and as she did, she smiled. Soon, like a baby, she had slipped into sleep.

2

The sun was just beginning to touch the still-life picture. That meant it was three o'clock. At four it would reach her chair. At five it would be at the fireplace playing hide and seek in the coal scuttle.

Claire Harper had never thought she would measure her days by the passage of sun through a room's furniture. But then she had never thought she would live in an old people's home.

That was one of the main things that had worried her when she had come to The Pines three years ago – that as her physical agility shrank, so too would her mind, that meal times would take on an undue significance, her bones become more important than the situation in Eastern Europe. She did not want to become a sour old woman who complained about the consistency of the gravy at lunch.

She had taken steps to prevent this. That was why now, for example, she was reading the business and finance section in *The Times*. Not because she wanted to, but because it helped sharpen her mind. She read the foreign pages too. All of them. Not just the interesting articles like the one about the unrest in Singapore following the hanging of a Filipino maid or the feature about American bounty-hunters, but the boring ones too. The ones about state visits and elections and what one politician had said to another.

The only page she did not read was the obituary page. When she was young and had known with a burning certainty that one day she would change the world she had loved reading this page. She had marvelled at the ingenuity of mankind. The fortitude. The fire. Now, though, now that she was old and knew with equal certainty that she had not changed the world and would not, she found it upsetting. The contrast between the lives of those written about and her own life was too stark, too pointed, too easy an invitation to regret.

Instead, she learnt poems. One a day. Not necessarily long poems or even poems she liked – she chose them at random from Palgrave's *Golden Treasury*. The learning was not an aesthetic exercise but a disciplinary one, a means of testing her memory and concentration, a mental warm-up before she tackled the crossword.

Today, though, she still had two more business pages to read before she chose a poem. And, whether it was the warmth of the afternoon sun or the article she was reading – a particularly turgid piece on foreign exchange markets – she felt drowsy. The French windows were open and every so often the sound of laughter from some of the other residents sitting outside in the garden drifted in together with the scent of roses and yesterday's lawn clippings.

Something in the laughter, the tone, the restraint of it, reminded her of a garden party her mother had once held. Her father had been a vicar and the party had been one of many her mother had been obliged to give to thank parishioners for their charity. On this occasion, the party had been for those on the flower-arranging rota and the guests were consequently all female.

She had been about five, she remembered, a small child with springy black hair and a passion for cars and catapults. She had been playing quite happily by herself away from the tinkly voices and the carefully arranged ankles and elbows when her mother, unwisely giving way to a rare urge to show off her daughter, had summoned her to hand round refreshments.

'Go and ask Miss Reeves if she'd like a piece of fruit cake,' she said. Claire, annoyed at being dragged away from her play, took the plate reluctantly.

Miss Reeves was sitting slightly apart from the rest of the group talking to Mrs Maitland, the church organist.

'Would you like a piece of fruit cake, Miss Reeves?' she asked.

Miss Reeves shook her head and said, quite clearly: 'No thank you, dear.'

'Here you are,' said Claire, handing her a very large piece.

'No . . . really . . .'

'Yes, you do,' said Claire, pushing the cake down.

'Claire, what on earth are you doing? Miss Reeves said, "No",' said her mother, rushing up and trying to take the plate.

'She said, "Yes". She said, "Yes",' insisted Claire.

A struggle followed, the plate slipped, and the cake tumbled to the ground, some of it rolling into the flower beds among the hollyhocks and night-scented stock. Her mother slapped the backs of her legs and she ran off crying to the end of the garden where she flung herself on the grass.

'I'm sorry . . . I'm ever so sorry . . . I don't know why she's like that,' apologised her mother, brushing the crumbs off Miss Reeves' lap.

'She's so contrary sometimes. So headstrong. She'll ask you the name of something and then, as soon as you tell her, she'll say it's called something else. The other day I told her not to go into the kitchen because the floor had just been washed and it was slippery. 'No, it's not,' she said. And in she ran and over she fell.'

The other women shook their heads sympathetically but not quite vigorously enough to make her feel free of all blame for her daughter's bad behaviour.

Later, that evening, after her bath, her mother gave her a talk.

'You knew Miss Reeves didn't want any cake, didn't you?'

Claire said nothing. Just drew up her bottom lip and stared.

'You did, didn't you?'

Claire thrust out her chin.

'I don't want that kind of thing to happen again. You mustn't say things are one thing if you know they are another. It's naughty. Do you understand?'

Looking back, Claire could not help marvelling at her obstinacy, the rootlessness of it. She smiled. The memory of that day was so clear. She could even remember the dress she had worn. And the game she had been playing. She had been burying marbles. The yellow one and the large clear one with pink spots. Covering them with petals.

She was so wrapped up in the memory she did not see the

door open or two people come in or anything at all until she felt something touch her arm.

It was Matron, Matron with a man, a tall man, a stranger. They were both standing looking down at her. She felt foolish and vulnerable as though caught talking to herself.

'I'm sorry . . . I didn't mean to startle you. You were miles away,' said Matron.

She struggled to her feet. There. That was better. She felt less exposed now.

'I wanted to introduce you to our new resident, Mr Mansley. Mr Mansley, this is Mrs Harper. She's been with us . . . oh, about three years. Is that right?' asked Matron.

Claire nodded.

'If you don't mind, Mr Mansley, I must just make a phone call. Tea is at four in the dining room. I'm sure Mrs Harper will show you if you can't remember the way.'

Left alone, they stood awkwardly for a moment until Mr Mansley indicated with a movement of his hand that they should sit down.

'I'm sorry . . . I'm interrupting you. You were reading.'

He pointed at the paper, spread open on the sloping reading tray bought from a mail order company which specialised in equipment for the disabled.

'No, not really. I'd almost finished.'

'I'm afraid I usually skip the business pages. I find them a bit dull myself,' he continued.

'Yes . . . well . . . I don't always read them myself.'

How could she say that she only read them because she didn't want to read them? It would sound odd. Maybe it was odd.

'I'm Peter, by the way. Peter Mansley.'

'I'm Claire. Claire with an "i".'

They smiled. He had nice teeth, she noticed. Straight, and almost certainly his own. Unconsciously, she felt with her tongue for the edges of her plate.

'Have you come from far?' she asked.

'Sussex,' he replied. 'Haywards Heath, to be precise. I commuted. I used to work in the City.'

'What made you choose to come here?'

'The space,' he said, smiling again, only this time it was more like a grin, a warm confiding grin.

'The wide open space. The castles, the sea, the history, the look of the land, the light, particularly the light. Also, I used to live here. Or near here. My father was a headmaster at Berwick. I went to school there.

'I suppose I shouldn't have let a thing like space influence me,' he added, almost more to himself than to her. 'After all, in a few years' time I probably won't be able to get out to enjoy it. But I needed a change. I wanted to be able to drive without seeing a supermarket or DIY store or drive-through fast food place. And my son lives abroad so that didn't come into it. Above all, I suppose, I didn't want to end up in Eastbourne.'

He paused then said: 'How about you? Do you come from round here?'

'No,' she said. 'No. In fact, I'd never been here in my life. I was living in London and like you I wanted a change. I chose Northumbria at random. Well, almost. I read about it somewhere. It sounded romantic and, as you say, full of history. I thought it would be a good place to . . . well, you know, a good place to live.'

'And die,' he added, picking up on the word she had been about to say but had dropped.

'Yes. And that too,' she agreed.

There was an awkward silence broken finally by the sound of laughter in the garden.

'I think maybe I'll take a quick walk before tea,' he said, standing up. 'There's a Japanese water garden, if I remember rightly. And a conservatory. Or was that at one of the other places I looked around?'

'No, you're right. There is a conservatory. I was there only this morning. The camellias are wonderful.'

She stood up too.

'I would offer to show you only I've already been for quite a long walk today and I'm feeling a bit stiff.'

'Don't worry, I'll be fine. I'll just have a quick look and then start my unpacking.'

'I think maybe some of the others are playing cards on the

terrace. Would you like me to come and introduce you? I can manage the terrace.'

'No, it's OK. I'll just pretend I'm a gardener. An old new gardener.'

They both laughed.

Alone again, Claire noticed that her tights were all wrinkled at the ankles and scowled. Her legs had grown so thin it was difficult to make any tights stay up, even the smallest size. Suddenly, she felt very cross with herself. Cross and old and ugly and itchy with heat. She picked up a phone on the table next to her, pressed some buttons and spoke into the mouthpiece.

'Oh, hello, Iris, it's Mrs Harper. Could you bring me a glass of still lemonade with ice? I'm in the yellow drawing room.'

She chose a ballad to punish herself for minding about her ankles. It was long and also she disliked ballads.

Outside, in the corridor, a young girl carrying folded blue check tea towels, stopped and glanced through the window at the top of the door. Another girl, carrying a glass of lemonade on a tray, came up behind and also looked through.

'Isn't it terrible?' said the girl with the tea towels. 'What some people have to go through. The hand life deals them.'

'Why, what about her life? What's been so wrong with it?' asked the other girl.

'Just about everything. You should ask her one day. She's a good talker once she gets going.'

Beyond the door, Claire memorised Walter Scott and remembered her mother. There was nothing wrong with her memory, she reflected. If anything, it was too sharp.

3

Claire could not remember the third line of the fifth verse. That troubled her. Normally, by evening, she was word perfect, however long the poem.

A member of staff came round with menus for the following day and she ticked kippers for breakfast and cannelloni for lunch.

That was one of the things that had attracted her to The Pines when she had been looking for somewhere to live. The amount of choice. The graciousness. The feeling that you were in a hotel rather than a home for people no longer able to cook and wash and clean for themselves.

Ironically, for the first time in her life, by a twist of fate that made her smile even now, money had been no object. And so she had looked for somewhere that would gladden her eyes if not her heart, somewhere with fresh flowers on the tables and a garden, a drawing room rather than a TV lounge. The Pines had offered all these and more – a library, billiard room, en-suite bedrooms and a kitchen on every floor. The carpets were thick, the furniture an elegant blend of antique and modern, the decor thoughtful – cheerful yellow in the drawing room, warm red in the dining room and cool blue in the bedrooms. Outside, there were gravelled paths and lawns, a rose garden, herb garden and water garden. Beyond them was the vegetable garden and beyond that a paddock with a goat and sometimes a donkey. There were concerts in the conservatory, visits by aromatherapists, a programme of talks and films and slide shows.

It was expensive, very expensive, but Claire had worked out

that she could afford to live there until she was ninety-five, an age which, according to her doctor, she was unlikely to reach.

A burst of laughter made her raise her head. Phyllis, the major's wife, was regaling a small group the other side of the room with a story of mistaken identity at the hairdresser's that morning. She noticed that Peter, the new resident, was among the group.

For some reason, she always thought of Phyllis as 'the major's wife', partly because it was the first piece of personal information Phyllis had volunteered, and partly because she looked so much like a soldier with her shiny shoes and red band-box jackets. She was wearing one of these jackets tonight, a particularly stylish one nipped in at the waist to show off her bust. Her hair, newly tinted and styled, gleamed like waves in moonlight.

Without realising it, Claire found herself feeling her own hair. It was her best feature – still thick and wavy and a lovely pure white. But it was also, as it always had been, and as her mother had always pointed out, totally unmanageable. She wore it to her shoulders now, restrained by a black Alice-in-Wonderland band, the only style she felt comfortable with and could manage on her own. She knew that most women her age had shorter, neater, trimmer styles and that Alice bands were worn by little girls in party frocks but she did not care. Tonight, though, she felt ridiculous and pulled savagely at the band, tearing it from her head.

There was another burst of laughter from across the room. Clearly, it was an amusing story. Claire tried to say the fifth verse again, faltered at the third line, looked down at the book and then snapped it shut with the page-turning tongs Catherine had bought her as a leaving present.

She missed Catherine. A brisk, witty woman, she had worked as Keeper of the Oriental Gallery in the Tower of London until failing eyesight had forced her to retire early. She had come to The Pines three months after Claire, by then almost blind, and the two women had become friends. She had been the only one able to put Phyllis in her place, the only one who shared Claire's love of books, the only good friend, in fact, that Claire had had there. If she were here now, thought Claire, she would tell me that Phyllis needs to tint her hair so that it doesn't look yellow.

We would gossip about Peter and talk about what we were going to do tomorrow. I would not feel lonely.

Catherine had left The Pines nine months before to live with her daughter in Oxford. She wrote at least once a week, usually in the form of a tape, but it was too far to visit often.

Her departure meant Claire had no one to confide in. It was not that she disliked the other residents. She did like them – or at least most of them. But there was no intuitive bond, no flying of sparks, no shared outlook. No one interested her in the way that Catherine had done, or made her laugh, or knew, without telling, when she felt down. And Claire had learnt that, this being so, it was best to keep a certain distance. To be polite but not too open. After all, The Pines was not, despite its appearance, a hotel. The other residents would still be there the next week and the week after that and the week after that. It was important not to make an enemy or give away too much. One didn't want to be vulnerable.

She was conscious of a light touch on her arm. Peter, the new resident, was standing by her chair.

'We're going to play cards. Would you like to join us?' he asked, pointing at the group near the window, now sitting down round a table.

'Oh! No. I . . . I . . . I can't. I'm afraid I . . . I . . . I . . .' she stuttered.

It was his height. All the other male residents were so small and shrivelled. She had forgotten men could be so tall.

'It's my hands. They're not very good at holding things. Particularly something like cards. I'd probably drop them all over the place.'

She held them up and he glanced down at the fingers, once so slender but now more like clumps of root ginger.

'Horrible, aren't they?' she said.

'I'm sorry, I didn't . . .'

'It's OK,' she interrupted, sensing his embarrassment. 'I don't like playing cards anyhow.'

'I'll let you get back to your reading then. Sorry about the mix-up.' He smiled, quickly and perfunctorily, a social smile, and rejoined the group at the table.

What do you mean, 'mix-up', thought Claire? Catherine would

have liked that. The euphemism of it. The maleness. We would have had a good laugh about it.

She noticed that Phyllis was shuffling the cards, her red finger nails moving in and out of them like snakes' tongues, and was suffused with sudden hate.

'Are you cold?' asked Janet, coming up behind her and sitting down in the chair to her left.

Janet was a former librarian and looked like one. A nervous, giggly woman with a fringe and a liking for baggy cardigans, she was harmless but irritating.

'No, why?' asked Claire.

'You were shivering, that's all.'

'Well I'm not cold. Hot, if anything.'

'I've asked for some Horlicks. Would you like me to order some for you too?'

'No thanks,' said Claire, aware that she was being unnecessarily curt but too distracted to care.

A few minutes later Iris brought in the Horlicks.

'Are you ready?' she said, turning to Claire. 'It doesn't matter if you're not. I can ask someone else to do you later. It's just that I'm going in about half an hour and I haven't got much to do until then.'

'No, I'm ready now,' said Claire.

'Are you sure? You're not just saying that, are you? I don't want you to feel you've got to go now.'

'No, really. I'm feeling tired. I was going to ring for someone anyway.'

She said goodnight to Janet and allowed herself to be led out of the drawing room and up the stairs to her bedroom.

Iris moved to the window to close the curtains.

'No, don't close them. I don't like to close them while it's still light,' said Claire.

'Don't you? Nor do I.' said Iris. 'In fact, in the summer I don't like closing them at all. I like to wake up with the light all around me. Quintin hates it though. He says he can't sleep.'

'Quintin's your boyfriend?'

'Yes. I'm living with him at the moment. At his parents' house. They've got a farm near here. Just outside Shilbottle.'

Iris slipped off Claire's shoes and tights and started unbuttoning her dress.

'Do you want your slip on or off?' she asked.

'Off, I think, please. It's so hot, isn't it?'

She had given up wearing a bra about six months ago after finally reconciling herself to the fact that her breasts, always small, were now so small as to no longer require support.

Iris fetched her nightdress and Claire held up her arms obediently.

'What does Quintin do?' she asked.

'He writes music.'

'What sort of music?'

'Not your sort.'

Claire raised her eyebrows and Iris, noticing, added: 'Or mine either. It's very loud and angry. There aren't any tunes or anything.'

She picked up the hairbrush and brushed Claire's hair then slid her hands down her neck and massaged the top of her spine.

'There. Is that better?'

Claire nodded, realising for the first time how tightly she had been holding herself.

Iris went over to the sink and squeezed a blob of toothpaste onto the toothbrush.

'How about you?' said Claire.

'How do you mean?'

'Well, this is just a holiday job, isn't it?'

'Yes, I suppose so. I've just graduated. At least I hope I have. We haven't had the results yet.'

'What did you do?'

'French and Spanish. I was at London. King's College. Quintin was too only he dropped out at the end of the first year. That was how we met. We were both in the same French set.'

'And what are you going to do now?'

'I don't know really,' said Iris, filling a glass half full of water. 'That's why I took this job. So that I could think things through without my parents badgering me to get a real job. Quintin wants me to go round the world with him. I've just inherited some money so I could afford it but I don't know . . . it's not that I don't like travelling, I do, but I like to have a purpose. It

all seems a bit aimless drifting from one place to another just so
you can say you've been there. I'm not sure I would enjoy it.'

She held out the toothbrush.

'Do you want to do it tonight, or shall I?'

'I think you better,' said Claire. 'The last time I did it, the
toothpaste ended up on my chin instead of my teeth.'

Iris brushed her teeth, handed her the glass of water so that
she could swill her mouth and then glanced at her watch.

'Right then. I'd better be off unless there's anything else you
need. Quintin's picking me up in ten minutes and I've got to get
changed first.'

'Are you going out?'

'Yes. We're going for a meal in Newcastle and then on to a
club. There's a group on tonight that Quintin wants to hear.
He's a singer too, you see, and apparently this group's singer
might be leaving.'

Claire switched on the bedside lamp and climbed into bed.
The sheets, she noticed, were new – pale blue with mauve
forget-me-nots.

'Is there anything else you'd like?'

'No, no, off you go. You don't want to keep him waiting.'

After Iris had left, Claire switched off the lamp and climbed out
of bed. There was a full moon and with the curtains open, the
room was still very light. She leant out of the window, mulling
over the day. It had started when she noticed her tights were
wrinkled, she decided. That was when she had begun to feel
grumpy.

A car roared up the driveway and skidded to a halt. The driver
jumped out, looked around, then leant possessively against the
car bonnet. It was a young man, Claire saw, a young man
wearing jeans, sunglasses and a clinging white T-shirt which
showed off the muscles in his arms. It was probably Quintin,
she realised, the boyfriend Iris had been talking about, and
she waited with interest. Sure enough, after a few minutes,
Iris appeared. Her hair, which a few minutes before, had been
tied back in a ponytail, was now loose, and she was wearing
a stretchy black mini skirt instead of the blue and white check
dress worn by staff at The Pines.

They kissed and Claire drew back, wary of being seen. Then

they both jumped into the car. There was a blare of music as a radio or tape recorder was turned on. The doors slammed, the engine started and the car moved off. Claire followed the headlights until they disappeared from view, picturing them in the restaurant – the bright lights, the noise, the glances that their youth and beauty would inevitably attract.

She turned and very slowly climbed back into her bed. She still could not remember the third line of the fifth verse.

4

Claire took Catherine's letter to read in the conservatory. She found that by doing this, moving around from room to room, from the library to the drawing room to the sitting room, she minimised the impression of restriction on those days when, like today, her leg was playing up.

It was another scorcher. The gardeners were already busy adjusting hoses and sprinklers before it became too hot to water. Someone – it looked like Iris – was hanging out sheets to dry on the washing line outside the laundry. Phyllis, immaculate in white slacks, a red and navy striped top, and red sandals, was playing croquet on the lawn.

'Hellooo,' she called, waving her mallet in Claire's direction.

Claire waved back but continued walking. She did not want to talk to Phyllis, mainly because she was afraid she would say something unpleasant. She had not forgotten the sight of those red finger nails flickering among the cards.

It was warm inside the conservatory, so warm that she stopped for a moment to readjust to the temperature. It reminded her of the first time she had been abroad. She had left London on a miserable drizzly afternoon in July. When she arrived in Rome it was dark. And yet, when she stepped outside, it was so balmy that she thought at first there must have been some mistake, that she had caught the wrong plane and was in Singapore or Malaysia or some other tropical destination.

She pressed the switch which turned on the fountain and sat down on her favourite bench at the far end where she was hidden from view. That was one of the things she liked best about the conservatory. The huge camellia bushes were so dense and leafy that four or five people could sit there, each without knowing that the others were there, and, if the fountain was on, without overhearing anything either.

She pulled the letter out of the envelope which, as usual, had already been opened for her. The handwriting was unfamiliar. Usually Catherine dictated letters to her daughter, Ella, if she did not feel like sending a tape. Maybe it was the new home help she had talked about in her last letter.

'I may be getting a guide dog,' wrote Catherine. 'I know I've always said before that I don't want one but Ella's persuaded me that it might be a good idea.'

She went on to describe the open-air performance of *Twelfth Night* she had been to at Magdalen College; the walkie-talkie her grandson, Luke, had made out of an egg box and milk bottle tops; the funny things he was saying now that he was beginning to talk properly.

'And I've joined a book club as well,' she wrote. 'It's amazing how many books you can get on tape nowadays. Every month we read a different book and then meet to discuss it. It's ever so interesting. You'd love it. Of course, we usually end up talking about ourselves as well as the books so it's very social as well. I've made two good friends through it.'

Claire put the letter down. The busy days described by Catherine made her wonder, not for the first time, whether she had been right to choose to live in a town as small and remote as Alnwick. It was not so bad now, during the summer. The holidaymakers lent the town a bustling air even when it was raining. Then there was the international music festival in a few weeks' time, the fair in the castle grounds, and numerous cream teas, church fêtes and open garden days. But in the winter it could be very bleak. The castle was closed, the library so tiny that she had long ago exhausted its shelves, and the streets empty except on market day. Several of the café and restaurant owners shut up altogether. The affluent spent the winter in their timeshare villas in Spain or Portugal, the less well-off took temporary shop or factory jobs in Gateshead or Newcastle. Maybe she should have chosen somewhere like Bath or Chester, she thought. They were busy all the year round. She could have gone to concerts there. Maybe even joined a book club like Catherine.

The sound of footsteps made her start. Someone else had come into the conservatory. She turned round and peered through the foliage surrounding her seat. She could just make out a figure settling into a bench in front of the fountain. It was a man but his back was turned so she could not tell who it was. Then the figure moved and she saw that it was the new resident, Peter.

Immediately, Claire felt flustered. If she went out now, he would see her and probably say something and, for some reason, after last night, she did not want to talk to him. But if she stayed, he might walk around after a bit and come across her and think she was spying on him. She twisted a lock of hair round the middle finger on her left hand, something she often did when nervous. In the end, she decided to stay where she was. He would probably go out after a few minutes, she thought. After all, it was very warm. Too warm almost.

The fountain stopped. It did this automatically after fifteen minutes to save unnecessary waste of power. Claire waited for Peter to switch it back on but he didn't. She realised that he probably didn't know about the switch. It had been a few weeks after her arrival before anyone had pointed it out to her.

It was very quiet without the sound of running water and she became worried that Peter would hear her. She could hear him clearly. First rustling something, then sighing, then clearing his throat. Then there was silence. She waited, not wanting to move in case she made a noise. Finally, curious to know what he was doing, she turned round again, this time very slowly, and parted the leaves. He was sitting holding his head in his hands, massaging his temples.

As she watched, he flung back his head, stretched his arms, yawned and stood up. She drew back hurriedly and picked up Catherine's letter, pretending to read it. He was coming her way. He must have heard her.

'Oh . . . hallo, I didn't know anyone else was here.'

She looked up, feigning surprise. He too was holding an envelope, she saw.

'I see you had the same idea,' he said, pointing at the letter in her hand. 'I hope I'm not disturbing you. I thought I'd have a look round, do a bit of exploring.'

'No, no, I'd just finished. Don't worry.'

He sat down on the bench opposite.

'It's from someone who used to live here,' she said, indicating Catherine's letter. 'She left nine months ago to live with her daughter.'

'Mine's from my son,' he said. 'He's sent me some coffee beans.'

'Coffee beans?'

'Yes, he deals in them. Buys and sells them. Look.'

He put a hand into the envelope and pulled out something. 'Smell them.'

He leant across with cupped hand, holding the beans up to her face.

'It's better if you rub them,' he said, doing so as he spoke. 'They're like garlic. They don't smell much until they're crushed. Here, smell them again.'

His hand was so close that she could smell the soap on it behind the coffee, see the ragged cuticle on his middle finger. The fingers were long and tanned – strong, capable looking fingers.

'They're from an island somewhere. I can't make out the name. Apparently, he's just bought the rights to the entire crop.'

He sat back. She was aware once more how tall he was and how small and thin she was in comparison. His legs almost reached hers without trying. Hers barely touched the ground.

'How about you? Do you have any children?' he asked.

'I did,' she said. 'I had a son. He's dead now though.'

His mouth shut like a door in the wind. She watched him, familiar now with the reactions – the embarrassment, pity, curiosity and fear – wondering which ones he would show.

'I'm sorry,' he said finally. 'I seem to be making a habit of this. Putting my foot in it.'

'You didn't put your foot in it,' she said firmly. She hated humbug. 'It happened a long time ago now. It no longer makes me cry.'

There was a long pause. Both studied their hands.

'Is that why you're here?' he said. 'Because of your hands?'

'Yes. I had a couple of strokes as well. The first was very minor but the second paralysed my left side. The leg is still a bit dodgy. But it was the hands really.'

She opened and shut them, then laughed lightly.

'I couldn't undo things. You know, buttons, laces, bottle tops. Then I started dropping things. Heavy, awkward things at first. Then light things as well. I just couldn't grip things any longer. I burnt myself twice and cut myself. The burns were so bad I had to go into hospital. But I still kept on insisting I could look after myself. What did it was when I locked myself out.'

'What?'

'Yes, I know. It sounds ridiculous, doesn't it? I didn't lose the key or anything. I had the key but I couldn't turn it. I asked a passer-by to help me. He looked nice enough but as soon as he'd opened the door he pushed his way in after me and started hitting me. I didn't keep money in the house but he wouldn't believe me. He turned the house upside down looking for it. Then he ripped the phone out so I couldn't ring for help. My home help found me the next day. It turned out I'd broken one of my legs and dislocated the hip on the other. That was why I couldn't move.'

Peter looked shocked.

'Yes, at the time it was terrible. More because of the shock than anything else. But, looking back, I think he probably did me a favour. If it wasn't for him, I might still be there, living off yoghurt and biscuits, unable to take my own blouse off if I spilt something on it. And, if I was there, then I wouldn't be here, sitting among these wonderful flowers.'

She leant back and buried her nose in one of the camellia blossoms.

'Well, yes, I suppose so,' said Peter doubtfully.

'Why are you here?' she asked. She felt bolder now, less daunted by his height. It was often like that, she thought. By exposing yourself, making yourself vulnerable, you became stronger, more confident.

'I had a couple of strokes like you,' he said. 'Neither was serious but they made me take stock. Quite simply, I decided better now than later. They say the third stroke is often much more severe. And once you've had two, well, you're almost bound to have another. I didn't want to inconvenience Tom – that's my son. He lives abroad, you see. It would be difficult for him to come back suddenly. This place seemed ideal. More like a hotel than an old people's home and yet, if you need it, the care's there. And if I do have another stroke, there's always The Willows next door.'

The Willows was a nursing home, run by the same group as The Pines.

'But you look so well, so fit. Don't you mind being surrounded by . . . well, by people like me, I suppose.'

He laughed.

'Come on. You're hardly geriatric. Besides, that's one of the rules here, isn't it? They don't take you on if you need intensive nursing.'

'Well, yes, but even so.'

She looked him up and down critically.

'I just decided that it was better to find somewhere now while I still had the energy and could look around properly and find somewhere I liked, than later when I might have had to take the first place that was offered.'

A defensive tone had crept into his voice. Claire, noticing it, changed the subject.

'Are you going out?'

She pointed to the rucksack lying near his feet.

'Yes, Bamburgh Castle. I thought if I got there early there wouldn't be too many other people even though it is the weekend.'

'How are you getting there?'

'My car.'

'You've got a car?'

She was surprised. No one else, not even the sprightly Phyllis, had a car.

'Yes, I thought I might as well keep it. At least for a year or so. Just while I get to know all the old spots again.'

Of course, she thought. He was a local. He had said so yesterday. His father had been a headteacher at Berwick.

'I used to love Bamburgh,' he said. 'The way the beach stretches into the distance. We used to take picnics there. I suppose they've ruined it now. Turned the sand dunes into an amusement arcade.'

'No, I don't think so,' she said.

The last time she had been there had been with Catherine.

They had taken a taxi late one autumn. There had been no one else on the beach and they had paddled in the sea, splashed one another, and written their names in the sand – two old women playing at being young and loving it.

'Well, I'd better be off or there'll be no distance left to admire,' he said. 'Just people's towels and windbreaks.'

They said goodbye, eyeing one another, each wondering whether they had said too much, given too much away.

After he had gone, Claire went over to the bench where he had been sitting. A coffee bean was lying on the seat. It must have rolled out of the envelope. She picked it up and rubbed it in her hand as he had done. Then she put it to her lips. It smelt warm and secret, tangy, like salt on skin, the inside of an armpit. She opened her mouth and bit into it and the bean exploded in her mouth – dark and bitter and evocative. She spat it out.

5

'Do you mind if I join you?'

Claire looked up, shading her eyes from the sun. Iris stood in front of her, a basket of peas in one hand, a colander in the other.

'No, of course not. There you are.'

She moved over, making room on the bench where she was sitting.

'What are you reading?' asked Iris, starting to shell the peas into the colander.

'It's about beekeeping,' said Claire, closing her book. 'How to handle them without getting stung, that sort of thing.'

'I didn't know you were interested in bees.'

'Nor did I,' said Claire, laughing. 'I found it at that bring-and-buy sale at St Paul's the other day. It was only 50p and in a good cause – Romanian orphans, I think – so I bought it. And actually it's very interesting.'

'Quintin would think you're mad,' said Iris. 'He doesn't believe in trying new things. I don't know why he wants to go round the world. He'll probably insist on eating hamburgers everywhere.'

'Didn't you have a good time then, last night?' asked Claire.

Iris glanced sideways at her, then grinned and bent down to pick up a pod that had fallen on the path.

'No, I didn't,' she said finally. 'Not really. I'm not sure why. Well, yes, maybe I am. I think it probably started when we were looking at the menu. I chose skate because I'd never had it before and Quintin chose chicken. I told him chicken was boring and that he should choose something more adventurous and he said he didn't want to try something new because he might not like it. I said that was the whole point – venturing into the unknown – and he said it was just a waste of good money. And so on and so on.'

She pierced another pod with her fingernail, pulled it open, held it over the colander and ran her thumb down the inside so that the peas broke free and fell, thick and fast, on top of the peas she had already shelled.

'I think it might have been OK later only he wanted to talk about us. You know, where we're going as a couple, what's going to happen next year, where I'm going to live, when we're going to get married . . .'

'He wants you to marry him?' asked Claire.

'Yes. He hasn't asked me yet. But he's made it pretty clear.'

'And you don't want to?'

'No. Not yet. Not until . . . well, not until I know what I want to do, until I've got a job. A proper job, I mean. At the moment . . . I don't know . . . at the moment I just feel so unsettled, so aimless. I've got all this energy but nowhere to put it. I feel like a windmill with nothing to mill . . . as if I'm rushing around flailing my arms to no purpose. If only I knew what I wanted to do, then I would have a goal, something to work towards, a framework, something to give everything meaning.'

'You want a vocation, you mean?'

'Well, yes, I suppose so. I've always rather envied people who wanted to be doctors or dancers or writers – people who felt born to do something. But the thing is I've never wanted to do any of those things.'

'Haven't you got any idea what you want to do?'

'Only vaguely. All I know is I want to help make people's lives better, to fight injustice and cruelty and poverty. I know that all sounds terribly naïve and starry-eyed but I really want to change things, to make a difference, and I know that if I'm going to do it, I've got to do it now, before I get sucked into marriage or a career and become pregnant or cynical or just tired, just tired of it all, and content to have a house and a husband and enough money to pay the mortgage.'

She stopped shelling peas and looked Claire straight in the eyes.

'Does that sound silly?'

Claire shook her head.

'No, it sounds very sensible. Very wise. People do . . . well, get sidetracked, lose sight of where they're going.'

Iris looked at her watch and then picked up another pod.

'I'd better hurry or Cook will come out looking for me,' she said.

Claire watched her. The slim deft fingers. The slight frown of concentration on her forehead. A reddish mark on her neck. A lovebite perhaps. Or maybe just a rash.

'Do you like him? Quintin, I mean?' she asked.

There was a long pause as Iris considered her question.

'Yes, I like him,' she said finally. 'And I think I love him. But sometimes . . . well . . . I don't know. Maybe it's because . . . you see, he's my first proper boyfriend so I haven't really got anyone to compare him to. But sometimes I think, "Is this it? Is this all there is? Is this what all the fuss is about".'

Claire smiled.

'And when I think of marrying him . . . well, I see it as an end rather than a beginning, a loss rather than a gain. I don't know. Maybe it's just that I'm too young to marry yet. After all, I'm only twenty-one.'

Claire moved along the bench so that her face was more in the shade of the cherry tree under which they were sitting. It was almost midday. Soon it would be time for lunch. Afterwards, she would have a nap and then, when she woke up, finish reading the paper. Later, she would learn a poem and then it would be time for tea. After tea, she would dictate a letter to Catherine and maybe go for a short walk if her leg felt better. At seven she would have supper and afterwards read or maybe listen to music in her room. Then it would be time for bed. Another day gone.

'I suppose you think that's old,' said Iris. 'I suppose in your day girls got married when they were much younger.'

'Well no, twenty-one wasn't old exactly but it certainly wasn't young,' said Claire. 'Most of my friends were married by the time they were eighteen or nineteen.'

'How about you? When did you get married?'

'When I was twenty,' said Claire. 'In 1940. The year after the war started.'

'How did you meet?' asked Iris, not looking at her, still shelling the peas, her fair head bent over the basket.

'In a register office.'

'No, I mean how did you actually meet?'

'In a register office,' repeated Claire, laughing. 'I know. People always thought it was funny. Especially considering my father was a vicar. My husband was a registrar, you see. I was his assistant. That's how we met. My mother heard they were looking for someone through a friend. Register offices were very busy at the time. Lots of people wanted to get married in a hurry before the man was called up or something. I thought it would be a way of doing my bit for the war effort.'

'What was he like?'

'Old,' said Claire. 'Much older than me. He was also short, slightly overweight, and he had a moustache which he twisted round his fingers. I thought he was ugly. And I didn't even like him much as a person at first.'

Iris looked up, a half-emptied pod clasped in her left hand.

'What happened then? What changed your mind?'

'We had an argument. He overheard me saying that when I got married I wanted to get married in a church rather than a register office and so he asked me if I believed in God. When I said I didn't, he exploded. I'd never heard anyone argue like him. With such force and conviction, with so much passion. I was scared but also fascinated. I didn't want him to stop. That's how it started. That's when I began to take an interest in him.'

A burst of laughter from the direction of the croquet lawn made her look up. Iris too looked up again. She had finished shelling the peas and was now sifting them with her fingers to see if there were any stray bits of pod.

Phyllis was still there, Claire saw. But she was no longer alone. Janet was there too and Tom and Colin and also Peter. He had changed, she noticed. He had been wearing a blue shirt when he came into the conservatory. Now his shirt was yellow.

'He's nice, isn't he?' said Iris. 'The new resident, I mean. Peter.'

Claire hesitated.

'I haven't really spoken to him much yet,' she said. 'But yes, he seems very pleasant.'

They both watched as Peter swung his mallet, driving the ball in one hard, fast shot straight through the final hoop and onto the end post. Everyone clapped and Colin slapped him on the shoulder. Clearly, Peter had just won the game.

'He must have been very good-looking when he was young,' said Iris. 'He still is.'

Again, Claire hesitated. She agreed with Iris but was reluctant to admit it, partly from an innate contrariness and partly from a desire to protect herself, although she wasn't quite sure what from.

'Yes, I suppose so,' she said finally. 'If you like those sort of looks. I think I prefer fair hair myself.'

'I don't,' said Iris. 'I like black hair. Black hair and brown eyes and dark, olive skin. That's my ideal.'

She stood up and brushed down her dress then picked up the colander and the basket.

'There. That's me done. I'm off after lunch and it's my day off tomorrow so I'll see you on Monday.'

Claire waved goodbye. The group on the croquet lawn had gone inside, the hoses and sprinklers had been turned off and the birds had stopped singing. Only the bees in the lavender still moved. The day, which had started so lightly with a letter from Catherine and the promise of sunshine, had become heavy, bloated.

She thought about what Iris had said. About the fierceness in her voice as she had spoken of her wish to help people, to make a difference, to change things.

'I was like that once,' she thought. 'I wanted a cause, a wrong to right, a battle to fight. And look at me now. What have I done? What have I changed? Who have I helped?'

She twisted her hands, pulling at them as if she could tug them back into shape, smooth away the knots and lumps.

'Why did I do it?' she moaned quietly. 'Why did I insist on doing it? Why didn't you stop me?'

The bell for lunch rang and she responded automatically, wiping her eyes and checking to see that her bookmark was still in place. As she stood up, she rearranged her face, replacing the past with the present, the memory of her husband with the expectation of lunch – spinach cannelloni, fresh fruit and coffee. The day had to go on. The only way was forward.

6 ∫

I know why I did it, of course. I did it because you didn't want me to. I did it to thwart you, to reject you, to show that you had no control over me. That's why I did it.

I didn't think so at the time. I thought it was because I loved him. It's only now, desiccated, purged of feeling, that I can see more clearly.

If you hadn't objected, I wouldn't have gone through with it. But when you said he wasn't right for me, I became determined to marry him.

I'm not blaming you. I'm not saying it was your fault. I'm just pointing out, in a matter-of-fact kind of way, what influenced my decision. How, in an effort to break free from you, I enmeshed myself still further.

I realise that I was difficult; that my refusal to conform, my insistence on experiencing everything first hand, must have been wearing. That time I stepped off the top of the stairs to see whether I could walk on air. That other time I put my doll in the oven with the roast chicken. You thought I did these things to provoke you, to test you, to attract your attention. But you were wrong. I did them because it was not enough to be told that I would hurt myself or that my doll would melt. I had to feel it myself, see it with my own eyes, smell the horrible, acrid smoke.

I realise too, although this dawned on me only recently, that the things you tried hardest to crush in me were the things you most feared in yourself. Also, that there was an element of jealousy in your attitude, an element of 'if I can't do as I want, then neither shall you'.

I'm not blaming you. I'm not blaming anyone. But . . . did you ever realise how much you swamped me? How stifled I felt? I used to dream about that, you know. About waking up and being unable to lift the blanket. About lying there suffocating, gasping for breath, thrashing around like a beached fish.

Of course, you weren't born to pour cups of tea. You were born to lead, to achieve, and above all, to do. You were a great doer, always busy, always organising. No one ever walked as fast as you. Or made so much jam. Or sat on so many committees. But it wasn't enough. I see that now. You were allowed to sit on committees but not on the ones that mattered, not on the ones that had money and power. Father was the one asked to sit on those. How that must have irked you – you who were so much brighter than him, so much more energetic and capable. You had the talent to run a government, to inspire and control a workforce of thousands. Instead, you were given Sunday School outings. How it must have chafed you, the pettiness of it all. The squabbles about who was to do the flowers for Easter, the tiffs over whose cake had sold first at the bring-and-buy stall, the weekly ritual of hearing Miss Boole describe the pain in her legs.

Even your name was all wrong. Was that why you called me Claire? Because it was sensible. Practical. A name for a girl who did things. I preferred yours, of course. I used to write it secretly, say it out loud in the bath, Lav-in-i-a. Once, when we were on holiday and a boy on the beach asked me my name, I even pretended it was mine.

I thought you didn't like him because he was only a registrar. Because his father had been a town hall clerk. Because he went to pubs and drank beer and didn't have a middle name. I thought you were being snobbish.

He loved it, of course. The uproar, the fighting, your refusal to come to the ceremony. It made me even more of a conquest. He felt flattered – as though the vicarage were a castle and he a knight in shining armour who had rescued me from the clutches of a wicked stepmother.

Father came. At least I think he did. How pale a memory he is now. I find it hard even to picture him. Whereas you, you are three dimensional colour, stereo sound. I see a scarf in a shop, a purple one, your favourite colour, and I think, 'She would have liked this.'

Why didn't you say what you really thought – that he didn't love me? Why didn't you tell me that?

Maybe I do blame you.

7

Peter shut the library door gently behind him. It was three o'clock in the afternoon – the dead hour when nearly everyone slept.

He was so quiet that Claire, sitting with her back to the door looking out of the window, did not hear him come in. He, for his part, did not see her because the broad, high-backed armchair in which she sat hid her from view.

He started looking at the books on the shelves nearest the door. Most were classics – leather-bound, gilt-edged editions of Dickens and Scott donated by one of the first residents, a former civil servant who had recently died after developing a chest infection. A book on the top shelf, a paperback novel by a contemporary author, caught his attention and he reached up to take it down, pulling first gently and then more strongly. There. He tugged the book free and in doing so, dislodged another, a heavy, hardback book which crashed to the floor, narrowly missing his face.

Claire leapt to her feet. Peter spun round, clutching the paperback.

'What happened? What was that dreadful noise?'

'It was just a book falling. Sorry. I didn't mean to give you a shock. I didn't see you there. Are you all right?'

'Yes. Yes, I'm fine.'

They both stood there, looking one another up and down like contestants at a boxing match, assessing potential weak spots.

Then, almost simultaneously, they relaxed and smiled. Peter stepped forward.

'I was trying to get this down.'

He held out the book.

Claire recognised it immediately. She had read it the previous week.

'There are some steps over there.'

She pointed to the other side of the room where an aluminium stepladder stood, propped against the wall.

'Yes, I saw them. But I thought I didn't need them. I thought I was tall enough. It's a mistake I often make.'

He picked up the hardback book and replaced it on a lower shelf.

'I don't,' she said. 'You don't. Not when you're my height.'

He walked over to where she stood.

'What do you mean? You're average, surely? For a woman, I mean.'

She shook her head, smiling.

'I'm five foot three. That's small. Even for a woman.'

He shrugged his shoulders.

'You look taller,' he said. 'It's probably because you're so slim.'

Skinny, she said to herself. You don't need to pretend. I know I'm too thin.

He ran his fingers along the spines of the books nearest.

'I always wanted to have a room like this,' he said. 'A room lined with books from floor to ceiling. We're supposed to want workshops, aren't we, us men? Little hideaways at the bottom of the garden where we can keep our tools and fiddle around with bits of wood and glue. But I always wanted a room like this. A proper library. I never had one, though.'

His brow darkened, as if he was thinking of other unfulfilled dreams. Then, abruptly, he changed the subject.

'What were you reading? Before I dropped the book?'

'I wasn't. I was just sitting. I usually have a rest at this time but I didn't feel like it today so I came down here.'

He began playing with the ends of the silk cord that held back the curtains, swishing them to and fro.

'Actually, I was thinking of my mother. About how much she influences me. Even now. Even though she's been dead for more than forty years.'

She paused. He was looking away. He had stopped playing with the curtain cord.

'Does your mother still prey on you like that? From the grave?'

'She probably would do,' he said. 'If I'd ever known her.'

He looked up. Looked her straight in the eyes.

'She died giving birth to me.'

She did not look down. She could not look down. To do so would be to give in to pretence and convention.

There was a long silence. Finally, he dropped his eyes.

'You haven't said sorry . . .'

'I know . . . I . . .'

'No, I don't want you to. It's just that most people do when they find out. But I suppose you know that. With your son, I mean.'

'Yes,' she said. 'I do know that. I know it very well.'

She too looked away. There was another long silence.

'I was going to have a coffee. After I'd found a book. Would you like to have one too? I thought I'd try the coffee my son sent this morning.'

'Yes, I'd like that,' she said. 'I'd like that very much.'

8

Claire entered Peter's room as a teenage boy might enter a
brothel – curious and reluctant at the same time. Although
most of the residents had their own sitting rooms as well as
en-suite bedrooms, few entertained in them. She had only ever
been into Catherine's and once, when she wanted to borrow
some shampoo, into Janet's.

A red sofa strewn with orange and yellow cushions stood
in front of the fireplace. Next to it, on a small low wood
table was a lamp with a beaten copper base which glowed
in the sun. There was a mirror above the fireplace, a rag rug
on the floor, a cork noticeboard on the wall covered with
postcards, newspaper cuttings and what looked like scraps of
material. Cardboard boxes of books lay on the floor, some
piled on top of one another. Pictures were propped against
the wall.

She was struck by the clutter, by the almost feminine pro-
liferation of objects – candlesticks, photo frames, china boxes.
There was even a vase of flowers on the desk in the corner.
Yellow freesias in a clear glass vase. Bill had never bought
flowers.

'Sorry about the mess. I haven't had time to unpack everything. Also, I haven't got enough shelves. A joiner's coming in
next week to make me some.'

He rushed around, shaking cushions and clearing away papers,
throwing open the window to admit the warm afternoon air.

Claire, still hesitant, hovered inside the door.

'Sit down. Please. Make yourself at home. I'll put the kettle on.'

She sat down, not on the sofa but on the funny, Edwardian-style chair next to it. As with most chairs, she had to sit on the edge to prevent her legs from dangling.

He had a fridge of his own, she noticed, even though there was one in the residents' kitchen a few doors away. He also had a sandwich toaster and a bottle of malt whisky with two – she noticed that particularly – crystal cut glasses. The door to the bedroom was ajar and she caught sight of the bedclothes, cream, with something blue, maybe the shirt he had discarded earlier, lying on them.

'Did you spill something? Weren't you wearing another colour earlier?' she asked.

Peter, busy in the corner spooning coffee into a cafetière, turned to face her. She could not see whether he was smiling.

'Yes,' he said slowly. 'Yes, I did. How noticing of you.'

He walked over and placed a tray on the coffee table in front of the sofa. The tray was round and flowered and made of melamine – the type sold in National Trust gift shops or quality department stores. He served the coffee in small glasses and offered her an oat cake spread with olive paste. She took one.

'I bought these in Turkey,' he said, picking up his glass. 'That's what they drink coffee in over there.'

'Really?'

'Yes, young boys carry round whole trayfuls of them in the streets, delivering coffee to the shopkeepers. That's why I bought them. To remind me. It was one of the best holidays I've ever had.'

There was a long pause. Claire, uncomfortable, cast around for something to say.

'Have you done much travelling?' she asked finally.

'A fair amount, I suppose. Most of Europe. Hong Kong, Australia, the States, India, the West Indies. I've never been to Poland, though. I've always wanted to go there. How about you?'

'I've been to Italy but that's about all. I didn't have the money to travel. Not when I was younger.'

There was another silence. Claire wondered how soon she could leave without appearing rude. She noticed that the coal scuttle was full and that there were ashes in the fireplace. He must have had a fire since he arrived, she thought.

'Are you going out again tomorrow?' she asked. 'It's supposed to be staying fine.'

'Yes, I thought I might go to Lindisfarne. In fact, I . . . well . . . I wondered if perhaps you'd like to come too.'

She swallowed abruptly, burning her throat.

'We needn't walk anywhere,' he added quickly. 'We can just go for a drive and then find somewhere to have lunch. A nice pub maybe.'

'It's not that. It's just that . . . well . . . don't you want to look up some of your old friends? I mean . . . you've only been here a few days.'

'Not really. Most of the people I went to school with have either moved away or died. Besides, I . . . well, I feel very lucky still to have a car, to be able to get out. It's nice to share it with someone else.'

Claire smiled. She had never been to Lindisfarne. She had meant to go. She and Catherine had even booked a taxi once. But then Catherine had felt unwell and they had had to cancel it.

'Well, if you're sure,' she said, looking up shyly. 'I'd love to go. Really love to.'

Peter poured her another glass of coffee and she sat back in her chair, right back, not caring if her legs dangled.

Later, washing her hands in her room before supper, she studied her reflection in the mirror above the basin. Her cheeks were flushed and her eyes shining. She pursed her lips, turning her face from side to side, and was not too displeased with what she saw.

It was half past six in the evening. She had missed tea, she had not finished reading the paper and she had not even started to learn a poem. For once, though, she did not mind. Seize the moment, she told herself, spraying her wrists liberally with eau de toilette – a Christmas present from Catherine. Routines were made to be broken.

9

Claire rose early and went for a walk in the garden. There had been a heavy dew and the hem of her nightdress was soon wet against her ankles. She picked a sprig of lavender and rubbed it between her palms, staining them blue. She was going out, she was going out, she was going out to Lindisfarne.

She bent her head to smell a rose, then another, then another, almost running between them. Everything was good, everything was wonderful. She would never be sad again, never dislike anyone, not even Phyllis, not even the women in the library.

She wanted to run, to sing, to whoop with joy. To turn cartwheels on the lawn, wear daisies in her hair, shout 'look at me, look at me' like a child on a wall.

John, the head gardener, was in the vegetable garden weeding runner beans. He looked up as she approached, clearly surprised. She waved and called out, noticing the look he gave her. He thinks I'm mad, she thought. He thinks I'm going soft in the head. Later, he'll probably have a quiet word with Matron. She giggled, almost losing her balance on the narrow path, hearing herself describe the scene to Peter later.

Back in her room, she ordered a light breakfast of tea and toast. Residents were allowed to have meals in their rooms but were not encouraged to because of the extra work it created. Claire rarely did so but today she told herself that she needed to. She wanted to dress herself – a task that could take her a long time.

Her clothes were laid out ready – a wool crepe dress, navy nubuck sandals, and a pink scarf to complement the dusty blue plum colour of the dress. She would wear the coral earrings and necklace her parents had given her for her eighteenth birthday, she decided. They would tone well with the scarf. Her hands trembled as she lifted up the dress. She could not eat the toast that had been brought and had managed only two sips of the tea. Her stomach churned the way it had done more than fifty years ago on the day she sat her matriculation exams. How dreary my life must have become, she thought, seeing herself with sudden painful clarity. To be so excited at a drive in the countryside. It occurred to her that she had left Alnwick only twice since Catherine's departure – once, to attend a funeral in London and once, to visit Durham Cathedral on a minibus trip organised by Matron. I must go out more, she told herself. I must meet more people. It's bad to be so confined, to have such a narrow existence. Last night, when I came back to my room, I felt almost drunk. And all I had done was talk.

She sat down at her dressing table and opened her cosmetics bag, arranging the pots and tubes and compacts in a row in front of her. The clasp on the first eyeshadow compact defeated her. The second opened but only to reveal a powder too dry and flaky to use. She seized a third, a green one. Green went with purple didn't it, she thought, wincing at the pain as her fingers snapped open the lid. She glanced at her watch. Eight-thirty. Peter had said he would call for her at nine. She began to feel panicky. She put on some green eyeshadow. Then some mascara. Then, holding her right wrist with her left hand to stop it from shaking, she defined her lips with a lip pencil and filled in the outline with red lipstick. No, no, it was no good. Her hands were too unsteady. The mascara looked like black clotted cream, the eyeshadow stood out in creases like the folds of a mountain, and the lipstick had bled, making her look as though she had been sucking lollipops. She looked like a clown, a grotesque paper mask bought at a carnival and found the next day, discarded, lying in the gutter.

She scrubbed the make-up off. If only Iris were here, she thought. She would know what to do. She would help. She picked up the phone to ring for another member of staff but then stopped. She didn't trust anyone else, she didn't want anyone else. Only Iris would do.

There was a knock at the door and she ran to open it. It was

Peter. As soon as she saw him, she felt overdressed. He was wearing cream trousers and a green, short-sleeved sports shirt. Worse, he looked relaxed.

'I'll be with you in a moment. I'll meet you downstairs, shall I?' she said breathlessly. And she shut the door.

She almost sat down and wept. She almost went and told him she was feeling ill and would not be able to go. She almost kicked off her shoes and climbed into bed.

But, instead, she reapplied some lipstick. Only a little this time, rubbing it in with her fingers and blotting it with tissue paper. Then she drew herself up to her full height, pulled in her tummy, picked up her stick and handbag, checked to see that her comb and purse were in the bag, and went downstairs.

The car was smaller and shabbier than she had imagined with a pile of what looked like shells and pebbles on the floor in front of the passenger seat.

Peter, who had been holding the door open for her, saw them before she did, and held out his arm to prevent her stepping in.

'Drat! Sorry. I'd forgotten those were there. I picked them up yesterday at Bamburgh. I thought . . . well . . . I thought they might be nice to look at or something.'

He found a plastic carrier bag in the back of the car and began to fill it.

'Look. Isn't that a lovely one? It looks like a French horn.'

Claire looked at the shell he held out to her but did not see it. The early morning frolic in the garden, the worry of dressing herself in time, the frustration of not being able to apply her make-up – all had taken their toll. She felt drained.

As they pulled out of the drive, she caught sight of Phyllis surveying them from the first floor landing window. But she was too worried to feel any triumph. She was thinking about lunch. She couldn't cut up meat. Or vegetables even. Not unless they were very soft. She had forgotten about that. She would have to ask for a sandwich. But what if they didn't have sandwiches? She hugged her bag, wishing she was back at The Pines, safe in her routine, writing a letter. Gradually, though, as they passed from the town to the countryside, her grasp relaxed. She had forgotten how bright the colours were at this time of year, how green the leaves, how yellow the fields. The road dipped, curved and entered a small wood. The trees on both sides of the road were so broad and tall that they met in the middle, creating a tunnel of shade. There was a warm, dank smell of last year's leaves steaming in the heat. Then they were out again, out in the open, and the air was hot and dry and dusty.

'Are you OK? You're not too cold? Tell me if you want me to wind my window up, won't you?' said Peter, not taking his eyes off the road.

Claire nodded, leaning out slightly so that her face caught the full rush of the air. Her left arm trailed against the side of the car and every now and again grasses from the verge touched it.

'Did you see that? That bird?' asked Peter, braking suddenly.

Claire looked round, startled.

'There. Back there. Sitting on the gatepost. I'm sure it's a falcon.'

He reversed the car slowly on the wrong side of the road until they were almost level with the gatepost. The bird looked in their direction but did not fly away.

'It's a sparrowhawk,' whispered Peter. 'A female sparrow-hawk.'

He took a pair of binoculars from the pocket in his door and handed them to her. She put them to her eyes and he leant over to adjust them for her, the hairs on his arms brushing against her, the smell of his skin in her nostrils.

The hawk tilted its head to one side. She could see the sharp, curved beak, the creamy breast ringed with brown.

'It looks like an owl,' she said. 'If you weren't here, I'd have thought it was an owl.'

At the sound of her voice, the sparrowhawk rose slowly into the air and flew to the far side of the field, settling on a tree.

'Sorry. I think I startled it. I didn't mean to speak so loudly.'

Peter smiled.

'It doesn't matter. There are lots round here. We'll probably see several more before the day's out.'

She settled back into her seat, drowsy now like a sun-lapped cat, feeling her mind empty, her shoulders relax. A combine harvester squeezed past them and she waved at the men on it. The youngest wore no shirt, she saw, his shoulders bare and brown, shiny with oil and muscle. She had not noticed men's arms when she was younger. Now though, now that she had no opportunity to do so, she wanted to touch them, to trace the rise and fall of the biceps.

They turned a corner and suddenly, there it was, the sea, right beside them, the whole horizon steeped with blue.

She sat up excitedly.

'Look! The sea! The sea!'

He turned to look at her and she blushed.

'Sorry . . . it's just . . . well, that first glimpse. It always surprises me, however many times I see it. It's as though I expect it to be smaller. Less blue, less intense.'

They passed through a small village called Craster.

'Isn't that Greek for castle?' she asked.

'Yes. Probably. I don't know. Look! Just look at that,' he said, pulling the car over to the side of the road.

She followed the direction of his finger and saw that he was pointing at the ruins of a castle, perched dramatically on the cliffs about a mile along the coast, the waves crashing on the rocks below.

'What is it?' she asked.

It was so beautiful, so perfect, it was almost eerie. She stared at it as if seeing a mirage, fearful it would disappear as soon as she blinked.

'It's Dunstanburgh Castle,' he said. 'The Earl of Lancaster built it. At least I think it was him. Have you never seen it before?'

She shook her head.

'Only in guidebooks.'

'I used to know the history of all the castles on this coast. When they were built, who lived in them, that sort of thing. We did a project on them at school,' he said.

'Can you reach it? Is there a footpath?' she asked.

'Yes. But it's quite a long way. I'm not sure that you'd . . .'

'It's OK. I didn't mean . . . I don't want to go there . . . I just wondered . . . have you been there?'

'A long time ago. With my father. He taught history. I think that's why he came here. To Northumbria, I mean. Because of all the castles and forts. He wasn't from here originally, you see. His family came from Liverpool.'

He frowned and glanced at his watch.

'Come on. We'd better hurry or we'll miss the low tide.'

He said nothing else until they reached Lindisfarne. The silence made her feel uneasy and she began to worry about the lunch again and also about her leg which had started to ache from being in one position for so long.

'I thought we'd see the castle first and then look round the priory after lunch. Is that OK?' he asked.

She nodded. He was a stranger again. Formal, stiff, kind. An English gentleman hedged around with politeness.

He parked as close as possible to the path leading to the castle and leant over to the back seat, bringing out a red tartan thermos flask.

They drank the coffee in silence, the car doors open, nodding at the sightseers who passed them from time to time.

'I've been thinking about what you said yesterday,' said Peter slowly. 'About your mother. How you still think of her. The power she has over you. It reminded me of my father.'

Claire kept still and said nothing, as though, like a lizard, the slightest movement might startle him into retreat.

He sighed and poured himself another half cup of coffee.

'You'd have thought . . . I mean it's supposed to be an adolescent problem, isn't it? The struggle to establish one's own identity. And yet sometimes . . . well . . . I feel I've only just begun.'

He looked away, out towards the sea. There was a long pause.

'It's difficult to believe, isn't it? That someone of my age should still worry about what his father thinks, about what his dead father thinks. But I do.'

He turned to face her, smiling wryly, and she, sensing that he had said all he was going to say for the moment, smiled back.

'Do you mind if I take a walk up? I won't be long,' he said.

'Of course not. I'm quite happy here.'

And she was. Her eyes and ears had been so starved of new sights and sounds that she felt intoxicated, bewildered almost, as though newly arrived in Manchuria.

She watched him until he disappeared from view then levered herself out of the car. She wanted to try out her leg, to make sure it didn't let her down. She walked to the stile at the end of the road and back again. It was OK. A bit painful but not enough to make her want to use her stick. She lowered herself back into her seat and closed her eyes, luxuriating in the sound of the waves breaking gently on the shore below, the breeze cool against her neck and cheeks, the knowledge that most of the day was still to come.

They ate prawns for lunch. Large, pink, plump prawns bought that morning at North Shields fish quay and served with granary bread and butter. He peeled them for her, every now and then washing his fingers in the bowl of warm water brought to their table for the purpose. A large party of French students had come in just after them and she watched them flirting and joking, the girls flicking back their long hair, the boys swaggering, hands in pockets. She felt she was on holiday, that the pub was a French café or Spanish bistro, that if she walked outside she would see yachts and windsurfers, beautiful people with tanned limbs, shops selling beach balls and sun cream.

She sipped her lime juice and Peter drank his beer. He began to tell her about the history of Lindisfarne, about Saint Cuthbert, the shepherd boy who became a monk, about the Viking raids which forced the monks to leave the island, about the foundation of Durham Cathedral.

She listened, but more to his voice than to the words he spoke. She had always been sensitive to voices and Catherine had taught her to be more so – to notice the pitch, the tone, the intonation that revealed the character. Now she felt his voice as one might finger a piece of material, enjoying the texture, the inconsistencies, the curious way he pronounced his 'r's.

Afterwards, they visited St Aidan's Winery, a shop selling jam and mead and plates saying 'Holy Island – the birthplace of Christianity in Britain'. Claire bought a packet of fudge for Catherine.

The priory was better preserved than she had imagined and also more interesting. They walked round it separately, catching up with one another at a point where the walls had collapsed to waist height, revealing the coastline beyond.

'What a place!' whispered Claire. 'No wonder they built a

monastery here. It makes you feel so small, so dwarfed, you can't help but want to pray.'

Peter nodded.

'It's a pity you can't bottle atmosphere, isn't it?' he said. 'Then again, maybe it isn't or this place would have been plundered long ago, exported abroad breath by breath.'

Claire laughed at the thought of bottled Lindisfarne air on sale at duty-free checkouts, consumed in bulk by jaded executives.

They bought ice creams from a man with a handcart outside the priory and ate them sitting on a rock looking out to sea. I am happy, thought Claire. I want to remember this, to preserve it. To look back wherever I am and be here again, licking ice cream, my mind washed clean and white like a stone on the shore, empty of worry.

They drove back slowly by a different route, Peter pointing out sights of interest on the way. She was impressed by his knowledge, by his memory for dates and names, by the way he did not make her feel ignorant.

Just before Alnwick they took a detour.

'There used to be a teashop at Howick that served wonderful Singin' Hinnies. Shall we see if it's still there?' said Peter.

He added that Singin' Hinnies were a local speciality, a sort of griddle cake, served hot with butter.

The teashop turned out to be the front room of a small fisherman's cottage. There were only four tables and all were occupied so they sat down outside at a table in the garden. A young girl came to take their order and Peter asked her if she was related to a Mrs Barnard – the woman who had run the café when he had first visited it as a child. The girl said Mrs Barnard was her grandmother and that she was living nearby in a nursing home. She offered to write the address of the home down when she came back with their order.

'There was only one table when I used to come,' said Peter. 'A big, long rectangular table. Everyone used to sit round it. It was lovely. You would talk to complete strangers. You had to. The owner – that girl's grandmother – she started the café after her husband drowned trying to rescue a friend. It was a terrible story. The friend survived. But her husband didn't. It turned out that he couldn't swim.'

The girl must have said something to the cook about Peter knowing her grandmother because their Hinnies, when they arrived, were much larger than those brought to the other tables. Peter spread them with butter but so quickly and unobtrusively that she barely noticed him do it.

Back in the car, he fumbled in a bag on the back seat and took out a small plastic case, about the size of one of her eyeshadow compacts.

'I'm sorry. I'll have to take my contact lenses out. They're starting to hurt,' he said.

Claire was surprised. She had not known he wore contact lenses. She had noticed he did not wear glasses but had simply thought that, like her, he did not need them. He balanced the case on the shelf above the glove compartment and with his left forefinger and thumb peeled back the eyelid on his right eye. She looked away so as not to embarrass him.

'There. All done.'

She saw now why he wore contact lenses. They concealed the broken blood vessels in the whites of his eyes and made the pupils look darker and bigger. A sudden wave of protectiveness swept over her. Old age had him too by the throat, she realised. He was just better at hiding it than most.

'I think maybe some grit blew in them when we were looking round the priory. They've been smarting ever since then,' he said.

He put the case back in the bag and took out a pair of glasses. Claire waited for him to put them on and start the engine but he just sat there, staring at the steering wheel.

'My father used to take me to Lindisfarne a lot,' he said finally. 'I think that's what made me think about him, about what you were saying yesterday.'

He looked at her, turning the glasses over and over in his hand.

'I felt I had to make up, you see. Make up for the fact that my mother had died. Try and please him as much as I could.'

She sensed a change in him. It was as if, by taking out his contact lenses, he had also removed some of his inhibitions. He was less wary, as if he had decided he could trust her, that she would not trample on any thoughts he might choose to expose.

'I wanted to go to art school but my father wanted me to get a job in a bank. I'd always done as he said before. This time, though, I didn't. I held out. I said I didn't like figures, that maths was my worst subject at school, that I would be unhappy, that I wouldn't be any good, that they would get rid of me. We argued like this for months. Then, finally, I gave in. I got a job in a bank and I stayed there for the next fifty years and all that time, all those weeks and months and years, I wished I'd gone to art school instead.

'I thought it was just the money. I thought he wanted me to get a job in a bank so that I would have money. So that I would be able to look after myself. So that I could afford holidays and nice clothes, a house with a porch.

'Then, after he died, I found his diary. A diary he'd kept when he was a teenager. I wasn't going to read it but then I did and I'm glad I did. Because it showed me it wasn't just the money. It was the security, the safety a bank could offer. His father was a docker in Liverpool and in that diary he wrote about watching him queue for the chance of a day's work. Sometimes fights broke out. Once a man was even killed. Killed over a day's work! Not a year's work or a month's work. Just a single day. He wrote about the look in his father's eyes when he was not chosen. About the humiliation of seeing him stand there, cap in hand, begging, begging to be allowed to break his back so that his family could eat. About his determination to find a job that offered a better future, how he would make sure his children found better jobs too.'

He unfolded his glasses, put them on and started the engine.

'I wish he'd told me this,' he said. 'It would have helped me understand. I still wouldn't have agreed with him but I'd have felt a lot better.'

Claire was so tired when they arrived back that she went straight to bed even though it was only six o'clock. At eight o'clock she ordered a glass of hot milk and some oat cakes, and asked for someone to come and undress her.

The woman who came was someone Claire had never seen before. They were often short-staffed at weekends, especially on Sundays, and had to take on staff from an agency in Newcastle.

She told Claire there was going to be a storm that night and, without asking, closed the window.

'Been out, have you?' she said, picking up Claire's hand-bag and stick from where she had dropped them just inside the door.

'Go anywhere nice?'

Claire, holding her arms up so that the woman could remove her dress, did not hear the question. She was too busy replaying the day in her mind. The woman put on her nightdress, brushed her teeth, put the milk and oat cakes where she could reach them on the bedside table and left. Claire continued replaying the day, moving moments around like jigsaw pieces. As she reached the last moment, the moment when Peter had turned off the engine and thanked her for coming with him, there was a loud clap of thunder. Claire smiled. It could rain now. She did not mind. The day was accounted for, every look, every word. All stored away. She lay in bed, her milk cold, a thick yellow scum on its surface, listening to the rain, holding the day to her like a coat, falling asleep in its warmth.

10

The next day it rained. Claire passed Peter once on the stairs but he seemed in a hurry and they did not speak.

It rained the following day as well and the day after that and the day after that. The shopkeepers began to say it was the wettest July they could remember and wasn't it a pity, what with the schools out now and that.

On the Friday she saw Peter again on her way to the library to order a new book. She stopped, expecting him to cross over the road to say hello, already deciding where they should have tea. But he merely waved and walked on. She was so disconcerted she forgot what she had come out to do and went back without going to the library.

She wondered if she had offended him and spent a miserable afternoon replaying the trip to Lindisfarne, seeking an explanation. But in the end she decided his behaviour had nothing to do with Lindisfarne. He had invited her out because he felt sorry for her. That was all. Sorry she could not play cards, had to walk with a stick and needed someone to cut up her meat. It had been the kind, gentlemanly thing to do and now it was done and he was getting on with his life. She scolded herself for reading more into the invitation than had been intended and made fun of herself in a letter to Catherine. She did not trust herself to send a tape in case the hurt in her voice broke through.

Thereafter, she avoided him so that he would not have to avoid her. This was quite easy. As well as the library and the yellow drawing room, there were also several other reception rooms – the Pink Room, so called because of the colour of its curtains, the West Room, and the Den, a small cosy sitting room with a thirties' style fireplace and a view over the back gardens. Sometimes she did not see him for days at a time, even at mealtimes. He went out a lot, particularly when it was fine, often returning only late in the afternoon. She reminded herself that he had been brought up in Berwick, that despite what he had said earlier he probably still had friends in the area, that no doubt he was visiting them.

Catherine wrote and said she had finally got a guide dog, that he was a black labrador, was called Vashti which was Persian for 'best' and that he let Luke ride on his back like a horse.

Iris heard that she had received a First Class in her degree and had an argument with Quintin because he refused to go to London for the awards ceremony. In the end he did go but was noticeably absent from the photos which Iris showed round afterwards.

A doctor gave a talk on homeopathy and Eric, the diabetic former research scientist who rarely talked to the other residents except when approached for help with crosswords, forgot to give himself his daily insulin injection and was found in a coma in the conservatory.

Claire discovered Gerard Manley Hopkins and began learning his poems, sometimes two a day, enjoying the difficulty they presented, the tightness of the syntax. The wet weather had made her hip ache, the one that had been dislocated by the young burglar, and for several days she had to use her stick and restrict herself to short walks to the paddock or herb garden.

The joiners came to put up Peter's shelves two weeks after they had promised and played their radios at high volume until Matron asked them not to. Shortly afterwards, one of them, perhaps distracted by the unaccustomed silence, accidentally drilled through a mains cable and had to be rushed to hospital with severe burns. Peter, who had been present in the room when it happened, gave an eye-witness account after dinner in the drawing room. Claire noticed him glance in her direction once or twice but did not show, either by look or gesture, that she was listening.

It stopped raining and was fine again and after two days the shopkeepers began to complain about the heat and how it made their feet swell. They preferred it when it was cool really, they said, although of course the sun was good for business. Claire found it increasingly difficult to sleep at night and went to see her doctor who prescribed fresh air and sleeping tablets. She took one of the tablets but felt sick and sluggish the next day and so threw the rest away.

On the Saturday, almost two weeks after the trip to Lindisfarne, she went shopping to cheer herself up. She bought a new flannel and toothbrush, some dried apricots from the health food shop, some notelets in Woolworth's and then, finding herself outside a clothes shop, the only clothes shop in Alnwick which sold dresses her size, went inside to have a look around. There was a green dress she liked. The green was very bright and the design youthful but she bought it anyway, high on spending.

Back in her room, she laid out her purchases on the bed. She had just finished admiring the notelets when there was a knock at the door. She looked at her watch. It was three o'clock. She was not expecting any visitors. Nor had she ordered any food or drink. She went to open it, brushing her hair quickly as she passed the dressing table, annoyed at being disturbed.

It was Peter.

'Yes?'

She held the door behind her. Unlike him, she did not have a private sitting room and so could not hide her slippers, the nightdress lying on a chair by the bed, the red knitted hot water bottle cover.

He waved something at her. It looked like a paper serviette.

'Mrs Barnard, that woman I told you about who set up the café in Howick, the one whose granddaughter we spoke to.'

She nodded.

'Well, she's living next door. Next door, would you believe it. Look!'

He handed over the serviette. On it was written Mrs Barnard's name followed by the address of The Willows.

'I never really looked at it when she gave it to me. I just put it in my trouser pocket. That's where I found it just now. I couldn't think what it was at first. Then I realised.'

Zita Adamson

She nodded again, unable to share his excitement but not wanting to spoil his pleasure by making this obvious.

'I thought we might go and see her. She might not remember me but there's a good chance she will. We did go there every summer.'

'What, now?' she asked.

'Yes. You're not doing anything, are you?'

She glanced back at the bed where her new dress lay beckoning. She had planned to try it on, to see which shoes went with it best, to have a bath and use her new flannel.

'Well, I was . . .'

Something in his eyes, a pleading look, a look she had seen before in other eyes but so long ago she had almost forgotten it, made her change her mind.

'No, not really. But don't we need to let the staff know we're coming? They might have visiting hours.'

'No, it's OK. I've already phoned. They say it's fine if we just turn up.'

He looked sheepish now, like a small boy caught firing his water pistol at the clothes hanging out to dry in the next door garden. She raised her eyebrows. So he had already phoned, had he? Clearly, he had assumed she would say yes. Or maybe she had been an afterthought, a comma pencilled in, not strictly necessary. In her mind she saw a cat toying with a bird, letting it go, then catching it again. Was that what he was doing? Playing with her? Picking her up and putting her down? Just for the fun of it? The insecurity she had banked down so successfully with routine flooded her mind and she knew, without looking down, that her tights were wrinkled at the ankle. How could she even think anyone would find her attractive, she told herself. She was sixty-eight. An old woman. She had white hair and false teeth and knobbled stumps for hands. And she was too thin. It had not mattered so much when she was younger, when her skin fitted her, when her limbs and mind had spoken the same language. She had been slim then. Trim. Muscular even. Now though, now that her skin was several sizes too large, now that it hung on her like a dustsheet on a chair, now that her limbs and mind communicated only fitfully, she was scraggy. A peg doll. Yes, that's what she was. A wooden peg doll.

'So shall we go then?' asked Peter. Again, his look reminded her of a small boy – a small boy pleading for an ice cream or a trip to the swings.

She arranged to meet him downstairs in the front porch in ten minutes. This would give her time to brush her hair properly, she thought, to 'freshen up' as her mother would have said. But when she turned round and saw her new green dress she decided to change as well. The speed and skill with which she accomplished this surprised her. So did the way her heart bounded. It had been so long since she had dressed for anyone else she had forgotten how pleasurable it was. She peered nervously into the mirror, blushed, then laughed out loud. She might be sixty-eight, she thought, but she was still vain. That much, at least, remained unchanged.

The first thing she noticed about The Willows was the heat. It was always warm at The Pines but it was also airy. Doors and windows were regularly opened, especially in the summer. Here, though, the air had a stale smell as though long past its best.

A male nurse wrote their names in the visitors' book.

'Have you come from far?' he asked

Claire stifled a giggle.

'No, not far,' said Peter. 'Just a short journey.'

'Well, you've picked a good day. She had a bad day yesterday. Didn't recognise her nephew. Ever so disappointed he was. He'd come all the way from Peterborough. She called one of the staff and said there was a strange man bothering her and could we ask him to leave. Quite awkward it was.'

They followed him into the residents' sitting room.

'There she is. Over by the window. The one with the shawl on.'

They followed the line of his finger to where a tall, bony woman sat watching a snooker match on the television.

'I'll ask someone to bring you some tea,' he said.

They approached the woman he had pointed out.

'Mrs Barnard? Mrs Barnard? It's Peter, Peter Mansley. I used to visit your café at Howick with my father, Eric Mansley.'

The woman motioned them to sit down but did not take her eyes off the television.

'He's just got the pink and black to go,' she explained, frowning with concentration.

'Go on. You can do it. Go on, go on. Yes! Yes! Yes! You've done it! You've done it!'

The television audience burst into applause and Mrs Barnard and several other residents joined in. Claire, sitting on the edge of her chair, the new dress showing more of her legs than she wanted, felt uncomfortable.

'Sorry. It was the last frame. I didn't want to miss it,' she said, turning to face them.

'Now. Who did you say you were? Peter? I don't think I know any Peters.'

'Peter Mansley, Eric Mansley's son,' said Peter.

'You'll have to speak up,' said Mrs Barnard. 'I don't hear very well, I'm afraid.'

Peter glanced at Claire and raised his eyebrows.

'Peter Mansley,' he said loudly. 'Eric Mansley's son. We used to visit your café at Howick.'

Mrs Barnard looked Peter up and down.

'Eric Mansley's son,' she repeated. 'Well I never. Who'd have thought you'd grow so tall. You were always such a puny little thing as a boy.'

Peter laughed.

'It was all those Singin' Hinnies you fed me,' he said.

Mrs Barnard turned and put her hand on Claire's knee.

'Do you know, he used to eat five at one go. I don't envy you feeding him all these years. His father used to say he ate him out of house and home.'

Claire blushed. Clearly, Mrs Barnard thought she was Peter's wife.

'But we're not . . . I'm not . . .'

'And do you have any children?'

'I . . . I . . .' faltered Claire.

'One,' interrupted Peter decisively. 'A boy. Tom. He works abroad.'

Mrs Barnard nodded and leant in Claire's direction.

'Children are such a comfort, aren't they?' she said.

'Yes . . . I . . . yes, they are,' she answered lamely.

'A worry too, mind. My eldest now – Janet – she's seventy-six but I still worry about how little she eats. She never had a good appetite as a child and she still doesn't. People don't change, do they?'

'No, I suppose not.'

She looked at Peter for help but he just smiled as if nothing was wrong.

'I've got six, you know. Four by my first husband and two by my second.'

'I didn't know you married again,' said Peter.

'Yes. I married Jack Phipps, the man my first husband died trying to rescue. It's funny that, isn't it, how things turn out? Jack, he felt so bad about what happened he used to bring me vegetables from his garden. The first runners. Baby carrots, new potatoes, the lot. He was married himself then, but Marjorie died. Cancer it was. Cancer of the lung.

'We got married four years later when I was forty. I didn't take his surname though. It was unusual not to in those days but . . . well, I felt too old for all that. I suppose it was after you'd left school. Maybe that's why you didn't know. I'd have thought your father might have told you, though. He came to the wedding. I'm sure he did.'

Peter looked annoyed, Claire noticed. Almost angry.

'Jack didn't have any children. Marjorie hadn't been able to . . .' She lowered her voice, addressing Claire. 'Something wrong with her tubes.'

'We knew it was a bit of a risk. Me being so old then. But we were lucky. They both turned out fine. Jack didn't live to see them grow up, though. He died in 1955, two weeks after my birthday.'

They both murmured their condolences.

'He drowned too, you know,' she added, nodding to herself. 'I lost both of them to the sea. Spiteful old vixen!'

Claire looked around the room. At The Pines, the residents were always busy – reading, knitting, playing cards, doing a puzzle or crossword, or talking. Here, though, people just sat. No one was watching the television now but it was still on. Was this the next stage, she thought? Slumbering upright until it was time for bed?

Mrs Barnard turned to Claire again.

'Has he told you about his parents? How they were my first customers.'

'No . . . I . . . you see . . .'

But Mrs Barnard did not wait for a reply.

'Ruth, that was his mother, she was on holiday with her parents. Staying at a guesthouse at Alnmouth, I think. And Eric, that was his father, he was on a cycling holiday. It was the first day I'd opened. I'd only done it to bring in some money. Jack was good to us but we couldn't live on vegetables. I only had the one table . . .'

'Yes, he's told me about that,' said Claire.

'Ruth and Eric were sitting on opposite sides of the table. I could tell they liked the look of one another so I invited her parents out into the back garden to see my sunflowers. Over eight feet high, they were. I think it was all the seaweed I fed them with. Anyhow, while we were outside, they swapped addresses. Isn't that right, Peter?'

'Yes. Yes, that's right,' he said absent-mindedly, as if not particularly interested.

'And the next summer, on exactly the same day, they came back and showed me their engagement ring.'

'So if it hadn't been for you, they might never have got married?' said Claire, leaning forward eagerly.

Mrs Barnard nodded with the proud, contented air of a hen who had just hatched ten chicks.

'And they came back every summer after that until . . . well . . . until Peter was born. And then Eric came back with Peter.'

She paused and pulled her shawl more tightly around her.

'It's terrible, you know. I don't remember things. The other day I didn't recognise my own daughter. I thought she was the . . . what do you call those people who . . . who make sure you can still move things?'

'Physiotherapist?' suggested Claire.

'Yes, physiotherapist. I thought she was the physiotherapist. At least that's what she told me afterwards. I wish people didn't tell me. Then I wouldn't know. That's the worst thing – knowing. At least if I was like that all the time I wouldn't know. I wouldn't be able to know. As it is, people visit and I think, "Did I know you last time? Was I me or was I that other me? Who did I think you were? What did I call you? What did I say?"'

She bent her head and Claire noticed that she was wearing a wig, that the skin underneath was shiny and hairless.

'I had cancer too, you know,' said Mrs Barnard, as if reading her thoughts.

'They gave me chemotherapy. My teeth fell out. Literally. I was just sitting there, not doing anything, and a tooth dropped on to my tongue. Half an hour later, another tooth dropped. By the end of the week they had all fallen out.'

She paused again, her hands playing fretfully with the ends of the shawl.

'I liked the pattern of it though. The symmetry. Both the men drowning and then me and Marjorie getting cancer.'

She sighed and leant back in her chair. It was clear to Claire that she was tired, that the emotion of recalling her past had exhausted her.

She looked at Peter.

'I think . . . maybe . . .'

Peter rose.

'Yes, we should be going. We don't want to tire you out,' he said.

'But you've only just arrived. You haven't had your tea yet,' said Mrs Barnard.

'No, really. It's ever so nice of you but we must go.'

Mrs Barnard grasped his hand.

'You will come again, won't you?'

They both nodded.

'And make sure you look after your lovely wife,' she added. 'Don't lose her like your father did his.'

Claire felt her neck and face flush hot. Why didn't Peter say something, she thought? Why did he just nod and smile? Mrs Barnard called after them.

'I'm ninety-three, you know. Ninety-three next month.'

'I'm sorry,' said Peter as they walked down the drive. 'I thought it best not to say anything. It obviously pleased her to think I was happily married after . . . well . . . after what happened to my parents.'

'That's OK,' she said, struggling to keep up. She wondered what they would do now. It was half past four. They had missed tea and it was another two and a half hours to supper.

'It's strange, isn't it,' he said, turning left towards the town, 'what parents do and don't tell you? I knew they'd visited her café before they were married but I never knew it was where they first met. No wonder it was so special to them.'

He stopped to cross the road and, without asking, took her arm.

'And then her second marriage,' he said, when they reached the other side. 'I wonder why my father didn't tell me about that. He must have known I'd have liked to go to the wedding.'

'Where . . . where are we going?'

Peter stopped and turned to face her.

'Sorry. I was rambling.'

He grinned. She noticed that the label on his shirt was sticking out at the back of his neck and resisted the urge to reach up and tuck it down.

'Are you hungry?'

'A bit. I could do with a cup of tea.'

'I had something stronger in mind. Wine and pâté and olives. I thought we could buy a picnic and take it back to my room. Light a fire maybe. What do you say?'

He looked away, as if preparing himself for her to say no.

'I say yes. A very big yes.'

'Good. Come on then. There's a wonderful delicatessen near here. I often get my sandwiches from it.'

They chose two cheeses each, salami, French pâté, black olives in oil and herbs, crusty white bread, spicy crisps with a yoghurt-and-cucumber dip and, for pudding, carrot cake still warm from the oven. Peter also put a bottle of white burgundy on the counter and some dark mint chocolates.

Back in his room, he placed the wine to chill in the fridge, unwrapped the food, and put on a tape of Elgar's Violin Concerto.

Claire looked around. It was tidier than it had been on her first visit although there were still some books and pictures piled against the walls.

'I collect driftwood from the beach,' he said, kneeling by the fireplace and pulling wood out of a plastic sack.

'It's a bit damp but it soon dries out in this weather.'

She sat down, on the sofa this time, and watched the fire take hold, the flames creep and flicker until they had devoured the light twigs and begun to eat into the wood.

'I like your dress,' he said, not turning round, adding wood to the fire, bit by bit.

She flushed with pleasure.

'Is it new?'

She hesitated.

'Yes.' Then, quickly, as if confessing something, she added: 'I bought it today. I didn't mean to. I mean, I didn't go out with the intention of buying a new dress. I just saw it and liked it and bought it.'

He turned, still on his knees, and looked at her, brushing the dirt from his hands.

'It suits you,' he said. 'The colour . . . it goes with . . . I was going to say it goes with your eyes but you haven't got green eyes. Or have you?'

He laughed and leant closer, peering up at her.

'Sort of green,' she said. 'Greenish-grey. The colour of the sea on a wet day in Margate.'

He arranged the food on plates and poured wine into the Turkish coffee glasses.

'I've got proper wine glasses if you prefer,' he said.

'No, these are fine. Just right.'

She felt in the mood to agree, to flatter him as he had flattered her. Again, she was touched by his thoughtfulness, by the way he buttered her bread without asking and peeled the rind from the salami.

They ate in silence, the room increasingly shadowy as the sun sank lower in the sky.

'I . . . I wanted to apologise for the other day. For going on like I did about my father. I . . . I . . . I'm not usually given to unburdening myself like that.'

He ran his finger round the rim of his glass so that it sang. Claire put down the bread she had been about to bite.

'I think it was all the associations. It was the first time I'd been back there since I left home.'

Claire stared. So he hadn't found her boring? He hadn't wished he'd invited someone younger and livelier?

He refilled their glasses and put the kettle on. Claire stretched her toes towards the warmth of the fire.

'I'm afraid I bored you,' he said, turning his glass round in the palm of his hand.

'No. You didn't at all. I had a lovely time. Honestly.'

'Really?'

'Yes, really.'

He had been so confident in the delicatessen, she thought. So self-assured and knowledgeable – the way he had surveyed the wines and asked to taste one of the cheeses. Now he looked so different. Like a fledgling flapping on the ground desperate to be back in its nest. What a strange mixture he was.

'Would you ... would you like to go for another drive then?'

'Of course I would!'

'Only there's the music festival at Rothbury next weekend. I thought you might like to go.'

She smiled with delight.

'I'd love to. Really love to. I've meant to go every year but somehow never managed it. I've either been doing something else or been ill and then one year I think I got the date muddled up.'

She leant back and took off her Alice band, running her hands girlishly through her hair. There would be ceilidhs and puppet shows, she thought. She had read about them in the glossy listings magazine that came out once a month.

He fetched the carrot cake and sat down next to her on the sofa. She shivered.

'Are you cold? I'll shut the window, shall I?'

'No, don't. Leave it. I love hearing the evening.'

He sat down again.

'So do I,' he said. 'There's a special kind of quiet, isn't there? Not like the quiet you get in the middle of the day.'

Claire finished her carrot cake and licked the cream cheese topping from her fingers.

'I thought you were avoiding me,' she said in a small low voice.

'I thought you were avoiding me,' he said.

They looked at one another and both laughed.

'What a pair of sillies,' she said.

Peter filled their glasses again and turned the sofa round so that they could watch the sun set. And they sat there and watched the light fade until it was quite dark and the still of twilight was shattered by the teenagers from three streets away racing their motorbikes.

11 ∫

Claire tipped her head back so that the water didn't trickle down her neck.

It was Monday afternoon and Iris was washing her hair. She liked having her hair washed – so much so that sometimes she asked Iris to wash it when it did not really need washing. When she was a child, she remembered, she had played hairdressers with Monica, the doctor's daughter. She had loved the endless brushing and combing, the plaiting and unplaiting, the feel of fingers in her hair.

Iris held up the bottle of shampoo Claire had bought that morning in Nelson's chemists. It had cost six pounds, almost twice as much as she usually spent on shampoo, but the woman in the shop had assured her that it was specially formulated for the 'older lady's hair'. Claire had doubted whether this justified such a high price but felt she had spent too long in the shop to leave without buying anything and so had bought it anyway.

She watched Iris pour some of the shampoo into the palm of her left hand and rub it into a lather. Then she closed her eyes.

'Did you do anything nice at the weekend? Go anywhere exciting?' she asked as Iris began to knead her scalp.

As she spoke she thought of the picnic in Peter's room, the invitation to Rothbury music festival. Her dress still smelt of wood smoke. She had taken it out that morning and sniffed it as a dog might sniff a lamp post, excited by the scent.

'I went camping in the Black Mountains near Brecon. Quintin, me, two friends from college, a girl I'd been at school with, and the drummer from Quintin's old band. We went on a couple of walks and looked round Hay-on-Wye – you know, that place on the Welsh border that has all the bookshops. And the rest of the time we just lay around eating and reading and talking.'

'Sounds lovely.'

'Yes, it was. Mum and Dad and the twins came over and took us out for a pub lunch on Saturday and then we drove back late last night.'

'Is that where your family live then? Herefordshire?'

'No, North Wales. Near Ffestiniog. Dad used to be a miner until they closed his pit down. Now he works as a guide at the visitor centre there. He's Welsh. Mum's not though. She's German. That's why I speak German. She used to speak it at home. She still does a bit – especially when she wants to get at Dad. It used to be quite mad sometimes – Mum shouting in German, Dad shouting back in Welsh and me and the twins shouting at them to stop in English. You wouldn't know she was German though, her English is so good. She came over here when she was about ten, you see. She was Jewish.'

Claire opened her eyes.

'They met on a march in London in the sixties. They were both carrying banners and the banners got tangled up and . . .'

'So did they,' interrupted Claire.

Iris laughed and began to rinse the shampoo out.

'Yes. They sneaked away from the march and went to see the Crown Jewels in the Tower of London. It was the first time Dad had been to London and he wanted to see the sights. Afterwards, they bought fish and chips and ate it in Mum's bedsit and the following weekend she went to Wales to watch him play in a rugby match.'

'And was it the first time they'd met Quintin?'

'No. They've met a couple of times before.'

'So you didn't have to worry about whether they would get on?'

Iris lathered her hair for a second time, rubbing it briskly between her palms.

'In theory, no. In practice, yes. I always worry about whether Quintin will get on with people because he can be so . . . so . . . well, so rude, I suppose.'

She paused, her hands dripping suds.

'I don't know . . . maybe it's got something to do with the way his parents treat him. They don't approve of half the things he does but they never really say anything. Just look on with a sort of amused detachment. They didn't plan to have him, you see. He was a mistake. They already had three children and then, just when they'd given away all the baby things and packed the others off to boarding schools, along came Quintin. Maybe they'd run out of energy or something by then . . . I don't know, but they treat him differently from the others. Sometimes it's as if he's not their son at all but a rather difficult weekend guest who has to be humoured. Apparently, they were terribly strict with the others and yet they give Quintin virtually everything he asks for.'

'What do they think of his music?' asked Claire.

Iris giggled.

'They hate it, of course, but they don't say so. Just let him get on with it. I think it would have been different if they hadn't had another son but Julian – that's Quintin's elder brother – he's interested in farming. In fact, he practically runs the farm now, and so they don't mind that Quintin isn't interested. In many ways, they rather like the idea of having a musician in the family. They've always been farmers before. Farmers or lawyers.'

She squeezed out a dollop of conditioner, rubbed it into Claire's hair, then combed it through, gently, holding it so that it didn't pull.

'And how is his music? Has he found a band to sing with?'

'No, not yet. He got quite excited the other week because the band we went to see in Newcastle phoned up and asked if they could hear him again but then their singer discovered his girlfriend was pregnant and decided not to leave after all.'

She reached out for a towel and wrapped it turban-style around Claire's head.

'So what does he do all day? While you're working, I mean?' asked Claire, standing up and walking over to the bedroom window.

'Not a lot. Gets up late, has breakfast, mooches round the farm getting in everybody's way, plays his guitar a bit and then drives into Newcastle. I think maybe that's why he doesn't like me working here. He doesn't like it that I come back and have things to talk about. He wants to be the one coming home even though he doesn't want a job.'

Claire sat down on the window seat and rested her feet on a tapestry foot stool made by a local textile student. She would have to do something about her feet, she thought, looking down at them. There appeared to be a corn developing on the left one and there was a lump, possibly a bunion, at the side of her big right toe.

'And he still wants you to travel round the world with him?' she asked.

'Yes. He's even found out about the visa requirements,' said Iris, not looking up, clearing the plug hole of loose hairs.

'And you still don't want to go?'

Iris swished water round the sink, then dried her hands and sat down at the opposite end of the window seat.

'It's not that I don't want to travel. I do. Desperately. Far more than Quintin. He just wants to do it so that he can say he's done it. So that he can tick it off, move on to another box. Sometimes I think that's how he sees life – as a series of boxes to be ticked off. I'm just another box only at the moment I'm bulging at the sides, threatening to mutate into a circle or worse.'

She stood up, fetched the hairdrier from the bottom shelf of the bedside cabinet and plugged it in. Then she unwound the towel from Claire's head.

'How would you like it today? Turned under or curly.'

'Turned under,' said Claire, wishing her toenails weren't so yellow.

She moved her head so that she was looking out of the window.

'There. Is that OK?'

'Fine,' said Iris. 'I'll turn you round when I need to do the other side.'

She switched on the hairdrier and began to dry Claire's hair, turning the ends under with a large comb.

'Did you go anywhere nice for your honeymoon?' she asked, raising her voice to make herself heard.

'Not really. We spent two nights at a farm in Devon. Then Bill had to get back for a meeting. He was quite high up in the local Labour party association at the time.'

'Devon. That sounds nice. All those winding lanes and high hedges.'

'Well, it wasn't. At least not when we went. For a start, it rained the whole time. I don't think I took my mackintosh off once. The farm was arable so there were no animals, not even chickens or ducks, and the farmer and his wife used to hide the bath plug so that we had to ask if we wanted a bath. The nearest village was a mile and a half away and all it had was one shop and one pub. We divided our time between them. I don't think I've ever written so many postcards in my life.'

A figure appeared on the drive outside. It was Phyllis, she saw. A moment later, Maureen, a pleasant if somewhat vacant woman in her seventies whose only interest was her son, Mike, a bailiff in Sunderland, joined her and the two women set off down the drive.

As she watched, a car turned into the drive, stopped when it drew level with the women and then, after a few minutes, moved on, swinging into a parking space next to Matron's car. Claire watched Peter get out of the car, shut his door, open the back passenger door and take out something – a bag and what looked like a board. Iris also noticed him and waved the comb in his direction.

'He goes out a lot, doesn't he? Almost every day if the weather's nice.'

'Yes, I think he likes going for drives,' said Claire. 'He used to live round here, you know.'

Her tone was deliberately casual. She did not want anyone to know about the meal on Saturday. It was her secret. Their secret.

'So he's got friends locally?'

'No, I don't think so. He just . . .'

She stopped, aware of the defensive tone in her voice.

'I think he's interested in local history. His father wrote several books about it. About Lindisfarne and the Roman sites.'

'Was that what he was then? Peter, I mean. A historian?'

'No, I don't think so,' said Claire cautiously. 'I think he told Maureen he worked in a bank. As an analyst or something – you know, someone who studies the markets, who predicts whether a company's profits will rise or fall.'

'What do you think I should do?' asked Iris, changing the subject abruptly, much to Claire's relief. 'Do you think I should go with Quintin?'

She turned off the hairdrier, wound the flex round the handle and replaced it on the bottom shelf.

'What would you do if you were in my place?'

Claire stared. People did not ask her for her advice. They told her their troubles, asked her to listen, yes, but not to advise them. Not even Catherine did that.

'I . . . I . . . I'm not sure. Why all the hurry anyway? Why do you have to decide now?'

Iris hung up the damp towel.

'I don't have to decide "now",' she said. She sounded exasperated. 'But I have to decide soon. I mean, if I'm not going to spend next year travelling then I'll have to find a job instead. A proper job. I don't want to spend my life cutting people's toenails . . .'

She broke off.

'Sorry. That sounded rude. I just meant that . . . well . . . this is hardly a career.'

Why do people attach so much importance to a career nowadays, thought Claire? Work used to be a bore, a means to an end, a necessary evil. Now it seems it is an end in itself, the source of all wellbeing and happiness.

After Iris had left, summoned by Cook to help prepare tea, Claire remained in the window seat thinking of her surprise at Iris' request for advice. She was surprised, she reflected, because she did not think herself worthy to give advice. And she did not think herself worthy because she did not think she had learned anything. She had changed, yes. She was less hasty, less contrary. She was not the same as the child who had insisted Miss Reeves wanted a cake. Nowadays, she did not have to experience everything first hand. She accepted the word of other people, partly because she had to. She was also humbler, more charitable, less ready to judge. Her hands had seen to that. It was difficult to be proud when you needed someone to brush your teeth.

She looked back at her life as one might look at a picture one was thinking of buying – critically, standing back, weighing it up. What she felt above all else, she decided, was a sense of waste.

When she died she would leave nothing behind, no sign that she had ever lived. There were no children, no grandchildren, no trees planted, no books written – nothing. It was not even as if she had been happy. She had been unhappy mostly. Sometimes very unhappy. And what had she to show for it? The ability to learn poems by heart and do crosswords. Two or three friends that she wrote to regularly. Six or seven others with whom she exchanged Christmas cards. That was it. Her total sum of achievement. That, and the knowledge that things passed if one waited long enough. That grief, fear, anger, jealousy – all passed, given time. That things passed. It seemed a mean return on so much hurt.

12

After the two nights in Devon they went back to Bill's house. She had been there before but only a few times and always at night. This time, she remembered, it was late afternoon. There were children playing outside and two women talking on the pavement, their shopping bags held upright between their feet.

She hurried in, anxious to avoid introductions to neighbours, the polite questions, the inevitable scrutiny of her dress and manner.

Bill went straight to his desk to prepare for his meeting. He was to make a speech, she remembered. An important speech. She hung up her coat on a hook in the hallway and brushed her hair in the bathroom.

There were dirty cups and plates on the table in the kitchen and what looked like the remains of a bowl of porridge, flecked with mould. She wrinkled her nose and saw with a pang of homesickness the kitchen at the vicarage. Her mother would have made scones or Scotch pancakes. There would be a fire in the sitting room, flowers on her dressing table and a hot water bottle in the bed. The towels in the bathroom would smell of sun and hay.

She washed the dirty dishes and then, so that she did not disturb Bill, went upstairs to the bedroom. She wanted to unpack but did not know where to put anything. There was no space in the wardrobe and none in the chest of drawers either and she did not want to move Bill's clothes without asking where she should put them.

'I'm going now.'

She must have fallen asleep. Bill stood in the doorway.

'I'll probably be back late so don't wait up,' he said.

She sat up to kiss him goodbye but he had already turned and left the room. After the front door had closed, she lay there for some time. She imagined the house being bombed and Bill coming to find her, tearing away the rubble with his hands. He would kiss her then, she thought.

Comforted by this, she went downstairs to make a cup of tea only to discover there was no milk. She could not go out to buy any because Bill had not given her a key. Nor had he told her where the nearest shop was.

She went upstairs to the bedroom again, opened the window and leant out. It was a beautiful summer evening. House martins swooped in huge curves from eave to eave while opposite, perched on a chimney pot, a blackbird sang. Down below, half obscured by the leaves of the lime trees which lined the street, three girls played hopscotch. A bee bumped into the bottom half of the window pane, staggered as if dazed, and flew off again.

She breathed in deeply, delighted by the novelty of it, the neat line of roof tops, the tiny front gardens. She still could not believe she was married and now, here she was in an Oxford suburb, alone, without milk or key. It was so absurd she laughed out loud.

A cough made her turn sharply. Someone else, a woman, was leaning out of the window next door. She was so close Claire could have reached out and touched her.

Seeing her turn, the woman nodded and smiled, confidingly, pityingly almost. It occurred to Claire that the woman must know she was Bill's new wife and must be wondering what she was doing, apparently alone on her first night back from honeymoon. She did not want the woman to know Bill had gone out and so, out of loyalty, she half-turned and spoke, as if to someone in the room with her. Then she returned the woman's smile and withdrew her head completely.

She was hungry but there was nothing in the kitchen except Bovril and porridge oats. She made herself a mug of Bovril and drank it in bed, naked, the sheets drawn up to her waist, watching the house martins.

Bill came back late as he had said he would and they made love. As always, she was excited by the sight of their two bodies together, the difference between them – his so thick and coarse, the skin so dark, hers so slim, the skin so soft, so white. How could she explain this to anyone, especially to her mother? That this was what attracted her to him – his very unattractiveness.

She was woken the next morning by the sound of the front door banging as he left for work. She was not going to work because she had given up her job to a twenty-three-year-old former soldier whose right leg had been amputated at the knee. It was Bill who had found the soldier and offered him the job.

'After all,' he told Claire after the man had accepted, 'you won't need to work after we're married.'

Looking back, she did not hold this against him. Or the lack of milk or a key of her own. What she remembered instead was that he had not washed the sheets. At the time, she did not think of it particularly, just changed them herself later that morning. But later, as the years passed, the lack of fresh sheets, the thoughtlessness it betrayed, clung to her like a burr on a sheep's coat.

13

Claire sang as she tidied her room. The sun was shining, Catherine had written to say she was coming to visit her soon, and she was going to Rothbury music festival with Peter.

She sprayed her wrists with perfume, eyed herself approvingly in the mirror and picked up the copy of Elizabeth Jennings' *Tributes* she had promised to lend to Peter.

They had been sitting in the garden the previous evening watching the dusk fall and she had quoted a few lines by Jennings she had memorised earlier.

> 'The subtle twilight, most things juxtaposed,
> Shadow and substance, pale moon facing sun,
> Stars like splinters from a hammered forge,
> A time for guesses, love words for the dark.'

Peter had been interested. He did not read poetry much, he said, and had never heard of Elizabeth Jennings. She marked a few poems now with slips of paper torn clumsily from the envelope of Catherine's letter. 'Chardin', she liked that one, the phrase 'a seize of sight'. 'A Living Death' also, the poem about a friend, once so wise and bright, now dulled by age and loss of memory.

There was no answer the first time she knocked and so she knocked again more strongly. Maybe he was shaving, she thought – playing the radio in the bathroom with the tap running and the door shut. She waited a few moments and then knocked a third time. There was still no answer. She glanced around to make sure no one was looking, then tried the handle. The door was locked.

She wandered down to the dining room where Iris was clearing away the breakfast dishes.

'You haven't seen Peter, have you?'

She noticed that Iris looked tired, that her dress needed ironing, that there was a yellowish stain on the front, but was too preoccupied to do more than notice.

Iris said no, she hadn't, and continued scraping bacon rinds into a bowl.

Claire looked in the drawing room but there was no one there apart from a cleaner dusting the picture frames. The Pink Room was also empty and so was the West Room. Tom, the former Second World War fighter pilot, a pleasant man, but difficult to talk to because of his severe deafness, was in the Den with his daughter, a woman in her late thirties who worked for a mental health charity. And the only person in the library was Eric. That left the garden.

A small group of residents sat on the terrace enjoying the sunshine. Colin, the rat-catcher who'd won the football pools, was among them. So was Freda who suffered from Parkinson's disease. There was no sign of Peter.

She walked purposely past them to the vegetable garden where the head gardener, John, was digging up new potatoes. They exchanged a few pleasantries about the weather and the state of Claire's hands. John's wife also suffered from arthritis, a fact he told her nearly every time they met. She asked him if she could have a carrot to feed to Minty, the donkey, and he dug her up several, shaking the earth off them before handing her them.

'Don't let anyone see you, will you,' he said, grinning. 'Or else they'll all be down here asking for carrots and there won't be any left for your lunch.'

Minty was not in the paddock but the nanny goat and her two kids were. Claire called to them, waving the carrots. The nanny goat looked up, still chewing, and eyed her suspiciously, its head slightly on one side. Claire called again, banging the carrots against the fence. The nanny goat ignored her and started eating again, watching her out of the corner of its eyes. Finally, exasperated, she threw the carrots over the fence and sat down on a bench overlooking the paddock. She was still clasping the

Elizabeth Jennings book and, after a while, she opened it. A poem called 'Presences' caught her eye and she read it.

'Trust is the child of hopefulness and love.
A guardian seraph drives me daily on.'

Drives. Drives. Drives. Of course! His car. Why hadn't she thought of it earlier? He had probably gone for a drive. She hurried to the front of the house and scanned the rows of parked cars for Peter's. No, it wasn't there. It was a violent orange-red colour, the colour of tomato soup. It was impossible to miss.

She walked slowly back to the garden. Colin and the others were on the lawn now, playing croquet. They waved at her and shouted at her to come and join them but she shook her head and held up her book by way of explanation. She did not feel like playing croquet. She was not very good at it and besides, her hip had started to ache.

She sat down in the conservatory and let the warm, scented air and the sound of running water soothe her. There was no reason for him to tell her where he was going, she told herself. There was no agreement between them, no bond, no shared history other than a car drive, picnic supper and a couple of walks. She had known him only a few weeks.

Calmed, she began to plan how to dispose of the rest of the day. She would go to Alnwick Castle, she decided. It had been a long time since she had been there and she enjoyed walking in the grounds. She would buy a present for Catherine's grandson, Luke. A wooden car, maybe. Or a packet of crayons. They had some nice toys in the gift shop. After lunch, she would read the foreign pages and listen to the classic serial on the radio. They were dramatising a book by Thackeray. She had heard the first episode last week and it had been excellent. That would take her up to four o' clock when she would have tea. The evening could take care of itself. A small quiet voice told her that Peter would probably be back by then but she ignored it.

The fountain stopped suddenly and she realised there were other people in the conservatory. She could hear voices, women's voices. One was Janet's. Claire recognised the way she sliced off words at the end like a gardener cutting a hedge. Snip, snap, snip, snap. The other voice was softer and lower. For a moment, she wondered if it belonged to Iris then remembered that Iris was in the dining room clearing away the breakfast things. It was Maureen, she realised, the woman whose mind Catherine had once described as candyfloss. Maureen had irritated Catherine, partly because of the way she nodded almost continuously and partly because of the way her mind wandered when she was talking – the way she meandered from subject to subject, seemingly oblivious of what anyone else said. Catherine herself was a rigorous thinker and talker – the result of a degree in classics and marriage to a philosophy professor. She enjoyed discussing things and was impatient with anyone who was unwilling or unable to justify a view they had expressed or a word they had used. Claire had admired this and yet had thought her view of Maureen slightly uncharitable. It was true that Maureen could be vague. But she had had a difficult life. Her husband had run off with another woman when their son was three. She had had to work night shifts in a factory to make ends meet. And besides, the reason why she was unable to hold a conversation with Catherine was because she felt intimidated by her. Most people did. Even Claire had been nervous at first. It was only later that she realised Catherine's habit of scrutiny, of holding remarks up to the light like a housewife examining fruit for bruises, was done out of fun and a love of inquiry rather than a desire to knock people down.

She stood up, anxious to have at least half an hour at Alnwick Castle before the coach tours arrived. Then she overheard Janet mention Peter's name.

'Of course, it's a big change from London. No wonder he goes out such a lot. He must find us all very dull.'

Claire sat down again, the Jennings book gripped tightly in one hand.

'I still can't understand what he's doing here,' said Maureen. 'You'd have thought he'd have preferred to have his own place.'

'Well, he has had a few strokes apparently,' said Janet. 'But yes, I agree with you, it does seem a bit strange. Maybe he just liked the idea of living in a home, of having a captive female audience. Some men do, you know.'

There was a pause, then Maureen said: 'Has anything else happened since . . . well, you know?'

She was referring to an incident a couple of months previously when Colin had returned drunk from a day out at the races and tried to kiss Janet.

'He hasn't . . . he hasn't tried to do it again?'

'No, no. Mind you, I'm not surprised, the way Matron talked to him. Apparently, she told him . . .'

At this point Janet lowered her voice and Claire was unable to hear what she was saying any more. The Jennings book slipped from her fingers and fell to the floor, landing on a dead camellia bloom. She did not pick it up. She was thinking of what they had said. About how Peter must be bored. They were probably right, she thought. She had forgotten what it was like to be in one's own house. To be able to dress at noon, eat breakfast at night and talk back to the television. She had found The Pines difficult at first – the set meal times, the organised games, the lack of privacy. But now, well . . . she had been there three years, after all. She had probably become institutionalised – had probably slipped, softly and easily, without realising it, into the habits that were expected of her. She had fought against it, was still fighting against it, but even so, it had probably happened. In a way, she thought, it was bound to happen. Maybe, she should just give up now – should cancel her paper and watch the telly news instead, commenting only on the newscaster's tie.

She picked up her book and walked slowly back to the house, limping heavily. Her hip was too bad to take her to the castle, she decided. She would have to lie down instead. As she passed the door to the dining room, she glimped Iris, now laying the tables for lunch, but felt too tired to stop and talk.

She slept almost immediately, dreaming vividly. In the last dream, the one she remembered when she woke up, she was running along a row of people stabbing them in the heart. To her surprise, the knife met no resistance. That was what she remembered – the ease with which she plunged it in and drew it out, the small gurgle as it emerged, the red froth against the hard grey of the blade. There was no struggle or violence. The people were nameless, blurs without faces or pasts. Even so, the dream was disturbing because it seemed so inexplicable. The dreams she usually had could be traced back to something she had done or seen or heard recently, to something she was worrying about or looking forward to. This, by contrast, was a bastard dream, a dream with no father, no name to explain its arrival.

Lunch was a quiet, gloomy affair cheered only by the arrival of Maureen's son, Mike, a large well-built man with a scar across his right cheek received when a tenant he was trying to evict had slashed it with a glass. He was rumoured to deal in drugs and stolen property. This, Phyllis had once told Claire, explained why he often gave Maureen electrical goods as presents and why he could afford to pay for her to stay in The Pines. Maureen, however, seemed either not to know or not to care where he got his money from. He was the best son a mother could hope for, she said.

The afternoon passed equally quietly. Claire wandered from room to room, unable to settle. Most of the other residents had gone to an open day at a nearby private garden and there was a sleepy, Sunday afternoon feel about the place. In the end, she joined Tom and Janet in the drawing room, unwilling to trust herself to her own company.

The residents who had gone to the open day came back just before tea, exclaiming about the heathers, and the size and blueness of the delphiniums. Claire looked up each time the door opened, expecting to see Peter. He did not usually stay out so late, she thought. He was usually away only for a couple of hours in the morning. Maybe he had had an accident. Maybe he had crashed the car.

After tea, she went back to the drawing room, ostensibly to complete the crossword she had started. The residents tended to gather here before dinner to talk about the day's events. After dinner they usually dispersed, some to their own rooms, some to the snooker room and some to watch television in the West Room, the only public room where there was a television. But between six and seven, they sat together – talking, reading, sewing, laughing. It had become a tradition.

She watched the door, glancing every now and then at her watch. By half past six almost everyone was there, even Eric who often went straight from his room to the dining room. He must have had an accident, she thought. There was no other explanation. She decided to find Matron to ask if she had heard anything. She stood up and walked towards the door. She had her hand on the handle, was already opening it when it burst open. Peter and Phyllis walked in. They were both laughing, their cheeks glowing, their hair dishevelled.

'It's OK. You see, we haven't missed it. I told you,' said Phyllis, nudging Peter and giggling.

'We didn't have a watch,' she explained, flopping down in the chair Claire had just left. 'We had no idea what the time was.'

'Where've you been?' asked Janet.

'You'll never guess,' said Phyllis, addressing the room at large. 'Kielder Water. Had the most marvellous time. Beautiful cruise and then a picnic by the shore. Peter's found this absolutely wonderful new delicatessen in town. The bread is simply out of this world. And then after lunch we went on a pony ride. I never thought I'd stay on I was laughing so much . . . I haven't ridden since I was in my teens. Legs feel like jelly now but it was worth it. We went right into the woods. It was really magical.'

Claire put out a hand to steady herself. He was all right. He hadn't had an accident. He hadn't crashed the car. He was fine. But why hadn't he said anything? And why had he taken Phyllis to the delicatessen, to the place where they had bought their 'sunset picnic' as they had since called it. It had been their place, their secret. Now everyone knew about it.

She looked up, her eyes blurred. There he was. Over by the French windows joking with Colin. She stared, trying to meet his eyes, to force him to look at her. But he didn't look up, didn't even seem to have noticed her.

The bell for dinner rang and everyone trooped into the dining room. Claire stayed where she was, pretending to fold up her newspaper. No longer hungry, nauseous at the very thought of food, she walked slowly up the stairs to her room. There, lying on her bed, she remembered how the day had started. She could no more sing now, she thought, than a cabbage could dance.

14

Claire had just finished her first mouthful of cold roast beef when the door burst open. Everyone looked round, shocked.

A young man stood swaying in the doorway. Claire did not recognise him at first. Then she realised it was Quintin, Iris' boyfriend. For a moment she thought he was ill or hurt and had come to fetch help. There was a strange look on his face, a look at once both scared and determined.

No one said anything. Two petals from the roses Iris had picked earlier in the garden dropped soundlessly on to the polished wood of the sideboard. Suddenly, Quintin stepped into the room and slammed the door behind him as violently as he had opened it. The residents flinched. Doors were not banged at The Pines unless by accident or a gust of wind.

'Where is she then?' he shouted. 'Which one of you is she feeding?'

His eyes moved round the room like a cloth scouring a pan. Back and forth. Back and forth.

'So we can all feed ourselves, can we? Aren't we clever? Where is she then? Wiping someone's bottom? Or has someone wet their beds? Is that it? Is it?'

He thumped the sideboard as he spoke. Several more petals, some pink, some white, fell. A murmur of disapproval ran round the room. Phyllis made to rise.

'Now look here . . .' she began.

'Sit down,' he screamed. 'Stay where you are. All of you. Just stay where you are.'

Phyllis sat down again slowly and wiped her mouth with her napkin. It occurred to Claire that Quintin was drunk. His face was flushed and he appeared unsteady on his feet.

'What's going on? Why aren't you all eating? Who's this?' said Tom, the deaf former pilot, waving his fork in Quintin's direction.

Sitting on his own with his back to the door, he appeared to have only just noticed Quintin.

'Shut up! Don't speak. None of you speak.'

The residents, at first curious, began to look worried. Someone dropped their cutlery. Janet tittered nervously.

Quintin began to walk around the room and their eyes followed him. He moved slowly, his thumbs jammed provocatively into the front pockets of his jeans, enjoying their attention.

'I want an answer, you see. An answer. That's what I want. Either she wants to go or she doesn't. Yes or no.'

The residents stared, clearly puzzled. Only Claire understood.

He stopped at the serving hatch where the joint of beef which Matron had carved only five minutes before still stood. Next to it were bowls of green, tomato, and potato salad, left out in case anyone wanted a second helping.

'We can still chew then, can we?' he said, pulling off a lump of meat and cramming it in his mouth.

He helped himself to potato salad, then, his fingers still covered in mayonnaise, scooped up a handful of sliced tomato.

'Not bad, is it, the food here? Still, I suppose meals are the highlight of your day, the only thing you've got left after the telly.'

Another murmur of disapproval ran round the room. He couldn't talk to them like this. They wouldn't let him. But still no one spoke.

Quintin grinned and licked his fingers clean, looking up after each loud suck, like a child daring his parents.

He began to walk round the room again.

'An answer. That's what I want. That's all.'

Janet, who had been fiddling with her glass, knocked it over accidentally, smashing it against her plate. The noise bit into the room. She looked up guiltily, then down at her lap.

Quintin walked over to her.

'I'm sorry, I didn't . . .'

'What's your name?'

'I . . . I . . .'

'Your name?' he insisted.

'Ja . . . Ja . . . Ja . . . Janet,' she stuttered.

'Janet's broken her glass,' he announced, as if no one else had noticed.

He held a piece of the glass up to the light then dropped it casually on to the floor.

'Oh, well. I suppose they're used to cleaning up after you. Your pooh, your snot, your sick.'

He walked back to the serving hatch and picked up the carving knife. The room, already still, became even stiller. Everyone watched the knife, the blade moving through the air as he waved it to and fro. Janet began to cry, quietly at first, then more loudly.

'Shut up! For God's sake, shut up, will you!' he shouted.

Claire saw Phyllis, who was sitting next to Janet, stretch out a hand under the table to comfort her, and felt a surge of warmth for her. Quintin stabbed at the air then swept the bowls of salad to the floor. A blob of mayonnaise flew up into the air and landed on the table where Claire was sitting with Eric.

The door opened, almost as violently it had done a few minutes earlier. Matron and Iris stood in the doorway.

'What was all that noise? What's going on?' demanded Matron.

'Watch out! He's got a knife,' warned Phyllis.

Iris stepped forward.

'Quintin! What are you doing? What the hell do you think you're doing.'

She stepped forward again. Quintin held up the knife so that the sharp end was pointing in her direction. She backed off, round a table. Quintin followed her.

'I want an answer. Yes or no. Will you or won't you?'

'For Christ's sake, Quintin. What do you think you're playing at? This is a home, an old people's home, and these are people, real people. You can't put them back in the cupboard when you've finished knocking them about.'

Matron watched helplessly. So did everyone else.

'Do you or don't you? I want an answer. Now.'

He stopped following her. Claire could hear him breathing. He was standing right behind her. She kept very still. She didn't dare look round in case the movement attracted his attention.

Suddenly she felt herself lurch backwards as Quintin yanked her chair away from the table. His arm was round her neck, forcing her head up, pressing against her windpipe.

'I want an answer. The right answer. And if I don't get it then . . . maybe . . . well . . . maybe . . .'

He forced Claire's chin up further so that the back of her head was pressing down against her shoulders. Iris rushed forwards. Claire saw Quintin's other arm, the arm holding the knife, move towards her exposed throat. Iris stopped.

'So what is it to be then? Are you coming with me or are you staying here – with this old crone?'

Don't panic, Claire told herself. Just breathe normally. In and out. In and out. That's it. Just concentrate on breathing.

'Quintin . . . please . . . let her go!' begged Iris.

He tightened his grasp round her neck, the hard bone of his wrist digging into her skin.

'Yes or no?'

There was a pause. Claire could not see Iris but she sensed that everyone else was looking at her, reading the struggle on her face. She wanted to call out, to tell her not to listen, not to give in, but she didn't have enough breath.

'I'm waiting.'

He was pressing so hard she wanted to gag. She swallowed, her throat dry and tight as a rubber knot. She was struggling now, fighting for breath. She was going to choke. She knew she was. She could bear it no longer. Her stomach contracted violently and she vomited, spewing sick over Quintin's arm.

He jerked the arm away and in the same instant Peter jumped on him, pulling him to the floor. The knife slipped from his hold and was seized by Eric. There was a violent struggle then Peter had his wrists, was kneeing him in the groin, and he was writhing, groaning, curling up like a chopped worm. Colin grabbed his legs and Phyllis threw a jug of water over his head. He thrashed about but was no match for Peter's bulk, and after a few moments became still.

Peter tied his hands behind his back with a napkin, knotting it tightly. Then he took off his belt and bound Quintin's feet.

'We'll take him outside,' he said to Colin. 'Let him cool off a bit.'

They carried him away. Iris followed. Immediately, the room erupted like a punctured balloon. Everyone started to talk at the same time.

'I thought he was going to kill me,' wailed Janet. 'When he took up that piece of glass, I thought he was going to cut my face.'

'Who was he?' said Eric, examining the carving knife as if it were an interesting archaeological find.

'Call the police!' shouted Tom. 'Quick! Before he breaks free.'

'Little thug,' said Maureen. 'I'll get my Mike on to him. He'll sort him out.'

'He could have killed us all. Gunned us down. You hear about it . . . perfectly ordinary people, people you talk to in the street, suddenly going mad and running rampage,' said Phyllis.

'What did he want?' asked Freda. 'I don't understand . . . what was he talking about . . . what answer did he want?'

Claire, her dress flecked with sick, said nothing.

'It's OK . . . he won't come back, it's over now, it's all over,' said Matron, putting an arm round Janet.

The door opened a third time. Everyone spun round, half expecting to see Quintin, another knife in his hand. But it was only Colin and Peter followed by several other members of staff.

'He's gone,' said Peter. 'Iris has driven him home. One of the gardeners went with her just in case. But I don't think he'll do anything. He seemed to have calmed down.'

He came up to Claire.

'Are you all right?'

She smiled, blinking.

'Yes, fine. Shocked and probably a little bruised but otherwise unharmed.'

She felt her neck, patting it gently with her fingertips, seeking out the tender spots.

'He was just frustrated,' she said. 'It can do that to you –

frustration, powerlessness. It can make you do mad things – things you wouldn't dream of doing normally.'

She seemed totally composed, as if it had been ten years not ten minutes since a young man had tightened his hands round her throat.

Peter knelt beside her and dabbed at the sick on her dress.

'You were very brave,' he said gently. 'Very brave indeed.'

He poured her a glass of water and handed her a tissue to wipe her face.

Her bottom lip began to wobble.

'Very brave,' he repeated. 'Very, very brave.'

She began to shake violently, as if his words had unlocked the fear she had, until then, suppressed so successfully.

'I didn't feel brave,' she said. 'I didn't feel brave at all. I was terrified. Absolutely terrified. I didn't know what to do. I didn't know whether to try to struggle free or stay still or what. I thought he was going to choke me . . . I thought nobody was going to do anything . . . I thought you were all going to just stand there and watch him . . . watch him kill me . . .'

She started to sob loudly. Matron and the others gathered round, offering sympathy and advice.

'She doesn't need a doctor,' said Peter, rejecting a suggestion from Phyllis. 'Or smelling salts or tranquillisers or anything. She just needs time to come round.'

He stood up as someone pressed against him.

'Please! Don't crowd her,' he said angrily.

'Don't you think we ought to take her to casualty?' ventured Matron. 'Just to make sure nothing is broken.'

'No. I don't,' he said firmly. 'Nothing is broken. Just bruised. Now please. Give her room to breathe.'

They moved back and Peter turned round to face Claire.

'Come on,' he said, helping her stand up. 'I'll take you upstairs. You need to lie down.'

He drew the curtains and removed her dress, rolling it into a ball inside out and placing it by the door. Claire, still crying, allowed herself to be helped into bed.

'I'll ring for some tea,' he said.

'You won't go,' said Claire, panicking. 'You won't leave me on my own.'

'I won't go anywhere,' he said. 'Not until you want me to.'

He phoned for some tea and biscuits then drew up a chair to the bed and sat down.

'I thought he was hurt at first,' said Claire. 'That he'd been hit by a car or something. Then, just for a moment, I thought he was joking and that he'd suddenly smile and say hello, that he'd leave us to finish our lunch. It was only when he shouted at Phyllis that I realised he was serious . . . and even then, I didn't think . . . I didn't think he would get violent.'

She relived the scene – the moment he had picked up a piece of Janet's broken glass, the moment he had grabbed the knife, the moment he had dragged her chair away from the table. Then she relived it again. And again.

As she spoke, Peter stroked her hand – softly, gently, rhythmically.

'I'm sorry . . . I'm sorry I keep going over and over it. But I . . . I . . . I just . . .'

Her voice caught and she started to cry again.

'There's no need to apologise,' he said. 'You must talk about it. You need to. It's the only way you'll get over it.'

The tea and biscuits arrived. Claire, still crying, heard Matron whispering to Peter at the door but could not make out what she was saying.

'I don't have to see a doctor, do I?' she asked when he came back to the bed.

'No. Not if you don't want to. Later on maybe. Just to make absolutely sure your neck's OK.'

He poured her a cup of tea and plumped up her pillows. Claire began to talk again. How the lack of air had made her feel dizzy, how she'd thought she was going to faint, how she'd known she was going to be sick, known she couldn't do anything about it. She talked fast, tumbling over the sentences, repeating herself, leaving out words, jumping back and forth.

All the time, Peter stroked her hands. And gradually she quietened, talked more slowly and coherently, until finally she was quiet. Peter rearranged the pillows so that she could lie down and she sank back gratefully.

'Better?' he asked.

'Yes, thanks. A lot, lot better.'

Neither spoke for a while. Then she raised her head slightly.

'Have you done this sort of thing before? Counselled people? You know, worked for the Samaritans or something?'

He shook his head.

'No. Why?'

'You just seem to know exactly what you're doing, that's all. I wondered if you'd been trained.'

'I worked in a bank,' he explained. 'Before I moved into management I worked in a branch in East London with the worst record for armed raids in the country. I had a gun pointed at my head twice in three months. So I suppose I know what it feels like.'

'Oh, I see.'

She let her head fall back on the pillows and yawned.

Peter stood up.

'You need to sleep now. You're exhausted.'

She nodded obediently, no longer afraid to be left.

'I'll be in my room if you need me. Just give me a ring. I won't go out.'

She nodded again, warmth spreading through her body, her limbs heavy and tired.

He took the tray of tea out with him and her dirty dress.

Alone, she snuggled down into the sheets, thinking, not of Quintin's hands round her throat, but of Peter's hands round her hands – the way he had touched them, as if they were beautiful, something to be cherished, something to be loved. And, cradled by this thought, she fell asleep.

15

Claire arranged a silk scarf around her neck so that the bruises which had come up overnight would not show.

'Are you sure they don't hurt?' said Iris, coming up behind her. 'They look awful. All purple and angry.'

'They look worse than they are,' said Claire. 'Like a lot of things,' she added, smiling at Iris in the mirror of her dressing table.

Iris did not smile back. She was exhausted. She had spent the whole of the previous afternoon arguing with Quintin, both of them alternately shouting and crying. Later, she had spent an hour with Matron offering mitigating excuses for behaviour she privately thought could not be excused. She had only just managed to keep her job. And it was only thanks to Claire's intervention that Quintin was not, at that very moment, either in custody or on police bail. Then, that morning, after an evening of suspicious questioning from Quintin's parents, she had had to face the residents. Tom had lectured her. Phyllis had been haughty. Maureen had muttered something inaudible under her breath. And Eric had looked at her for the first time.

Claire touched her arm.

'The doctor said I was OK. Honestly. He said I might find it a bit tender chewing or biting things for a few days but that otherwise I was fine.'

Iris placed her hands on Claire's shoulders and squeezed them lightly.

'I'm sorry. I really am.'

'But you mustn't be. There's no need to be.'

How could she tell Iris that she felt happier now than she had felt for a long time? That yesterday when she had woken up she had phoned Peter and found him waiting as he had promised. That he had come to her room and read her extracts from Elizabeth David's *French Provincial Cooking*. That he had asked the kitchen to send up some soup and fed it her himself, spoonful by spoonful. That they had talked and laughed and drunk tea. That later, after the doctor had come and gone, he had helped her dress and taken for a ride in his car. That they had parked by the sea at Alnmouth and sat there, the doors open, listening to the waves, talking about colours.

'I like green best of all,' she said.

'Why?'

'Because Spring is green. New things, growing things. I think that's why. Because it symbolises hope, renewal, freshness.'

'I like purple,' he said. 'It was the colour of the king's cloak in the dressing-up box at school. I loved that cloak. One day I even hid it in the cloakroom so that no one else would be able to find it and wear it instead of me.'

She laughed at the thought of a young Peter cavorting in purple velvet.

'Purple and green,' he mused. 'They go well together. Complement one another. I've always thought that.'

She smiled, absurdly pleased, and suggested a walk along the shore.

How could she tell Iris, that without Quintin's outburst, none of this would have happened? That she would have spent the afternoon in the garden reading Marcus Aurelius.

'It's not your fault. You mustn't blame yourself,' she said.

'But it is my fault,' said Iris. 'If I had told him one way or the other he wouldn't have come. He only came because he wanted an answer. Because he was so frustrated and upset. He only came because he loved me.'

'No, no, no!'

Claire turned urgently as though to prevent an accident, a child falling from a window, a glass bowl slipping and breaking.

'He came for himself not for you. He came so that you would feel guilty and say yes.'

She could not bear the idea of Iris making the same mistake

as she had done, confusing violence with passion, selfishness with love.

'But maybe I should say yes. It's only one year. One year out of my life. I don't know why I'm making such a big thing of it, building it up so much, talking about it as though it will change everything.'

'Because maybe it will. Things do. Look at me. I got married and that was it. My whole life set in aspic. Everything affected by that one decision. I didn't think it would be like that. I never dreamt it would be like that. But it was.'

'Did your husband do things like that? Like Quintin did yesterday?'

Claire frowned and pulled at her mouth.

'He behaved in such a way that he made me feel at fault when in fact he was.'

'How do you mean?'

'I mean that he would come home very late without telling me and then, when I objected, make me feel I was being unreasonable. I would end up apologising for being upset that the dinner I had spent two hours cooking was ruined.'

'But that's terrible.'

'Yes, but what was more terrible was that, at the time, I did not know it was terrible. I thought it was my fault. That everything was my fault. That if only I tried harder, cleaned the house better, cooked nicer meals, everything would be OK.'

'Was that why you left him?'

Claire did not answer.

'I'm sorry . . . I didn't mean to pry.'

'No, it's OK. I was just thinking what to say, that's all.'

She paused again then said: 'I left him because he didn't love me. Because I saw that he didn't love me, understood it quite suddenly one day.'

The phone rang and Iris answered it.

'They need me downstairs,' she said, replacing the receiver. 'Cook's been stung by a wasp. They want me to help out in the kitchen.'

'You won't rush into anything? said Claire quickly. 'Please, promise me, you will think about it, won't you?'

Iris kissed her lightly on the forehead.

'I promise,' she said.

Alone, Claire turned to face her dressing table again. In the mirror, next to her own reflection, she saw that of her mother, a pained, sad expression on her face.

'You tried,' said Claire. 'You couldn't have done anything else. It was my life, I had to do it, I had to make the mistake.'

16

I left him because he repelled me. That was one of the reasons. Because the grossness which had first excited me – the gusto with which he ate, the lust for my skin, my small, white, round breasts – ended up by disgusting me.

Towards the end, I jumped when he touched me, as if scalded by an iron. I started playing music at meal times or going to the lavatory so that I would not have to listen to him chewing or watch him mash his food.

At night, when he clambered on to me, his skin clammy with sweat, the round roll of his belly enveloping me like a soft rubber ring, I recoiled like a slug from salt.

I would lie there, not daring to refuse, allowing him to pummel me, to squeeze my breasts, to spread my legs wider and wider, to enter me, not caring that I was still dry, too selfish to wait.

Afterwards, when he had come, when he was lying there, beached, with that self-satisfied grin on his face, all I wanted to do was heave him off me, open the window, breathe cold, pure air, wash myself clean again.

My mother, even in those first few weeks, knew I was unhappy although, tactfully, she did not say anything. She would visit on market days after Bill had left for work, carrying small thoughtful gifts – a bunch of white sweet peas picked that morning to put on my dressing table, two brown eggs from my favourite hen, a cheese and tomato flan so that I wouldn't have to cook that evening. More importantly, she would bring me news, light-hearted gossip about the people in the parish. Before, when I had lived there, I had despised village life, called it petty and parochial, claustrophobic even.

Now though, now that I could walk down the street in a new dress without anyone noticing, far less caring, I clung to my mother's words as if to a raft, interested in the smallest event, the slightest, most insignificant disagreement between my former neighbours.

Bill did not like my mother visiting. When he came home on the days she had been, I would always say I had seen her, anxious not to hide anything in case he accused me of duplicity. Immediately, he would start to prowl around – to look for signs of interference. He would refuse the food she had cooked, would say it was too rich or that he was not hungry. At night, he would complain that the flowers she had brought were aggravating his hayfever and would take them downstairs. In the morning, I would find them in the bin, their white fragrance squashed into yesterday's rubbish.

My mother must have sensed that her visits were causing difficulties because after a while she started suggesting that we should meet in town. We had morning coffee in the lounge of the Swan Hotel and talked about the things that were safe to talk about – who had been called up, who was on leave, the bitterness felt by Jack Rogers because he had not won first prize for his onions in the crafts and produce show. Often, my mother would produce tickets for an extramural lecture or a lunchtime organ recital in Christ Church. Or she would take me boating or help me choose material so that she could make me a new dress.

I was grateful for these distractions but also resentful. I did not want my mother's pity. She had told me not to marry Bill and I had done so. And now it seemed she had been right and I had been wrong. And I disliked this – that she seemed to know me better than I knew myself. Looking back, knowing what it is to be a mother, I can see that she felt my unhappiness almost as keenly as I felt it myself, that all she was trying to do was cheer me up, take me out of myself, help me see that my decision was not final.

It must have been terrible for her to watch Bill chip away at me. For that is what he did. Day after day, like a savage bird, he pecked at the sense of worth and identity she had nurtured so carefully all those years.

Above all, he decried my efforts at housekeeping. I had thought it would be easy. The house was tiny, there were only two of us, and Bill's salary, although not huge, was adequate. But I had no experience of budgeting or planning. Also, I did not know the price of things. At the vicarage we had bought few groceries apart from flour, sugar, salt, soap, bacon, tea and coffee, and the odd joint of beef or ham. We had grown all our own vegetables, made all our own jams and marmalades, kept our own chickens, and with the help of Kitty, the village girl who helped my mother in the house, baked all our own bread and cakes. Milk, butter and cream came from neighbouring farms, usually in the form of gifts. So too, when they were in season, came apples, pears and plums.

Now, in a two-up, two-down terraced house with a back yard just big enough to hang up three of Bill's shirts, I began to discover how difficult and expensive it was to make ends meet when there were no beans or potatoes a few yards away waiting to be picked or dug. I bought indiscriminately, not thinking of menus or what would go with what, an easy prey for stallholders anxious to get rid of four pounds of rhubarb by lunchtime. The result was that I would run out of flour or milk in the middle of making a sauce, discover I had no eggs when I wanted to make an omelette or realise, just as the shops closed, that I had cabbage, carrots, peas and cauliflower but no meat or fish.

I was not much better at washing and cleaning either. I would put off washing Bill's shirts for days then, suddenly, wash them all at once only to find that it was raining and that I had nowhere to dry them. Several times we ate supper sitting on cushions on the floor, the chairs occupied by wet clothes and the windows steamed up, listening to the gentle plip plop of water dripping from Bill's shirt sleeves into the saucers given us as a wedding present by my father's Aunt Madge.

I could have asked for advice, should have done so, but I was too proud and shy. Besides, the other women in the street, the woman next door I had seen on my first night leaning out of the window, the woman on the other side, all seemed much older and wiser with children or jobs. I had suggested that I too should get a job. They needed more workers in the local munitions factory. There were signs everywhere asking for women to volunteer. But Bill had ridiculed the suggestion, had asked what chance I had of making ammunition correctly when I could not even make an apple pie.

'They make bullets,' he said. 'You need to have your wits about you. If you put the casings on the wrong way round, they don't work. I've heard of stories like that, of soldiers getting dud ammunition, soldiers at the front, mind, and only finding out when it's too late. You don't want to have that on your conscience.'

I suspected he did not know what he was talking about, that, like me, he did not know one end of a bullet from another but I also feared he might be right and so I never applied for a job.

Now, of course, I can see that Bill's real worry was not that I might turn out dud bullets but that I would no longer be dependent on him. Because this was the surprising thing. The very qualities that had first attracted him to me, my independence, my boldness, my forthright opinions, were, once we were married, the qualities he tried hardest to obliterate. He had enjoyed arguing with me when I was his assistant, had liked the fact that I was confident enough to disagree with him, had even made deliberately provocative statements to arouse my anger. But when I became his wife, he changed. He no longer wanted me to have a life of my own with my own interests and opinions. He wanted me to be part of his life, a shadow, an echo, a sounding-board for *his* opinions.

I realised this quite clearly one night when we were walking home from a play. I can no longer remember what the play was or why it had been staged. There were few plays in those days because they were felt to be an extravagance. Besides, most of the actors and stage managers had been called up and the theatres taken over by the Ministry of Defence. Partly on account of this, because it felt such a luxury, I was excited. I had enjoyed the anticipation, the dressing up in smart clothes, the animated chatter in the interval. I had also genuinely enjoyed the performance. And so, as we walked away, away from the bright lights and the knots of people still gathered outside, I squeezed Bill's arm.

'It was disappointing,' he said.

I removed my hand as if he had slapped it.

'I enjoyed it,' I said.

'It was disappointing,' he said again, as though repetition would ensure agreement.

He spoke with finality, like someone shutting the lid on a coffin, closing the subject for ever. And suddenly, as we walked along, our footsteps loud on the cold November pavements, my coat flapping loose as the bottom button escaped from a loose buttonhole, I saw with terrifying clarity that he was not interested in me, that my thoughts and feelings were of no more importance to him than those of the man he bought his evening paper from.

I stopped abruptly. He continued walking then, after a while, looked back and stopped too.

'What are you doing?' he called.

'I'm not happy,' I said quietly, too quietly for him to hear.

'What? I can't hear . . . hurry up . . . I'm cold.'

'I'm not happy, Bill,' I said, bending down, willing myself to speak louder.

'What? What are you saying? For God's sake, Claire, hurry up. It's freezing!'

I straightened up and joined him.

'I was just fastening my coat,' I said. 'One of the buttons keeps coming undone.'

Back home, I made cocoa. He said it was too weak. I cursed my lack of courage.

17

It was my father's death, though, that really convinced me.

It was January 1941. We had been married six months and I had learnt how to cook a roast lunch without burning the meat or letting the vegetables go cold.

The day started badly when I took a mouthful of tea and discovered the milk had gone sour. I ran to the sink and spat, running the water until the brown liquid flecked with white lumps had all gone. Later, I wanted to dispose of the day in the same way – to wash it down the plughole, swish it away, watch it disappear forever. At the time, though, I merely made a fresh pot of tea which I drank black, weak, with a teaspoon of sugar. I switched the radio on and the lamps. It was one of those dull, gloomy days which never seem to get properly light.

I spent the morning cleaning – dusting, ironing, and washing the kitchen floor. By that time, I had grown reasonably proficient at housework. Bill had not yet complimented me on the state of the house – he never did – but he had stopped making comments about how he needed to open the windows to see out properly. After lunch, I made the pastry for the steak and kidney pie we were going to have for dinner and scraped some carrots, leaving them to stand in a saucepan of cold water. Then I wrote a shopping list. I needed to collect Bill's shoes from the cobbler's, buy potatoes and find some thread to mend the tear in my red skirt. It was a difficult colour to match – a pinky purplish red rather than a pillarbox scarlet – and I had already tried the local haberdashery shop without success.

As I set out, it started to drizzle. Not enough to justify an umbrella but enough to be uncomfortable. It had rained the previous day as well and the day before that and there were puddles on the pavements where the water had not yet drained away. A mile down the road I trod on a loose paving stone which squirted mud all up my legs. I thought about going home to change but decided not to. I was almost in town by then and going home and coming out again would take at least half an hour.

I went to collect Bill's shoes first. The cobbler could not find them and I had to wait, perched on a stool, the damp creeping up my legs, while he opened brown paper bags and held up shoes for me to identify. He found them finally, lying in his workroom, still unmended, and promised to work on them straightaway so that I could pick them up later.

I went next to the market and bought potatoes, ignoring the efforts of the man selling them to induce me to buy cabbage and swedes as well. I was wise to stallholders by then. Or at least I thought I was.

The red thread proved more difficult. I tried three haberdashery shops, all without success, then found some in a fourth, discovering at the same time that I had left my potatoes behind somewhere. I traced them to the first shop, went back to the cobbler's and was splashed on my way out by a car driven by a young man in evening dress, probably a student and almost certainly drunk, accompanied by four female passengers.

By now thoroughly damp and fed up, I made my way home, deciding on the spur of the moment as I passed Blacks, then Oxford's only department store, to revive myself in the perfumery. I was at the Max Factor counter, I remember, admiring the shape of the bottle containing their newest fragrance when one of the assistants approached me. I don't know what she looked like – at the time I was aware only of a pointy bosom, hair piled high like stiffly-whipped cream, and a voice designed to intimidate.

'Madam . . . excuse me, madam, but one of your bags appears to be leaking.'

I looked down. She was right. A dirty trickle of water was dripping from the potato bag on to the thick, maroon pile of the carpet. I blushed, mumbled something about being splashed by a car, and headed for the door, catching sight of myself in a mirror as I went, a lick of wet hair hanging over my forehead, my stockings spattered with stains.

And it was in this state, humiliated, wet, tired, the palms of my hands scored with red lines where the handles of the bag had dug into my flesh, that I arrived home. I dropped my shopping, kicked off my shoes, went upstairs to change and made myself a hot drink.

So it was only later, after I had been home about an hour, when I went to pick up the shopping, that I noticed the telegram on the mat.

'Matthew died yesterday. Please come. Mother,' it said.

Matthew was my father, the man who cut such a vague, shadowy figure beside my mother, who always looked puzzled, as if he had just found a zebra in the garden, as if life was not quite what he had expected it to be. I had thought that maybe, after my marriage, I would get to know him better but this had not happened. The two or three occasions when I had made arrangements to see him on his own, without my mother, he had cried off at the last moment, saying he had urgent church business to attend to.

My mother had never referred to him as 'Matthew' when speaking to me. He was always 'your father' just as she, when referred to by him, was always 'your mother'. The fact that she had done so in the telegram – that she had, for once, blurred our roles, written as if to a friend rather than a daughter, spoke more than ten pages.

I rushed upstairs, packed an overnight bag, wrote a note to Bill, turned off the meat cooking on the stove, grabbed an umbrella, put on my coat, looked round for my keys and only then, as I glanced at my watch, did I realise that I had missed the last bus to our village, that I would have to wait until the next day.

Bill came home an hour later after I had borrowed a neighbour's bike and cycled to the nearest hotel to phone Nesfield Hall, the only house in our village with a phone. I had asked the housekeeper to send a message to my mother saying I would catch the first bus the next morning.

He put on his slippers and sat down and, as usual, started

to complain about the number of ceremonies he had had to conduct that day.

'It's indecent – the way we're expected to pack them in,' he said. 'It's more like a cattle market than a register office. I had to call the police this afternoon. One lot of relatives started fighting with another lot. They'd all been waiting outside in the rain getting more and more irritable and apparently someone started comparing the brides' looks. It got very nasty. One of the bridegrooms had to be taken to hospital. It wasn't serious, though. Only a broken arm. I married him later.'

I nodded, distracted, the telegram piercing my thoughts like a poisoned arrow tip, wondering what my mother was doing.

I think it was about halfway through the meal when he asked me what was wrong. I opened my mouth, was about to say something, to blurt it out, when something stopped me. I wanted him to guess, to know without being told, to comfort me without being asked.

'Nothing,' I said.

'There is. I can tell there is. You've hardly said a word all evening.'

I shook my head and got up to hide the tears swelling in my eyes.

He tried again later after I had done the washing up and we were sitting down – him with his evening paper, me with my red skirt and sewing box.

'Go on. Tell me. There's something bothering you. I can tell there is.'

I wanted to tell him. I wanted to so much. But I also wanted him to reach out, to take me in his arms, to offer me sympathy even though he didn't know why I needed it. As soon as he did this, I knew it would all come out – the terrible day, the potatoes I'd lost, the shoes which hadn't been mended, the woman in Blacks and then the telegram, the telegram announcing that my father had died before I had got to know him. But he didn't. He didn't even reach out to stroke my leg with his foot as he sometimes did when we sat together in the evenings.

Instead, he folded his newspaper neatly and looked at his watch. It was half past eight, time for his evening pint.

'Well, if you won't tell me, I can't help you,' he said matter-of-factly, standing up and putting on his cap.

I stayed in my chair, his words reverberating in me like shook steel, and as the door shut, something hardened in me. I decided then that I wanted to leave him.

18

My father had killed himself. Had gone upstairs to his study after evensong, removed his shoes and wedding ring, and taken 120 sleeping tablets prescribed, ironically, after the death of his own father five years before.

The sermon he had preached at evensong had been about doubt, about its value in fostering humanity and humility, about the importance of remaining open to new ideas. This could be difficult, he said. It was very tempting to become closed, to retreat to the safety and warmth of old ideas, to shut the door on change. Fighting this temptation required constant vigilance, he said. It was a daily battle. But one could go too far in this battle. Too much doubt, too much openness could eat away one's inner core. It was important not to undermine one's beliefs so much that, like a building with no foundations, one was at risk of toppling over.

The coroner made much of the sermon at the inquest, implying that my father had killed himself to escape the religious doubts that were tormenting him – doubts brought on largely as a result of the war. 'This was a man racked by uncertainty,' he said, 'tormented by the idea that the God he had devoted his life to, might not exist. For most of his life he managed to overcome these doubts but when the war started and one by one his parishioners started losing husbands, sons and brothers, he found it more difficult. When he heard that two young men in his parish, two former choirboys, had both been killed at the front, he sank into a deep despair. It was in this mood, this sorrow at the suffering of those in his pastoral care, that he took his own life.'

My mother, elegant in black crepe at the back of the magistrates' court, sniffed dismissively at the suggestion that my father had been suffering a crisis of faith.

'He was just depressed,' she said. 'He always had been.'

Besides, she said afterwards, he had not even particularly liked the two young men mentioned by the coroner. As choirboys they had never been able to sing in tune and were always turning up late for practice. He had only taken them on to please their mothers.

She had not been worried when my father failed to reappear from his study that Sunday evening. He had always kept odd hours and had recently become even more reclusive, often spending the whole night reading or writing.

In fact, it was only thanks to Mrs Frampton, the blacksmith's wife, that my father was discovered on Monday. She had come to arrange a time for her youngest son's christening service and refused to leave when my mother said my father was working.

'I can wait,' she said, settling herself down at the clean scrubbed table where my mother was making bread.

And so my mother had reluctantly rubbed the dough off her fingers and knocked at my father's study door, gently at first, then more strongly, and finally quite loudly, calling his name at the same time – 'Matthew! Matthew! Mrs Frampton's here to see you.'

I think the thing that upset her most was that he had removed his wedding ring. She took this as an accusation, a sign that he blamed their relationship for the unhappiness he had always felt but, until his death, never been able to express.

She said this at the funeral – that in her view my father had been a deeply unhappy man all his life. The fact that he had been a vicar had made it worse, she said, because he had felt it was his role to comfort, to minister rather than be ministered to. He had shored his grief up, she said, banked it down in the traditional English manner with smiles and pretence until finally he had run out of sandbags.

The reporters had liked this metaphor and had scribbled my mother's words down frantically. But there was no evidence to support her view that my father was what is now known as a manic depressive. He had burnt all his private papers before swallowing the tablets and had been to his doctor only twice in the previous ten years – the first time when he could not sleep following the death of his own father and the second time when his left ear had become blocked with wax. In a written statement to the court, the doctor said my father had never complained of depression.

And so, in the end, the reporters, like the coroner and my father's parishioners, chose the religious crisis explanation and ran the story under the headline 'Vicar Gives Up on God'.

The villagers, in fact, were scandalised by my mother's suggestion that my father was unhappy. Many took it as a personal affront implying that they had been particularly trying as parishioners.

'I don't know what she means,' said Mrs Frampton. 'He wasn't sad. Why, I saw him laughing only the day before he died. Roaring with laughter he was.'

Of course, I learnt all this only much later. At the time, on that Tuesday morning, bouncing along on the 9.30 a.m. bus, I did not know why or how my father had died, only that he was dead.

It occurred to me on the journey that he might not have had a heart attack as I had first assumed, that he might have had an accident, have fallen off while riding, been knocked down by a car, or slipped on the ice and cut his head. But I did not, even for one second, suspect suicide. Despite this, I was not particularly surprised when my mother told me. I mean I was surprised, of course. I was horrified. But what surprised me much more was the picture that emerged over the next few weeks of the relationship between my father and mother. You see, I had always thought they were happy. Happy as a couple and happy as individuals. I had never known that my father was depressed. I had not even thought him particularly moody. And I had never seen the blackness which, according to my mother, had gripped him virtually all the time. After years of silence, she suddenly became quite open on the subject.

'I tried to get him to talk about it. It would have been better if he could have been angry, if he had shouted at me even. I wouldn't have minded. But he couldn't. He called it the monster. "The monster is very big today," he would say. That was all.'

She said my father had first threatened to kill himself two days after their wedding when they were sightseeing in Florence. She had always known that one day he would carry out his threat.

Her words stunned me. For I had, until then, in my youthful idealism, thought that marriage and happiness were synonymous. I had felt it was a sin, an aberration, to feel unhappy as I did. The discovery that it was not an aberration, that other married people were unhappy, my own parents even, strengthened the decision I had taken the previous night – to leave Bill and live on my own.

19

Claire watched the wasp collide with the window yet again and wished irritably that someone would come and deal with it.

Peter had warned her that she might feel worse, both physically and mentally, after a couple of days and he had been right. She had woken up that morning with aching limbs, a thumping headache and a feeling of quite extraordinary tetchiness.

That day's paper lay untouched on the table next to the chair in which she was sitting in the Pink Room. There was also a cup of milky coffee, undrunk, a thick scum on its surface. She looked at her watch, calculating how long it would be before Peter returned from the dentist's.

It was another hot, cloudless day. Already, at barely ten o'clock, her feet were starting to swell. She could feel the lining of her skirt sticking against the backs of her thighs. That morning, on the radio, there had been a story about water companies setting up standpipes in the streets of Bradford. Northumbria, apparently, was not as short of water as Yorkshire but, even so, there was now a hosepipe ban in force and notices in the local newspapers urging people to take showers instead of baths and to water their gardens with washing-up water.

The wasp banged angrily at the window. Claire watched, increasingly exasperated.

'It's open. Go on. Oh, you stupid thing! You've flown right past it again.'

She stood up, seized her newspaper and tried to steer the wasp towards the gap at the bottom of the window. But it just buzzed even more frantically than before then suddenly flew straight back into the room towards her. She shrieked and stepped backwards, catching her ankle against the base of a standard lamp.

At that moment, the door opened. Claire looked up angrily, expecting to see Matron or Iris or one of the other staff, ready to demand the wasp's instant removal. There was a flurry of something black and wavy. A tall woman followed. The anger on Claire's face melted, first into astonishment, then into delight. She ran forward and the two women hugged.

'Catherine! What a lovely surprise! Oh . . . I am glad to see you!'

She stepped back, looked the woman up and down, then hugged her again.

'And you look so well, so brown, better than I've ever seen you look.'

The black flurry waved his tail furiously and pushed his nose against Claire's legs. Catherine pulled him back.

'Stop it! Vashti! You're not do that. You don't need to inspect her. I already have done. Many times. Usually late at night under the influence of gin!'

Claire laughed and patted the dog who grinned back at her then suddenly snapped at the air.

'What was that?'

'A wasp. I was trying to get it out. He's swallowed it!'

Catherine laughed.

'Are you sure he'll be OK? It won't sting him?'

'No, no. He's always eating them. Ella calls him the pest control officer.'

Claire led her to the window and ordered a pot of tea, and a bowl of water for Vashti.

'Why didn't you tell me you were coming? I know you said you were going to come and see me soon but I didn't expect you to turn up out of the blue like this.'

Catherine smiled.

'I didn't tell anyone,' she said. 'Not even Ella.' Ella was her daughter, a tall immaculate woman whom Claire found even more intimidating than she had once found Catherine.

'I waited until she had left for work and the nanny had taken Luke to playgroup. Then I packed my bag and called a taxi to take me to the station.'

'But why?'

'I wanted to see if I could do it. It was a challenge. A test, if you like. Both for Vashti and for me.'

At the sound of his name, Vashti, now lying on the floor at Catherine's feet, began to thump his tail again.

'If I'd told Ella she'd have done everything for me – found out the train times, the connections, the numbers of the platforms, everything. I wanted to do it on my own.'

'But what if something had happened? If there'd been an accident?'

'I had a letter in my bag saying who I was, where I was and giving Ella's work and home numbers. Besides, nothing did happen. There was one dicey moment when I discovered that we'd got on a train going to Birmingham. They'd changed the platform numbers at the last moment and I'd been concentrating so hard on negotiating the stairs I hadn't heard the announcement. But we managed to get out in time and find the right platform. It was a real adventure. I felt such a sense of achievement when we arrived at Newcastle. I almost cheered.'

The tea arrived and Claire asked about Ella, her son-in-law Jeremy, and grandson Luke.

'Ella's fine. She's handling a test case against the government at the moment. Something to do with UK employment legislation which breaches an EC directive. Anyhow, it's keeping her very busy. Jeremy? Well . . .'

She rolled her eyes dramatically. Claire giggled. She had forgotten how theatrical Catherine could be.

'He's beginning to talk like a suit as well as wear one. All that gobbledegook you hear politicians come out with on the news about empowerment and dialogue, re-engineering and personal interfaces – well, he's a past master at it. Still, his employers seem to like it. He's just got promoted.'

'And Luke?'

Catherine smiled.

'Luke is pure sunshine – a bottomless well of delight. He gives me so much joy – honestly, I can't tell you how much. It's so different being a grandmother to being a mother. I don't know whether it's just that you're not responsible for them, that you can hand them back when you get fed up with them but, well,

I wouldn't say this to Ella, but in a way I enjoy Luke so much more than I did her.'

Claire frowned.

'He's started saying all sorts of long words. Last week he announced that his jigsaw was "frustrating" only he didn't say it properly so it came out as "fustating". He's also started picking up words from the radio and television. The other day I was in the sitting room with him listening to a natural history programme while he did some colouring. One of the presenters said the word "nipple" – they were talking about the feeding habits of monkeys – and after a while I noticed that Luke, who was right the other side of the room, was saying "red nipple, green nipple, pink nipple, purple nipple". He was still saying it when the nanny showed in someone from the guide dog association who had come to see how Vashti and I were getting on together.'

Claire laughed, first at the idea of Luke saying 'purple nipple' and then simply because it was good to laugh, because she was happy, because Catherine was there. She was still laughing when the door opened again and Peter came in. She introduced him to Catherine.

'I won't stop. I just came to see how you were,' he said.

'Don't rush off. Stay and have a cup of tea with us,' said Claire. 'We can ring and ask for another cup.'

'No, I won't if you don't mind. I think I need to take a couple of paracetamol.'

Claire felt guilty. She had been enjoying herself so much she had completely forgotten his dentist appointment.

'How was it? Was it painful?'

'No, fine. Just a little tender now that the anaesthetic has started to wear off. I'll tell you about it later.'

He left the room and the two women sat down again. Claire poured the tea, aware that Catherine was studying her, listening to her movements.

'He seemed nice.'

Claire hesitated. 'Nice' was not a word that usually featured in Catherine's vocabulary. Was she being tactful?

'Genuine,' added Catherine. 'A genuine sort of person.'

Claire smiled, relieved.

'Yes, he is,' she said.

'What did he mean, though, about coming to see how you were? Have you been ill or something?'

'Well . . .'

She dropped her voice to a conspiratorial whisper.

'You do realise, I hope, that you are talking to someone who has narrowly escaped being strangled.'

'What!'

Claire told her about the attack.

'So Peter saved your life?' said Catherine when she had finished.

'Yes, well, I suppose so. I hadn't really thought of it like that.'

'Come on,' said Catherine, standing up. 'I'm taking you out to lunch. Now we've got two things to celebrate – my first long-distance journey on my own and your dramatic rescue.'

They went to Barley Hall, a small hotel a few miles outside Alnwick, set among yellow barley fields with gardens running down to a stream and a view of a mill. They sat at an open window overlooking the gardens and drank cold, very good white wine with prosciutto and fresh bread. Afterwards, Claire had salmon with lime butter while Catherine, who had always had a hearty appetite, had potato gnocchi with red pesto. Vashti lay under the table, eating crumbs of bread. The waiter suggested that they might like to drink their coffee in the garden and they agreed, choosing seats in the shade near an ornamental pool, a white cat sunning itself at the edge.

'Tell me then,' said Catherine, putting down her coffee cup, feeling for a safe place at the side of her chair. 'Are you in love with him?'

Claire blushed, began to protest, to ask who 'he' was and to laugh evasively until a look from Catherine silenced her.

'I like him,' she said finally. 'I like him very much.'

Catherine said nothing for a while, then leant over, took her hand and squeezed it.

'I'm glad,' she said simply.

'If I was . . . what . . . I mean . . . would you think . . . do you think at our age . . . well . . .'

Catherine interrupted her crisply.

'It's never too late either to love or to make love,' she said and smiled wickedly.

'In fact, I thought I might place an ad in one of the Braille magazines myself. "Old man with young dog sought for talks and walks."'

'You wouldn't!'

'Why not? I thought it might be rather fun devising tests to judge their suitability. I'd rule out everyone who told me their star sign. That would get rid of at least half of them straightaway.'

A waiter arrived with the bill and the news that their taxi had arrived. Claire saw Catherine off on the bus. Then, even though it was not far to walk, she caught another taxi back to The Pines. Her leg had started to ache again and she wanted to lie down. The excitement of seeing Catherine had exhausted her.

Peter was in the hallway when she walked in. She could not tell if he had been waiting there or just passing through.

'There you are,' he said.

'Yes. I've just seen her off on the bus. She's staying the night in Newcastle with friends and then catching the train back to Oxford tomorrow.'

'Did you have a good time?'

'Wonderful . . . we talked the whole time. It's always like that. It doesn't matter how long we don't see one another . . . we just pick up where we left off.'

'You certainly seemed to be enjoying yourselves when I came in.'

She looked closely at him. There was something peevish about the way he had spoken, something grudging as though . . . as though . . . It occurred to her suddenly that he was jealous and this realisation, the knowledge that she, with her lumpen hands and scrawny legs, was the object of his jealousy, made her blood run hot.

'I'm sorry your tooth hurts,' she said, smiling.

'You don't look sorry,' he said, still sullen.

She burst out laughing, unable to restrain herself any longer.

'Come on,' she said, taking him by the hand. 'Tell me what you thought of Catherine.'

20

Rothbury Music Festival was not what Claire had expected. She had imagined something rural and charming – harp recitals by girls with long hair, spinning demonstrations, folk dancing and strawberry teas.

Instead, she found herself in an open air amphitheatre littered with beer cans. At the bottom, lay a huge stage. At the top, was a giant funfair. The air rocked with noise – with screams from the teenagers being spun senseless by the funfair rides, and music, or at least sound, from the band on stage.

She stayed close to Peter as she picked her way among the bodies, mainly young, sprawled on the grass. It wasn't that they looked threatening. They didn't. Many had babies and young children. A man with hair shaved in a chessboard pattern and an orange octopus tattooed on his back was even changing his baby's nappy. But they were so different. And the clothes they were wearing were so extraordinary – velvet witches' hats, earrings in their navels, patchwork pantaloons, thigh-high leather boots. It had been a long time since she had seen people dressed so unconventionally.

Peter led her to a small round tent marked 'Information'. Outside, the names of the bands performing that afternoon were scrawled on a large blackboard.

'There's another stage over there,' he said, pointing to a structure halfway between a wedding marquee and an Indian tepee. 'And another one behind those trees.'

Claire surveyed the scene in front of her – the thousands of people, some dancing, some talking, some fast asleep in the sunshine. The metal of the beer cans glinted like water. A man on stilts walked past. A small boy sold two girls tree-shaped badges to raise money for a rainforest protection group.

Her eyes met Peter's. He raised his eyebrows. So did she. Then, both at the same time, they started to laugh.

'It's not what I was expecting,' she admitted.

'Nor me. Do you want to go?'

'No. Not unless you do. It could be rather fun. For a short while, at least.'

'Good. Come on then. Let's explore.'

They bought vanilla fudge and cans of soft fizzy drink and walked slowly round the ground.

'Have you ever been on one of those?' he asked, pointing at a ride called the Terroriser which flung its passengers at high speed in every conceivable direction before depositing them on the ground again.

'No. I went on some dodgem cars once at the seaside. Apart from that, I've only been on merry-go-rounds. And I always used to feel dizzy on them.'

Another man on stilts walked past them and disappeared into a tent striped red and white. There was a notice outside which they stopped to read.

'Juggling. Three o'clock. The amazing Mr Wiggle-Waggle and his assistant Nimble Nancy.'

'Oh . . . shall we come back and see it? I love juggling . . . I bought some balls once but I wasn't very good. I suppose I didn't practise enough. I could never get beyond three.'

He noticed the incredulous expression on her face.

'Sorry . . . would it bore you?'

'No, no, I'd like to see it. I was just surprised. That's all.'

'People in banks often do funny things in their spare time,' he said. 'At one time, my colleagues included a glider pilot, a man who'd launched his own medieval re-enactment society, a woman who was training to climb the mountain K-2 and a parachuting enthusiast. I suppose it's the safety of the nine-to-five lifestyle. It forces you to look for excitement elsewhere.'

They stopped near the stage behind the trees. It was smaller than the first stage and the band on it was playing music which, although not to Claire's taste, was relatively tuneful.

'Shall we listen for a bit?'

Claire nodded.

He took off his rucksack, spread the green tartan, plastic-backed picnic rug he had been holding and sat down on one side of it. Claire sat down on the other side, noticing as she did so, the smiles on the faces of the couple entwined behind them.

'They're laughing at us,' she said. 'I suppose we must look funny. Like two sticks of rhubarb in a rose bed.'

'Let them laugh!' he said. 'Who cares? Anyhow, wait till they're our age. I bet they won't be going to rock festivals then.'

'Is that what this is? A rock festival?'

He nodded and handed her a leaflet he'd picked up.

'It's usually very traditional. Folk singing, ceilidhs, that sort of thing. But apparently this year the organisers decided to change the theme on a one-off basis to attract more young people. The proceeds are to go towards a new youth centre.'

'Goodness! My first rock festival. Catherine will be impressed!' said Claire, handing him back the leaflet.

Peter lay back and closed his eyes. After a while Claire lay down too, careful to maintain a distance between their bodies, a hand on her skirt to prevent it blowing up.

It was warm in the sunshine and she soon felt drowsy. The music was really quite pleasant, she decided.

'What's the group called? The people playing now?' she asked.

Peter opened his eyes and sat up slightly.

'I don't know . . . wait a minute.'

He consulted the leaflet.

'Cows Don't Dance,' he said.

'What!'

'Yes. Funny name, isn't it? Still, I think it's almost obligatory for rock bands to call themselves something odd.'

'Actually they do,' she said dreamily, closing her eyes.

'What?'

'Dance. Cows, I mean. When they're let out to pasture for the first time after a winter cooped up inside. I saw them once. Great big cows with udders reaching almost to the ground leaping around like lambs. It was an extraordinary sight.'

He lay down again and she opened her eyes a crack and looked at him. He was so close she could see the pores on his skin. There was the faint white line of a scar above his right eyebrow. She had said she liked him. But was that all, she asked herself? Did she feel something more, something stronger? She closed her eyes. She did not know. It was all so strange. So unexpected. Like finding orchids in a station waiting room.

'Margaret – my wife – liked music,' said Peter.

Claire, startled, opened her eyes wide then closed them again when she saw that his were closed.

'She played the piano. Not brilliantly. But competently. Very competently.'

Claire imagined Peter sitting in summer twilight listening to his wife play Chopin's piano concertos.

'What was she like?'

'Tallish. Largish – she wasn't fat but she had a big frame. Brown hair. Grey eyes. She was good with plants – loved gardening. She was a country girl really. She was brought up in the country and I think she'd have liked to live there if circumstances had turned out differently.'

'Did she work?'

'She was a nurse. That was how we met. Corny, I know, but true. I'd been injured by flying shrapnel after a building was hit near my lodgings. Nothing serious. Just a few gashes here and there. She cleaned me up and I invited her out.'

He hadn't said that her eyes were beautiful, thought Claire. Was that because they weren't or because one didn't say that sort of thing to another woman?

Someone made room for them on the front bench just behind the rows of children seated on the floor.

'You know you're old when people start giving up their seats for you,' whispered Peter.

'Yes. I went white early so I've had it for a long time,' she whispered back.

Mr Wiggle-Waggle and Nimble Nancy appeared and started to juggle, first with balls, then with plates, and then with skittles. They wore white satin tunics and trousers with large pink spots, and pointed shoes with bells. Their faces shone with make-up grease.

'Now, we need some helpers,' announced Mr Wiggle-Waggle. 'Two girls, two boys and two grown-ups.'

Arms shot up all over the audience as the children vied for attention. 'Me, me! Over here! Me!'

Mr Wiggle-Waggle chose apparently at random.

'You, you. The boy in the red top. The girl with the curly hair. The man with the beard. Yes, you. No need to be shy. And you . . .'

Claire suddenly realised that he was talking to her, that his hand was on her shoulder, that Peter was smiling, encouraging her.

'No, no, I couldn't, please, don't . . .'

'You don't need to do anything. You just need to stand still,' said Mr Wiggle-Waggle.

'Oh, go on, it's only a bit of fun,' urged Peter.

'That's the spirit. Do it for your husband,' said Mr Wiggle-Waggle.

'He's not . . .' Claire started then stopped. Why not, she thought? Why was she making such a fuss? And, infused with a sudden, devil-may-care recklessness, she stood up and followed Mr Wiggle-Waggle into the ring.

He stood them in a line. Claire was at one end, next to the girl with the curly hair. The man with the beard, the other 'grown-up', was at the other end, next to the boy in the red top.

'Stand very still,' he said. 'No wobbling, no wiggling and above all, no waggling. If you need to laugh, laugh sideways like this.'

He demonstrated a sideways laugh, jerking violently from side to side like the pendulum of a clock. The children tittered nervously.

'Ready!' said Mr Wiggle-Waggle. Nimble Nancy nodded.

'One, two, three, go!'

They began to throw one another skittles behind and in front of the line of helpers. Claire froze. The faces in the audience dissolved into a blur of open-mouthed wonder. The skittles were going to hit her. She was sure they were. They were getting closer and faster. That one almost touched her nose. She tensed into herself, trying to make herself as flat as possible. They were flying past now. Faster and faster. She felt dizzy. She could no longer see. She closed her eyes. Peter's words spun round her head – 'Margaret – my wife – liked music. She played the piano. Brown hair, grey eyes. A country girl really. Margaret – my wife. Good with plants. My wife. Margaret.'

'OK. Well done. Give them all a big round of applause,' shouted Mr Wiggle-Waggle.

It was over. She opened her eyes. Everyone was clapping. She stepped forward, tottered and almost lost her balance.

'Steady there!'

Mr Wiggle-Waggle caught her by the arm. One of the girls, the one with curly hair, began to cry. Nimble Nancy thrust something into her hand. She could not see Peter. For a moment, she panicked. Then she heard his voice.

'Claire, Claire, over here.'

She turned. He was waving at her, smiling proudly like the parent of a child who had won the 800-metre race at the school sports day.

She sank into her seat.

'Are you OK? When you closed your eyes I thought you were going to faint. It looked terrifying.'

'It was terrifying. I thought they were going to hit us. I'm sure one grazed my nose.'

'What's that?'

She looked down at her hands then held up the object pushed into them by Nimble Nancy.

It was a dog, a dog made from twisted yellow and red balloons with felt-tip eyes and nose.

'Here. You have this. They don't allow dogs where I live,' said Claire, offering the dog to a girl with pigtails sitting at her side. The girl shrank back shyly against her mother who took the dog and thanked Claire, apologising for her daughter's shyness.

'Come on! I'll buy you a cup of tea to steady your nerves – if they sell such a thing here.'

They could find no tea at the stalls outside the children's tent but a man directed them to the funfair where they bought a bag of hot doughnuts and two polystyrene cups of dark brown liquid. They ate and drank standing up, blowing on the doughnuts between mouthfuls to cool them, walking slowly among the rides.

'We ought to try one really. Just one. Just so that we can say we've been on one,' said Peter. 'What about that one?'

He pointed to a wheel made of replica eighteenth-century carriages.

'It doesn't go very fast and you stay the right way up the whole time. Look, it's stopping. Come on!'

He grasped Claire's arm and pulled her, protesting, to the back of the queue of people waiting to go up.

'I don't like heights. I never have done,' she said.

'But it doesn't go very high.'

'It doesn't look very high from here but it will do when you're up there.'

They were still arguing when they reached the front of the queue. Peter took hold of her arm. She shook him off.

'In you go,' said the man controlling the ride, helping them step into a carriage. She sat down and clutched hold of the railings that ran behind the seats. The man bolted the door shut. They began to rise into the air. Peter moved closer and put an arm round her. They rose higher then stopped as more passengers got on and off.

'Look! Look at the view. There's the church and there's that place we passed where they were selling pine furniture. And isn't that the sea? Over there, look!' said Peter.

Claire followed the direction of his finger. She could see something shining but could not tell whether it was the sea or merely the horizon shimmering in the heat. The carriage rose higher and she tightened her grip on the railings. They were not even moving properly yet and already she felt scared. She allowed Peter to draw closer so that the back of her head was resting against his chest. The carriage swayed in the breeze. They were almost at the top now.

'You're shivering. Here, put this round you.'

He took the rug out of his bag and wrapped it round her shoulders. The wheel began to move. He had been right. It did not go very fast. But the carriages swayed as they moved and she could see chinks of light through the wooden floor and sides.

'I only married Margaret because she was pregnant,' he said.

Claire jerked forward but his arms held her back. She could feel the warmth of his body through the blanket.

'I had been called up to the front. I thought I might never see her again. I almost didn't. It seemed the only thing to do.'

The wheel stopped moving. Their carriage came to rest two stops from the top. Down below, a child, seemingly miles away, dropped his ice cream and began to cry.

'She found out she was pregnant on the Tuesday and we were married on Wednesday afternoon. On Thursday morning I left for France. It was 1940. I didn't see her or my son, Tom, for five years.'

Their carriage was at the top now, swinging dangerously in the wind. She felt sick. Why was he telling her all this? She didn't want to hear it. She wanted to get off, to walk on firm ground.

'We were both carried away. There was a sort of fervour in the air. Everyone was getting married,' he said.

She knew, she knew. He didn't need to tell her. She had worked in a register office, seen the proud young girls burning to be widows, the young boys dreaming of medals.

'We would never have married if she hadn't been pregnant,' he said. 'We were . . . well, we were just very different.'

The carriage moved down, stopped, then moved down again. She could see the face of the boy who had dropped his ice cream now, see the white mark on the ground where it was melting.

'We weren't suited to one another,' he said. 'We both knew it, but at the time it didn't seem to matter. Neither of us thought I would come back.'

The carriage moved down further. The man controlling the ride unlocked the door of the carriage in front of them. The passengers, a teenage boy and girl, jumped out giggling.

'I wanted to tell you,' said Peter. 'I wanted you to know.'

They were down. At the bottom. The man was unlocking their door. She relaxed her grip on the railings and unwrapped herself from the rug. Peter released his arms. He stepped out of the carriage, then turned and held out his hand. Claire took it.

'Let's go home now, shall we?' he said.

They walked slowly up the field to the gate where officials were checking the tickets of those coming in. They were still holding hands.

21

The hot weather continued. The grass turned first yellow, then brown, and then disappeared altogether in some places, leaving patches of dust like holes at the elbow of a much worn jersey. The beech trees put out large clumps of mast to increase their chances of survival. John, the head gardener, cursed and muttered as he struggled with watering cans. The lettuces were burnt to a frazzle, he said. And the French beans would be uneatable.

'All that work gone to waste. I don't know why I bother. I don't. Really, I don't,' he said.

Phyllis announced that she had heat exhaustion and retired to her bed for a week with a tapestry kit bought by her niece on holiday in Majorca. Iris took a fortnight off to visit her family in Wales and came back looking even more drawn and worried than before. Claire heard someone mention something about Quintin and drugs but could not find out whether it was anything more than a rumour.

The only ones who did not complain about the heat were Peter and Claire. Claire, in particular, lapped up the sun as though she had spent the last ten years of her life in a cellar with no windows. Each morning she woke with a sense of foreboding alleviated only when she drew her curtains and saw that the sun was once again shining. It was as if she felt that the rain, when it finally came, would wash away her happiness along with the silt in the gutters.

She had never known such contentment, such peace, both of mind and body. She even caught herself looking at her hands, not with pride, but with acceptance rather than the usual frustration she felt when she saw her misshapen knuckles.

She still read the paper and learnt poetry. But she did not do so with the same discipline she had once subjected herself to. Sometimes she skipped the business section. And she put away Blake and Wordsworth and other poets she had never enjoyed and instead read those she genuinely liked such as Donne and MacNeice. Anything in the paper which she found particularly interesting or amusing she cut out to show Peter later. He did the same with his paper.

They compared cuttings after lunch sitting in the garden in the shade of the cherry tree drinking iced tea from a jug. The jug was green and yellow, dappled like light on leaves. It had a saucer on top to keep the wasps out. Afterwards, if it was not too hot, they would visit Mrs Barnard next door at The Willows or walk into town. They bought orange and passion fruit lollipops and ate them walking along, licking furiously to stop the juice dripping on their clothes. They chose houses from estate agents' windows, arguing about the respective merits of a double garage or a conservatory. They admired the Meissen china collection in Alnwick Castle.

If they were too tired to walk they read to one another in Peter's room with the curtains half drawn. Or else they listened to the afternoon play on the radio, Claire on the sofa, Peter on the Edwardian-style chair, his legs raised on a footstool.

Often, after supper, they would drive to the coast to watch the sun set over the sea. They held hands openly here, free of worry about what people might say. For Claire was nervous of what Matron or the other residents might think of their friendship, even though no one had said anything or even appeared to notice that they spent an undue amount of time together. Once, when she could not sleep, she had got up in the night, found the brochure about The Pines which she had been sent four years ago when she had first started looking at residential homes, and re-read the paragraph which said it took only single residents. She had re-read it several times since then but had not yet found the courage to show it to Peter.

If they did not drive to the coast they drove inland instead, exploring country lanes with the help of a road map Peter had bought in the tourist information office. Once, when the sun was very low, they took a turning not marked on their map which led them through a small wood, over a stream, past a farm and a row of cottages and then down a dusty, increasingly bumpy track to a church.

'It's derelict,' said Claire. 'Look, the door's all boarded up.'

'Let's have a look,' said Peter.

The wall round the churchyard had fallen down in places but the gate still hung on its hinges. Raw planks, defaced with the usual teenage 'I woz 'ere' messages, were nailed across the church door. A notice, covered with a waterproof jacket, and tacked firmly to the wood with rusty drawing pins, informed visitors that St Margaret's was no longer in use, that the nearest church was St John's in Edlingham – two and a half miles away, Holy Communion at 8.00 a.m. and 10.15 a.m. every Sunday – that the Rev. Michael Prudhoe could be contacted at the Vicarage there.

'What a pity,' said Claire, running her fingers over the stone of the lintel. It felt warm and rough like the skin of an old man sitting in the sun.

'Yes,' said Peter. 'Mind you, it doesn't look as though it ever had much of a congregation. Just that farm back there and a few cottages.'

He wandered down the path and into the graveyard. Claire followed him, stopping to read the inscriptions on the tombstones, calculating how old people would have been when they died.

'It's terrible, isn't it? They all died so young. You had to have twelve children just to increase your chances of seeing a few survive to adulthood.'

Peter, crouched a few feet further on in front of a headstone which had keeled over to one side, nodded. Several of the words on the headstone had crumbled away and he had to trace the letters with his finger to read them, a giant purple foxglove dusting his arm with pollen as it moved from side to side.

'She had six children and they all died before her,' said Claire pointing to a headstone on which was inscribed 'In memory of Martha Heddon, a loving wife and mother, 1810–1849. Also of William 1831–1840, Joseph 1838–1842, and Edward 1839–1847, sons of the above. And of Elizabeth 1829–1835, Mary 1833–1837 and Jane 1845–1846, daughters of the above. May their souls rest in peace.'

'This one is even worse,' said Peter. 'It doesn't even give the children's names.'

Claire moved to his side and crouched down next to him, pushing the foxglove back so that she could see more clearly. She read the inscription out loud, hesitantly at first, then more confidently as the lettering became easier to decipher.

'To the loving memory of John Rees, died 1834, aged 52. Also Clara Rees, wife of the above, died 1831, aged 47. Also their nine children – all died in their infancy.'

She stood up and brushed her skirt free of the grass and seeds which clung to it. A purple butterfly flew past, then a small yellow one, then two cabbage butterflies. A bee landed on the foxglove and began to extract pollen. It was a beautiful clear evening, still warm, but cool enough now for the many wild flowers flourishing in the graveyard to release their perfume. She could hear water running somewhere, possibly the stream they had crossed earlier, and beyond it a blackbird, its voice coursing pure and clean as a mountain spring.

She walked back to the church and sat down on a wooden bench, checking first to see that it was not rotten. She felt heavy and languid, as though her head was too large for her body to support, as though, like a ripe peach, it might twist off and fall with a soft thud to the ground. She leant back and stroked the church wall behind her. It was flecked with lichen and brown moss, dry and crusty like an old scab. Peter, she saw, was at the far end of the graveyard, examining a tombstone surrounded by broken railings. The grass and flowers were so high that if he knelt down she could hardly see him, just the top of his head, the thick dark grey hair falling forward over his forehead. It was badly cut. She had told him so once and he had laughed, amused by her interest in his appearance.

He walked back towards her and she watched him lazily – the long, powerful stride of his legs, the large, strong hands swinging loosely at his sides, the slight stoop in his shoulders. He was smiling slightly, his eyes screwed up against the sun, and for a moment she saw him in a different light, as more man than Peter – a man returning from a day's hunt, triumphant, eager to show off his kill. Then he was sitting down beside her, familiar again in red shirt and cream trousers creased neatly at the front.

He was particular about his clothes, fussy almost, a fact she had noticed and teased him about.

'There were fresh flowers back there so someone must still come here,' he said.

'Where? Which one?'

'That small white marble headstone. Over there, under the tree. There. Do you see it?'

'Whose is it?'

'I don't know. Someone who died when they were twenty, six years ago. You can't tell whether it was a man or a woman because it only gives the initial – S.'

'Sarah,' said Claire.

'Or Susan.'

'Or Samuel or Stephen or Simon or Sophie.'

'The flowers were quite fresh. Pinks. Only a day or two old. And they were in a proper vase. Not just a jam jar. A white china vase.'

The sun was very low now, a large red eye watching them. The blackbird had stopped singing and the air, which only a few minutes earlier had been thick with bees and butterflies, was now empty and still. Claire shivered. There was something expectant about the way the sun hung there, as if something was going to happen, something that would shatter the quiet, would splice it apart like a log ripped in two.

'Twenty years old. Just twenty years. Not even a proper adult yet. I wonder what happened.'

'Cancer or a car accident, I expect,' said Peter briskly.

'I've never been really ill, apart from the strokes and arthritis and they're not really an illness. I've never even had chicken-pox,' said Claire.

Peter looked away. A bat swooped low over the churchyard, turned, circled twice, then flew over their heads out of sight.

'Have you? Been really ill, I mean?'

Peter said nothing. His fingers were tapping the arm rest as if he were trying to pick out a tune, she noticed. Sometimes they stopped moving as though he had lost his way then began again, rising and falling, one at a time.

'Peter?'

'Yes,' he said, still looking away.

Claire repeated her question.

There was a long silence. The bat, or possibly another bat, reappeared. There were long shadows in the grass now but still the sun hung on the horizon, ominously large. Claire stared at it, fascinated, watching for the dark to puncture its perfect roundness, for the red to spurt out, to dissolve into pinks and purples.

'I have been once.'

She turned to face him, frowning. For a moment she had forgotten what she had asked him.

'What? What did you have?'

'Malaria.'

'Malaria! In England!'

'I wasn't in England at the time. I was in Thailand. It was during the war. I was a Japanese prisoner.'

'Was that . . . was that why you said you almost didn't come back? Why you didn't see your wife and son for five years?'

She spoke gently, tentatively, as if cleaning a bad wound.

'Yes.'

'What . . . what happened?'

She didn't really want to know but she had to ask in case he wanted to tell. It was important to ask, to invite people to talk. She had learnt that.

'I was a junior officer in the ninth battalion of the Royal Northumberland Fusiliers. We had been evacuated from Dunkirk and were on our way to the Middle East when the Japanese bombed Pearl Harbour. We were diverted to Singapore instead and arrived there in February 1942. A week later we were told to surrender.'

He spoke flatly without emotion, as if reading from a script, as if the events he was relating did not concern him personally.

'We were sent to a holding camp first, then to a work camp in Singapore town. We had to clean up places. Mainly of bodies. There were bodies everywhere. Heads stuck on poles wherever you went. After seven months we were sent to Thailand by train. It took five days to get there. Most of us had dysentery by then and there was nowhere for us to defecate. We had to sit in our own mess. Four men died on the journey.'

Claire could hardly make out his face even though the red yolk of the sun was still intact. Only the tapping of his fingers, now fast and furious, told her of the feeling that lay behind his words.

'They sent us to Ban Pong to work on the Burma railway. We had rice to eat. Nothing else. Only rice and that was always full of dust and maggots. We slept on the floor in bamboo huts. In the rainy season the latrines overflowed and we had to sleep squatting or standing up, raw sewage swilling round our feet. I was ill then. Ill all the time. Everyone was. Cholera was rife. So was dysentery. But malaria was the main killer. That was when I was "really ill". When I got cerebral malaria. The Japanese didn't care how ill you were though. We were just human fodder. They even brought out men on stretchers and made them break stones, men who were dying, who could hardly lift the stones they were supposed to be breaking . . .'

His voice caught suddenly like a kite in a tree. Then he freed himself, went on.

'Our bones went spongy because of the bad diet, our cuts went ulcerous – sometimes so badly they went right back to the bone. We used to go down to the river to let the fish eat away the dead flesh.'

Claire shuddered.

'It wasn't recommended,' said Peter dryly. 'But it gave us some relief even if it was only temporary.'

Claire glanced towards the horizon where the sun still clung, full and heavy, refusing to leave. Peter was silent. She turned back to look at him and saw that his fingers had stopped moving. She waited. Finally, he spoke again.

'One particular memory still . . . still haunts me. Some men tried to escape. Friends of mine. They tried to persuade me to go with them but I wouldn't. I was too weak. It was just after I'd had malaria. I could hardly walk. They were weak too. They had no food, no map, no supplies of any kind but they wouldn't listen. They were determined to go. And they did.'

He stopped. Claire waited again.

'They were caught less than half a mile away and brought back to the camp. The guards beat them in front of us, insisted that we watched while they hit them round the head with rifles and sticks. I tried to look away but one of the guards saw me and screamed at me to watch. And so I watched, trying not to see, looking but not looking, wishing that I was blind, that everything was black, that the whole world was dark.'

He stopped, the control in his voice disintegrating, the emotion now clearly audible. And at that very moment, the sun, as if this was what it had been waiting for, dropped out of sight. The darkness fell quickly and softly, folding around them, hiding the edges of things.

'I still have nightmares about that. The seeing and the not seeing. Trying to show the guard that I was looking so that he would not beat me too but trying also not to look, to look beyond what I was seeing.'

Claire stretched out, took his hand in hers and squeezed it tightly. Then she reached up to stroke his cheek. It was wet. He was crying.

'I've never told anyone about it before,' he said.

Claire continued to stroke his cheek until she felt his jaw loosen and the tension drop from his shoulders. Then she turned and cupped his chin in her hands, drawing his head down. She hesitated as if unsure then, quite slowly, pulled his chin towards her and kissed him full on the lips.

'I've never done that before either,' she said.

22

Suddenly, it was autumn. The hedges lost their sharp focus and became blurred and soft – a tangle of briar and bramble. The pale golden honey colour of the stubble fields gave way to ploughed brown, the earth turned up in thick wedges, seagulls wheeling overhead. Matron turned on the heating and asked Iris to put out extra blankets. Cook served apple and blackberry crumble for pudding.

The health of old Mrs Barnard began to fail rapidly. She lost the sight in one eye, could only hear if you shouted, and developed a rare heart condition. The staff said she needed both hips replacing. The doctor said she was too old and would not survive the operation. Her relatives bought her a walking frame and then, when she grew even weaker, an electric wheelchair. Eventually, she was carried from her bed to an armchair mid-morning, after the staff had had their coffee and biscuits. Finally, this too stopped and she was left in bed all day, turned occasionally like a sausage on a barbecue so that she did not develop bed sores. Peter and Claire visited her often. She still thought they were married.

Peter continued to go out alone in his car most mornings. He never told Claire where he went and she never asked. She had thought at first that he drove to the sea, to walk and be alone, to skim stones on the water. But then, as the weather deteriorated and he still went out, she began to wonder if this explanation was correct, to fear that he might be visiting someone, an old friend, a woman friend, someone he had not told her about. She became increasingly suspicious.

Iris was sullen and moody. She still dressed Claire and brushed her hair but she did so quickly and efficiently, not lingering as she had done before, not asking about Claire's past. The stories about Quintin and drugs continued. Someone said he had been arrested by the police. Another that he was on bail. Claire wanted to ask Iris if the rumours were true. She wanted to know whether she had agreed to travel round the world or whether she was looking for a job. She felt a sense of responsibility towards her. But Iris avoided her.

Undaunted, Claire waited. Her opportunity came one afternoon when, walking to her room, she passed the laundry and glimpsed Iris inside ironing. She went in and sat down.

'Shall I keep you company?'

Iris grunted and moved her lips in what could, if one didn't know her, have been a smile. Her hair needed washing, Claire noticed. And her cardigan had gone all baggy at the elbows. It was only good to throw away. And yet she had been so clean and bright when she first came to The Pines. Like a new penny. To see her had been to feel that the window had been opened, that one was breathing fresh air, tasting sea spray on one's lips.

'I used to hate doing the ironing. Now I couldn't do it, of course. It's one of the few things I don't miss.'

Iris concentrated on the collar of the shirt she was ironing, pressing the iron down, grinding it into the fabric. Claire looked away, summoning up her courage.

'How's Quintin?'

Iris looked up sharply then down again, stabbing at the shirt now as if it were a pin cushion and the iron a pin.

'Not very well. He's . . . he's . . . he's in hospital if you really want to know. In a detoxification unit.'

So the rumours had been right, thought Claire. Or at least partly so. She did not ask Iris which drug or drugs Quintin was addicted to because she knew it would mean little to her. There were so many of them now and they all had so many different names and so many different ways of being taken.

'He comes out next week. I'm going to take some time off to nurse him. We're moving into one of his parents' farm cottages. They want us to. It was their idea.'

She spoke rapidly now as if this was what she had been waiting for – an opportunity to confess. Claire looked up sorrowfully. Their eyes met.

'What's the matter? Why are you looking at me like that?'

She folded the shirt quickly and added it to a pile on the large scrubbed table to her left. Then she took another shirt from the laundry basket on the chair to her right and began ironing it.

'Don't do it.'

'Don't do what?' asked Iris, not looking up.

'Move in with him.'

'Why not? He needs me. Besides, I . . . I . . . I like him. We get on together. Why shouldn't we live together? I'm twenty-one. You were already married at this age.'

'He doesn't need you. You need him.'

She had never spoken to anyone like this before but the sight of the baggy elbows, the unwashed hair, the bitter smile on Iris' face, spurred her on.

'You're using him as an excuse because you're afraid to find out what you really want. You're frightened it will be too difficult. Scared you will fail.'

Iris gave a shrill, false laugh.

'Scared! Scared! What do you mean, "scared"? What am I scared of?'

'Yourself. You're scared you won't meet your own high expectations. You want to do things, to make a difference, to matter. Isn't that right? Isn't that what you told me? But you're scared you won't succeed and so you're giving up, stopping before you've even started, burrowing yourself in this backwater.'

'I don't know what you mean,' said Iris, folding the second shirt, 'I like my job here. I feel I'm being useful. I never said I wanted a career.'

'You never said you wanted a career but you never said you wanted to iron shirts either. You know you don't.'

She was angry now. She would say it all. She had to. It was her duty. Her hands writhed like fish in nets, urging her on.

'You believe in things. You care about right and wrong. You've got energy, talent, fire. So go on then. Use them. Find yourself a proper job. A job which will change the world. That's what you want to do. Isn't it? Isn't it?'

'Don't talk to me about a proper job,' shouted Iris, slamming down the iron. 'Look at you! What have you ever done with your life? You could have been a teacher, a professor even. You're far cleverer than most of my lecturers were. But what did you do? Nothing. So don't tell me what to do. It's my life. Not yours. And I'll do what I want with it.'

There was an acrid smell of burning. Both women looked at the ironing board where the iron lay face down on a shirt which Claire recognised as one of Peter's. Iris seized hold of it, revealing a large brown scorch mark.

Claire stood up.

'I know I've wasted my life. I just don't want you to waste yours too. That's all.'

She was already outside in the corridor when Iris replied.

'And don't think I don't know what's going on with Peter,' she called out. 'Because I do.'

23 ∫

Back in her room, Claire did not lie down as she had planned. Instead, she walked up and down like an animal in a cage. Up and down. Up and down. Up and down. Her eyes were glazed.

Why had she interfered? Why had she been so brutal? She had accused Iris of timidity, had implied she was a coward. Why? She had no right to give her advice, had been wrong to think she had. Iris would do as she pleased, regardless of what anyone else said or did. That was how it was. That was how it always was with young people. That was how it had been with her.

All she had done was hurt her. Now Iris would probably never speak to her again. She would ask Matron to be transferred to other duties so that she did not have to dress and undress Claire. Someone else would take her place, someone with large hands who would pull at her hair when they brushed it.

She had spoken out of vanity. Because she thought Iris would listen to her. That was why. She saw it now. How foolish. How childish.

She picked up a printed 'entertainment' list of the talks and outings Matron had arranged until Christmas, glanced at it, and put it down again. Then she picked up a miniature bottle of perfume Catherine had given her. She turned the bottle round in her hand. It was so small, so perfect, it reminded her of a miniature dolls' tea set she had had as a child. It had been white with pink roses and a gold rim round the edges of the cups and saucers. Her father had bought it for her on one of his rare trips to London. He had bought fresh figs for her mother. They had been dark purple, wrapped in straw, plump and soft to the touch like a newly-beaten pillow. Her mother had protested, had said it was ridiculous, a waste of money, but you could tell from the way she stroked them that she was pleased really.

There had been an argument later about the tea set. She had been playing with it on the lawn, feeding her dolls lavender sandwiches when her mother had called her in. Afterwards, she had played inside and forgotten about the tea set. The next day, after a night of heavy rain, one of the cups was missing. Her mother had scolded her and said she didn't deserve to be bought nice presents. But her father had intervened and promised to buy her another cup. Then her mother had accused her father of spoiling her and they had begun to argue.

Was that right? Had her father really stuck up for her? It seemed unlikely. But she was sure he had done. She could see him now, standing in front of her mother like a coat, warding off her disapproval. Or was that later, on a different occasion? She stopped pacing the room and stood still, grasping in her mind for a hold, something solid that would prove her memory right. Her forehead tightened and at the same time her fingers, still holding the perfume bottle, relaxed, opening wider and wider until the bottle slipped through them. As it hit the floor, the stopper flew out, and perfume began to leak on to the carpet. Claire watched the stain grow larger and larger until it was the size of a small orange. Finally, when the bottle was almost empty, she knelt and pressed the tips of her fingers into the stain, then the insides of her wrists. It would be a shame to waste it completely, she thought. She rubbed her wrists together and smelt them, first one, then the other, flooding her nostrils. Maybe her father had played a more active role in her childhood than she realised, she thought. It was difficult. Memory, like a driver in a car accident, could be an unreliable witness.

She stayed kneeling on the carpet watching dust motes until her legs began to ache then rose, clutching at furniture for support, and made her way to the window seat. It was a beautiful autumn day, very blue and still. She pressed her face against the windowpane, her hot cheeks thirsty for the cold of the glass. The trees were already specked with gold like the first small freckles on a child's nose.

A figure emerged from the front of the house and began to walk up the drive towards the parked cars. She watched lazily, envying the stride – the confident, easy, forward motion of the legs. Peter walked like that, she thought. But it couldn't be Peter because he was in his room. When she had said she was tired and was going to rest, he had said he was tired too. But it did look like him, very like him. The figure stopped and looked up at the sky and as the head tilted back, she saw that it was Peter. She pressed her face more heavily into the glass. Was it him? Surely it couldn't be? But yes, it was. It was only because she hadn't expected to see him that she hadn't recognised him instantly. What was he doing? Where was he going? Why had he said he was going to lie down if he wasn't? Had he changed his mind? Or had he to planned to go out, had he lied to her?

Peter walked up to his car, unlocked the driver's door, took off the jacket he was wearing and threw it on to the passenger seat. Then he walked round to the back of the car, unlocked the boot and bent in. He seemed to be rearranging something but she could not see clearly. After a few moments, he straightened up, looked round briefly at the house, then walked back to the driver's side and climbed in.

Claire watched him drive away, straining to see which way he turned at the bottom of the drive. He turned left which could mean anything. It was the way to town but it was also the way to the coast and to Berwick.

Maybe he knew she would feel threatened. Maybe that was why he had not said anything. Maybe it was just an old friend, someone he had lost touch with but was now seeing again. But every day? Every morning? And now the afternoon as well? No, one did not see a friend that often, even a good friend, even a very good friend. It had to be something more than that. Her fears, like a slack sail finding wind, began to swell and grow. He was hiding something from her. She knew he was because otherwise he would have told her where he went in the mornings. It was not like him to be secretive. That was her weakness. He was open and frank. Why, look how much he had told her about himself – about Margaret and his son, Tom; about his relationship with his father; the time he had spent as a prisoner of war. She knew far more about him than he knew about her. He didn't even know the name of her husband. Was that because she hadn't told him or because he hadn't asked?

Maybe she knew more about him because she wanted to know about him, because she was interested. Maybe he wasn't as interested in her as she was in him.

She pressed a palm against her forehead as though to stop the doubts escaping and coursing through her veins. What was this other woman like? Was she tall? Strong? Yes, probably. She imagined her striding down a beach, clambering over sand dunes, throwing pebbles in the sea, doing all the things she couldn't.

The woman began to take shape in her mind, to acquire clothes – a long, stylish raincoat which flew out in the wind – and a hairstyle, a short cropped look which emphasised her cheekbones. She taught sculpture and had a professional massage every fortnight. People paid to buy her work – not handsomely but enough to finance a holiday once a year in Calabria or Galway. She was a member of the Royal Academy and of Amnesty International. Several of her friends were actors and artists. She loved cooking.

With an effort, Claire wrenched her mind free. Peter had gone to post a letter, she told herself. Or he was buying a present for a friend's birthday he had forgotten. He would be back in ten minutes. Twenty minutes at the most. Or maybe half an hour. It might be difficult to find a parking space.

She turned her hurt round like a piece of dough, kneading it and shaping it as though it would look different from another angle, would be more manageable. Why are you so upset, she asked herself? All that has happened is that a man you have known for a couple of months, a man who has made you no promise, given you no indication that he does anything more than like you, has gone out in his car without telling you?

A quiet voice rustled in her mind like a snake in dry leaves. I am upset because I am jealous. 'And why are you jealous?' Because . . . because . . . because . . . 'Say it, say it, say it out loud.' Like a nun whipping her back, she forced herself to speak. 'I am jealous . . . because . . . because I love him.'

The words bit into the air. Stuck in her throat. But as soon as she had said them she felt better, calmer, as if a splinter had been plucked from her mind, its poisonous threat removed. She began to think about Peter, to meditate on why she liked him, to puzzle out what it was that made her glad to see him, that made her feel, in his company, comforted – confident that all would be well.

She liked his mouth, she thought. The mobility of it. She liked too the way he lifted his eyebrows to express surprise or interest. The way he listened. The way he didn't interrupt her halfway through an account to narrate a similar experience of his own. The way he didn't switch off. She had never once had to repeat herself.

Then there was the way he noticed things. The shapes of things. Textures. Colours. A lone tree in a field of corn, its green circled by gold, set off by it, like a ring on a white finger. A hedgerow soft with dog rose and tangled old man's beard. A sky yellow with the threat of bad weather. He was like Catherine's guide dog. He helped her to see.

The tea bell rang down below in the hall, far away in the world where people were finishing crosswords and marking that night's TV schedule with red biro. Claire ignored it. She was worried now. Had he had an accident? Had something happened to his contact lenses, something which had prevented him from seeing that the car in front had stopped, was turning right, pulling in to park . . . ? They had been hurting him recently. He had even worn his glasses once or twice in the evenings, even though he hated wearing glasses and never wore them except in an emergency.

The sun had moved round. It was getting cold. She glanced across the room to the chair where her bed jacket lay, judging the time it would take her to reach it, put it on, walk back again. She decided against it. She did not want to miss him.

There was a spot on the road beyond the drive, the road down which Peter had driven, which was visible from the house. She concentrated on this, focusing on it until it bled like the speared yolk of a fried egg, running into the sky and the fields. Something red appeared. Her heart jumped. But then she glimpsed it further on, on the other side of the drive, driving away, heading towards Rothbury.

She focused instead on the end of the drive but this too quickly blurred. She looked away, into her room, focused briefly on the perfume bottle still lying on the floor, then looked back. A car was coming up the drive. But it was white, not red. She watched it swing into a parking bay and a short, bald man get out. It was Maureen's doctor, she saw, come to check on her weak chest.

She looked back at the end of the drive. Nothing. Not even a delivery van or the boy on the bike who delivered the afternoon papers taken by Colin and Freda. Maureen's doctor came out and drove away.

Then, suddenly, when she was not looking, when she thought she had been, there it was, Peter's car, that unmistakable shade of tomato soup red, already halfway up the drive. She ran to the door, then came back and sat down again. He had already parked, she saw, and was putting something in the boot of the car. She got up again and went to look in the mirror. She would give him five minutes, she told herself. She would wait until she was sure he was in his room.

But she didn't wait long enough because when she walked down the corridor, there he was, in front of her, unlocking his door.

He heard her footsteps and turned round, grinning when he saw that it was her.

'Where've you been? I thought you'd had an accident . . .'

She was doing it all wrong. Showing him how much she cared. How much he mattered. She had meant to be dignified. Calm.

'I'm sorry . . . I thought you were asleep . . . you said you were tired. I wouldn't have gone out if I'd known you were awake.'

Claire made herself as tall as possible.

'I'd rather know. I don't want you to have to go on pretending like this. Just tell me.'

Peter looked puzzled.

'Tell you what?'

Claire stared at him, exasperated. Did he think she was a complete fool?

'Where you go every morning, where you've been just now . . . who you see. That's what!'

'You think . . . you think . . .'

'I don't know what to think. That's what I'm saying.'

He frowned then raised his eyebrows and she decided that she did not, after all, like the way he did this. There was something mannered about it, exaggerated, as if he was making faces in a mirror.

'I'll show you, then. Come on.'

He seized her by the arm and led her back down the corridor, down the stairs and out the front door. He wasn't . . . no, he couldn't . . . surely he wasn't going to take her to see the other woman?

They approached his car. Claire started to pull away from his hand. She wouldn't go. She didn't want to. How could he possibly think she would? Out of the corner of her eye she glimpsed Janet and Phyllis staring goggle-eyed from the drawing-room window.

'It's in the boot,' said Peter, finally releasing her arm so that he could unlock the boot. Claire stepped back. But nothing jumped out. Nothing moved even. Peter leaned in and unzipped what looked like a flat, black suitcase.

'Here it is.'

Claire stepped back again. He was holding up a large piece of paper and on it, half-drawn, half-painted in watercolour, was a picture of the churchyard at St Margaret's where she had kissed him. She stepped closer, stretched out a hand as if to touch it. He had got the colours just right. The air. It was so real. She could almost feel it against her cheeks. The heaviness of it, thick with heat and insects. There was the bench on which they had sat and there the white marble headstone with the pinks in the white china vase. There was even a bat at the very edge of the paper, its wings taut with flight. She fancied that she could hear the blackbird too, could feel the warmth of the stone, the crustiness of the moss as she ran her fingers over the church wall.

'It's . . . it's . . .'

'It was for your birthday. I wanted it to be a surprise.'

'It's beautiful.'

What pleased her most was that it was all as she remembered it – that he had not seen it differently. Even the sun, full, red, ever so slightly threatening, was right.

'I was worried I wasn't going to finish it. Before the weather got too bad, I mean. That's why I went out this afternoon as well as this morning.'

'Is that . . . is that where you've been going then?'

'Recently, yes. Before that . . . well . . . look.'

She saw that there were more paintings in the black case. A

haystack. Grey roof tiles stained with gold. A wall, half fallen down. Tall trees meeting in the middle to form a green arch over a road. A clump of cow parsley.

'You haven't . . . there aren't any of the sea.'

'No,' he agreed.

'It's just that I'd have thought you'd have wanted to paint it. That . . . well . . . I mean, it's so wonderful, the coast round here.'

'I'm working towards it,' he said. 'Field by field, wall by wall. I might reach it in about twenty years' time.'

He smiled then leant towards her.

'Actually, I'm not sure I want to paint the sea. I love looking at it and walking by it, but I'm always glad I can get in my car and drive away from it after an hour or so. I'm not sure I'd like to have it on my walls. I find it . . . well, I suppose I find it frightening. The endlessness of it, always changing, always moving.'

He replaced the picture of St Margaret's in the black case, zipped it up again and locked the boot. They began to walk back to the house.

'Why didn't you say if that's all you were doing? Why did you keep it a secret?' asked Claire.

He stopped walking.

'I didn't . . . I didn't want people to ask me about it. I didn't want to deal with that. With their interest or pretence of interest. I didn't want them coming up to me, looking over my shoulder, saying they liked it or they didn't like it or had I thought of this or why didn't I try that. It wouldn't matter so much now but when I first started to paint again, just before I came here, I was so nervous, so self-conscious, that one ill-chosen remark would have done for me. I'm not strong like you.'

'Like me?'

'Yes. I'm weak. I give up. Give in. If I'd been stronger, I would have held out against my father and gone to art school. I wouldn't have got married. I wouldn't have stayed in the bank in a job I hated, that I always had hated. I would have had a different life.'

They started walking again.

'But you're right, I should have told you. I was going to but I kept on putting it off. I wanted to have something good to show you, something that I felt was worth showing. Then I decided to paint you a picture for your birthday, that I would tell you like that.'

They were inside now, walking up the stairs. Tom passed them on his way downstairs, then a new temporary resident, Leslie Shaw, a retired tax inspector from Cheltenham who was spending a month at The Pines while his bungalow was redecorated.

'I'm sorry . . . I didn't realise that you thought . . . that you . . .'

He glanced sideways at her. Her cheeks were red. But it could have been the effort of climbing the stairs.

They stopped at the top. Claire was out of breath.

'Isn't it funny? Here we are, almost seventy years old, and it's only now that we're finally doing what we've always wanted to do.'

'Yes,' she said bleakly.

He turned to walk down the corridor to his room.

'I'll see you at supper. I need to change first.'

He walked briskly away. Claire turned and walked up the opposite corridor which led to her room. It was dark inside but she did not switch on the light. His words banged against her mind like a ball in a slot machine. We're finally doing what we've always wanted to do . . . always wanted to do . . . wanted to do . . . to do . . . do . . . do . . .

Maybe he was doing what he had always wanted to do. But she wasn't. She didn't even know what she did want to do. Still. After all these years. She wished suddenly that he had not shown her the paintings, that she had been right, that he had been seeing another woman. It would have been easier. She had been prepared for it in a way that she was unprepared for this – this emptiness, this sense of waste.

24

He thinks I'm strong. 'I'm not strong like you.' That's what he said. I'm not though. I never have been. Strong-willed maybe. But that's not the same thing. That Friday in 1941, for example. I was not strong then.

It was a typical April day – breezy but warm too – the kind of weather when you're not sure whether to wear a coat or just a cardigan. I went to the shops to buy some liver and a loaf of bread. Several people nodded to me on the way. I was known by then. I'd even drunk tea in my neighbours' kitchens.

Mr Webb, who lived three up from us, was weeding his front garden. Mrs Fellows, on the other side of the road, was beating a rug on the wall. It was that sort of day – a day for whistling and rolling your sleeves up, a day for doing. Even the birds seemed busier than usual.

On my return, instead of cutting out a skirt for my mother as I had planned, I decided to spring-clean. I flung open the windows, tied an old scarf round my head and went up to the bedroom where there were several boxes I had not yet unpacked. I emptied them on to the bed and began to sort the contents into piles, stopping every now and again to re-read an old letter or try on a necklace I'd forgotten I had. I was reading a letter from my father, I remember, a letter he'd sent when I was about twelve and had gone to spend a week at Eastbourne in a boarding house run by a friend of my mother's, when the doorbell rang.

I assumed it would be one of my neighbours or someone selling something and so did not bother to remove my headscarf or wash my hands. But when I opened the door, I found a smart man in a suit, clearly not a tradesman, and behind him, a young couple, the woman carrying a baby.

'We've come to look round the house,' said the man in the suit. 'Your husband said you would be in.'

'The house?'

The man seemed puzzled by my surprise.

'You are Mrs Harper?'

'Yes.'

'Good. Well, if I could just show Mr and Mrs Ball round. It shouldn't take long.'

The young couple smiled.

I let them in, torn between embarrassment at my appearance and confusion as to why they wanted to look round the house.

'You're . . . you're . . .'

'Mr Sharp from Sharp and Saunderson estate agents,' prompted the man in the suit, pumping my hand vigorously. 'I take it you weren't expecting me.'

'No. My husband didn't say. He must have . . . it must have slipped his mind.'

'Easily done. Very easily done. Specially at a time like this.'

Then he turned and began to enumerate the physical characteristics of the kitchen – its size, the clothes drying rack, the pantry, the gas cooker, the curtains. He spoke fast as if reading from a list. I wondered if he was an auctioneer as well as an estate agent. The young couple nodded, smiling whenever he paused. The baby, cocooned in white blankets, slept.

We went upstairs into the bedroom.

'I see you've started packing already,' said Mr Sharp, looking at the bed.

I blushed. There was a pair of my knickers on the chair next to the bed, discarded the previous night, and not yet put in the laundry basket. I hoped nobody else would see them.

'Where are you moving to?' asked the woman. Her husband was talking to Mr Sharp about the chimney, asking if it had been swept recently.

'I . . . I . . . I . . .'

How could I say I didn't know, that I didn't even know I

was moving? It would look ridiculous. They would think I was mad.

'We're not quite sure yet,' I said, taking refuge in the plural pronoun. 'It depends on various things.'

'Bradford. Isn't that it? Isn't that where your husband's new job is?' broke in Mr Sharp.

I stared. What else had Bill told him? That my favourite colour was green. That my father had committed suicide. That the smell of boiled celery made me nauseous.

'Yes. We think so,' I said slowly. 'It hasn't been confirmed yet.'

I turned back to face the woman.

'I'm sorry about the mess . . . only . . . well . . . you know what it's like.'

It was quite easy to lie, I thought. It was just a matter of keeping going really. That was the main thing.

'Oh, don't bother about that. We've been three months now in our flat and we're still at sixes and sevens. Mind you, it didn't help moving in a week before he was born,' she said, shifting the bundle of blankets higher up her arm.

I asked the name of her son and she told me he was called Charles, that he was fourteen weeks old and had just started on solids, bless him.

'I'm Lilian, by the way. My husband's Philip.'

'Claire Harper,' I offered in return.

We smiled at one another warily like new girls on our first day at school. She told me her husband had inherited some money from an aunt, that that was why they were looking to buy, that they wanted somewhere closer to Magdalen College where Philip worked as a gardener.

'The army turned him down because of his kidney condition,' she added in a loud whisper. 'I can't say that I was sorry.'

I offered to make a pot of tea but Mr Sharp was already leading them downstairs and towards the front door. The baby started to cry.

'We won't stop, thanks,' said the woman. 'It's time for his lunch. He gets a bit irritable if you keep him waiting. Don't you, my little pudding face?' she said, hauling the baby upright against her shoulder.

Mr Sharp apologised for disturbing my packing and said he would be in touch. I showed them out.

After they had gone, I sat down at the kitchen table and put my head in my arms. I didn't even know where Bradford was.

25 ∫

Bill said nothing when he came in. Just took off his coat and sat down to read the paper until dinner was ready. I finished mashing the potatoes, wiped my hands on the piece of square green towel which hung from a hook at the back of the kitchen door and called him in. He sat down. I waited until he had helped himself to the potatoes. Then I spoke.

'Someone came to look round the house today. A couple. Philip and Lilian.'

'Oh good. The estate agent said there had been a few inquiries.'

'You didn't tell me the house was for sale.'

'No, I didn't want to . . .'

'You made me look ridiculous.'

'I only . . .'

'You only didn't tell me. I didn't know what he was talking about. I didn't know anything. The couple asked me where we were moving to and I said I didn't know. But the estate agent knew, didn't he? You'd told him. But not me. Oh no, not me. Because I'm only your wife. It doesn't matter what I think, what I want to do, what I feel . . .'

'I don't think . . .'

'No, you don't. You don't think I exist. Not as a person. A separate person. A person with my own thoughts and feelings. I'm just a name, a wife, a provider of food and clean floors and a hole for you to stick when you feel like it.'

He frowned.

'Well, you can find someone else to stick because I'm going. I'm going home.'

And I seized his plate and hurled it at the oven where it

smashed, the gravy flying up and splattering the glass front of the door.

Bill stared at the broken pieces. He hated wasting food unless it had been grown or bought by my mother. Also, liver and onions was one of his favourite meals. He wiped his mouth carefully, even though there was nothing to wipe, then went and fetched his coat. At the door he turned.

'I was going to explain but I see little point trying to do so in your current frame of mind.'

The door shut. I stayed sitting there for a few moments, hearing the slam of the door, seeing the tight primness of his lips. Then I ran upstairs, grabbed my pillow and pounded it against the bed. I wanted to shout, to scream, to swear obscenities, but the walls were thin and, despite everything, I still cared what the neighbours thought.

Finally, exhausted, I crept downstairs. I picked up the liver and onions from the floor and made myself a cup of tea.

Bill came in at eleven and sat down in the sitting room in his usual chair. I went and stood behind him. I had brushed my hair and put on lipstick.

'I'm sorry,' I said.

He said nothing.

I knelt beside the chair.

'I'm sorry I lost my temper.'

He turned and smiled, then touched the top of my head and patted it lightly.

'That's all right,' he said.

'I could make you a sandwich,' I offered. 'We've got some ham.'

'No, it's OK. I had something to eat while I was out.'

He stood up. He did not say why we were moving or when or what his new job was in Bradford.

'Come on. It's late. Let's go to bed,' he said.

So we went to bed. And as always, when we had argued and I had apologised, we made love and he was even more aggressive than usual, ramming home his victory with each thrust of his body.

That's how strong I was.

26

I could not have gone home even if I had wanted to because my mother was leaving. A new vicar with a wife and four young sons had come to replace my father. My mother was going to Coventry to work for the Women's Voluntary Service. She told me so in a letter.

I went over the next day to help her pack but she had already done most of it. She had put the good furniture in storage and sent the rest to be sold at auction.

'I won't need furniture where I'm going,' she said.

We were standing in my old room, the only room in the house she had left untouched. I sat down on the bed which creaked as it had always done.

'They've found me a room in a boarding house. I won't need anything more. After all, I'll be out during the day.'

She was going to help the families whose homes had been destroyed by the November air raids. She was also going to work part-time for the city council. It would be mainly typing, she said, and clerical work. But someone had to do it.

'But why Coventry? There's work here too, isn't there? Why do you have to go so far?'

'The boarding house is run by the widow of someone who used to work in the housing department,' she said, not answering my question. 'That's where I'll be working. A Mrs Draper. She's got two sons at the front as well, poor woman.'

The doorbell sounded and she ran to answer it, shouting back that people had been visiting her all week to say goodbye, that she had cakes coming out of her ears, and bookmarks and handkerchiefs.

I lay back on my bed, nuzzling my old pillow. Outside, through the window, I could see the branches of the elm tree waving in the breeze, the new leaves breaking out like beads of green sweat.

My father had read bedtime fairy stories to me in this room. *Little Red Riding Hood. The Princess and the Pea. The Magic Porridge Pot.* His wolf voice, I remembered, had been particularly good. I wondered if he had thought about me before he killed himself. Had he tried to imagine what we would feel – my mother and I? Or had he blacked us out, concentrated on the bottle of tablets, focused on swallowing just one more and then another and another?

I jumped up and went to the window. Below, on the path beyond the porch, my mother was talking to Mrs Cawood, the mother of Kitty who used to help in the house. Kitty was married now and living outside Reading. She had one child, a girl, and was expecting another. I watched my mother as she talked, noticing the way she moved her hands to emphasise a point, and I realised, with surprise, that she was still young, that she was probably still capable of bearing children, that she might meet someone else. Mrs Cawood said something and my mother laughed, throwing back her head so that I could see her throat, the smooth tight whiteness of it. I moved away abruptly, sick in my stomach.

There was a paperweight on my desk I had saved up to buy. Also, a varnished papier-mâché tray for holding pens and pencils, and a blue-and-silver toffee tin full of old stamps. I opened the drawers, two on the right and three on the left. All were full. I went to the wardrobe and opened the door. A pair of purple suede gloves fell out and landed on the floor at my feet. I picked them up. The thumb on the right hand was slightly stained but otherwise they were in good condition. I turned them over then replaced them on a shelf. I was supposed to be sorting through things, deciding what I wanted to keep and what I wanted to give or throw away. But I had not realised I had so much.

I closed the door and went out onto the landing. The door to my parents' room was open, the sunlight streaking the floorboards like a long, thin mistake. I tiptoed in. The mahogany dressing table with the oval mirror was gone. So too was the matching wardrobe. I could see the marks on the floor where their legs had stood. There were bright patches on the wall where pictures had once hung, protecting the wallpaper from the glare of the sun. Only the bed remained and beside it, a straight-backed chair with a pair of brown walking shoes tucked underneath.

A small trunk lay next to the chair, half full of clothes. I rifled through them. There was a skirt I had not seen before, in her favourite colour, purple. I held it up, imagining her wearing it, seeing the cloth swing from side to side as she strode about her work. Further down, beneath her green twinset and the mohair scarf she wore when it was very cold, there was some new underwear, silky camisoles in cream and peach pink, lacy white knickers. I held these up too, seeing again the smooth tightness of her throat, the powerful arch of her body as she threw back her shoulders. Then I threw them back, not even trying to replace them properly, and went downstairs.

The dining room was bare. So too was the sitting room. I tried to imagine them as they had been, with our pictures and rugs and vases, but failed. Like sullen ashes, they refused to rekindle. The new vicar, I saw, had already brought some of his possessions. A box full of books. A small desk. A chest for holding linen or towels. He had even hung a picture on the sitting room wall, a portrait of a middle-aged man with pink, overfed cheeks.

My mother came in behind me. She was holding a large bunch of daffodils, the first I had seen that year, and her mouth was still turned up at the corners from laughing.

'Aren't these lovely?' she said, holding up the flowers. 'Mrs Cawood brought them.'

'Yes, I saw.'

'She said it was to put the sunshine in my heart, that yellow was the colour of cheerfulness. I didn't know that. Did you?'

I pointed to the portrait on the wall.

'Couldn't they wait? You haven't even moved out yet.'

'Oh, I don't mind. I said they could. It's easier to move bit by bit than in one large go – especially with four young children.'

I sniffed disapprovingly, a trick I had picked up from her.

'Have you done it already?'

'Done what?' I asked, even though I knew what she meant.

'Gone through your room. Decided what you want to keep.'

'No. I'm not going to. You do it. You keep what you want –
what you want to remember me by.'

The hand holding the daffodils dropped to her side. She looked
puzzled. I waited for her to insist, for her eyes to spark and her
chin to rise, as they had always done in the past. But she just
shrugged.

'OK. Let's have some lunch.'

We ate boiled eggs and bread and butter in the kitchen, the
only other room in the house apart from my bedroom which was
still fully furnished. For pudding we had Mrs Frampton's famous
fruit cake, made with real eggs and butter, washed down with
tea. My mother seemed subdued and said little, no longer talking
excitedly about her new job. She had rammed the daffodils in a
chipped jug, not even bothering to cut the string which bound
them together. Later, when she was out of the room, I arranged
them properly in a vase and set them in the centre of the table.
But she did not appear to notice.

After lunch, I went into the garden and swished at things with
a stick. Our old gardener, Dick, had died the previous summer
and there were no young men in the village to replace him.
Neglect was rampant. The roses had not been pruned. The
smooth lawn where I had played with my rose-patterned teaset
had grown choppy. The ground in the orchard was slippy with
the pulp of last year's apples.

I went back inside. My mother had cut Mrs Frampton's fruit
cake in two and was wrapping one half up. She tucked the ends
of the paper over neatly then placed it in my basket.

'You might as well,' she said. 'I can't eat it all. Just say you
made it yourself. He won't know.'

She took the daffodils out of the vase, retied them with string,
wrapped newspaper round the wet stems and placed these too
in my basket.

'I think you need them more than I do,' she said.

She walked with me to the bus stop even though it had clouded
over and looked as though it was going to rain. Two people were
already sitting in the bus shelter – an old man I had not seen
before and the postmaster's widowed sister. My mother nodded
at both.

It began to drizzle and we moved into the shelter, standing as far away from the bench as we could, conscious that everything we said was being listened to. The handle of the basket began to dig into my arm.

Finally, as the drizzle turned to rain, the bus arrived, its windows steamed up, its sides splashed with mud. The postmaster's widowed sister got on. Then the old man. My mother turned to me. She opened her mouth to say something, hesitated, then drew me towards her, snuffing out the unspoken words with the pressure of her large, warm shoulders.

I had to wipe the window with my sleeve to look out. Even then, the rain on the outside of the glass made it difficult to see so that my last glimpse of her was blurred, fractured – like a photo torn up and then reassembled so that you could still see the joins, the white scars where the tears had been.

When the bus stopped in Oxford, I took my basket and set off for home, taking a long indirect route through the outdoor market. The traders were packing up for the day, unfastening their awnings and stacking the crates of unsold vegetables in piles. I picked my way through the slimy black mess of turnips and cabbage leaves trodden underfoot. There was a sweet, sourish smell which made me want to gag. As I reached the end of the market and stepped on to clean pavement, someone wolf-whistled. I did not look round to see if it had been aimed at me.

A bit further on, I dropped the daffodils on the road and waited, pretending to look at clothes in a shop window, until a car passed and squashed them flat. I did not want to take the cheerfulness meant for my mother.

27 ∫

I went to Coventry to see my mother later that year after we moved to Bradford to an ugly rented house with dirty windows. I cleaned the windows for the first week then, when I saw how quickly the passing traffic made them dirty, I stopped. Soon, I liked it that I could not see out. It seemed right, a fitting symbol for how I felt at the time.

After three weeks, I still had not found enough courage to go into the city centre. I bought food at the small parade of shops three streets away. If we did not need food, I walked past the shops, memorising street names so that I could retrace my steps. The houses I passed on those walks were small and squat and red – like the lumps of beef the butcher chopped up for stewing. Usually there would be a cat somewhere with a belly which almost touched the ground when it walked. There were women too, just as there had been in Oxford, but I found them unfriendly. They would stand in clusters on the pavement replaying conversations they had had the previous evening with their husbands or neighbours. When I approached, they would stop talking but they would not move aside. So I would step off the pavement onto the road and I would see them looking at me, appraising my skirt and hair, deciding that I was overdressed, that I came from the South, that I did not belong. Those were the days when ugly women thrived, when it was unpatriotic to look as if you had spent too much time making yourself look nice.

Occasionally, in between the red houses, there would be a school or a small scrubby park with one or two swings, often broken. I never reached the countryside or even a glimpse of it. It was forty minutes before the houses began to thin.

I wondered, on those walks, whether my mother felt lonely too, but when I saw her I knew, immediately, that she did not. She was wearing trousers but that was not, on its own, why she looked so different. Her hair had changed. It was looser, tousled almost, as if rumpled by wind or someone's hand. She wore no make-up, not even lipstick, and yet despite this, she looked younger, years and years younger. She stood there on the station platform waiting for my train to arrive and then she saw me and started to walk towards me. I saw her too and I also began to walk but then I stopped, disconcerted. Then I was in her arms, my head against her shoulder, and when I stepped back and looked at her again, I could no longer see her as she had been, only as she was, laughing, saying I looked pale, her own skin glowing.

We put my bag in a left luggage locker and set off for a place she knew where you could have a good lunch cheaply, including pudding. She told me this as she walked, dodging shoppers, whisking in and out of side streets, up alleyways, round corners and then, so quickly that I almost lost her, down two steps and through a glass door. There was a small pot of toothpicks on the table. I had never seen them before and did not know what they were for until I saw a man using one.

The room was like nothing I had ever seen before. It was not a tearoom or a café or a restaurant but somewhere between all three. If anything, it reminded me most of the dining room in the London club I had once visited with my father and a friend of his. The walls were red but a warmer, more orange red than the houses in Bradford. At one end, there were two easy chairs and a sofa on which a young man reading a newspaper sprawled as though sitting in his own kitchen. Behind us, on a small table against the wall, two middle-aged men played chess in between mouthfuls of Welsh Rarebit. 'Now you've got me,' said one as the other captured his knight. 'I should have spotted that.'

I felt as if I was in Paris or Berlin not Coventry on a rainy day in October. It was only just midday but already all the tables apart from one had been taken. The air sang with talk, with laughter, with the flash of eyes and minds meeting one another, grappling, excited. I breathed in deeply, filling my lungs. I realised I had barely spoken to anyone apart from Bill and shopkeepers for months.

My mother waved to someone on the other side of the room. A woman in a purple sequinned hat waved back, then shouted out, 'Is that your daughter?' Several people turned round and looked in our direction. I felt myself turning red but my mother just smiled and nodded, not seeming to notice my embarrassment.

'Come on then, what shall we have? The stews are always good, especially the Lancashire hot pot.'

I took her advice and chose the hot pot. She ordered hot tongue with mustard sauce and mashed potatoes. For pudding, we had stewed Victoria plums with a caramel topping. I noticed that the waiter, a small wiry man with narrow hips which weaved in and out of the tables like a needle through soft cloth, knew my mother's name. Here you are, Mrs Langley. Have you finished, Mrs Langley? Anything else, Mrs Langley? I watched him while my mother talked about her work – the bureaucracy, the petty, internal politics, the difficulty in maintaining adequate funding.

'I'll show you if you like, I'll show you where I work. It's not far from here,' she said.

Outside, it was raining. People were bumping into one another with their umbrellas and getting wet and cross. I looked at them pityingly as if they belonged to another species. The warm weight of the hot pot lay snug in my stomach, the sweet taste of caramel in my mouth.

My mother opened the door to the building where she worked with three keys which she jangled proudly. Inside, there were four doors, all closed and a flight of stairs covered with green linoleum curling up at the corners. We went up to a large landing. My mother took off her coat and hung it on a peg, then poked her head round one of the doors leading off the landing.

'Nobody there,' she said. 'I was hoping to introduce you to a few people. Never mind. I'll show you the storeroom.'

I followed her through another door, down a corridor, and up two steps into a huge barn-like room divided into aisles by shelves full of clothing and shoes.

'Often, they have nothing, you see. Just the clothes they stand up in. We find out what they have left and then make them up a bag with the essentials – a change of underwear and clothes, soap, toothbrush, a small towel, pen, paper, blankets. The clothes are all second-hand apart from some of the women's underwear. We're always low on bras, particularly in the smaller sizes for some reason. We keep pocket mirrors too for the women and powder compacts. And, if possible, we give the men razors so that they can shave.'

I walked along the aisles, glancing at the shelves, amazed by their size and number. When I had thought about my mother and her new job, I had imagined her answering the phone in a poky office or distributing the odd parcel of baby clothes to young mothers. I had never imagined her involved in an operation as big as this clearly was.

As I walked, my mother talked. She said her job was to help make sure that people whose homes had been bombed had somewhere suitable to stay. She also helped them obtain new ration books or other official papers.

'It's a bit like the church flower-arranging rota really, only on a larger scale.'

I took a camisole from one of the shelves and held it up. It was of a soft, silky material with thin, insubstantial straps.

'Of course, I wouldn't ever have got the job if it hadn't been for Duncan.'

I dropped the camisole on the floor.

'Who's Duncan?'

'He came to the funeral. Tall, black hair, bushy eyebrows. He works for the council.'

I could not remember him.

'He told me about the job then and asked me to think about it. I used to work with him, you see. Before I was married. In London. We were both in housing then. That's why he thought I might be interested.'

She picked up the camisole, folded it and replaced it on the shelf, her fingers caressing the shiny material. As I watched, I saw again the new underwear I had found in her trunk and my mind flooded with suspicion, coursing through my thoughts like an infection.

The door opened and two women came in laughing, their hair

wet from the rain. My mother introduced us. One of the women, a Mrs Thornton, asked what plans we had for the afternoon and said she hoped my mother was going to treat me to tea at Hepworths. The other woman, a Mrs Bentley, nodded and said: 'You must be very proud of her.'

I smiled, acknowledging the compliment. Then I realised that she had addressed me, that she meant I, the daughter, should be proud of her, the mother. My smile faded.

28

We went to buy my mother a coat in Hepworths, the department store where her colleagues had recommended the teas.

'How do you like this?' she said, trying on one in camel cashmere which flowed behind her like a bridal train.

I had not bought any clothes since moving to Bradford and so was surprised to see that rationing, introduced a few months earlier, had had so little impact, both on the quantity and the quality of the coats for sale.

'Or what about this?' she said, slipping out of the camel coat into a jaunty red one with brass buttons.

She giggled as she looked at herself in the mirror.

'You'd never lose me in a crowd.'

A sales assistant, busy the other side of the room advising a customer on raincoats, glanced at us reprovingly.

'No, no. This. This is the one. The film star look. What do you think?'

She flung off the red coat and plunged her arms into the sleeves of a dark charcoal-coloured coat with a broad, fur collar.

The sales assistant, now wrapping up a raincoat, glanced again in our direction.

'Mother. Please! They'll ask us to leave.'

She walked away from me then minced back with small tottering steps, clutching the fur collar to her throat.

'Pleased to meet you,' she said, proffering her right hand. 'Lavinia Langley's the name.'

I stared. I had never seen her behave like this before. She had always been so sensible and practical at the vicarage, always the first one to take her geraniums in before the frosts, the first one to make a Christmas cake. Now I felt as if I was the mother and she the child, foolish and giggly.

The sales assistant came towards us.

'Can I help you?' she asked, her face smooth and blank as glass.

'Not yet, thank you,' said my mother, smiling charmingly. 'We're just looking at the moment. If you could hang this up, maybe.'

And she slid out of the fur-collared coat and handed it over carelessly as if she bought a new coat every week, as if she were indeed a film star. I smiled apologetically. But the assistant did not need my smiles.

'Our coats for the more mature lady are over there,' she said, pointing to a rail of drab browns and greys. 'You might find something more suitable.'

And she was right. We did. We found a black coat with a velvet collar which made my mother look even younger than she had done on the station platform. I was doubtful about whether the collar would wear well but my mother liked it and bought the coat, talking so pleasantly as she paid that she even managed to coax a smile from the assistant.

Afterwards, upstairs, dutifully eating the teas we had been recommended, my mother said: 'I may not buy another coat. It's funny that – to think it may last me. Until I die, I mean.'

'But you're only . . .'

She broke in crisply, quoting the average age at which women died and the average length of time one could reasonably expect a coat to last.

'So you see,' she said. 'It may well be the last.'

I looked down at my plate and rolled the scone crumbs together into a ball. The air smelt of perfume and the boredom of women who, despite rationing and air raids, still had too little to occupy their minds. Next to us, an old woman with liver-spotted hands fed a Pekinese dog jam from a teaspoon.

I squeezed the ball of crumbs between my fingers. My mother began to talk again. She had bought tickets for a film, she said. The best seats in the house. She hoped I hadn't seen it yet. It was the one starring . . . I listened, pleating my napkin into a fan, wanting to ask if she still believed in God, if she thought about dying.

I suspected that the answer to the first question was no when, the following morning, after a cooked breakfast served by Mrs Draper and eaten at the same table as the other lodger, a girl who also worked for the council, we did not go to church. I had assumed that we would go just as we had always done, kneeling when bidden, intoning the responses in the loud, clear voices befitting a vicar's wife and daughter, daydreaming during the sermon. I had even brought a dress on purpose, the sort of dress one wore to church – high-necked, long-sleeved, waistless. Instead, my mother suggested a picnic in a park.

'It's too nice to stay indoors. A waste,' she said, pointing outside to the brilliant sunshine, the light dancing off the dew on the small patch of grass in Mrs Draper's back garden.

So we took corned beef sandwiches and gingerbread squares and ate them on a bench overlooking a children's play area, a good one with swings which worked and two slides, not like the ones I had seen in Bradford.

The ducks approached as soon as we sat down, scrabbling round our feet, catching crumbs before they even touched the ground.

'No one feeds them any more,' said my mother, breaking off a crust and throwing it in the direction of a small female duck which had been chased away by the others. 'People use up their stale bread themselves.'

The crust landed near the feet of the small duck but was grabbed by a drake before she could swallow it. I broke off another crust and threw it towards her and this time she caught it. We both watched, satisfied, as she gulped it down.

The dew had dried now and the air no longer felt cold when I breathed in. My mother took off her new coat, folded it, and laid it across her lap so that the velvet collar hung down and brushed against her legs.

'Summer's paid us a last curtain call,' Mrs Draper had said that morning when she served us our eggs.

And she had been right. It was unseasonably warm. The park started to fill up as people finished their Sunday lunch and came outside to take the air. We watched them as they passed us – young couples, old couples, families, toddlers staggering their first unsteady steps to cries of admiration. Near us a father, probably a soldier on leave, played cricket with his two young sons, glancing at his wife every now and then for approval, unable to stop himself competing, even against a six-year-old.

My mother asked me about the house, whether I liked Bradford and whether I had made any new friends. I said I had not. We talked about jobs. I said that Bill wanted me to get a job in the Post Office but that I fancied something more interesting. The local paper had run a piece about the need for more women to train as bus drivers, I said. My mother, registering no more surprise than if I had said I preferred carrots to cabbage, agreed that this might be more enjoyable.

I asked her more about her job, about the people she worked with, about the bombs, how often they came, what had been hit so far. We talked also about the village. Kitty had had her baby, my mother said. A boy this time. Both were doing fine. Monica, the doctor's daughter with whom I had played hairdressers when I was small, had married a pilot.

'He's quite high up apparently,' said my mother. 'His family come from somewhere near here. Warwick, I think. Or maybe Evesham. I'm not sure.'

Ted, Mrs Frampton's eldest son, was home on extended leave after being shot in the knee. They had nearly had to amputate the leg and still might have to.

At half past two we set off for the station. I had brought my bag with me so that I would not have to go back for it. We drank watery tea in the station tearoom at a table still littered with the cups and saucers of the previous occupants. The girl who served us explained that the other waitress on duty, Peggy, had been rushed to hospital with a burst appendicitis, and that was why she was so behind. A cat escaped from a travelling basket and broke three plates before she was caught and restored to her owner. We did not talk.

When the train drew up, I found a seat by the window and then came out again to say goodbye.

'Thank you for coming,' said my mother, pressing something into my hand.

I looked down and saw that it was a present, a small rectangular shape wrapped in green paper and tied with ribbon. The guard blew his whistle. I climbed back on the train.

'Let me know about the bus driver's job,' she called. 'And don't worry, it will all . . .'

A door slammed, shutting out her words. The train began to move and I went back to my seat. There was no one else in my carriage and so I unwrapped the present at once, tearing the paper in my hurry to see what it was. It was a book, a book with a black, mock leather covering and the words 'Baby's Book' in gold lettering on the front. It was a book about me. Inside, my mother had recorded my weight at birth, my first smile, word, step, haircut and all the other milestones of a child's early years. But she had also recorded other things. She had written about the birth, how the first sight of me had disgusted her, how she had refused to hold me, how guilty she had felt about this later. She had written about the things that made me laugh – gentle splashes in the bath, leaves moving above me when I lay in the pram under a tree – the things she liked about me and the things she did not like. She had felt oppressed by me in those first few months, she wrote. Stifled, tied down. At night, she had dreamt of leaving me somewhere, of running off, free, glad, her feet and heart light.

I read the book from cover to cover and then I sat and looked out of the window and wondered why she had given it to me. And, as I thought about this, with the book in my lap, loosely wrapped again in the green paper, it occurred to me that my mother had not once mentioned Bill's name. Nor had she suggested what I should or should not be doing, how I should be making friends, what sort of job I should be looking for.

In the past I had always resented her willingness to give advice – the way she made me feel she could live my life so much better than I could. Now though, now that she had not done this, I felt hurt instead of pleased. Also, I resented the fact that she was so busy. That was my role, I thought. She should be at home, drawing in, reflecting, waiting for grandchildren, not going out, meeting new people, starting a new life. I felt usurped.

29

Long drifts of leaves piled up in the lanes. Mist hung around the house, sometimes so thick that when Claire and Peter drove out to Alnmouth, they could hear the waves before they could see them. Once, Claire forgot her gloves and wore Peter's instead, her tiny warped hands like shrivelled beans in a pod inside the sleek brown suede fingers.

The cold kept Peter inside, painting still lifes instead of fields. He had finished the painting of St Margaret's and taken it to a shop in Newcastle to be framed. Claire visited him in his room at eleven o'clock for a twenty-minute coffee break. She was careful not to arrive earlier or stay longer or to ask to see what he had painted that morning. He rarely offered to show her unless it was almost finished, out of a fear that an incomplete work had an energy which could be dissipated by exposure. She understood this.

While he was painting, she read, usually in her room or in the library, shunning conversation or Scrabble or invitations to look at someone's daughter's holiday snaps. She had returned to her old routine of learning a poem a day although she now chose them from a wider source. Peter had given her the *Penguin Book of Women Poets*, also slim paperback volumes of young modern poets. She marked the poems she liked in these new books with a green asterisk and then handed them to Peter who marked the ones he liked with a red asterisk. Sometimes there were two asterisks by the same poem but often there were not. It interested Claire to see which poems he had chosen and to speculate why. She liked to think he was similarly interested in her choice.

Occasionally, if the sun was shining and she had finished

learning her poem, she went on a walk. She wore her slip-on ankle boots and shuffled through the leaves, enjoying the sound they made. People were right, she thought, when they said it was getting warmer. Years ago, autumn had started in September. By November, the trees were bare. Now, at the end of October, the trees were still half full, the leaves on some only just beginning to yellow.

If she felt up to bending, she gathered acorns and twigs for Peter's fire, and conkers, shiny as new peeled eggs, for his mantelpiece. She took care to keep her eyes open, to see everything fully, to describe it to herself silently, grappling for the right word, the exact description, so that she would be able to describe it later to Peter. She wanted him to know that she was learning.

If the sun was not shining and she had decided to learn her poem later, in the afternoon, she looked through old magazines, tearing up pictures for a collage she was doing of the sea. She had never done a collage before and so was doing it secretly in case it turned out badly, storing the torn paper in old shoeboxes to keep the colours separate. The fractured nature of a collage appealed to her. Besides, it did not require hands which could stay steady for long periods of time.

One evening, when she was sitting in the drawing room after dinner, hunting for more green in a copy of *Homes & Gardens*, Peter came in. She could see at once that he was agitated.

'Tom's coming,' he said, sitting down beside her.

'Your son Tom?'

'Yes.'

'When?'

'He's not sure. Tomorrow probably. It depends on meetings and things. He's over here on business.'

She folded down the corner of a page advertising a sparkling green drink and tucked the magazine into the side of her chair, between the arm and the cushion.

'Have you just spoken to him?' she asked.

'Yes. He's going to call again tomorrow. He doesn't know when.'

Leslie Shaw, the new temporary resident, approached them smiling and invited them to play cards. Peter shook his head.

Claire, who disliked drawing attention to her hands, felt herself turning red.

'I can't . . .' she began.

'I could hold them for you,' said Peter.

'But you . . .'

'I'd like to,' he broke in.

Phyllis and Colin, who were already sitting at the card table, looked surprised when Claire sat down next to them.

'Peter's offered to hold the cards for me,' she explained.

'What a good idea! I don't know why we haven't thought of it before,' said Phyllis.

She was wearing frosted pink lipstick and matching nail varnish and a cream, ribbed turtle-neck sweater.

Claire smiled by way of reply. She had felt more kindly towards Phyllis after learning that the fine bust she had always envied was, in fact, false. Apparently, Phyllis had had a double mastectomy four years ago after developing breast cancer. The arrival of Mr Shaw had also helped because he sat next to Phyllis whenever possible, so distracting her from Peter. Clearly, he thought the bust was real.

Colin explained the rules of the game they were to play while Mr Shaw dealt the cards. Peter picked up Claire's cards and divided them into suits, leaning close to her so that no one else could see them. Colin played a card first. Then Phyllis followed by Mr Shaw. Then it was Claire's turn. She leant sideways to point at a card, her hand brushing against his, the hairs at the bottom of his arm tickling the soft underside of her wrist. She was so close that the outside of her right leg touched his left leg. She could hear him breathing. It was faster than usual, she thought. That phone call from his son had disturbed him. Mr Shaw won the trick, taking the Queen of Hearts played by Phyllis with a King of Hearts and making suggestive play of his conquest.

More cards were played, spinning across the smooth wood of the table. Peter and Claire's hands moved around one another like courting birds, avoiding direct contact. His breathing was slower now, his forehead smoother, the frowns ironed out like wrinkles from a sheet. The others talked about the Americanisation of Hallowe 'en, whether MPs should be forced to disclose their earnings outside the House of Commons, and

Maureen's health. She had been in bed five days now with a chest infection and, according to the doctor, showed no sign of improvement. Phyllis said she had overheard Matron say that her son, Mike, was coming to visit her the following day. Mr Shaw, who had enjoyed exceptionally high cards, won the game and immediately suggested another.

Claire looked at Peter.

'If you want to. My hands are yours.'

'Well, no, I think . . .'

Claire followed Peter to the French windows. He had opened the curtains slightly and was writing something in the condensation on the glass. As she drew closer she saw that it was a smiling face with a mop of tight curls. He drew another face, a sad one this time with no hair, then rubbed them both out with the flat of his hand, wiping it dry against his trousers.

'Let's go outside and look at the sky.'

'What, now?'

'Yes. There's a harvest moon. Bright orange. Like the pumpkins we saw in the market yesterday. I saw it out of the landing window when I was coming downstairs.'

He unlocked the French windows and they stepped outside, staying still for a few moments until their eyes had adjusted to the dark.

'I was thinking about dying the other day,' he said, no longer avoiding contact, his hand on hers, grasping it firmly. 'About what I would miss, the things that have given me most pleasure apart from people. And I realised that one of the things was the sky. So I decided to look at it more, to make a conscious effort to look at it every day, both when it was light and when it was dark.'

She squeezed his hand. No man had ever talked to her like this before, about the sky and dying. They had talked about what they had read in the papers or heard on the radio or done at work that day. The weather. The future of the mental hospital up the road. Why the health authority should never have closed it anyway. But they had never indicated, not even by so much as a pause or a look in their eyes, that they knew they would not live for ever.

'I'm cataloguing them. Sky by sky. Shade by shade. The next

time I have to fill in a form and state my job, I think I'll put archivist. Sky archivist.'

She could tell he was smiling even though she could not see his face clearly. He had a tendency to do that, she reflected. To mock himself. As if he feared someone else might do it, as if he wanted to pre-empt them.

'What I need now is one of those split skies. You know, all cloudy on one side and brilliant sunshine on the other. Half-dark, half-bright. I can remember them but not clearly, not the details, not where the threat stops and the promise begins.'

He led her down the steps into the garden to where the moon hung, full and heavy like the udder of an unmilked cow.

'It's already less orange,' he whispered.

She shivered and he drew her towards him so that she stood in front of him, facing away, his long arms passing over her shoulders and around her body, the warmth seeping through.

'Why's that?'

'I don't know.'

It was very still and quiet, so quiet that they could hear the noise of Minty the donkey eating hay in his shelter beyond the vegetable garden.

Suddenly, a rocket cracked the silence. Peter and Claire watched the bright speck wriggle up the sky then explode in a shower of blue and gold dust which fell slowly, gracefully, melting into the dark like snowflakes.

There was the noise of someone opening a window at the back of the house and, without saying anything, they separated, moving into the shadows.

'I don't know the names of the stars either,' said Peter, after they had heard the window close again.

'I've always wanted to. For years I've cut out night sky charts from newspapers and bought myself books on stars. I've got a whole shelf of them upstairs and yet I still only know the ones that everyone knows – the North Star, the Plough, the Seven Sisters.'

'We could learn them. Together,' said Claire.

'Yes. We could,' he said, but not enthusiastically, she thought, not as though he wanted to, as though he had given up all hope of achieving that particular dream.

She shivered again.

'Come on. Let's go in. You're cold.'

'No. I don't want to go in yet.'

'Well, let's go into the conservatory. We can still see the sky from there and it will be warmer.'

He turned the fountain on and they sat and watched the water rise and fall in the still, perfumed air.

'Will you go out to lunch with Tom?'

'Maybe. If we do I want you to come too.'

She noticed the use of 'want' rather than 'would like' and was comforted.

'Won't you want to be on your own?'

'No. It's better if there's someone else.'

The fountain stopped. Claire waited for Peter to turn it on again but he didn't.

'I never told him what to do,' he said. 'I mean, of course, I told him not to pick flowers in the park and things like that when he was small. But when he was older and making choices, about what he wanted to study at university and what he would do afterwards, I left him to make up his own mind. I'd resolved not to put pressure on him in the way my father had on me. I thought he liked this, that he enjoyed the freedom it gave him. Then two years ago, he phoned me up one morning very early. It must have been late at night where he was phoning from. I think he'd been drinking. It sounded as though he had. Anyhow, he said I'd never given him any advice. That I'd been a rotten father. That he would never treat a son in the way I had treated him, as though I'd learnt nothing, had nothing to pass on, no tips on what to do or not to do, how best to live. Then he put the phone down.'

There was a long pause. Claire wondered what her son would look like if he had lived and what he would be doing, whether they would be on good terms.

'There's still time,' she said. 'When he marries. When he has children of his own. Often they become closer then, when they realise the sacrifices you have to make, the sacrifices you made for them.'

Peter shook his head.

'He won't marry. He says he doesn't want to make anyone

unhappy the way I made his mother unhappy. He told me that too on the phone. He's able to talk on the phone, you see, or at least, to say things, things he wouldn't be able to say to my face.'

'Does he have a girlfriend?'

'Lots. A new one every week, it seems. But they never last. He doesn't want to commit himself. If they don't go of their own accord, then he goes. Once he went to South Africa for two months just to get rid of a girl who wouldn't give up. She got hold of my number and phoned me every night for a week. I couldn't tell her where he was because I didn't know. In the end, I had to take the phone off the hook.'

He stood up and switched the fountain on again. She watched him, hugging herself to keep warm, wishing her mother had lived longer, that they had known one another when they were both older.

Peter sat down again.

'Will you tell me about your son?'

The question took Claire's breath away as if she had plunged into a pool of cold water and come up gasping, spluttering, her whole body in shock. She felt like a bare electrical wire or splashed petrol – dangerous, liable to ignite at the slightest spark.

She stared at the fountain and saw in the water the book her mother had given her at Coventry railway station. Name: Claire Langley. Weight: 7lb 5oz. Height: 84 cm. Circumference of head: 35 cm. Disposition: Obstinate, strong-willed, contrary.

She wondered what she would have written if she had kept a similar book about her son. Would she have wanted him to know how she felt about him? Would she have been brave enough to tell him?

The fountain stopped again and once more it became quiet so that her words, when she spoke, fell like pebbles down a well, clear and distinct.

'Yes. If you like. But it's not a happy story.'

'You don't know yet. It hasn't finished.'

30

'His name was Harry, Harry Harper, and he had muscular dystrophy. Last year they finally found out what causes it. But there's still no cure.

'I didn't notice anything wrong at first. Nor did the doctors or nurses at the hospital. He was a beautiful baby. Everybody said so. Black hair – but straight, not wavy like mine. Green eyes. And a funny, pointy little face. A pixie face.

'He crawled at the normal age. And walked. Earlier than most. But then, when he was about two and a half, I noticed that his walking, instead of getting stronger and faster, was getting weaker and slower.

'I took him to the doctor. But he said there was nothing wrong and asked me how I felt, whether I was depressed, as if I was the one who needed help.

'I took him back to the doctor three months later. By then I knew there was something wrong. He'd started to go floppy if he'd been walking or standing for a long time, as if the weight of his own body was simply too heavy to support. The doctor said the same as he'd said before. That it was easy to be anxious especially if one was on one's own . . .'

'You were on your own?' interrupted Peter.

'Yes,' said Claire, knotting her hands, watching the beech mast she had collected the day before crackle and spit in the fire.

They were in Peter's room. He had lit candles first and then the fire, found cushions for her head and a rug to cover her legs, and made hot drinks. They had drunk the drinks while the fire was gathering strength and her fingers and toes warmth. Then he had turned out the main light so that the room was lit only by the candles and the fire and she had started to tell him.

'Sorry. Go on.'

The fire spat violently and a spark flew out, landing on the rag rug. Claire watched it glow for an instant, then fade, leaving a tiny black scorch mark. She went on.

'He said there was nothing to cause any concern, that I shouldn't compare Harry to other children because they all developed at their own pace, that I should come back in twelve weeks if I was still worried.

'I went away but I didn't go home. I went to see another doctor. I didn't tell him about the first one. I just explained what was wrong. He was a young man, I remember. There was a photograph of a small child, a boy, probably the same age as Harry, on his desk. Maybe that was why he listened. He didn't say much – just nodded and wrote something down every now and again – but, at the end, he said Harry would have to go into hospital to see a specialist.'

She paused and readjusted a cushion that had slipped sideways.

'We saw the specialist three weeks later. He asked me some questions and then he asked Harry to do things like run across the room. After about an hour, at half past four – I know because there was a clock on the wall and I remember looking at it and thinking that Harry would soon want something to eat – he took me into his office and told me that Harry had Duchenne muscular dystrophy, a gene defect which caused progressive muscle weakness. He said he would not be able to walk in five or six years' time, that he would grow weaker and weaker and more and more deformed and that he would die at about fourteen, probably from cardiac failure or infection.'

She paused again and held up her hands in front of her, the palms facing outwards, then placed them in her lap, one on top of the other.

'He was right about nearly everything. Harry could no longer walk when he was eight. By the time he was eleven he couldn't stand without support. At the end, he couldn't even raise his head. The only thing he was wrong about was the age at which he died. He lived until he was twenty, until he was a young man, a young man with the same dreams as any other young man but with no hope of ever fulfilling them. He still had the same black hair and green eyes. But his face and body were no longer those of a pixie but a goblin. He was hideously deformed. When I wheeled him outside for a walk, the children who lived nearby used to scream and run away. "Here comes the troll," they said. "The troll! The troll!".'

She hid her face with her hands, her eyes swollen with tears. After a few moments she felt Peter's hands on top of hers. She pressed her face into them and he rocked her gently, forward and back. When he felt her quieten and the pressure of her face slacken, he lay her head back and fetched her a glass of whisky. It was malt whisky, a drink she had not tasted for more than thirty years, and she greeted it like an old friend, rolling it round her mouth, exploring it, seeing if it had changed.

'I went to a sports day once at his school. He went to a normal school until he was about seven. It was an egg-and-spoon race. I don't know why they let him enter. He was last, way behind everyone else, and the other children who were watching started to laugh. I was crying. I couldn't bear to look. Then a man, I don't know who it was – I couldn't find him afterwards to thank – ran forward and took him by the hand and helped him finish.'

The memories were bubbling furiously now, coming up for air, jockeying for position like racehorses at the starting post.

'There was no help then. No grants to help you buy a wheelchair or adapt your home, no special needs teachers or family care officers or respite care. Nothing. I never met anyone else with muscular dystrophy until after Harry had died. That was the worst thing. The isolation. Not having anyone to talk to who knew what I was going through. Someone came once a month and gave him physiotherapy. And my neighbour looked after him for three hours on Thursday afternoons so that I could shop. They were the only people I saw – that I knew by name – for twelve years. When he died, I felt as though I'd been in prison. Everything had changed. I didn't know the names for things, the way to dress and behave. I couldn't even speak properly. I stammered when I asked for a ticket on the bus.'

She was aware that Peter, sitting down again in the Edwardian tub chair, was looking at her but avoided meeting his eyes in case the expression in them, the sympathy she had felt in the touch of his hands, made her falter. She did not want to stop. She wanted to unload those memories, to throw them overboard like unwanted cargo, to watch them disappear, the distance between herself and them growing further and further.

'He made models. Built boxes out of bits of cardboard and fabric, anything he could find really. I would show him things before I threw them away in case he wanted them. At first, he made them by himself. Later, when he began to lose the use of his hands, I helped. He told me where to stick them. He would have been an architect, he said, if he had lived.. That's what he wanted to do, to design houses.

'I . . . I . . .'

Her tongue stumbled, tripping over itself in its hurry.

'The worst thing was when someone was kind. One Thursday, coming back from the shops, facing another week in the house on my own with him, someone helped me onto the bus with my bags. And I cried. I sat down and wept because someone had been nice.'

She paused, remembering the way Harry had looked when she had returned from those trips – relieved that she had come back, angry that she had gone, jealous that she had been able to go.

She remembered other looks too – the worried expression on his face when he had told her at the age of nine that he was going to die, as if she didn't know, as if the news might come as a terrible shock; the fury when she had put a jumper on him without asking if he was cold; and worst of all, heartbreaking to see, the wistful longing when once, shortly before Christmas, it had begun to snow and through the window in the light of the street lamps they had seen a group of boys throw snowballs at one another, whooping with delight when a throw hit home.

She had wanted it to be all over, had felt guilty for feeling this. Then, when the years dragged on and he grew weaker and weaker, she became angry, as if God was tormenting him, sucking the life out of him like a boy blowing birds' eggs – slowly, methodically, drop by drop. She had prayed then, prayed for him to die and yet despite this, she had dreaded his birthdays, knowing that each one brought his death closer.

When he did finally die she had felt bereft. Had howled like a cow whose calf had been killed. Had wandered round the house, aimless, unable to concentrate, unable to stop herself walking in circles.

'He was so bright, so sharp. It was like watching a butterfly trapped in a bear's body. It would have been better if he had been dull and slow. I wouldn't have felt the cruelty of it so much then, the waste, the terrible, appalling waste. Or maybe I would. I don't know. One can't know.'

She was no longer aware of Peter or where she was or even that she was speaking out loud. Peter held himself still.

'One Thursday, instead of doing the shopping, I had my hair cut. I had it cut really short, the shortest it's ever been. It was silly, childish. But I wanted to shock him, to show him I had my own life, was my own person, that I did not have to consult him before making a decision. He was hurt, I could tell he was hurt as soon as I walked in the door and even though I pretended to be surprised, I wasn't because that's what I had wanted – to hurt him.

'It wasn't like that all the time. But sometimes, just occasionally, I would see my life with the eyes of an outsider – the endless repetition, the hoisting and lifting, the drudgery of it all, and I would see also how it might have been, how it was for other people, and I would feel bitter then, eaten up with it. I would feel guilty afterwards, there was so much guilt then, guilt that he had the disease in the first place, guilt that I couldn't do anything about it, that no one could, that I couldn't look after him better, that I didn't have enough money to run a car or pay for a taxi to take him swimming regularly as the doctor said he should.

'That's why I had the test – the test to find out if he had inherited the dystrophy from me, if I was a carrier. I had to have it done privately because by the time they knew how to do it I had started the menopause. The NHS doctor said there was no point doing it as I could no longer have children. I didn't even try to explain.

'I was glad when they told me I wasn't a carrier and that Harry had probably developed the dystrophy through a mutation in his own gene. It's silly but it made me feel a lot better.'

A coal shifted in the fire and a handful of ash fell through the grate. Claire did not seem to notice.

'It would have been so different if he had been born now, with the television and computers. All those places he would have been able to see, places he could only read about. He might have been able to study, to go to university even. They do now. I've read about it. It's all so different.

'I did my best. I tried to act as though he had a future, as though there was a point in him learning things, even if it was only for his own sake, to help him lead a fuller life.

'I wish he'd seen the sea, though. That's what I think of now, more than anything. That I'd managed to take him to the sea so that he could see it for himself, the waves crashing on the beach, the enormity of it, the endless frightening rhythm. I knew he wanted to see it but I didn't realise how much until he talked about it on his twentieth birthday. Then I decided I would do it whatever it cost, even if I had to pay for a taxi to take us all the way there and back, but I was too late. He died a week later.

'Maybe that's why I came here. To be near the sea. As though somehow I can make up. As though I can see it for him. I don't know. I don't know.'

Her eyes closed and her head dropped. Her lips continued to move but no sound came out and after a few minutes they too became still. Peter watched her. When he was sure she was asleep, he rose and very gently, very slowly, removed her shoes. Then he tiptoed into his bedroom and came back carrying two blankets with which he covered her, equally gently and slowly. Finally, he leant over and kissed her lightly on the forehead. She stirred but did not wake up, a slow smile dawning on her face as though acknowledging the kiss. Peter smiled back.

Peter's son did not phone the next day as he had promised. Nor the day after. He did phone the following day but Peter was out, having his eyes tested, and he rang off without leaving a message.

'He's doing it on purpose,' said Peter.

'He's probably just busy,' said Claire.

'You don't know him. He's like that.'

He struck angrily at the sand, gouging out a hole with his heel. Claire walked away. It had rained during the night and the air had a freshly laundered feel. She breathed in eagerly, enjoying the way the breeze lifted the curls at the back of her neck, delighting for once in her frailty, in her heightened sense of the sea's power. The rain had swollen it, making the waves slow and heavy; dangerous, like a pregnant woman or a sleeping snake.

She looked back. Peter was still kicking at the sand, his hands in his pockets, his shoulders hunched disconsolately. He looked like a small boy who'd been told off, she thought, and smiled protectively.

'Come on!'

A woman walking her dog beyond Peter looked up as though the cry had been directed at her and then, when she realised it hadn't, looked down again. Peter too looked up.

'Come on,' she cried again, only this time she held out her arms as well. Peter began to walk, slowly at first, then faster until by the time he reached her he was almost running.

'He wants to keep me waiting. To unsettle me. It's a tactic. That's what he does. He's always done it.'

Claire gazed at the sea, wondering if the black speck she could see on the horizon was a boat, a bird, or nothing at all, just a figment of her imagination. She took Peter's hand.

'He's got a lot to do. You said yourself how many meetings he had to attend.'

'It's as though he's playing a game of chess. All his life he's been like that, as if people are going to attack him, to take things from him, and the only way he can prevent it is by attacking them first, taking things from them.'

'Have you looked at the sky today?'

'No.'

He looked at her and then up at the sky. She looked up too and they both stood there, drinking it in, the immense bright blue splashed with white.

'How extraordinary,' he said, not looking down. 'I don't think I've ever seen clouds look quite like that. It's as though someone's thrown a bucket of milk and it's splattered everywhere. Look at those streaks over there. They look lit up from above or behind, don't they? Like pictures in an art gallery.'

She looked down and saw that his face had been rinsed clear. They began to walk again.

'Maybe you're right,' he said. 'But I still wish he'd phone or leave a proper message. Then at least I'd know what was happening.'

A couple passed them, the man with a small girl sitting on his shoulders crying that she was cold.

'Come on, I'm cold too. Let's go and have tea at Howick. That'll warm us up,' said Peter.

But when they arrived at Howick they found that the teashop was shut. A sign hung on the garden gate. *Closed for winter*, it said. *Open again, April 20*. Peter stared at it disbelievingly.

'It never used to shut when Mrs Barnard ran it,' he said, his face clouded over again.

'It was open the whole year. And she made the Singin' Hinnies herself. Everything was home-made then. Even the butter.'

They drove back in silence. Claire thought about Mrs Barnard. The doctor said it was just a matter of weeks now but then, as one of her relatives had pointed out to Claire, he had been saying that for months. She wondered what sort of funeral there would be and whether it would be what she would have wanted. It was too late to ask her now. It was difficult to know if she could even hear.

'Peter?'

'Yes,' he said, changing down, indicating to turn right into the drive.

'I want to be cremated and my ashes scattered at sea.'

'Haven't you written a will?' he asked, not taking his eyes off the road.

'Yes, but just in case there's any confusion. I wanted you to know.'

'OK. I know,' he said and turned right.

She leant back in her seat and smiled to herself. That was another thing she liked about him. That she could say things like that and not be asked why.

32

Claire and Iris were talking again. It had started when Claire went into her room one day and found Iris looking at the collage. The door was open and she walked in quietly, and Iris, who was leaning over the desk, her back turned, did not notice her. She gave a small cough. Iris looked up and she was so pleased to see Claire, to be able to voice what she was thinking, that she forgot they were not talking.

'It's beautiful. Really lovely. The waves. The roll of them. You've made them so real.'

Claire, who had not yet shown the collage to anyone, who had not even told Peter she was doing it, was so delighted that she too forgot they were not talking.

'Do you think so?'

'Yes. You feel as if you're there, standing on the shore, buffeted by the wind.'

'It's not meant to be frightening. It's a celebration. I love storms, you see. I always have done. I used to run out into the garden and dance when I was a child. Once I went out in my pyjamas. It was pouring with rain and there was the most incredible sheet lightning. I can still remember it. The whole sky kept on turning pale violet. Someone saw me from inside and brought me in. My father, I think. I was wet through and I'd torn one of my pyjama legs. I overheard our cleaning woman talk about it the next day in the kitchen. She called me a little pagan. I didn't know what "pagan" meant and I asked my mother and then I got into more trouble for listening to people's conversations.'

Iris propped the collage up and stepped back to look at it from a distance.

'I didn't know you were an artist as well as Peter.'

'I'm not. This is the first collage I've ever done.'

'But you must have done one before. How did you know what to do?'

Claire shrugged her shoulders.

'I didn't. I just stuck a piece of paper down and if it didn't look right, I pulled it up and stuck another one down. If it wouldn't come up, I stuck something over it.'

Iris lay the collage flat and picked up the duster she had been using to clean the desk. Claire sat down. She had forgotten what she had come into her room for.

'I'd like to do something like that,' said Iris, twisting the duster round one hand. 'To make something.'

'Why don't you then?'

'I can't . . . I wouldn't know where to start.'

'I'll show you then. Come on. I'll get the paper out.'

She started to get up but Iris waved the duster at her.

'No, I will. Tell me where it is.'

'At the bottom of the wardrobe behind the shoes in those small boxes. You could help me sort the colours if you don't mind. They're getting dreadfully muddled. I've been meaning to do it for ages but it's such a fiddly job.'

Iris knelt down and found the boxes. Then, still kneeling, she tipped them out and sorted the paper by shade. Light blue, dark blue, bright blue, cobalt blue, blue grey, blue green, blue black, blue white, turquoise blue, petrol blue.

Claire watched.

'I think you need a few more boxes.'

'I've got some,' said Claire. 'I asked Cook to save me some.'

She fetched a plastic carrier bag from behind the door.

'Here you are. I don't know if they're the right size. I haven't looked to see yet.'

She handed Iris the bag and their fingers touched. Iris smiled.

'I'm sorry about what I said.'

Claire knew she was referring to their exchange in the ironing room.

'I'm the one who should be sorry. You were right. It's nothing to do with me. It's just that sometimes when you care about someone you . . . well . . . you . . .'

Iris stood up.

'It wasn't your fault. I overreacted. It was just that I was so tired. I was going into Newcastle every other night to see Quintin. Sometimes I didn't get back until after midnight. And then I was up again at six. I didn't mean what I said about . . .'

Claire interrupted. She did not want Iris to repeat what she had said that afternoon about 'knowing about Peter' – the implicit threat. She did not want to think about what would happen if people began to talk.

'How is he?' she asked.

She had actually seen Quintin in Alnwick a few days before but did not like to say so. He had not recognised her and she had been so shocked by the change in his appearance, the weight he had lost, the dead putty-like look of his skin, she had not said hello.

'All right. A bit woozy, but I think that's mainly the tablets. He's on antidepressants and various other things.'

Claire sat down again.

'He's out of hospital then?'

'Yes. He came out last week. He has to go back once a week for a checkup.'

Iris sat down too, but on a chair this time, facing Claire. She seemed a lot older than when she first arrived, thought Claire – as if three years had passed rather than three months. She looked at her face, at the first traces of wear, the small lines under her eyes and wondered what would become of her. Would she marry Quintin, would she have children, would she remember her, the talks they had had, the stories she had told? Or would her memory fade like a scar, vivid one day, paler the next until all that was left was an outline, visible only in certain light? Probably the latter, she thought, wrenching herself back to the present.

'And how long do they think it will take? For him to recover completely, I mean?'

'Well, he's better now really. But he's lost a lot of weight and he's also very low – very depressed. I think it would help if he had more to do or if we lived somewhere that wasn't so isolated. We have thought of moving into Alnwick but then of course we'd have to pay rent which we don't at the moment and it would be difficult to manage on what I earn. I think he gets quite lonely. I'm out nearly every day, you see. And his father and brother are busy on the farm. His mother's very good. She usually pops in once a day to see him but she's quite busy herself and anyhow I'm not sure she's the best person for Quintin to see. She's one of those very brisk, efficient people. I think sometimes she makes him feel rather inadequate, as though he should pull himself together and go out and find a job.'

'Is that what he wants now then? Has he given up the idea of joining a band?'

'Oh, no. In fact, he still spends most of his time writing songs. He's bought this computer programme where you can compose music and then play it back to yourself. But I think he finds it increasingly difficult not to have a job – to have no role. It didn't matter in London because half of his friends didn't work either. But now he's up here and they're down there and anyhow most of them have gone back to college or become merchant bankers or something.'

She spotted three pieces of stray paper on the floor next to Claire's chair and knelt down to file them in the correct boxes.

'I think I'd like to do one of a field. There's one near us that's just been ploughed. I pass it every day on the way here. I think I'd like to do that. The earth standing up in great brown slabs, all shiny where it's been sliced by the metal. Do you think it would be too difficult?'

Claire said no, she did not.

'Good. I'll start collecting browns then. I'll look out for blues too. You could do with some more turquoise.'

33

Peter had not told her what Tom looked like or shown her a photo, which was why, when she met a man on the drive, she did not know it was him. In her mind she had pictured a younger, more modern version of Peter – a tall, dark man with expensive clothes and the look of living fast. This man was sandy and freckled and his clothes had the comfortable, lived-in look of a farmhouse kitchen. Also, although not small, he was definitely not tall.

'Can I help you?' she said.

He was staring at the ground as if he'd dropped something.

He looked up and grinned.

'I doubt it,' he said.

Claire did not know why she did what she did next. Looking back, she blamed both the grin, which maybe unconsciously reminded her of Peter, and her shopping bags, which were heavy. She had walked into town and bought Christmas presents – a novel for Catherine, a toy dumper truck for Luke, a novelty bone for Vashti, and *Othello* on tape for Peter. He did not like compact discs.

'Try me,' she said, putting down her bags.

He grinned again, only this time, instead of metamorphosing into a frown, the grin stayed and broadened, spilling from his face like jam from a doughnut.

'Have you lost something?'

'Yes.'

Claire looked down. She was good at finding things. Once, when she was nine, she had found a gold earring of her mother's in a crack between two paving stones in the front porch. It had fallen off one evening as her parents left the house to have supper at Nesfield Hall and had been given up as lost for good.

'Not that kind of thing,' he said, no longer grinning. 'I've lost my courage.'

She might, at that point, have walked away. She might have picked up her bags, smiled politely and walked away, telling Matron once she was safely inside that there was a strange man at the end of the drive, that he was behaving very oddly and that maybe someone ought to keep an eye on him to make sure he didn't do anything. She would have walked away. On any other day, she would have. But on that day, on that particular morning, she didn't.

She looked at him and she saw the appeal in his eyes behind the self-mockery and for some reason she remembered a lecture her mother had once given her on charity – how one didn't need to seek out people to help, how there were always people among one's friends and acquaintances, people one came across in the ordinary course of events. She saw too that he had shaved that morning, that his clothes, despite their lived-in look, were clean, and that he did not look like someone who would rape an old woman or steal her purse. More importantly, she saw that they could be easily seen, both from the road and the house.

'Why don't we sit down? There's a bench over there.'

She pointed up the drive to where to a bench stood, set back in a small paved area surrounded by rose beds.

He picked up her bags.

'Weren't you going in?'

'Yes, but not to do anything urgent. Nothing that can't wait.'

They sat down. Claire adjusted her coat so that it covered her knees. The man smiled at her, put his hands in his pockets, took them out again, crossed his legs, opened his mouth as if to say something, and then shut it again. She began to feel awkward.

'I hope . . .'

'What did . . .'

They both stopped.

'Sorry. After you.'

'No. You were first,' said Claire. 'Please. Go on.'

'I was just . . . I was just going to say that I hoped you didn't think I was in the habit of doing this – of loitering outside old people's nursing homes . . .'

'Residential,' Claire corrected him. 'You have to go next door if you need nursing.'

'Residential. Sorry, residential.'

He burst out laughing – a huge hearty roll of a laugh that wrapped round Claire like a hug.

'I'm sorry. I don't even know you. It's ridiculous. I don't know what I'm doing. I think it's just I'm very tired.'

He moved as if to stand up.

'Why have you lost your courage?'

He looked at her sharply then leant back and sighed.

'It's nothing. It's just . . . it's just that I should have told someone something. Something about myself. But I didn't. Now I've got to tell them and I can't because I can't explain why I didn't tell them in the first place – why I've kept it a secret.'

A squirrel ran out from behind a tree and eyed them curiously, its head on one side. The man laughed his warm, rolling laugh again and it darted off, stopping to look back once it was at a safe distance.

'Sorry. I'm being a bit evasive.'

He ran his hands through his hair and turned to face her.

'The thing is, I got married a year ago and I didn't tell my father. Now my wife is pregnant and I've got to tell him. I mean a wife is one thing but a grandchild – well, I can't not tell him that.'

'Why didn't you tell him you were going to get married?'

He wrinkled his nose, once, twice, then three times.

'I don't know. You know how these things are. You try to unravel them afterwards, to find an end, a reason, and you can't. It happened very quickly. That was partly why. One minute we weren't married and weren't particularly thinking of getting married, and the next minute we were. We were also halfway across the world in a country he'd never visited before and didn't want to. And there was no ceremony or anything, no flowers or white dress or reception, nothing to invite him to. It was just a quick service in a register office. The witness was the waiter from the bar next door. There were probably other reasons too, personal reasons. But I never meant not to tell him. I just thought I'd keep it to myself for a bit. But then another week went by and another week and it seemed more and more difficult. And now it seems impossible. I've come all this way to tell him, I was on my way to tell him when you saw me, but I don't know what to say, I don't know how to explain.'

'Don't explain then,' said Claire. 'Don't even try to.'

He was about the age Harry would have been if he had lived, she thought, and she wondered whether he would have kept it secret if he had married, if he would have wanted to keep her out, to hurt her, to show he did not need her approval.

'But I have to.'

'You don't have to. Besides, he'll be too busy thinking about being a grandfather to be angry.'

'Do you think so?'

Her mother would have made a better grandmother than a mother, she thought. She would have been less stifling, more able to concede that her grandchildren were people in their own right, with opinions and feelings which might differ from hers. It had always amazed her how someone so open-minded about religion and politics and even morality, could be so narrow-minded when it came to her own daughter, so intolerant of difference.

'Yes,' she said. 'I know I would.'

'Maybe you're right. I'll think he make a better grandfather than he did a father.'

She looked up quickly, suspecting him of mocking her, but he gave no sign that he had read her thoughts.

'We probably all make better grandparents,' she said slowly. 'It's an easier job. Not so messy.'

'You're right. I'll just tell him. I don't know why I'm making such a big thing of it.'

Their eyes met and they smiled.

'Come on, you're getting cold. I mustn't keep you any longer.'

'No, I'm fine. Really.'

'You're not. Look, you've got goose pimples.'

He pointed to the gap between the end of her coat sleeve and the cuff of her glove.

'Well yes, I am starting to feel a little bit chilly.'

He stood up and handed her the shopping bags.

'Thank you for listening. You've helped me find it again. My courage, I mean.'

She laughed and made a joke about having sharp eyes and said goodbye. She turned round once when she reached the door and saw that he was standing where she had left him. She waved and went in, expecting that in a few minutes he too would turn round, walk back to the end of the drive and go on to wherever he was going, wherever he had been going when she had met him. She went upstairs, washed her hands and put away the presents in a cupboard to be wrapped later by one of the staff. The dumper truck was quite large and she had to clear a space for it and as she did so she came across an awkward shape wrapped in a plastic bag. She took it out and unwrapped it. It was one of Harry's models she had kept, a strange sculpture of cardboard and paper decorated with sweet wrappers. She sat down and turned it round in her hands, remembering him making it, the awful cheap toffees they had had to eat to supply the wrappers, his irritation when they had run out of glue one day.

She sat there and she looked at the model and she thought of her son. She did not look out of the window or go downstairs as she had meant to do after she had taken off her coat and put away the presents. And so she did not see that the man she had been talking to did not turn round but instead walked straight on towards the house and rang the bell and asked for Peter Mansley.

34

Claire did not put Harry's model back in the cupboard but placed it on a shelf near the window where she could see it when she woke up in the mornings. It was better than a photograph, she decided. Happier. More positive.

Afterwards, she went next door to The Willows to read Mrs Barnard stories from the local newspaper. She did not know whether the old woman could hear her but reasoned that if she could, she would probably be interested.

The staff had moved her again, this time to a room at the back of the house with no view and an unfortunate choice of maroon wallpaper. Claire had questioned the move but had been told – somewhat acerbically, she thought – that there was no point giving Mrs Barnard a room with a view when she could not see, and that anyway, the new room was closer to the lift. She could not fault the physical care – the room was always spotless and Mrs Barnard had no bed sores – but she had decided that she did not want to move to The Willows if her health deteriorated. She would rather be looked after by staff that smiled, she thought, even if she could not see them smiling, than have a clean mantelpiece.

She read Mrs Barnard three stories, one about the failure of Alnwick traders to give enough support to the town's Christmas lights appeal, another about a Rothbury schoolgirl who was trying to raise money to go on what was described as a 'trip of a lifetime' and a third, about a farmer near Shilbottle who wanted to turn some disused farm buildings into light industrial units. She described the look of the sky the previous day when she and Peter had walked on the beach at Alnmouth, how they had gone for tea at Howick but found it closed, how disappointed Peter had been. She thought she saw the old woman's eyes flicker when she mentioned Howick but she might have imagined it.

'I'll come again tomorrow,' she said, lifting the old woman's hand, dry and light as dead leaves, and gently squeezing it. 'And I'll bring you my collage, the one I told you about. I'm finding the waves hard. It's difficult to get the movement right, to make them look angry enough. But, even so, I'm quite pleased with it.'

She went next to feed Minty, cutting through a gate at the bottom of The Willows' garden. The goat in the field beyond had kidded, she saw. She could see a little head poking out of the wooden outhouse. She would have to walk round later and find out how many she had had.

On her way back she passed John, the head gardener, clearing leaves from the flower beds and humming 'Land of Hope and Glory' at the same time. He inquired briefly about her arthritis and told her at length about his wife's. A boy two doors down from him had been blinded the night before, trying to light a faulty rocket, he said.

'It's the same every year. If you ask me, they shouldn't sell them. People should go to public displays. Then it wouldn't happen.'

Claire nodded, although privately she thought nothing could rival the pagan joy of stomping round a fire in the gloom and shadows of one's own back garden.

Peter met her in the hallway as she wiped the mud off her shoes.

'Where've you been? I've been looking for you everywhere.'

'I've been . . .'

'It doesn't matter. It doesn't matter now. Come on. Tom's here. We're going out to lunch. It's all booked. I phoned up and they said we could have a table as long as we got there by twelve thirty.'

'But I'm not dressed . . . I haven't got my handbag.'

'You don't . . . we can't . . .'

'I need my handbag,' she interrupted firmly.

'All right. I'll wait for you here.'

She slipped on a jacket and sprayed some perfume behind her

ears. There was no time to do anything else. She would have to put some lipstick on when she got there, she decided.

Peter, as promised, was still in the hallway.

'Where is he?' she whispered.

'Outside. By the car. He's waiting for you. We've both been waiting.'

She followed him out of the door. He had the agitated air of a teacher shepherding fifty children up Oxford Street the day before Christmas Eve, she thought. She had never seen him look so fraught.

A man was standing next to Peter's car with his back to them. He turned round only when they were a few feet away so she had no time to prepare herself. It was the man who had lost his courage. The man with sandy hair. That man was Peter's son. The man she had talked to. The man who was worried about telling his father he was married.

She registered the alarm in his eyes as he too recognised who she was. But Peter noticed nothing, introducing them hurriedly and rushing around unlocking doors. She saw him find a paint brush on the floor and poke it out of sight underneath the driver's seat. Clearly, whatever else had been said, he had not told Tom about his painting.

'I'll go in the back,' she said.

'No, please. You go in the front. There's more leg room. You'll be more comfortable.'

'I don't need more leg room. Look at me!'

He did look and he grinned, conspiratorially, she thought, as though they had reached an agreement.

'Well, anyway, I'd like you to sit there.'

And he got into the back quickly, leaving Claire no choice but to climb in next to Peter who was already fastening his seat belt, starting the engine, acting as though they had five minutes to catch a train ten miles away.

He drove fast with the choke out too far, leaving it out even when the engine had warmed up. Claire could just see the top of the man's head in the make-up mirror on her sun visor. She could not get used to the idea that he was Tom. Had he told Peter, she wondered? Was that why he was so tetchy?

'You don't look at all alike,' she ventured when it was clear no one else was going to initiate conversation.

'Yes, no wonder you . . .' the man began.

She interrupted him, alarmed that he was going to reveal their meeting earlier that morning.

'I would never have thought you were father and son.'

'Tom inherits his colouring from his grandmother. From his mother's mother,' said Peter, braking violently, forcing her to grab the handle above the door.

Tom said nothing.

Claire tried again.

'Where are we going?' she asked brightly.

'The Blue Lion at Warkworth,' said Peter, not taking his eyes off the road. 'I haven't been before but the food's supposed to be good. There was a review of it in last month's *Northumbrian Life*. Phyllis went there on her birthday. Do you remember?'

'Yes, I think so,' she said, straining to see more of Tom than his hair and the top half of his forehead.

'When did you arrive?' she asked, turning slightly in her seat.

'Last night. Very late. My hire car broke down about seventy miles south of Newcastle. It took an hour for the breakdown people to arrive and another two hours for them to tow me here. I was going to call but it was half past eleven by the time I'd found somewhere to stay so I just went to bed. That's why you . . . that's why I'm on foot today. The car's at a garage. It's supposed to be ready this afternoon.'

She asked him where he had stayed and he told her he had found a lovely bed and breakfast run by a former television executive and his wife.

'They've got a smallholding. You know, goats, pigs, chickens. I had two of their own eggs for breakfast and some bacon they'd cured themselves.'

Claire expressed interest. Peter was silent.

She asked next about his business, how his meetings were going, whether the English climate was a shock after . . . where was it, where was it he lived?

'Kenya. I've got a house in Nairobi. But I'm hardly ever there. My job involves a lot of travel.'

'Yes, won't that be a problem now you're . . . I mean, don't you find it tiring, all the plane flights?'

Tom said no, he didn't, that he loved travelling and wanted to do as much as possible while he could.

Still Peter said nothing. Claire wanted to comfort him, to stretch out a hand and let it rest on his, but she didn't dare. She wondered what he had said when he had told Tom he would like someone else to have lunch with them, how he had described her.

They turned off the road on to a freshly gravelled driveway. Ahead of them, shining in the beam of several floodlights, stood a long low building with a horseshoe shaped opening at one end. A wooden sign showing a blue, gold-maned lion hung over the opening. Peter looked at his watch.

'Only five minutes late. We'll be OK, I think.'

A light drizzle had started to fall, making the ground slippery with dead leaves. Despite this, Peter did not offer to hold her arm as he usually did but strode ahead, whistling. Claire followed more slowly, smiling nervously at Tom who had opened the car door for her, wishing she was back at The Pines, safe in her room, reading the paper.

Inside, the other customers seemed to be either businessmen or childless, moneyed women in their forties with a liking for gold sequins. Claire felt dowdy and looked for a sign to the ladies. Her jacket did not go particularly well with her blouse and there was a greenish brown mark on her skirt, she saw, probably made leaning against the fence to feed Minty.

They bought drinks at the bar – fruit juice for Peter, sherry for Claire and beer for Tom – and sat down at their table. More polite, stilted conversation followed, punctuated by shouts of laughter from a group nearby enjoying an early office Christmas party. Finally, Claire could bear it no longer.

'Are you OK?' she asked Peter. 'Only you seem a bit quiet.'

'I'm fine. I'm fine. It's just that . . . well . . . actually Tom has just told me some rather extraordinary news.'

He paused. Claire waited, her eyes fixed on his face.

'He's married and his wife is expecting a baby. I'm going to be a grandfather.'

'Really! How wonderful! Oh, Peter, I am pleased! Why didn't you say so earlier?'

'I think he was letting it sink in, getting used to the idea.'

Claire allowed herself to look at Tom.

'Congratulations,' she said, shaking his hand so strongly that it hurt, trying to squeeze the glint out of his eyes.

'When is it due?'

'About six weeks' time. The second week of January, we think.'

She turned to Peter.

'A grandfather, then? How do you feel about that?'

'Shocked. But pleased. Pleased really.'

She looked at Tom as if to say 'I told you so' and raised her glass.

'Here's to your grandchild then. To his happiness and health. Or hers!'

They all drank. Tom proposed a toast to the grandfather and they drank again. Claire waited for Peter to propose a toast to the parents but he said nothing. After a few moments, just as she had opened her mouth to propose one herself, he excused himself.

Tom and Claire looked at one another, then they smiled, slowly at first, then more broadly and finally, like buds breaking into flower, they burst out laughing.

'I never for a minute . . .'

'No. Nor did I. It just didn't occur to me. You looked so different from Peter. Besides, I wasn't expecting you.'

Now that she knew he was Peter's son she could see that there were some physical resemblances. He had the same long, graceful fingers and his hair, although a different colour, had the same texture. Above all, he had the same smile – the infectious, laughing grin of a dog or small boy.

'How is it going? The pregnancy, I mean? Is your wife well?'

'Oh, yes, Charlotte's fine. Absolutely fine. But then she's not the invalid type, if you know what I mean. She felt a bit tired for the first three months but after that there's been no stopping her. She's still working and shows no sign of giving it up. She'll probably go into labour wearing a hard hat.'

'A hard hat?'

'She's an engineer,' explained Tom. 'She works on water projects mainly – drainage, irrigation, sewage treatment, that sort of thing. That's how we met. My car broke down near a site where she was working and one of the locals said they would fetch someone who would be able to mend it. They came back with Charlotte.'

'And did she mend it?'

'Yes. But it took her more than two hours. It was a big job. I think she would have mended it though, however long it took. I was a bit surprised, you see, when they turned up with a woman and so she felt she had to prove me wrong.'

'And will you stay out there? In Kenya?'

Tom drained his glass and wiped the foam from his upper lip with the cuff of his sleeve. His shirt was open at the collar and a few sprigs of chest hair peeked over the top button. It was curly, she saw, like golden parsley.

'Yes, I think so. We both feel our future's there. I . . . I've never really felt at home here. People don't laugh enough. And there's so little sense of . . . well, otherness – God, spirits, ghosts – call it what you will. Besides, Charlotte's parents live out there.'

Claire raised her eyebrows inquiringly.

'They're missionaries. They're retired now. But her father still takes a few services. They live north west of Nairobi, near a place called Nakuru.'

Another vicar's daughter, she thought. She wondered if Charlotte was an only child as well, if she too had had to hand round refreshments at gatherings for the faithful.

She wanted to find out more about the pregnancy, to ask if they knew whether it was going to be a girl or a boy, if Charlotte was going to have it at home or at hospital, if they had chosen a name yet – all the small, important details which another woman would have volunteered without being asked. But she did not want to embarrass Tom and besides, Peter was coming back, asking if they wanted another drink, looking black.

The food arrived and the waitress asked if they wanted wine with their meal. Peter shook his head but Tom nodded.

'But haven't you got to drive later? You don't want to have another accident?'

'It wasn't an accident, Dad. The car broke down.'

'I just don't . . .'

'We'll have half a carafe of your house red, please.'

The waitress, who had been looking uncomfortable during this exchange, disappeared quickly before anyone could contradict her. Claire concentrated on grinding pepper.

The food was good if somewhat lukewarm and Claire made appreciative remarks, hoping to thaw the atmosphere. But no one reciprocated. What was the matter? Why didn't Peter say anything? Was he upset? Or were they always like this? Was that what he had meant when he said they didn't get on? She began to feel cross that he had invited her. It wasn't fair. Besides, it was a waste. She was so tense she could hardly swallow let alone enjoy what she was eating.

Peter cleared his throat to speak and she breathed a sigh of relief. At last. He was going to talk, to ask about his daughter-in-law, to show an interest in what his son had been doing since he had last seen him.

But instead he began to talk about a programme he had heard on the radio the previous evening about the role of the historian – about how yesterday's history created today's politics, how there were no heroes today because people couldn't agree on who should be looked up to, how in Roman times heroes were as important as the Gods, how you could be imprisoned for making a disrespectful remark about them.

'There's a square in London, you know, where they're supposed to be erecting a new statue. They've spent ten years trying to decide who the statue should be of, asking people to fill in questionnaires and things, and now they're going to build a fountain instead so that they don't offend anyone. They say a statue would be too politically sensitive.'

Claire looked down at the remains of her lamb in puff pastry with pearl barley and tomato sauce. Why was he doing this? Why was he behaving as if he saw Tom every other week, as if he had nothing new to say to him, as if he had not just learnt he had a daughter-in-law? Was he doing it deliberately? Was he trying to be hurtful?

They drove back to Alnwick in silence. Claire folded back her sun visor so that she would not glimpse Tom's face, so that she would not see the compressed lips, the tight-set shoulders, the hurt. She wanted to hit Peter.

He collected his bag from the bed and breakfast and they drove on to the garage. Claire and Peter waited in the car while Tom went to pay. Neither spoke. After about five minutes, Tom came back to the car. They got out.

'Well, that's settled. It wasn't as bad as I thought it was. Something wrong with the carburettor. At least, I think that's what he said. Charlotte would have known. But then she would have been able to mend it.'

He smiled, but it was a sad smile, nothing like the way he had grinned earlier. Claire saw that he had buttoned his shirt up to the top against the cold and felt a rush of maternal warmth. She wanted to hug him, to send him off with fruit cake in a tin and instructions to drive carefully and phone her when he arrived, but instead she shook his hand and said how nice it had been to meet him. Tom clasped Peter by the shoulder but so quickly and lightly that their coats barely touched.

'Which is the best way out? I turn left, do I, and then right at the end?'

'Yes, then left at the big roundabout and then straight on. It's signposted after that,' said Peter, sounding warmer now, conciliatory, as if he wanted to make up.

Tom got into his car and waved and drove off and then they climbed back into Peter's car and drove off. A low creeping mist had begun to fall and Peter turned on first the heater and then the windscreen wipers, making it difficult to talk, even if they had wanted to – which they did not. Claire thought of Tom's wife, Charlotte. She imagined her striding round a construction site, her fair bobbed hair clipped out of her eyes, pointing at plans, gesticulating, mattering. She sighed.

They stopped at a red traffic light and a man crossed the road carrying a Christmas tree sheathed in plastic. On the pavement a child flung a yellow velour elephant out of his pushchair. It landed in the gutter where it was rescued by a girl in pink snowboots, probably the boy's sister. Claire watched the mother tell the child not to throw the elephant out again and the child ignore her. This time the toy landed further out in the road and was almost run over by a bus. The mother fetched it and rammed it into a shopping tray underneath the pushchair between a cauliflower and a brown paper bag. The child began to cry. Two hundred yards up the street a group of boys fooling about outside a greengrocer's pushed one boy into the road. Peter slammed his foot on the brake.

'Stupid little idiot. He could have been killed.'

He sounded his horn and the boy waved at them jauntily before bending down to pick up the books that had fallen out of his bag. He took his time, not caring that he was holding up the traffic, cocky, untouchable, conscious that his friends were looking on.

The shops ended and they turned on to the road that led to The Pines. It was so gloomy it was almost dark even though it was only half past three. All the cars had their lights on. They passed the spot where Claire had seen Tom looking at the ground and the bench where they had sat and talked, and drew up next to Iris' new car, a present from Quintin. Peter turned the engine off. He did not say anything but he did not move either. Neither did Claire. They sat there in silence, not looking at one another, their breath misting up the windows. Another car drove up and parked. A door slammed and they heard footsteps on the gravel walking towards the house.

'Why?'

'Why what?'

'Why did you treat him like that?'

'Like what?'

She rounded on him fiercely.

'You know what! He came all this way to see you, to tell you that he's married, that he's having a child. And you treated him like a salesman, as though you couldn't wait to get rid of him. He wanted you to be pleased, to share his happiness and you didn't even ask to see a photo of his wife – your daughter-in-law, the mother of your grandchild.'

'Yes, because that's what he wanted! Because if I had, he'd have got his way. As usual!'

'What do you mean "way"? You behaved as if you didn't care, as though you were more interested in a radio programme.'

'You don't understand.'

'But I do. I do. You're jealous, aren't you? Jealous that he's married someone he loves, jealous that he's doing a job he likes, jealous that he's happy when you weren't because . . . because of him. That's it, isn't it? You blame him, don't you? Because if he hadn't come along you wouldn't have had to get married and you wouldn't have had to do a job you didn't like to support a wife and child.'

She had not meant to say this. She had not even known that she had thought it, but she could see from the two hectic spots of colour on Peter's cheeks that she had angered him, that maybe her accusation was more accurate than she had supposed.

'You don't know what it's like. You don't have any idea what it's like. You can't do because you haven't got a son, because . . .'

He stopped. Claire bit her lip. When she spoke again, her voice was low and careful.

'You're right. I don't have a son now but I did have. You do have one but you don't deserve to. No wonder he wants to stay in Kenya.'

She unfastened her seatbelt, opened her door and closed it again, quietly, not slamming it. She would not give him that pleasure.

Matron was in the hall talking to a new member of staff, a girl called Angela. They looked up when she came in and made as if to say something but she lifted her hand in greeting and walked on, up the stairs. She did not stop until she had reached her room, until she had Harry's model in her arms, clasped tight against her chest.

'Harry. Oh, Harry, Harry. Dear Harry. My beautiful boy. My pixie. My puddle. My precious pumpkin.'

The cardboard began to crumple under the pressure of her arms. Two of the sweet papers came unstuck and floated down to the floor. Claire only squeezed tighter.

35

Iris picked up a shiny blue sweet wrapper from a pile at the back of Claire's desk and held it up to the light.

'Were you thinking about this for the sky? For the bright bit?' she asked.

Claire looked at the wrapper. Harry had once touched it too, she thought. He had probably held it up to the light as well, had stretched it taut and smooth, admiring the peacock blue sheen. That was why she had kept it. It was creased now, marked with lines, but the colour was still strong.

'No, not really. It came from something else. They all did. From something my son once made that fell apart the other day.'

Iris stood up, crossed the room to where the collage lay on the coffee table and, after a few moments' consideration, placed the wrapper on one of the few remaining patches of white.

'It would be good. Look. The shimmer makes it seem as if the sun is breaking through.'

Claire got up to look.

'Yes. Maybe. Leave it there. I'll have a think about it.'

The suggestion appealed to her. Harry would have liked it, she thought. He had always encouraged her to make something of her own. He had told her she was good with colours, at knowing what would go with what.

'We could set up as a team,' he had said once. 'I'll design houses and you can decorate them. "Harper's Homes". We could call ourselves that.'

And she had nodded and smiled even though she knew he would never have a home of his own let alone design one for anyone else.

Iris sat down again at the desk.

'Sorry. I interrupted. Go on.'

Claire was dictating a letter to Catherine to say she would like to accept her invitation to spend Christmas in Oxford.

'Where was I?'

'You've just told her that you're going to arrive on Christmas Eve.'

'Oh yes. Tell her I'm catching the train that gets in at five forty – I think that's the best one – and that there's no need to meet me. I can easily get a taxi.'

Catherine had sent her a tape almost ten days ago inviting her to join her family for Christmas but Claire had decided to speak to Peter first and ask what he was doing before she replied. Now, though, there was little chance of finding that out. They had not spoken since Tom's visit.

'Do you want it to go first or second class?'

'First, I think. It always takes longer at this time of year because of the Christmas post.'

Iris handed Claire the letter to read and sign while she addressed the envelope and found a stamp.

'Are you still not talking?'

Claire frowned and continued reading.

'OK. I know you don't like talking about it but really! You're both behaving like . . . well, like . . .'

'A pair of teenagers?'

'Yes.'

'Well we are,' said Claire. 'Inside, that's what we are. Just you wait. You think you change when you get old – that you don't feel the same things or about the same things, as if your heart as well as your hair turns grey . . .'

'No, I don't.'

'You do. Everyone does when they're young. I did. But the thing is you don't change, not the real you – the thinking, feeling you.'

'He's stopped painting.'

Claire turned away and began to tug at the bedspread, pulling it smooth. Then she walked over to the window as if she had not heard.

'Look! They're bringing in the Christmas tree. What a lovely big one. It's a bit early though, isn't it? Or maybe it's not. It seems to have crept up this year.'

'I went in the other day to clean his bathroom and he was packing all his paints into a box. When I asked him what he was doing he said he was throwing them out.'

There was the sound of an ambulance siren. Iris folded the letter and began to lick the envelope.

'It's coming in. It's coming here.'

Iris sealed the envelope and jumped up to look.

'What is it? What's happening?'

The siren had been turned off now but they could hear the noise of the ambulance being driven at speed up the drive.

'I don't know. It's stopping. Someone's getting out. A man. Matron's there. He's getting back in again. They've obviously come to the wrong place.'

Iris opened the window and they watched the ambulance turn round and drive back towards the road.

'It's going next door. It's going into The Willows. It must be someone there.'

Claire felt a sharp stab of alarm. She had been so upset since Tom's visit she had not been to see Mrs Barnard. Nor, so far as she knew, had Peter. She walked over to the phone.

Iris closed the window and turned round.

'What's the matter? Who are you phoning?'

Claire held up a hand to silence her.

'Hello, it's Mrs Harper from The Pines next door. I saw the ambulance go in and I was a bit worried. I thought it might . . . 'Oh. Yes. I see. She . . . ? Yes. Thank you. Goodbye.'

'What is it? What's happened? What did they say? Has someone . . . ? It wasn't . . .'

Iris went to comfort Claire but she was already on her way to the door.

'I've got to tell him. I don't want him to find out from someone else. She meant such a lot to him. She knew his parents. She knew his mother.'

She knocked once at Peter's door and then opened it before he had a chance to reply. Peter jumped up from the sofa, letting the book he had been reading fall to the floor.

'It was for her. The ambulance that came. Mrs Barnard. She's died.'

36 ∫

They sent me her coat after she had died, the one we had bought together. I imagined them wrapping it up, those women we had met, or others like them, their red, swollen hands capable with brown paper and string, hands that had held babies and made pastry, had pressed the soil in firm over winter bulbs, those hands now touching the coat of my dead mother.

It had been a stray bomb, not meant for anyone, thrown overboard because the pilot had failed to find his target. But it had killed my mother.

She had been walking home from the factory where she worked three shifts a week sewing parachutes – a job she had taken on in addition to her work for the council and Women's Voluntary Service. There were fragments of cloth in her hair and clothes, threads of bright green and yellow clinging to her skirt. She only worked there because other women wouldn't – because they preferred to do more difficult, dangerous work which was better paid.

It was dark and, like everywhere else, there were no street signs and for some reason, even though she knew the way, my mother had taken a wrong turning and got lost. I thought about that as I tried on the coat – the pilot losing his target, my mother losing her way, both of them losing their lives. For the pilot had been shot down seconds after dropping his bombs.

The coat was too big. It hung around me in folds. Like a shroud, I thought, stroking the velvet collar which I had thought would wear too quickly.

I had thought it was a Christmas present. The postman had knocked at the door and handed over the big, brown parcel and, after I had thanked him, I had seen that the postmark was from Coventry. I had started to open it, had already begun to tease open the knots when there was another knock on the door. This time it was the telegram.

I thought about that too – the delay that had caused the telegram to arrive after the parcel instead of before, what I would have felt if I had opened the parcel first, had ripped the paper off to find the stiff, thick folds of the coat, her coat, still new.

There were other things too in that first parcel. Her hairbrush. A small black velvet evening bag containing a few necklaces, none of them valuable. Her watch. And a picture of myself aged about ten, standing proudly outside a wigwam I had made from runner bean sticks at the bottom of the garden. I could not remember ever seeing the photo and I held it up to look at it more closely, surprised that my mother should have chosen to have this image of me rather than a more conventional confirmation or wedding picture. My hair was in two knobbly black plaits and I was wearing a fringed hessian sack and a headdress made from fencing wire and chicken feathers. I looked triumphant.

I held that photo in the drab kitchen of our rented house and thought 'I didn't know her. I was just starting, just beginning, and now she's gone and it's too late, I'll never know her.'

There was no one I could tell this, no one who would understand what I meant, not even Bill, especially not Bill, and this realisation made me do what I had decided to do all those months ago. I ran upstairs and changed into the black suit I had worn for my father's funeral. I put a black armband on too. Then I packed a small suitcase. I packed quickly, pulling drawers open, rifling though their contents, hurling clothes on to the bed. I placed the wigwam photo on top. I needed something to keep my courage up.

There was a copy of the previous day's paper downstairs in the sitting room and I opened it and turned to the back, looking for the 'Accommodation' page. There was a long list of rooms to let, most with little to choose between them. One, however, stood out. 'Room in house with orchard. Women only. Free in exchange for help with trees and reading.' I was intrigued. Was the owner blind, I wondered? And what did she, or maybe he, want to be read? Newspapers, poems, novels? I liked reading, even then, but it was the orchard that attracted me as much as the promise of books. The cramped back yards of terraced housing had come as a rude shock after the space of the vicarage garden – the lawns, the rose beds, the herb garden, the vegetable patch, the herbaceous border with its hollyhocks and lupins, the lavender bushes that I used to reach out and touch as I walked past. I missed the garden but most of all I missed the orchard – that cool green shady place where I used to go in summer to be alone.

I cut out the address and put it in my jacket pocket. Then, on second thoughts, I tore out the whole page. The room might have been taken already, I reasoned, or impossible to find. It would be as well to have something to fall back on.

I caught a bus into the centre of Bradford and then another bus to Heaton, the suburb where the house was. Finding the street proved more difficult. The first person I asked for directions, a young girl serving in a corner shop, turned out to be from Birmingham. She had only arrived in Bradford the week before, she said. She was just staying with her aunt while her mother recovered from a miscarriage. The second person, an old man with a black labrador, said he had never heard of it. The third person, a woman waiting at a bus stop with a basket full of cauliflowers, said she had heard of it but was not sure where it was. I was beginning to despair when another woman, also standing at the bus stop, who had overheard our conversation, came forward. I needed to turn left at the butcher's, she said. Then up the hill, second right, and left at the big house with black railings. It was straight on then for quite a way until I came to a small parade of shops. In the middle of the parade was a lane. It was down there, she said.

I found the butcher's and the hill and the second right turning but not the big house with black railings. And what did she mean by 'big' anyway, I thought, putting my suitcase down at the end of the street and massaging my aching palm. The houses were all big. I retraced my footsteps. I found a house with railings about halfway back down the street but it was no bigger than its neighbours and the railings were more rusty than black. I turned left anyhow. Three hundred yards further on the street bent sharply to the left and ended in a T-junction. The woman had not mentioned this. She had said to go straight on for quite a way. I put my suitcase down again and leant against a low wall fronting the pavement. Almost immediately someone began to bang at a window in the house behind the wall. I looked up. There was a woman waving something at me, a duster probably, and gesticulating. It took me a few moments to understand what she meant but then I realised. She didn't want me to lean against her wall! I straightened up and seized my suitcase, two spots of angry colour in my cheeks. I turned right at the junction, crossed the road and walked straight into someone, my eyes too blurred with tears to see properly.

'Look where you're going!' said a woman's voice crossly, picking up the shopping bag I had knocked to the ground. She must have noticed the black clothes then and the state of my eyes because her tone softened.

'Are you OK, love? What's the matter? Do you want to sit down?'

'I'm okay. I just . . . I . . .'

And I burst into tears, the grief which I had so successfully dammed all morning erupting in front of a complete stranger.

'There, there, come on, it's OK, it'll be OK . . .'

The woman folded me into her bosom and patted me on the back until my sobs became quieter and less frequent.

'Here you are.'

She handed me a large, white, man's handkerchief and I blew my nose.

'I don't know where I'm going and there may not be a room anyhow when I get there and I keep asking people directions but half of them have never heard of it and the other half say they have but when I follow their directions I get lost and then this woman starts shouting at me because I'm leaning against her wall . . .'

I began to cry again.

'Wait a minute, wait a minute. Where are you trying to go?'

I told the woman the name of the street I was looking for.

'Why, it's just there!' said the woman, delighted that she could help. 'Look.' And she pointed up the road to a small parade of shops, obviously the same parade of shops the other woman had mentioned. 'You see that gap between the ironmonger's and the wool shop?'

I nodded.

'Well, it's there. What number do you want?'

'Fifteen.'

'Mrs Flowers,' said the woman triumphantly. 'I know her. It's on the left-hand side. Lovely old lady.'

I thanked her, considerably cheered, both by her directions and by her description of the woman I was about to see.

The house looked gloomy from the outside with a tall laurel hedge and a dank rectangle of lawn, half choked by dead leaves. I walked up the steps to the porch and rang the bell. There was a semicircle of stained glass set above the door and a strange collection of tubes and bits of wood dangling from a hook in the ceiling. I turned and pulled gently at one of the bits of wood and immediately stepped back, startled by the noise the tubes made as they moved against one another.

'It's a wind chime,' said a voice.

I spun round. A small woman stood in the open door. A very small woman. Smaller even than me. She wore a purple tweed skirt and a lilac cardigan and her white hair was twisted into a perfect chignon.

'I've come about the room . . . the room advertised in the paper.'

The woman smiled and showed me in.

There were more strange objects in the hallway. A grotesque mask with gaping holes for eyes. An enormous metal vase or urn filled with dead rose petals. A woven wall-hanging in soft pinks and browns showing what appeared to be a tiger hunt.

The woman must have noticed my interest because she waved her hand in their direction.

'They're from India. My father had them shipped back. He was a silk merchant.'

She showed me into a room at the back of the house and went out again. The room was bright and sunny and filled with other unusual objects. A prayer wheel inlaid with turquoise stone. Three ceramic tiles with an abstract design in black and white. And a piece of fretted woodwork which looked as though it had once been part of a door. Clearly, her father had been extremely acquisitive. At the end of the room, on either side of a small coal grate, there were bookshelves from floor to ceiling. All were full.

The woman came back in again carrying a tray with tea things and a plate of shortbread.

'Have one,' she said, handing me a plate and the shortbread. 'I made them yesterday with some extra butter.'

It was almost four o'clock and I had not eaten since breakfast. I took one gratefully.

'Mrs Flowers,' she said, holding out a hand. 'May Flowers. My parents lacked imagination.'

'Claire Harper,' I said, taken aback by her openness. 'Mrs,' I added.

Mrs Flowers looked sharply at my black armband and poured out the tea.

'Is the room still free?'

'Oh yes, you're the first person who's come about it. The advertisement only went in yesterday.'

She sipped her tea.

'Do you work?'

'No,' I said, scalding my mouth by swallowing too fast. 'Not yet,' I added quickly in case she should disapprove. 'I haven't been in Bradford long.'

'Only I thought if you didn't work you could read half an hour in the mornings and half an hour in the evenings.'

She put her teacup down.

'It's my eyes. They're going. I can still see to get around but not well enough to read. Or at least not without straining them. Now the doctor has ordered me to stop reading. And I don't want to. I like books, you see. They're the only thing I've got left. That's why I put the advertisement in.'

'And the orchard?'

'Yes, the orchard. Come on, I'll show you.'

There was a small garden first, nothing spectacular, but it had a lavender bush, I saw, and some well cared for rose bushes. There was a hedge at the bottom with a narrow gap at one side. We squeezed through, twigs and leaves clawing at our clothes, and burst out the other side. And, instantly, as if it had been waiting, a thrush began to sing, its voice tumbling through the dusk, clear and pure as a mountain spring.

'Oh!'

'Do you like it?'

I nodded, too amazed to speak. For it was the most beautiful, magical orchard I had ever seen. The ground ran down towards the west at such an angle that it captured the most of the vanishing sunlight. The trees looked golden against a black sky, each branch and twig distinct, as if they had been painted or etched. There were about thirty to forty of them, planted haphazardly in such a way as to suggest mystery and adventure, to invite one to wander, to touch and to taste. I was already imagining it in summer, the thick overlapping shade, the different-hued bark and leaves, the feeling that one could be anywhere, anyone.

Mrs Flowers pointed to the tree nearest to us, one of the oldest looking, a species I did not recognise.

'That was the first. I planted that when I was three. It almost died four years ago in those bad frosts we had early on but it managed to pull through.'

She pointed to another tree set further back, its trunk contorted at a crazy angle.

'That was the second. Russet apples.'

'You planted them all yourself?'

'Yes. One on every birthday from when I was three to when I was thirty-six. They were my father's present to me.'

'What a lovely idea!'

'Yes, it was. Only I didn't think so at the time. Not when I was three. I wanted a doll with real hair and petticoats that stuck out.'

Our eyes met and we both laughed. I decided I would take the room if she offered it.

'It needs about two hours' work a week here. More in the summer and autumn, of course. I did have a gardener but he's gone now. Volunteered in the first week. He always was a bit odd.'

She turned and began to walk back towards the house.

'As for the reading, I thought we could start with Conrad. Have you ever read *Lucky Jim*?'

I shook my head. She was talking as if she had offered me the room. Or was I jumping to conclusions?

'Good. We can discover it together then.'

We squeezed back through the hedge into real life, Bradford, and dusk, so thick now that I could barely make out the back of the house.

'Does that mean . . . the room . . . can I take it?'

'Yes, of course. Unless you don't like it. I forgot. How silly of me. You haven't seen it yet.'

The room was large and pleasant, with flowered wallpaper, chintz curtains and a white bedspread. Best of all, it had a view over the orchard.

Mrs Flowers showed me the bathroom and the cellar where I could shelter during air raids if I wanted to.

'I don't bother, myself,' she said. 'I'm too old to go fumbling about in the dark.'

I wanted to ask about meals. Would we eat together or would she expect me to eat on my own? Would she even allow me into her kitchen to cook?

'I'll let you unpack now while I make us something to eat,' she said as if she had read my thoughts. 'We'll talk about what you want to do about meals later.'

I put the wigwam photo on the table next to the bed and grinned at my ten-year-old self. I had done it. I had left him. I was free. And I had not been asked what I was doing or where I was from or who the black armband was for or any other of the questions I had been expecting and dreading. I lay back on the bed, smiling triumphantly as I had smiled all those years ago, exhausted, muddy, tired, but glowing with the success of achieving what I had set out to do.

Two weeks later I discovered I was pregnant.

37

Claire reached out, picked up a small handful of specially softened earth which she dropped on the coffin, and moved on. Behind her she heard the soft thud as another mourner did the same.

It had been a short service. The vicar, a prematurely bald young man with spots, had never met Mrs Barnard. But he had been well briefed by relatives. The Singin' Hinnies, the famous, prize-winning sunflowers, the six children she had brought up virtually single-handedly – all had been mentioned in the address. So too had her energy, the enormous gusto with which she had approached life, and the cheerful determination which had inspired so much respect in her friends and relatives.

Many of those relatives were here now including, apparently, grandchildren from Bexhill, a nephew from Rome and a great niece from Hong Kong who had made a thirty-six-hour journey in order to attend the funeral.

She watched them as they stood around in groups, most of them in black or dark blue or grey but a few in brighter colours, one even in brilliant yellow, in honour of the sunflowers perhaps. There were children too, at least twenty of them, right down to a tiny baby strapped tight against his mother's chest in a sling. There must have been more than a hundred people in all.

How many would be at her funeral, Claire wondered? Four, five, six at the most. Catherine; possibly Joyce, her friend from London, if she could find someone to look after her bedridden husband; Iris, if she was still at The Pines; Peter, maybe.

She looked sideways at him. He was standing with one of the

daughters – Janet, she thought – nodding politely at something she was saying. That was how he was, she thought. Charming but cold, fenced round with selfishness. Tom's visit had been useful in that respect, she reasoned. It had shown him in his true colours before it was too late – before she had enmeshed herself too deeply.

He glanced up, saw her looking at him and came towards her.

'There's food back at the tearoom. Everyone's invited, apparently. Janet wants to know if we're going.'

It was one o'clock. She had not eaten since breakfast and had had only half a slice of toast then. Even so, she did not feel hungry. Besides, they were not family. They could not even call themselves good friends. Look at how they had neglected her during that last week. She could not forgive herself for that.

'I don't think I will,' she said, stepping back, conscious that his hand was hovering near her arm. 'I don't mind if you want to, though. I'll wait in the car.'

'No, I don't want to,' he said quickly. 'I just thought you might want a drink. A cup of tea or something.'

'No.'

She could see he was disconcerted but she stood her ground, not adding anything, either by look or movement.

'Right. I'll . . . I'll go and tell her then.'

After he had gone, she held up her right, ungloved hand and examined it. There were traces of earth on her fingertips and a few fragments of grit lodged under her nails. Back in her room, there was the paper she had been saving to read to Mrs Barnard. She had already marked the interesting stories with a red marker pen.

She thought of the staff at The Willows clearing out Mrs Barnard's room, piling her possessions into boxes and bags. Her toothbrush. Her flannel. The knitted pink panther she had won at a raffle on holiday in Scarborough. The wooden tea caddy engraved with her name that had been a wedding present from her best friend, Agnes. They would have put them in higgledy-piggledy. The dirty laundry with the clean, jewellery with shells collected by grandchildren, her papers with her wash things, not caring if the jewellery was scratched or the damp from the flannel made the ink on the papers run, because she was dead, dead, her eyes large and staring, the flesh sucked out so that you could see how she would look when the skin went and all that was left was bones. The idea made her feel savage. That it should amount to this. A whole life squeezed into a few carrier bags.

The sound of a child crying interrupted her train of thought. A small boy playing hide and seek among the graves had fallen over and bumped his knee. There was a large grass and mud stain on his trousers. She watched a woman, probably his mother, roll the trouser leg up and inspect the damage. It couldn't have been bad because after a minute the boy was off again, calling out to the other children.

Of course, in Mrs Barnard's case it didn't amount to a few bags, she thought. It amounted to all these people. To the boy running. To her daughter Janet worrying about whether she had prepared enough food. To the great-niece from Hong Kong thinking about the boyfriend she had left behind, a Vietnamese law student living in a refugee camp. It amounted to their laughter, their hopes, their warm blood. It amounted to the future. In her case there would be the bags only.

Peter signalled to her from near the gate towards which most of the mourners were now moving. She looked round at the grave. The man who had been holding the tray of earth, a verger perhaps or someone from the undertakers, was wiping it clean with a cloth, ready for the next service. She said a last silent goodbye and fell in line.

He was already sitting in the car waiting when she reached the gate. She opened the door on the passenger side and got in slowly, cursing the pride that had prevented her from bringing her stick.

'Where do you want to go?' he asked.

'I don't know. Not back. Not yet.'

'No. Me neither.'

He started the engine.

'Where are we going?'

'You'll see.'

And she did. He drove to St Margaret's, the abandoned church where they had kissed, sitting on the bench outside, the bats swooping round them.

The gate had come off one of its hinges since their previous visit, she noticed. Peter had to lift it to open it. There was also more writing on the wooden planks boarding up the door. Clearly, they were not the only people to feel an attraction for the place. Without talking, as if by pre-arranged plan, they walked to the small white headstone where there had been pinks before. There was a wreath now, handmade, holly and ivy and laurel leaves twisted round a metal coat hanger.

'It must be a lover,' said Peter. 'Only a lover could be so devoted.'

'Or a mother. A mother could easily,' said Claire.

'But not a father.'

'I didn't mean that.'

'It's probably true anyhow, even if you didn't mean it.'

He turned and walked away, but not angrily. Claire knew he was thinking of her claim that he did not deserve to have a son. The holly on the wreath was bursting with berries, she saw, the sign of a harsh winter to come. Or was it the other way round? The fruits of a bad winter the previous year? She could never remember. She went after Peter.

She found him standing in front of a headstone which had fallen over.

'Wasn't this up when we came before?'

She looked at the lettering and saw that it was the headstone erected in memory of Martha Heddon and her six children. It had snapped sheer off its base, probably as a result of the sharp frosts they had been having. There were other signs of decay as well. The stone wall separating the churchyard from the fields had tumbled down in one place, the stones spilling on to nearby graves. And the wooden bench where they had kissed had rotted. There were only three planks left where there should have been four.

They sat down on it anyhow, holding on to the arm rests in case it collapsed, staring straight ahead of them.

'Were you thinking of your funeral? About who would come? How many?'

She turned to look at him.

'Yes.'

'I was too. Tom wouldn't come. And yes, you're right. He has good reason not to.'

She looked away again.

'I . . . I . . . there's something I want to tell you, Peter.'

His name sounded odd on her lips and she realised it was the first time she had said it out loud.

'I'm going away for Christmas. I'm going down to Oxford to stay with Catherine and her family. I'm sorry. I would have told you before only . . .'

'No. Don't be sorry. I'm glad. Well, not glad exactly but . . . well . . . I'm going away too.'

'Oh?'

Her voice was small and cold and hard, like a pebble washed up by the sea.

'Yes, I'm going to Yorkshire. Phyllis's niece has rented a farmhouse near Grassington. There was a spare bedroom so Phyllis asked me if I'd like to go and I said yes. It seemed better than staying here.'

She told herself she should be pleased he would not be spending Christmas with Matron and those residents without relatives or friends kind or guilty enough to invite them to stay. But she wasn't. She felt irritated. She had been prepared to be apologetic, remorseful, propitiatory even. Now she couldn't.

'I thought Phyllis was going to stay with Mr Shaw.'

Leslie Shaw, the retired tax inspector from Cheltenham, had finally left The Pines without, as some people had thought probable, a new Mrs Shaw on his arm. However, he had invited Phyllis to spend Christmas with him.

'He's got pneumonia apparently. He's in hospital. Not expected out until the New Year. And then he's going into a nursing home for a couple of weeks to convalesce. At least I think that's what Phyllis said.'

The prospect of Peter spending two or three undiluted days with Phyllis's bosom, false or otherwise, disturbed her. Phyllis, she thought, was one of those women who felt incomplete without a man, as though she had lost an arm or a leg. And yet evidently she found the hunt more satisfying than the kill. She had been divorced three times.

'You don't mind? I won't go if you don't want me to – even if you do still go to Oxford.'

The generosity of this offer released her from the green noose that was starting to tighten round her thoughts. She laughed.

'No, no, of course I don't mind. It'll be good for us both to get away. A nice change. Which day are you going?'

'Christmas Eve.'

'And coming back?'

'The day after Boxing Day.'

'Me too. That's OK then. We'll have the New Year to look forward to.'

'Yes.'

Claire looked at him.

'Iris says you're giving up painting.'

He turned to face her.

'Yes.'

'Are you?'

'No. Not now.'

'What do you mean?'

'Not now we're talking again.'

A warm glow spread through her.

'I'd like to paint you.'

She laughed.

'Don't be silly.'

'No, really. You have a beautiful face – a face that has lived.'

'Hasn't everyone our age?' she teased.

'No, they haven't. Some people have faces that have died, that have been dying all their lives.'

Their heads, which had moved closer during this conversation, moved closer still until their mouths touched. Peter kissed her.

But it was the compliment rather than the kiss that she relived later. It had been more than forty years since a man had remarked on her appearance.

38

The last person to remark on my appearance was Bill. He had come to take his son away as he had warned he would do in the letter he had sent through my lawyer when I was eight months pregnant.

'I will come for him when he is nine,' I read, sitting in the shade of the Russet apple tree, the sky above me blue mouthfuls between green lips. At the time, his assumption that the child would be a boy had angered me more than his threat.

Mrs Flowers came out soon afterwards to join me and settled in the wicker armchair that was dragged in under cover every night in case it rained. She was too old to roll around on rugs like me, she said, eyeing my shape benignly.

Dear Mrs Flowers. What would I have done without her? When I told her I was pregnant she opened a bottle of vintage port to celebrate instead of throwing me out as I had feared. She brought me tea and biscuits in the morning to ease my stomach. She begged and borrowed extra meat and vegetables so that I would have a nourishing diet. And when I went into labour, she was there, pressing cold cloths into my forehead, telling me over and over again 'Come on, you're doing well, you're almost there, just a little bit longer.' The midwife thought she was my mother. At moments, delirious with pain, so did I.

I waited for her to arrange her cushions and then handed her Bill's letter. While she read it, I leant back and gazed at the apples I had been going to pick but would now not. Like me, they were swelling daily. Some would be ready when my baby was ready, in the first week of September. I placed my hands contentedly on my taut roundness and made plans. We would have apple pie, I thought. Apple pie with cream and brown sugar. We would eat it in front of the fire. I would make it. It would be my present to Mrs Flowers.

'Does he mean it, do you think?' she asked, handing me back the letter. 'Will he really try to take the child away?'

'Yes,' I said, rolling a blade of grass between thumb and forefinger. 'But only if it's a boy. He wouldn't want a girl.'

I was right. It was a boy. And Bill did come.

He came on Harry's birthday. I had not told him the date but he must have found out. It wouldn't have been difficult. After all, he was a registrar.

Harry was in the living room arranging stamps in the album I had given him. I was in the kitchen decorating his cake. It was a clown cake, chocolate with yellow icing, brown Smarties for the eyes, red liquorice for the mouth and a pink joke nose I had bought in a toy shop on a Thursday afternoon shopping trip.

We were living in Ruby Close then, in the red-brick terraced house I had bought after Mrs Flowers' death. Her house had gone to a great nephew – she had wanted it to stay in the family – but the rest of her estate, or most of it, had gone to me. It had not made me rich. But, combined with the money I had inherited from my mother, it had bought me a house, and left me enough to live on.

I had just started to pipe Harry's name when there was a knock at the door. I finished the 'H', knowing from past experience that there would be an unsightly blob if I stopped in the middle. Then I straightened up.

'Come in. The door's open,' I called, thinking it would be Mrs Stocks, the neighbour who looked after Harry on Thursday afternoons. She had promised to look in after she had put the vegetables on for her husband's tea.

He looked sheepish. Sheepish and sly, as if he had stayed later at the pub than he had promised and was thinking of an excuse.

'Hello, Claire,' he said, as if somehow by naming me he could put me in my place, third row, second from the left, a face in a picture – his wife, the mother of his child. He had refused a divorce.

I said nothing. Red icing dripped from the piping gun I held in my hand, spoiling the 'H'. I did not notice.

He shut the door behind him and came further into the room, looking round in a teacherly way, as though he was going to give me marks out of ten for the way I had arranged things, the places I had chosen to put the strainer and the bread bin.

'You're looking well,' he said. And I was angry then, the adrenaline come from nowhere, my fingers tight round the gun, wanting to squirt him in the face. For I knew I was not looking well, that my skin lacked colour and my hair shine, that I had the white hair and rounded shoulders of a woman five, even ten years older.

Harry's voice came from next door.

'Mum. Who is it? Is it Mrs Stocks?'

Bill looked at the door which led to the sitting room and smiled a slow, greedy smile. I put the piping gun down on the table and wiped my hands on my apron. The sharp knives were in the drawer in front of me. It would only take a few seconds to pull one out if he tried anything, if he decided to . . . if . . .

'Aren't you going to finish it?' he asked and pointed at the cake.

I felt for the handle of the drawer without looking down. There. There it was. I eased it open. Just an inch or two.

'What do you want?'

My voice came out like footsteps in a dark alley. Tap, tap, tap. I heard it as though I was someone else.

He smiled again – a slow, simpering smile. I pulled the drawer open another few inches.

'Aren't you going to introduce me? Aren't you going to show me my son?'

He came closer to the table, so close that I could smell him. I stiffened. He was plumper than he had been, but all over, not just on his stomach, like a sleek, round mole. His skin was redder too, all except his fingers. They were as white as they had always been, the soft, white maggoty fingers of a man who had never worked outside. I saw suddenly that he was wearing his wedding ring and was revolted. How dare he? How dare he come here fawning and creeping? How dare he spoil Harry's birthday?

'You've come to take him, haven't you? Haven't you?' My fingers closed round the handle of a chopping knife.

The simper slipped from his face like a cup from greased fingers.

'You've had him for nine years. It's my turn now. Don't you think?'

His tone was sharp but the blade was sharper still. I tested it, feeling it lightly with my finger tips.

Harry called out again from the other room.

'Mum. Who is it? Why don't you say anything?'

'He's got you running round him in circles, hasn't he? He needs a man. I'd soon stop that.'

I smiled bitterly.

'You'd soon stop what?'

'Being at his beck and call. There's no point spoiling them. They never learn to stand on their own two feet otherwise.'

'Their own two feet?'

'Yes. What's so funny?'

I cackled with laughter. It was a horrible sound, savage and cracked, not like a laugh at all, and it must have alarmed Harry because his voice became more insistent.

'Mum! What's happening? Why don't you answer? Mum! Come here!'

There was a loud bang.

'Help! Mum!'

The vegetable knife dropped from my hand. I rushed into the sitting room, jabbing myself against the open drawer in my hurry, giving myself a bruise that would last for weeks afterwards, a purple reminder.

But Harry had not fallen off his chair as I had feared. It was his stamp album. The contents of the South African page lay scattered on the floor – a yellow bird against a turquoise background, a red-spotted butterfly, a cherry tree in blossom. Harry looked in bewilderment, first at me, then at the strange man beside me. The memory of the ring on the maggoty fingers fuelled my rage. I held it before me as I ran to Harry and lifted him off his chair.

I turned to face Bill. He was still smiling but less confidently now, no longer in control. This was not what he had planned.

'Go on then. You have a go. Make him stand on his own two feet.'

I pulled my arms out from beneath Harry's armpits and pushed him towards Bill. He clutched at the air, searching frantically for something to grab hold of. I stepped back briskly, away from him. His legs tottered, swayed, then folded beneath him like Plasticine. Bill's smile vanished.

I ran to Harry. He was crying now but I picked him up and pushed him off again, brushing his fingers from my clothes. He fell again, harder this time, screaming with rage and pain and fear. Bill, ashen-faced, stared at the mangled heap he had come to take away. He swallowed, opened his mouth as if to say something, then turned and strode out of the room. I ran to Harry and half-dragged, half-carried him to the sofa. Then I went after Bill. By the time I reached the back door he was already at the third lamp post. He did not look round at the corner. I shut the door, locked it and leant back against it. Harry was sobbing in the other room. In front of me, on the kitchen table, lay his unfinished birthday cake. The 'H' was ruined.

39

Iris was late again today. I heard Matron telling her off. She said she'd overslept and promised to buy a new alarm clock. But later, when I asked her about it, she admitted it was Quintin. He had woken her up at three in the morning, grinding spices to make a curry.

I wish I could help her. But I can't. I know I can't. It's like watching someone stand on the edge of a cliff. You know it's dangerous, that if they move forward, their feet will touch air, their bodies drop like a thrown stone, down, down, down. But they don't know this. They don't see. They stand there quite calmly, gazing round as if they're at a garden party, their feet firm on Kent soil. You want to cry out, to rush forward, to grab their arm. But you know you can't, that you might startle them, that they have to see the cliff with their own eyes, to turn round voluntarily.

She's lost interest. That's the worst thing. When she first came she was so curious, so sparky, like a firework shooting in all directions. She was always asking questions. Now she doesn't. Or at least not many.

Peter's the one who asks questions now. I'm telling him everything, everything I can remember about Mother, Bill, Harry – my life before I came here. They're not in any order, the memories I tell him, either chronological or otherwise. There are some things, sometimes quite important things, that I can't remember. Harry's death, for instance. I know it sounds odd but I really can't remember that much about it. The detail, I mean. How he went. Whether I was with him or whether I just found him. I can't even be sure that he died at home. He went into hospital so many times towards the end. He might have died there. I'm not sure.

And yet other things, apparently trivial things, I remember as if they happened yesterday. *Peter Pan*, for example, the play I took him to see when he was about six. I remember that. He talked about it for months afterwards, especially the crocodile with a clock in its tummy. He would pretend to be the crocodile when I tucked him up at night, tick-tocking with his tongue and then snapping at my nose. He wanted to go to Never Never Land too. I think he thought we could catch a bus there.

Sometimes, things come back to me as I'm telling them. Just now, for instance. I suddenly remembered that, after seeing Peter Pan, Harry started to call himself Peter. He did it for months, refusing to answer if I called him Harry. It upset me, I remember, because I knew he would never grow up to be a man, even if he wanted to.

I talk when he's painting me – the real Peter, the man Peter. It gives me something to do. Sometimes, if I get to a bad bit, he stops and gets up to give me a hug or take my hand. I wonder whether perhaps I am making things sound worse than they really were so that this will happen more often.

Another thing. An odd thing. Or maybe not so odd, given my age. Occasionally, I finish a story and look up, expecting to see Peter or Iris, and realise I've been talking to myself, either in my head or out loud. I'm not sure which. It's as though I'm trying to make sense of everything, to piece things together, to understand why my life has been as it has been and not as it might have been.

The other day, for example. The story about the time Bill came to take Harry away – I was sure I had told it to Peter and yet later, when I referred to it, he looked puzzled and I realised I must have told it to myself, relived it in my head.

I think, possibly, that I am scared, that Mrs Barnard's death has unnerved me, that I am worried about what I will find, there, on the other side – or what I will not find, what I will not be there to find.

Above all, I am frightened that I will be called to account, asked to justify the things undone – the languages unlearnt, the stars unknown, the lands untravelled. Maybe that is why

I scour the paper with increasing frenzy, pore over my collage, drum poems into my head – as if I am cramming for an exam, making up for lost time.

I have this dream in which I am standing in a queue. At the top of the queue there is a man, I think it is a man, with weighing scales, the old-fashioned sort with brass weights. They are very big, these scales, almost as tall as the man.

The queue shuffles forward and I see that people are putting things on the scales. I can't see the things but they must be there because the scales move. Sometimes more and sometimes less but always a bit.

Finally, it is my turn. I look down. There is nothing in my hands. I know there isn't but I reach out towards the scales anyway, hoping there will be something when my hands touch them.

A cry tears the air like ripped cloth. I look down. The scales have not moved.

40

When Harry died, I went to London. I sold the red-brick house in Ruby Close, I put my furniture into storage and I caught a train from Bradford to Leeds and from there to London, King's Cross. It was a Thursday evening in April 1962, it had been raining, the pavements were wet, and I felt I had entered another world.

At the time I did not know why I went to London. I just went, moving like a sleepwalker, my arms and legs acting unasked. Later, I understood better. Nobody knew me in London and I knew nobody. I was on my own – a forty-two-year-old woman with white hair and a healthy but not unlimited bank balance. The newness, the strangeness, the very difficulty of everything took up all my energy. I had no time to grieve and, in a way, no need. I had been grieving for twenty years already. His death had ended it, like a corpse found, physical proof that all was, indeed, over.

Each day I did battle, struggling to make sense of the new sights and sounds and smells which assaulted me, even at night, the police sirens wailing in my dreams as another bungled burglary ended with a chase through the capital's back streets. Long hair, patterned shirts, bare midriffs, slogans, marches, posters – I crept around, marvelling at them all, both excited and afraid.

It was as though I had been in prison. Everything had changed. The food, the prices, the way people dressed and talked, the look of the buildings even, the design of prams. I had forgotten how to talk, how to buy a loaf of bread, how to ask on a bus for a ticket. 'A return to Marble Arch. Yes, Marble Arch. No, sorry, I don't have any change.' 'A small white, please, and one currant teacake.' I practised phrases in my head like a student learning a foreign language, praying that the shop assistant would not ask me if I wanted the loaf slicing or the teacake buttering.

On that first night I caught a taxi to the hotel where I had booked a room. It was a small hotel but clean and reasonably quiet and the room I was given overlooked a narrow side street with three lime trees, all coming into leaf. I cleaned my teeth, turned back the bedclothes and unpacked my suitcase. Although small, the hotel was expensive, at least by my standards, but I had budgeted for a stay of up to two weeks while I found something suitable to rent.

There was a full-length mirror in the room and I undressed in front of it, folding my clothes carefully, one by one, until I was naked, looking at myself, surprised. I was not such an awful sight, I told myself. Running round after Harry, lifting and pulling him, had at least kept me trim. If anything, I was too thin. I turned sideways, eyeing myself critically, and then climbed into bed, the stiff, clean sheets cold against my warm skin. It was the first time I had ever gone to bed without wearing a nightdress. I had always worn one at home and later, after I had married, always worn one with Bill. He had removed it once or twice at first, but then, finding it easier, and quicker, just pulled it up. I knew then as I lay there shivering, hugging myself, goosepimpled against sheets someone else had washed, that I had started a new life.

The next day I found a job. And a flat. I did not intend to. I had planned only to get my bearings, buy a street map, and find out how the Underground worked. But a heavy shower of rain forced me to shelter in a shop. It was a department store – a big one with two restaurants, a terrace café, beauty salon, pet department and a space five times the size of my hotel bedroom devoted solely to handbags. Later I was to discover that people, mainly women, spent the whole day there. Enterprising mothers who couldn't afford to take their children to the pictures or zoo would take them to the pet department instead to watch the fish and choose which rabbit they would like if they could have one, if they lived in a bigger house, if they had a garden. The children would ride in the lifts, play with the electrical train set in the toy department, and eat knickerbocker glory with raspberry sauce in the café. Other women, women with more money and no children, or children who had grown up or gone away to boarding school, would meet friends for coffee in the first floor restaurant, have a haircut or manicure in the beauty salon followed by lunch in the third-floor restaurant, then try on some clothes in the afternoon, buy some cosmetics perhaps, one of the new lipsticks.

I did not know this then as I wandered around, looking for umbrellas, finding them finally on the first floor, among the ladies' separates. There were plain or patterned umbrellas with wooden or plastic handles, curved or straight. I reached instinctively for a plain black one but then put it back, telling myself to choose one I liked, not one I thought I ought to buy. In the end, I chose a pink one, pink with white dots like confetti on a church floor. It was a statement, another visible mark of the change I was undergoing.

'You're brave,' said the woman at the cash desk. 'I saw these and liked them but then I found myself buying a navy one the same as I'd had before.'

I blushed and busied myself finding my purse. When I had found the right money I held out my hand. I wasn't looking properly and my hand collided with something on the counter, a cardboard notice, knocking it to the ground. I apologised and picked it up and as I did, I saw that it was advertising a staff vacancy. 'Assistant wanted. Mon-Fri, 9.00 a.m. to 5.30 p.m.,' it said. 'Suit mature lady, 40 to 50. Apply here.'

'Is it still . . . are you still looking for someone?'

I pointed at the notice, amazed at my boldness.

'Yes, we only put it up just now.'

The woman looked at me more closely.

'Why? Are you interested?'

'No, I mean, well . . . yes, but . . .'

'You could have a word now, if you wanted. Miss Carter's in her office. I've just seen her. I would if I were you. They tend to go quite quickly. The pay's good and people like to work here. It's got, well, you know, a bit of class. It's not like working at the Co-op.'

And so, somehow, five minutes later, I found myself in a poky, windowless room telling a woman I'd never met before about my life. I got the job. The accent helped and the fact that my father had been a vicar. So, too, probably, did the neat grey suit I was wearing, the suit I'd bought twenty years earlier when I got the job at the register office.

Joyce, the woman at the cash desk, found me the flat too. Her brother-in-law was in property, she said, when she discovered I was staying at a hotel. She was sure he would be able to find me something. He was coming round that night. She would ask him, and leave a message at my hotel.

The flat he found was small, more of a bedsit really – the bed was in a small alcove off the sitting room, separated only by a curtain – but it was convenient, only twenty minutes' walk from work, and close to a fruit and vegetable market and a park with swings and a boating pond. I think it was the pond which made me take it. I would be able to sit on a bench on Sunday afternoons, I thought, and watch fathers adjust sails and rudders and pretend they were doing it for their sons.

I stayed there a year and then I bought a house of my own in south-east London. It was a terraced house again but larger, sunnier, with a prettier garden, also close to a park. I had to take out a mortgage to buy it but it was only a small mortgage and Joyce was right, the pay was good, so I still had enough money for treats.

At first, I behaved like a tourist – eating in Soho, seeing the Crown Jewels, feeding the pigeons in Trafalgar Square. Later, my pleasures became more cultural. I took fewer boat trips up the Thames and went to more museums. I discovered the Royal Academy, the Royal Opera House, the National Theatre. I went to *Swan Lake* and *Tosca*. The names Wesker and Pinter and Osborne began to mean something. I went to other places too. Buckingham Palace, the House of Commons, the American embassy, Downing Street. I watched the cars draw up, the big black cars, and men get out – politicians, statesmen, civil servants – men that mattered, men with power, men who could change things. Later, when I bought a television, and I saw these places on the screen, I would think, 'I've been there, I stood on that very spot, I've seen that man,' and I would feel so excited, so proud, as if I too mattered.

And my job? Yes, my job. I know it doesn't sound much – a shop assistant in ladies' separates – but I loved it. The security of it, the luxury, the order of everything. No one was more zealous at making sure everything was where it should be, arranged according to size, the skirts with the skirts, the scarves with the scarves. I would walk around, folding and refolding, more critical than a general inspecting his troops, pouncing on the least crease or tuck.

I was good with customers too, knowing when to offer help or advice and when to hold back, to allow someone to browse at leisure. After two years, I was promoted to a senior assistant, responsible for marking up sales items, putting out new stock, and dressing the mannequins. Joyce became my friend. She brought me rock cakes on Monday mornings, invited me to her son's wedding, and confided in me about the pornographic magazines she had found in her husband's tool shed. I made other friends too. Michael in the food hall used to bring me leeks and carrots from his East End allotment. Christine, one of the beauticians, would cut my hair for free. Even Miss Carter gave me a card on my fiftieth birthday.

Outside, in the streets, I held my head high. I knew who I was. I had a home and a job. I belonged. It was me now who gave people directions, who explained how the Underground worked, who told tourists the quickest way to get to Madame Tussaud's. I did not think of Bradford or of Bill or even of Oxford. They were another country.

I had not seen Bill since the day he came to take Harry away. He did not come to the funeral although I had finally, after much indecision, sent him a note with the time and date. Someone had told me he was living with another woman, a younger woman. They had not told me her name or age and I had not asked. I did not think I would ever see him again.

So you can imagine my shock when I came out of the stock room that March morning in 1967, my arms full of the new season's look, and found him there, waiting, leaning against a mirror. He stood out like a green cloud. First, he was a man and men were rarely seen in ladies' separates except at Christmas and, sometimes, before Valentine's Day. Secondly, he was dirty.

One of the pink linen shift dresses I was holding slithered to the floor. I did not pick it up. With my mind's eye I saw my house, the sunlight on my pillow in the morning, snowdrops coming out in the garden. I saw the mantelpiece with the wooden box Mrs Flowers had given me, its inside smooth and worn as a door knob. I saw the rag rug on the floor, the sofa all comfortable with cushions, the home-made marmalade in the kitchen. I saw these things and as I watched, they came apart like a half-knit jumper pulled into nothing, undone. I would not let him. I would not. It was my life. Mine.

I picked up the dress and strode towards him.

'What? What is it? What do you want?'

The smile hovering on his lips vanished and he lowered his eyes.

'I . . . I . . . I just wanted to say hello . . . to find out how you were.'

I was surprised by the conciliatory tone but did not show it.

'I'm fine. So now you know. Anything else?'

He lifted his eyes.

'Can't we go somewhere and talk? Just for a few minutes.'

I ignored the appeal in his eyes.

'Why? There's nothing to talk about.'

I began to hang up the dresses on a nearby rail. I felt strong and powerful and slightly guilty. He followed me.

'Please! Please, Claire.'

I saw Miss Carter come out of the lift on the other side of the floor and it occurred to me that if I refused he might make a scene.

'OK,' I said quickly. 'I'll meet you in five minutes in the self-service café on the top floor. Next to the toys. Go on then.'

I found Joyce in the stock room and told her I was going to have a coffee with an old friend who had called by unexpectedly. I would be about half an hour, I said.

Bill had chosen one of the tables tucked out of sight, I saw with relief. No one would be able to see us unless they came right into the café. I took a tray and helped myself to cups, saucers and teaspoons. At the drinks counter I asked for a pot of tea for two. Then, on reflection, I went back to the food counter and took one of the Danish pastries.

Bill proved as hungry as I had suspected, finishing the pastry before I had even poured the tea, clearing up the crumbs on his plate with a moistened finger. While he ate, I watched, studying him properly. He was more changed than I would have thought possible. It was not just that he was unshaven, that his skin was spotty, his clothes stained. There was also something unwholesome about him, like an apple the worms have got. He looked ill. Ill and thin and tired.

'You've lost weight.'

'Yes,' he said, picking up his tea and slurping it noisily in the way I remembered. Clearly, some things had not changed.

'What's happened?'

He told me he had been sacked for conducting a wedding ceremony while drunk. He had called the bride Brenda instead of Belinda and told the groom he should have chosen the bridesmaid instead, she was much prettier. Some of his old manner returned while he told this tory and he even smiled once or twice, but timorously – like a dog wagging his tail that expects to be hit. I asked him if he was still living in Bradford and he said no, he had moved to London but when I asked him where, he became evasive. It was half past ten in the morning and I could smell the alcohol on his breath.

He fiddled with the handle of his teacup and I wondered how he had found me and why he had come and, as if reading my thoughts, he asked me for some money. I gave him what I had, all that was in my purse – more than a week's salary – and he left, not hiding his hurry.

I watched him go, tripping over his shoelaces, looking back to see if I was following, smiling sheepishly, and I felt no triumph, no pleasure that he had come to this. I did not like him but I still felt for him.

He had not asked me for my address or given me his but I did not worry. I knew he would be back.

41

Bill returned sooner than I had expected, three weeks later to the day. This time, he did not hover in the background but walked straight up to the counter where I was serving a customer and burped noisily. The customer, a Gloucestershire doctor's wife in London to buy a suit for her son's wedding, looked round. Bill smirked and she turned back hastily, raising her eyebrows. I continued to wrap her outfit, a navy and white skirt with matching jacket which she had taken almost two hours to choose, and hoped she would think Bill was a customer.

He was cleaner than before but, if possible, looked worse, the white, spot-marked skin stretched tight over his face like a sheet on a hospital bed. I bundled the clothes into a bag and took the woman's money. Bill burped again.

'I'll be with you in a minute, sir,' I said loudly, willing him to move away, to sit down somewhere, praying that Joyce and Miss Carter would not see him. The customer clutched her handbag more tightly and edged sideways, her lipsticked mouth pursed with distaste.

Joyce came out of the stock room, saw Bill waiting and asked if she could be of any assistance.

'I'm waiting for her,' he said, jerking his head in my direction.

She looked at me and I nodded quickly, not meeting her eyes, not saying anything, my fingers in the till as stiff and wooden as clothes pegs. She stood there uncertainly for a moment or two then, seeing that another customer needed help, walked away.

'There you are. I hope the wedding goes well,' I said, finally locating the correct change. The woman took it and left, looking back when she was at a safe distance.

Bill came straight to the point.

'Can you lend me some more money? Just till the end of the month. I'll pay you back then.'

We both knew that 'lend' was a euphemism for 'give', that he had no intention and, for all I knew, no means, of repaying me.

'How much?'

He told me and I went to fetch my bag from where it was hanging in the stock room, the third hook on the left, my hook.

I counted the money outside the lifts, seeing the treats I had promised myself that month disappear with each coin – a new raincoat, supper out with Joyce, a soft, blue bathmat.

'There. That's all I can afford. I'm not giving you any more. Do you understand? This is the last time.'

One of the lifts opened and he got in. He looked at me and I looked at him. We were like two empty envelopes turned inside out – bare, blank.

It was not the last time. He came again a fortnight later and then increasingly frequently, first every week or ten days, then every two or three days. The money I gave him was no longer 'treat' money but money for food and bills. One day I laddered my tights at work and could not afford to buy any more. I rubbed soap into the ladder in the ladies' cloakroom and hoped Miss Carter would not notice. She did. Without asking, Joyce took over from me if I was serving a customer when he arrived. But sometimes she was serving a customer herself and could not help. Those were the times I dreaded.

I went overdrawn at the bank and began to receive letters from my manager drawing my attention to the fact. One morning, on Friday, June 21 – I remember both the day and the date, the day because it was Friday, the first day of the weekend, the date because it was the first day of summer – I received a letter from my building society warning me that if I did not pay a certain sum by a certain date, they would initiate proceedings to repossess my house. I folded the letter, put it in my bag and went to work.

Bill arrived an hour later while I was advising a customer which colours suited her complexion. Joyce was helping a girl choose a dress for her twenty-first birthday and Miss Carter, armed with a clipboard, her stiff-collared shirt speared at the top with a silver pin, was stocktaking nearby

'I like green but I always think it makes me look a bit sallow. What do you think?' said the woman, holding up a blouse the colour of pickled gherkins to her chest. She was right, the blouse did made her look sallow, but then she was sallow.

'I think . . .'

'The pink is nice as well though . . . very fresh and summery but maybe it's a bit too fresh,' interrupted the woman, putting down the green blouse and holding up a pink one instead. 'I don't want to look like mutton dressed up as lamb.'

She tittered, confident of being contradicted.

'Well, don't buy it then,' said Bill loudly, plonking himself down on a chair a few feet away.

The woman's mouth fell open. I saw Miss Carter look up in astonishment from her clipboard.

'Excuse me,' I said.

I went up to Bill, the memory of the letter lying in my mind like an unexploded mine.

'I'm serving a customer. Can't you see? Go to the lifts. I'll come when I've finished.'

'No. I'm not going anywhere. I've got as much right to be here as she has. I'm just looking,' he said, affecting a high-pitched, counties voice. 'Isn't that what they say?'

He got up and began to walk around, clearly the worse for drink.

'Ooh! Very nice.'

He fished a flowered miniskirt off a rail and held it up.

'A bit short, perhaps. What do you think?'

Everyone was watching now – Miss Carter, Joyce, the girl she was serving, two elderly women who looked like sisters and Milly, the other assistant on duty. A small crowd had also gathered at the edge of ladies' separates where the china and glass department started.

He flung the skirt on the floor and grabbed a handful of the shift dresses I had been putting out when he appeared for the first time, back in March.

'Who wants these anyhow? They're disgusting. Tarts' clothes. And as for the colours.'

He held up a lime-green one.

'It's like snot!' he said, throwing the dresses on top of the skirt. Someone, probably the girl Joyce had been serving, giggled nervously.

He ran his hands along a shelf of cardigans and swept them to the floor. He was enjoying himself now, liking the attention, the horror on everyone's faces. I knew I had to get him out quickly, before he hurt someone or himself.

'You shouldn't be here anyway. None of you should. You should be at home, looking after your husbands, cooking their dinners, not spending their money on this ... this ... this frippery!'

He tripped on one of the cardigans, flung out his arms to steady himself, failed, and fell, pulling a rail crashing down on top of him. Miss Carter stepped forward.

'Do you know this man, Mrs Harper?'

Bill groaned, his legs wrapped round with lambswool twinsets. 'Yes.'

'In that case, would you please ask him to leave? Quickly.'

I went to the stock room and took the letter from the building society out of my hand bag. When I returned, Bill was standing up, leaning against a mirrored pillar. The railing must have caught him as he came down for there was a gash above his right eye, bleeding heavily. I took out my handkerchief and handed it to him together with the letter. He took it and stuffed it in his pocket, holding the handkerchief against the cut with his other hand.

'I want you to go now and I don't want you to come back again ever,' I said quietly. 'If you do, I will call the police.'

He looked at me dully and without answering, turned and limped off, the crowd in the china department parting to make way for him.

When he had gone, I went to fetch my coat and bag from the stock room. I apologised to Miss Carter for the disturbance and said I would be taking the rest of the day off. To my surprise and relief, she did not ask me to explain further.

On my way home, I called in at a branch of my building society and made arrangements to pay back the interest I owed. I had had a few domestic problems recently, I explained. Now they had gone.

42 ∫

I did see Bill once more after that, two years later, a few weeks before Christmas. It was a Saturday afternoon, about half past four or five. I had been shopping to buy presents and tree decorations and had decided to catch a bus home instead of the tube so that I could see the lights in Oxford Street.

It was raining outside and the bus was full and at every stop there was much good-humoured jostling as people struggled to get on and off. I sat by the window, my feet snug and warm in fur-lined boots, my shopping on my lap – a tray for Joyce to carry meals to her husband, recently paralysed after an accident at work; a blue, gold-spotted angel for the top of the tree; a beeswax candle for the table by the window; half a dressed crab for my supper and a piece of baklava, dripping with honey, for pudding. I thought contentedly of the pleasant evening I was going to spend writing cards and listening to the wireless and smiled understandingly at the young mother opposite struggling to keep hold of her wriggling baby.

The people getting on were very wet now and the windows had begun to steam up. I rubbed mine with the sleeve of my coat, glad I had thought to bring my umbrella, the same one I had bought all those years ago, pink with white dots. Outside, the pavements were thick with shoppers hurrying home, collars turned up against the rain. I watched their shut-in faces, speculating idly about their lives, about the contents of their bags, about what they would be doing that evening.

Bill saw me at exactly the same moment as I saw him. He was standing under a shop front, no doubt waiting for the rain to stop. There was a bag by his feet but it looked old and crumpled, not like the shiny new bags carried by everyone else. After a few moments, he waved.

The conductor rang the bell and the bus pulled out. Bill picked up his bag and began to run. I kept my arms by my side, not showing I had recognised him. The bus gathered speed and Bill ran faster, his mouth moving. I sat still. Another bus overtook him, drenching him with water as it drove through a large puddle. He stopped running and dropped his bag. I stared through him, my face hard as stone. Then we turned a corner and I could no longer see him. I did not wipe the window again.

Three years later a policeman knocked at my door one evening in May. He asked if I was Mrs Harper, Mrs Claire Harper, formerly of Ruby Close, Bradford, and when I said I was, he asked if he could come in, said he had something to tell me.

We sat at my kitchen table and the policeman told me Bill had died six weeks earlier. It had taken them this long to trace me, he said. I asked what the cause of death was and he said it was liver failure. He was young and embarrassed and clearly anxious to be off but I pressed him for more information. Where had he died? Who had been with him? Had they buried him already?

The policeman said Bill had been found in a shop doorway by a newsagent arriving for work one morning. He had been taken to hospital where he had been certified dead on arrival. His body had been kept in a mortuary for two weeks but then, when they could find no relatives, cremated. He had had a bag with him when he had been found. Various personal possessions had also been found in the clothes he was wearing. I could pick them up by calling in at the local police station. I should ask for Sergeant Cooper.

I offered him a cup of tea but he said no, thank you, he had another call to make that evening. He took out a pad from his coat pocket, tore off a page and wrote down the address of the police station. I thanked him and saw him to the door where he apologised for bringing me bad news. I could tell he had expected me to cry.

I rang in sick the next day and went to the police station where I was told that Sergeant Cooper was on holiday. I explained the purpose of my visit and was asked to take a seat in a waiting room with orange plastic chairs and an eclectic pile of reading material including *Angling Weekly* and the Catholic magazine *The Tablet.* Forty minutes later, I was handed a crumpled plastic bag, tied at the top with string, very similar to the bag Bill had been carrying when I had last seen him.

I took it home and emptied the contents on to the kitchen table. There was a pair of red walking socks, very dirty and smelly; a striped, long-sleeved cotton shirt, also very dirty; a grey T-shirt, badly stained; and a brown, Shetland wool jumper. There was also a small roll of sticking plaster, a book of cartoons with the cover and some of the first pages missing, three extremely long shoe or boot laces, a tin of talcum power, a piece of towel and a smaller plastic bag. Inside this bag were several pens and pencils, a pair of scissors and tweezers in a red, mock leather case, two bars of soap, one still wrapped, and a wallet, empty.

I spread the things out, hunting through them. I was looking for an earring, an old hair slide or ribbon, a fragment of my handwriting, anything that would show he had still thought of me, that he had wanted to remember me. And when I found nothing, nothing at all, not even a photo, that was when I began to cry, not for him, not because he was dead, but for me, for the youth and love I had planted in such stony, hostile ground, because I was still hoping.

43 ∫

I spent seven more years working. They were good years but not as good as the previous seven. My elation at being in London had worn off and I found myself increasingly irritated by tourists, their stupid smiling faces, their rucksacks banging into me, catching me on the leg, bruising me. A property developer bought the house next door and rented it to five, possibly six, young people. They neglected the garden, filling it with bikes, a broken fish tank, a piece of rolled-up carpet which turned black with mould. The front door banged incessantly.

In the summer, sitting outside on my scrap of brown lawn, trying not to hear the music being played four doors down, I would think of Oxfordshire countryside – bluebell woods, full hedgerows at dusk, skylarks singing in a rinsed blue sky, cow parsley in June, the white froth of it, the dank damp smell of wild garlic growing.

My friendship with Joyce deepened and yet I felt lonelier than when I had first come to London. I began to mind being on my own, to miss having a partner to whom I could talk about the mother who tried to shoplift a doll for her three-year-old daughter, the seventy-year-old woman who made a scene in the beauty salon because she said her new haircut made her look old, the man who bought all the cheese in the food hall for a party he was having. I started to notice couples, to envy their closeness, to be jealous. Sometimes, when I saw two people in the street holding hands, I had to look away.

The arthritis started in 1975, five years after Bill's death. I didn't know it was arthritis at first, I simply put it down to old age. My fingers didn't hurt, they were just slower and clumsier. It took me longer to write, longer to operate the till, longer to fold clothes. It was Joyce who suggested I should see a doctor. She was watching me one day as I buttoned a customer into a dress. 'You should see someone about your hands, you know,' she said afterwards. 'They might be able to give you something. You can't go on like this.'

At the time, I was slightly offended, especially by the phrase 'like this'. But when I thought about it, when I watched myself at work, I realised she was right. So I went to the doctor and was given some tablets and for a while, about five or six months, I did improve. Then suddenly I became much worse. Everything was a struggle. It took me twice as long as anyone else to dress and undress the dummies. Zips and buttons were a torment. I began to avoid customers even when I could see they needed help.

The end came when a pushy young girl with bad breath decided to try on a cream silk dress fastened at the back with tiny mother-of-pearl buttons. I got the dress on but could not get it off. The girl became impatient. She strained and shifted, stretching the fabric tight across her shoulders, making it even more difficult to prise the buttons out of the silk loops enclosing them.

'Is anything the matter?' she asked tetchily, craning round to see what I was doing.

'They're just a bit fiddly, that's all,' I explained. 'If you could try and keep still please.'

I applied myself to the first button again, willing my fingers to move, to obey, to do what I was telling them to do. They refused. I tried again. Still nothing. The girl tut-tutted with exasperation. I yanked desperately. There was a dreadful tearing sound, the girl shrieked and I felt someone elbow me aside. It was Miss Carter.

'If you could wait in my office, please,' she said, not looking at me, swiftly unbuttoning the ripped remains.

Half an hour later, I took my coat off the third hook from the left for the last time and went home. I made myself an enormous comforting lunch of mince and mashed potatoes and went to bed and cried. I was fifty-seven. I had no job, no husband, no children and I hated the woman next door and the row of clean white nappies on her washing line telling me her grandson was staying again.

I had my first stroke four years later looking at blinds in a bathroom shop. One minute I was comparing colours, wishing I had brought a tape measure with me, the next minute I could not see and had pins and needles down the left side of my body. It lasted only a few minutes but I went to the doctor's just in case. I thought there might be something wrong with my eyes.

The doctor said I had had a mild stroke caused by a blood clot which in turn had been caused by high blood pressure. He gave me tablets to reduce the blood pressure and told me not to put too much salt on my food.

The second stroke, three years later, was more severe. This time, my left side was paralysed. I could not talk properly, found it difficult to swallow and had no control over my bladder. I spent three weeks in hospital and two months in a convalescent home in St Albans. Even so, I made a remarkable recovery. Two weeks after going home, I progressed from a walking frame to walking sticks and a month later, from two sticks to one. My home help, a knobbly little woman from Hull called Vera, put my success down to a fighting spirit. 'You've got grit, that's what it is, real grit,' she would say. Soon I was able and confident enough to walk without a stick at all.

But as my legs got stronger my hands got weaker. The arthritis bit deep into them, twisting and curling them like a wind-warped tree. Sometimes they were so clumsy they were no better than wood. They weren't like that all the time. It was like now. I had bad days and good days. But the bad days became worse. I wasn't just slow and awkward any more, I was dangerous. I would drop things – knives, glasses, cups of hot tea. Once I couldn't turn the tap off after running a bath. The most difficult thing was cooking. I cut or burnt myself nearly every meal time. Twice – I think I told you earlier – I burnt myself so badly I had to go into hospital for treatment. Vera tried to persuade me to go into a residential home. I was a liability, she said, my own worst enemy. I did once make an appointment to see one of the council homes in the area but it was so depressing I decided I would rather never eat a cooked meal again than live there. There were other nicer homes but they were private and expensive and beyond my means.

The letter from the solicitor came in the second post one day, shortly after Vera had gone, leaving me tongue sandwiches wrapped in the fridge for my tea. It informed me I had inherited the estate of the late Mr John Bedford, Bill's mother's cousin's son. I phoned the solicitor that afternoon and saw him the following day when I discovered that Mr Bedford, a financial adviser in a small provincial firm, had made several extremely clever or perhaps just lucky investments on the stock exchange. I was rich. Very rich.

Later, I discovered that if I had divorced Bill, if he had agreed to my request, the money would have gone to a charity for old racehorses. That made me laugh – the irony of it.

I started to think seriously about residential homes then and saw The Pines a few weeks later. Two months afterwards I moved in.

So now you know what happened, why they shake their heads sometimes, and point, and say 'She's had a terrible life, of course – really terrible.' That's everything more or less. We're up to here. Now.

44 ∫

There was kedgeree for breakfast on Christmas Eve, the butter on the surface still melting, pale cream against the yellow rice. Claire took some but managed to eat only two mouthfuls. She kept listing the contents of her suitcase in her head. New green dress to wear on Christmas Day, knickers, tights, easy-fastening bra, trousers in case they went on a walk, presents for everyone, wash things, make-up, nightdress – she needed a new one but it would have to wait until the New Year – earrings to match each outfit, a brooch to go with the dress – she would have to ask Catherine or her daughter to put it on – and what Peter called her baby-doll outfit, the pale pink skirt and matching cardigan. He was right, the colour was very 'pretty pretty' but she had worn too many drab browns and greys when she was young. Besides, pastel shades suited her now. They went with her white hair.

The door opened and she raised her eyes expectantly but it was Tom not Peter. She looked down again quickly, hoping to discourage him from joining her – she was sitting at a table for two – but the next moment heard the sound of the chair opposite being pulled out.

There were very few in the dining room that morning – Janet, Eric, Maureen and Colin at the table for eight in the middle, and three others over in the corner. A lot had left the previous day and a few before that even, their friends' or relatives' cars churning up the gravel as they wheeled round on the drive. Hardly anyone was going to be there for Christmas Day itself – just poor old Freda and one or two others.

She tried to make conversation with Tom, asking him when his daughter was picking him up and how many grandchildren he was going to see over Christmas, speaking slowly and clearly, conscious that he relied more on lip reading now than on the fragments of hearing left to him. As usual, though, it was hard work. When Tom could not read her lips, he guessed and often he guessed wrongly, giving wildly inappropriate answers. Claire tried not to show she had noticed when this happened. She knew some of the other residents avoided him because he was so deaf and that this upset him. He was a gregarious man by nature and it pained him to feel cut off, to be unable to join in conversations intelligently.

The door opened again and this time it was Peter, festive in red corduroy trousers and a green long-sleeved shirt. Claire had persuaded him to have his hair cut at what she described as a good hairdresser and the result, she thought, made him look him even more distinguished. She watched anxiously as he made his way to a seat, looking not at him but at the other women, studying their faces.

He helped himself to cereal, poured a cup of coffee, and sat down next to Janet. Tom asked her how Catherine was getting on with her new guide dog and she answered him, trying to overhear the conversation at the table behind. She heard the word 'Dales' and 'isolated', then Colin's voice cutting in. He had heard the weather forecast that morning, he said. Apparently there was going to be snow, particularly in Yorkshire.

'Ooh, a white Christmas! I can't remember the last time we had one. Can you?' said Maureen.

'You'd better take a spade with you, Peter,' she added. 'Otherwise you might have to spend the New Year in your farmhouse as well as Christmas.'

The fork Claire had been fiddling with slipped from her fingers and fell into her tea, splashing the kedgeree left on her plate. She did not want it to snow. Peter would be cut off. People always were in the Dales. She had read about it in the local paper when she lived in Bradford. Besides, the roads would be dangerous.

'I'll get you a clean cup,' said Tom, lifting the fork out and placing it on his side plate.

Claire stared at him as if trying to decipher what he had said then pushed back her chair.

'No. Thank you but I must rush. I've remembered some more things I need to pack. I knew I would forget something.'

Peter caught up with her at the top of the stairs.

'What's the matter? Why did you rush off like that? Are you all right?'

There was a white mark on his collar, she saw, toothpaste probably or maybe paint that had not washed out. The need to be alone with him, just the two of them, the world shut out, hit her like a blow to the stomach.

'You will be careful, won't you? You won't do anything silly if you get snowed in?'

Peter clicked his tongue in exasperation.

'We won't get snowed in . . . Colin's making it up. I heard the forecast as well this morning and they didn't say anything about snow. Sleet – that's what they said. Sleet turning to rain.'

'Are you sure?'

'Yes, it's just Colin. He's jealous. His son hasn't asked him to stay this year and so he's trying to make himself feel better by convincing himself that everyone who's going away will have really horrible, difficult journeys.'

'He's not going to his son?'

'No. I thought he was too. So did everyone. He only told Matron last night. He said his daughter-in-law had flu or something.'

Claire looked concerned.

'Don't worry. He'll be all right. It's Freda I'm worried about,' said Peter. 'She won't be able to get away from him.'

Iris waved at them from the other end of the corridor.

'What's she doing over Christmas?'

'Going home. I was really pleased until I discovered that Quintin was going with her.'

'Is he still not right?'

Claire snorted derisively.

'Right? He's just about as wrong as you can get.'

She pushed open the door to her room.

'He's blackmailing her – that's what he's doing. He can't bear it that she's working and he isn't and so he's doing everything he can to stop her. You know she's been late arriving three times already this week.'

'No.'

'Yes. He's started sleeping later and later in the mornings and so he isn't tired at night. He keeps her awake playing music or clattering around in the kitchen. The other night he started making a curry at three in the morning. He woke her up to ask where the cardamom pods were.'

'Why doesn't she just leave him? She doesn't need to stay there, does she? Surely she can afford to rent a bedsit.'

Claire glared at him. Why was it that men were so black and white? Did they really not see the grey and the green, those murky, shifting colours shading off between one and another, a pond's surface, changing? Or did they see them but pretend they didn't?

'She feels responsible. I mean he is ill, genuinely ill, as well as everything else. She feels she can't just walk out and leave him. Besides, she still cares for him even though she no longer loves him – because she no longer loves him. She feels she's partly to blame – that if she still loved him he wouldn't be ill.'

'But that's ridiculous. He's been taking drugs for years . . .'

Claire held up a hand to stop him.

'I know, I know. Come on. Let's not talk about him any more. Not on our last morning.'

Peter took hold of the hand and pulled her towards him, gently at first, then with a sudden jerk so that she lost her balance and fell against him, her head on his chest. He held her there tightly and she let him, relaxing into his arms, the buttons on his shirt pressing against her face.

'It's only two days,' he said, stroking her hair with the bottom of his chin. 'We'll see one another again on Monday. We'll have a special meal in my room by the fire. I'll order a takeaway from that new Chinese. You like Chinese, don't you?'

Claire nodded, pressing her face closer, not wanting him to see the tears which had sprung to her eyes.

'But what will they say? What will Matron say?' she asked.

'Who cares what they say? Or what they think? It's none of their business.'

Claire bit her lip. She had had another dream last night in which Matron had 'found out'. She had come rushing into the dining room when they were having breakfast, had exposed them publicly as lovers, and asked them to leave. 'You know the rules,' she said coldly. 'No couples. Especially not unmarried ones!' The worst thing was that Catherine had been there, sitting next to Phyllis, smirking triumphantly.

'Claire? What's the matter?'

He held her away from him so that he could see her eyes then pressed her even more firmly against him. She struggled free, wiping the tears away.

'I . . . I . . . I've got something for you. You're not to open them until tomorrow.'

She went to the desk where the presents lay – the tapes of *Othello* and the sea collage, wrapped, first in tissue paper, then in newspaper, and finally in purple crepe paper, decorated with gold stars.

'What are they? Can I feel them?'

'No. You'll guess.'

'I won't guess that one,' he said, pointing to the large bulging rectangle of the wrapped collage. 'What on earth is it?'

'You'll soon find out. Now, out of my way. They're not heavy. I'm going to put them in the car. Make sure someone else takes them out, won't you?'

She picked them up, trying not to show her disappointment at his failure to announce that he had a present for her.

'The car's open, is it?'

'Yes. I'll just get my bag and I'll follow you down.'

Phyllis was in the hallway giving Angela, the new member of staff, instructions about the plants on her windowsill.

'The blue one likes to be kept dry. It won't need watering at all until I get back. The others will probably need a little bit, especially the pink one at the end. That gets very thirsty. Oh yes, and the white cyclamen needs to be watered from the bottom – in the saucer, I mean. Otherwise it will rot.'

She smiled graciously as Claire passed, fussing with the yellow silk scarf which contrasted so effectively with her fuchsia pink trouser suit. She could afford to smile, thought Claire, tripping over the doormat and almost dropping the presents. Peter would probably admire her colour sense later, sitting next to her in the car, driving off together. Maybe he would even compare it unfavourably in his mind with hers.

She looked down at the brown skirt she had put on that morning. It was drab. She knew it was. And the length was unflattering too. She was so small she needed to wear skirts either on the knee or just above it if she wanted to avoid looking as though she had raided the dressing-up box. But it was comfortable. Extremely comfortable. That was why she had chosen it. She did not want to spend six hours travelling wearing something that felt tight or restrictive.

She shrugged her shoulders. That was how she was – more interested in comfort than appearance. She had always been like that. Once, she remembered, sledging during the Christmas holidays, she had cut the ends off some empty animal feed bags and tied them round her boots. The other children had sniggered. But, after two hours, she was the only one who still had dry feet. If Peter didn't like it, he could . . . She left the thought dangling like a spider, bunched up against the cold, a small black mark against the white of the ceiling. Some women, she reflected, always looked elegant no matter what they were wearing or doing. Her mother, for example. Tall and large-boned, she could have been mannish. Instead, the adjective her appearance most frequently prompted was 'striking'. Once, visiting her at the vicarage while living in Oxford, she had found her in the garden, digging potatoes. She was wearing gumboots, a man's tweed trilby hat, and a raincoat she had rescued from a scarecrow in Norfolk saying it was too good to waste on birds. Tied round her forehead to keep the hair out of her eyes was a strip of the blue-and-white checked tablecloth she had been cutting up earlier for dusters. Other people wearing the same outfit would have looked ridiculous. Her mother looked magnificent – like a lost migrant bird from another continent, a bird which had no place in rural Oxfordshire, which had merely stopped to feed and rest before it flew on to somewhere hotter and more exotic.

She put the presents down on the roof of Peter's car and turned the handle of the boot. It was locked. She tried the other doors. They too were locked. She put her hands in the pockets of her cardigan and waited. The sky, she noticed, was dull and thick and grey like bloodless skin. A snow sky.

A tinkly laugh made her turn round. Phyllis was coming down the front steps carrying a large square cosmetic case. Peter was behind her, carrying two cases. He too was laughing, presumably at something Phyllis had said, but he stopped when he saw Claire.

'Sorry. I thought it was open. I must have locked it again. You should have come inside,' he said, rushing forward.

'It's OK. I've only been waiting a minute.'

She placed the collage upright in the boot and stood back to let Peter arrange the cases.

'Do you want me to put that in my bag? Then all the presents will be together,' said Phyllis, pointing at the wrapped Othello tapes still lying on the roof of the car.

'Yes, OK,' said Claire doubtfully.

She watched as the purple parcel disappeared into a large carrier bag of presents, all wrapped with the same paper – silver with green Christmas trees. It looked like the sort of cheap, inferior paper sold by scruffy, cheerful men in the doorways of empty shop units, thought Claire, reproaching herself instantly for being snobbish.

'I want that in with me, if you don't mind. It's got things in it for the journey,' said Phyllis as Peter stowed a canvas drawstring bag in the boot.

'I treated myself to a tin of butterscotch,' she added, turning to Claire. 'I find one's throat gets so dry on long journeys.'

'Yes, I suppose so. It's a long time since I've been on one,' said Claire.

'There. That's everything then. Is there anything else to go in?' said Peter, slamming the boot shut.

'No. Just my handbag,' said Phyllis. 'Oh yes, and the poinsettia for Sandra. Angela said she'd find me a box to stand it in so it wouldn't get bashed about. I'll see if she's found one. Won't be a moment.'

Her shoes were totally unsuitable for a weekend in the Dales, thought Claire, watching her totter back to the house. She'd never be able to go on a walk. But then maybe she didn't want to.

'What time does your coach go?' asked Peter, after a moment's awkward silence.

'Eleven. A taxi's coming for me at half ten.'

They both looked at their watches which said half past nine. A whole hour, thought Claire, to spend thinking about him and Phyllis, alone in a car together.

'I'll ring you tonight,' he said. 'There's no phone in the cottage but there's a phone box in the village apparently. I'll ring you after supper, shall I? About half past seven?'

'Yes. Or a bit later even. My train doesn't get in until twenty to six and it will probably take me another half an hour or so to get to their house. It might be better to leave it until after eight when Luke will have gone to bed and it will be less hectic.'

'OK.'

He put his hands on her shoulders and leant down.

'Goodbye then. Happy Christmas.'

She kissed him lightly, avoiding his mouth, conscious that Phyllis was walking back towards them.

'Here we are then,' said Phyllis, her eyes flickering from face to face like a snake's tongue. 'One poinsettia. I can never keep the dratted things alive. But they do look very festive even if they do only last a few weeks.'

Peter took the box from her and placed it on the floor behind his seat. Phyllis opened the front door on the passenger side and got in.

'Goodbye then. Give Catherine my regards.'

'Yes. I . . . I . . . Drive safely, won't you?'

She waved until they were out of sight and then walked quickly back to the house. She was not wearing a coat and was beginning to feel cold.

The door to her room was ajar although she could not remember leaving it open. She shut it behind her, thought about asking Iris to come and clean her teeth and decided to do it herself. It would take a long time – manipulating a toothbrush was one of the jobs she found more difficult – but she had an hour to fill. And it would be better than sitting doing nothing, imagining.

It was not until she had finished, some eight or nine minutes later, that she saw them, the presents, lying on her bed. There were three of them, one soft and bulky, one small and hard and rectangular, and one the size of an envelope. All were wrapped in shiny green paper. She went up to them slowly. So he hadn't forgotten. And he had remembered that her favourite colour was green as well. There was a card too, handmade, an abstract pattern in green gouache. Inside, at the top, he had copied out two lines from Marvell's poem 'Thoughts In A Garden'—

'Annihilating all that's made/To a green thought in a green shade.'

Underneath he had written, 'To dear Claire, my green thought, who has helped me grow more in six months than I have done in as many years, Love Peter.'

There was a knock at the door. Claire hurriedly covered the card and presents with her eiderdown before she answered. It was Iris.

'Thank goodness you're still here. It's Catherine, your friend. She's on the phone. She tried ringing your number first but said there was no answer.'

As she spoke, she walked towards Claire's phone which stood on the small table next to her bed and picked up the receiver.

'It must have been knocked off,' she explained, replacing the receiver carefully. 'There was no dialling tone. Just a clicking sound. Do you want me to put her through now?'

'Yes please. I hope there's nothing wrong. She didn't say what it was about?'

'No, but she said it was urgent. She was worried you might have already left. I'll put her through now, OK?'

It was less than a minute before her phone rang but in that time Claire had already imagined that Luke had been run over and killed, Vashti poisoned, or Ella, Catherine's daughter, diagnosed with cancer.

The truth, when it came, was not as bad as any of these but still serious. Luke had meningitis. He was OK, said Catherine, they had found out in time, there was no danger now but he would be in hospital for a while. They had all been given antibiotics and told not to see friends or relatives for a week. It meant they could not have Claire to stay.

45 ∫

Claire was brisk and bright on the telephone as she knew she had to be. Yes, of course, she understood, she said. No, she didn't mind. Well, obviously she did in a way. She'd been looking forward to seeing everyone, especially Catherine. But she'd come down in a month or two. They'd have a second Christmas then. February always needed cheering up anyhow. No, there'd be no problem about staying. It wasn't as if anyone had been going to move into her room while she was away. Catherine wasn't to worry. There'd be plenty for her to do. There was a trip to a carol service that afternoon and a special Christmas Eve dinner of pheasant and chocolate soufflé. Afterwards, some of the residents at Maple Court, that residential home that had opened the year before near the castle, were coming over for a little party. It would probably be quite jolly.

Reassured, Catherine rang off, having promised to phone the next day to let Claire know how Luke was.

Claire replaced the receiver very slowly and gently, as if it was old china, so thin you could see the sun through it. She would not tell Matron yet, she thought. She needed to prepare herself, to arm herself against the inevitable sympathy, the kindness that was often more difficult to bear than indifference.

She began to pace the room. The tinsel lantern, hung up by Iris the previous day, had fallen down. She kicked it out of her way, not seeing it, seeing instead Peter in the car and beside him, Phyllis, handing him butterscotch, making him laugh, flashing her pink nails. She saw the sky opening out as they drove south, the grey giving way to blue; Peter leaning forward to turn some music on and Phyllis dancing to it, or pretending to, giggling; Peter's hand on the gear stick, the size of it, large, male, the skin stretched taut over the hard knuckles.

She saw this picture and she ran it through her mind and then she reran it, like a film director trying a different angle, wondering what she had missed the first time.

After the eighth take she became aware of the crushed lantern under her feet, unrecognisable, flattened like a bird on the road, a mess of pink and silver. She picked it up and dropped it neatly into the bin. Then she unpacked the bag which Iris had packed so carefully earlier, making sure it was balanced, that it would not tilt and be awkward to carry.

Matron was out so she left a message with Diane, one of the agency girls helping to provide cover while the staff took their Christmas breaks, and walked into town. Normally, she loved Christmas Eve – the anticipation, the feverish, last-minute activity, the sense of shared purpose. Today, though, she felt like a mourner at a wedding. In the market, as she walked slowly past the pyramids of oranges and apples, one of the traders called out: 'Cheer up, love, it might never happen.' She stared – she had not realised her gloom was so transparent – and the man's smile faltered.

'Have a pear,' he added, holding out one. 'Beautiful and juicy, they are. Go lovely with a bit of Stilton. Go on. Have it on me. It's Christmas, isn't it?'

Claire backed off.

'No, thank you. I don't like pears,' she lied. 'But thank you, anyhow.'

After only half an hour the jollity drove her back to her room. Here she found a scribbled message from Iris and a present. 'Sorry to have missed you,' said the message. 'My mother phoned to say it was snowing down there so we decided to leave a bit earlier than we'd planned. Very sorry to hear your trip to Oxford has been called off. Hope you manage to have a good time here. See you on Tuesday. Love Iris.'

She ate ham sandwiches for lunch followed by Christmas cake and Wensleydale cheese. Diane and another of the agency girls served and cleared it away. Cook was having a couple of hours off to decorate her tree and make the stuffing for her own family's

Christmas dinner. She was cooking for twelve apparently as well as cooking lunch at The Pines.

Later, she put on her coat and scarf to go to the carol service. She checked she had some loose change for the collection, and then, at the last minute, decided not to go after all. She did not want to cry. Not again. Not in public.

There were crackers for dinner, red scented candles on the table, and a tape of festive music playing from a ghetto blaster on the sideboard. Colin wore a tie with a holly sprig design and Matron a silver satin blouse. Even so, it was a sad, stilted occasion, the empty chairs a reminder of other people in real homes, sitting next to friends and relatives.

Claire excused herself from the party afterwards, saying she had a headache. She took off her shoes and lay on her bed in the dark waiting for the phone to ring. Through the open curtains she could see the moon, half-eaten, slipping in and out of cloud. Every so often she glanced at the fluorescent hands of her alarm clock and picked up the receiver to make sure there was still a dialling tone. Eight o'clock. Half past eight. Quarter to nine. Nine. Ten past nine. Quarter past nine. The intervals between her glances grew shorter. He had decided to wait until after dinner. No, the phone box in the village was not working. They were still having dinner. It was taking longer than he had expected because Phyllis and her niece had not been able to make the oven work at first. There was no phone box and no other house nearby. He had driven to another village but there was no phone box there either. He had used up all his loose change talking to Catherine about Luke's meningitis. He had forgotten. He had not forgotten but he was enjoying himself too much to want to break off to phone her. There was a fire, a real log fire, and someone was filling up his glass and anyhow it was too late now, she would have gone to bed. He would phone her in the morning.

The sound of laughter and music from the party drifted upstairs, hardening her loneliness. She could remember only one time when she had felt as isolated. It was soon after Harry's death. She had gone for a walk and found herself on a road running over a motorway. She had stood at the side of the road and hung over the rails looking down at the cars. She must have stood there some time because a police patrol car had driven up and stopped and a policeman had got out.

'Are you all right?' he asked.

'There're so many of them, aren't there? All going somewhere. All with something to do. Where are they all going?' she said.

The policeman looked puzzled.

'It's OK. I was just daydreaming. Just thinking. That's all.'

'Oh well, there's no law against that. Just as long as . . . just as long as you're OK.'

He got back into his car, shut the door, and drove off and she watched him. It was only later, walking back to her empty, childless house, that she realised he had not stopped by accident, that someone had seen her and called the police, had thought she was going to jump. The thought made her smile.

At ten she decided he would not phone. Not now. But she still waited another half hour. The minibus arrived to collect the residents of Maple Court. She heard the sound of doors slamming. Someone called out 'Happy Christmas'. She waited a bit longer, looked at the clock. It was eleven.

She undid her skirt and climbed into bed with the rest of her clothes on, hugging herself. The curtains were still open and in the moonlight she could see his presents where she had put them on the desk. They stood out like some arrangement of prehistoric stones, unknown, mysterious, waiting to be misinterpreted. She got out of bed and threw them into her wardrobe, down on the floor among the shoes and boxes. She would not open them. Whatever colour she was, green or pink, she was clearly not in his thoughts tonight.

46

Claire checked the phone as soon as she woke up even though she could see the receiver was on properly. There was still a dialling tone.

No one came to dress her and she did not ring for help, venting her disappointment on buttons and armholes. She had been intending to wear her green dress but changed her mind, putting on instead a scarlet wool crepe shift dress she had bought in a sale two years before and never worn. Looking at herself in the mirror, she could see why she had not worn it but decided to keep it on. She needed to distract herself.

She combed her hair, powdered her nose, dabbed perfume on her wrists, and thought, 'He would have got through by now if he had tried. He has not tried. He does not care. It is Christmas Day, I am sixty-eight, and I am in love with a man who does not love me back. To hell with him!'

The phone rang and she almost knocked over a chair in her hurry to reach it. It was Catherine. Luke had had a good night. The doctors thought he might be able to come out of hospital earlier than they had first expected. They were all going in later to open their Christmas presents with him. Ella was there already. She had spent the night there.

Claire tried not to let her disappointment show. Yes, she was fine. Absolutely fine. She was just about to go down to breakfast.

'Nobody's phoned for me, have they?' she asked, hearing the anxiety in her voice and knowing Catherine would hear it too.

'No, were you expecting anyone?'

'Peter said he might ring. That's all. I just wondered . . .'

'Do you want me to give him a message if he does call?'

'No. He'll know where I am. It's not as if there's anywhere else for me to go.'

Catherine changed the conversation back to Luke and what the doctors had said, how one of the hospital porters was going to dress up as Father Christmas later to visit the children's wards. Claire hurried her along, thinking, 'He might be ringing now. At this very moment, he might be standing in a phone box, putting coins in, hearing an engaged tone.' When she rang off she half expected the phone to ring again immediately. But it didn't.

Breakfast was late. Cook was not coming in until ten and her replacement, a boy called Malcolm, clearly found it difficult to cook bacon and egg and see to the turkey at the same time.

Afterwards, there was an awkward hour or so to fill. Claire tried to do the bumper newspaper crossword kindly provided the day before for readers with no chestnuts to peel or sprouts to prepare. Colin played patience by himself, slapping the cards down on the table with inordinate force. Freda hovered pathetically until Claire felt obliged to talk to her even though she had exhausted the topics on which Freda felt able or willing to converse on her second, or possibly even first, day at The Pines.

At eleven there was sherry in the drawing room. Matron gave out presents from under the tree while her sister, Brenda, a fat barrel of a woman who ran a successful wedding dress business in Warrington, handed round mince pies.

'So sorry to hear about your friend's little boy,' she said as Claire unwrapped a sponge bag in a violent pattern of red and yellow poppies.

Her small round inquisitive eyes stared at Claire as if seeking the loose thread that would make her unravel.

'Yes,' said Claire, imagining her extolling the virtues of lemon-coloured bridesmaids' dresses. 'And pink, you couldn't go wrong with pink, it always looked lovely. Mauve could be nice too – on the right skin.'

The brides' mothers would like her, she thought. They would find her stout shape comforting, would see her as someone they could trust, someone they could depend on. She probably wore a wedding ring at work even though she wasn't married. It would be expected.

'And so disappointing for you,' went on Brenda tactlessly. 'You must have been looking forward to going away.'

'Yes,' said Claire bleakly. 'Yes, I was.'

There was a tap on her shoulder. It was Diane, the agency girl.

'Sorry to interrupt you, Mrs Harper but there's a telephone call for you. Would you like to take it in here?'

'Yes. No. In my room. No, I'll take it in the library. I'll take it there.'

He might be in a call box, she thought. His money might have run out by the time she reached her room.

The library phone was near the window on a table where they kept reference books – a dictionary, a thesaurus, a road atlas bound in maroon leather. She drew up a chair and played with the cover of the atlas, flicking it open and shut. The phone rang – once, twice, three times. She picked it up.

'Hello?'

'Claire. It's me.'

'You said you would phone.'

'I couldn't get the car out. We were snowed in.'

'What?'

'Haven't you heard the news?'

'No . . .'

'We've got seven inches of snow. It started just after we arrived and didn't stop until eleven. I tried to get the car out but we're half a mile down a farm track. The wheels just spun round. I'm sorry. I tried.'

'Why couldn't you walk into the village?'

'I did. But there wasn't a phone box there after all. Just a bus stop and a parish council noticeboard.'

'What about the people in the village? Don't any of them have phones?'

'Not the two I asked,' said Peter testily. 'I didn't knock on any more doors because by then it was half past eleven. I was cold and tired and I thought you'd be in bed in Oxford. I didn't want to disturb everyone. How was I to know this was going to happen? That Luke was going to catch meningitis? You're being unreasonable. Claire? Claire, are you still there?'

'Yes.'

'I'm coming back. I'm setting off now. I'll be with you by teatime.'

'Don't be silly. You can't do that.'

'Why not?'

'But the road? You said it was blocked.'

'The farmer's been up it this morning with a tractor and cleared it. He says the back roads are a bit slippery but that the main roads are fine.'

'But Phyllis? How will she get home?'

'Sandra can take her to a station and she can catch a train.'

'But there's no need. I'm fine.'

'You're not fine. I can tell by your voice. And even if you are, I'm still coming back. I don't want you to be on your own.'

'OK,' she said, suddenly easy in her gladness.

'Claire?'

'Yes.'

'Thank you for the eyes.'

'For the what?'

'For the collage, the collage you gave me of your eyes.'

'It's not my eyes, it's the sea.'

'I know. I'm joking. It's just that it reminds me of your eyes, the way they look when you're angry.'

'You've never seen me angry.'

'Well, maybe not what you call angry . . .'

'Do you like it?'

'It's fantastic. I'm going to put it next to my bed so that I can see it when I wake up, so that I can lie there and look at it and be glad I'm in bed, all cosy and warm. It's so angry, so raw – it makes me shiver just to look at it.'

'But you do like it?'

'I love it. I only wish I'd done it.'

'Good.'

'Have you . . . have you opened my presents yet?'

'No, not yet. I . . . I . . .'

'You were too cross with me.'

'No, I . . .'

'Go on. Admit it. You were.'

She started to laugh.

'OK, I was. Just a bit.'

'Well, make sure you've opened them by the time I get back. It'll be about four or five. OK?'

'Yes.'

She replaced the receiver and hugged herself. He was coming, he did love her and he liked the collage. Everything was lovely, everything was right. Freda wasn't boring, the sponge bag wasn't ugly, and Brenda wasn't nosy.

She walked upstairs to her room and felt for the presents on the floor of the wardrobe. There they were. The soft one and the small, rectangular one. Where was the envelope? There it was. Behind her black patents.

She locked the door and drew the curtains and opened the presents in the light of her bedside lamp. The soft one was a nightdress – cream, silky, elegant and the right size too. He must have asked Iris or one of the other staff. The small rectangular one was a box of watercolour paints. 'So that we can go out together next summer,' said a piece of paper Sellotaped to the lid. The envelope contained two dress circle tickets for a production of *Peter Pan* at the Theatre Royal, Newcastle. There was also a card confirming a reservation for bed and breakfast for two at the Crescent Hotel. 'I want you to be my Wendy,' said the accompanying note. 'Only I want you all the time, not just for one week in the Spring.'

Claire buried her face in the slippery richness of the nightdress. 'You already have me,' she whispered. 'If only you knew.'

47

Peter arrived back just as it began to snow. Claire, who had sitting near the window for more than two hours, her radio tuned to a local news station so that she would hear regular traffic and weather reports, saw a car turn into the drive and guessed that it was him.

He must have run up the stairs because by the time she had stood up, turned off the radio and glanced in the mirror, he was there, opening the door, rushing in, gathering her towards him.

'More, more!' he said, laughing, refusing to let her go.

She gave in, relaxing her body, the tension slipping out like butter in a hot pan.

'You're all cold!'

'I know. The wretched heater packed up. I had to wrap the travel rug round me.'

'You had no heater! In this weather! You must be absolutely frozen.'

'I'm sorry,' he murmured, gently lifting her hair at the back so that he could kiss her neck underneath. 'I did try to phone you. I really did.'

'No, I'm sorry. I shouldn't have been so tetchy.'

'You should, you should. You had every right to be,' he said, kissing all the way down one arm and then the other.

Claire giggled. Who cared what Matron thought? He was here and he loved her. She was sure he did. Or almost sure. Why else would he drive more than a hundred miles to see her when he could have been sitting in front of a log fire drinking whisky?

'I didn't stop once . . .'

'Peter!'

'I know, I know, I know I should have done. But I kept on thinking, "Just another half an hour. Just ten more miles." And then suddenly I was only forty miles away and it didn't seem worth it.'

He buried his nose in her hair and breathed in deeply.

'I didn't want to,' he whispered. 'I didn't want to delay seeing you, not even by a second.'

They kissed again.

'Did you open the presents?'

'Yes. They were wonderful. Thank you. How did you know what size I was?'

'Ah well, I had my spies. And you don't mind seeing *Peter Pan*? Only there's nothing else on at this time of year. The woman at the box office said it was aimed at adults as well as children. She said it was a Christmas show rather than a pantomime.'

'No, it will be lovely. I haven't been to the theatre for . . . oh, I don't know how many years. Cartainly not since I've been here.'

'I've got some oat cakes and smoked Wensleydale in the car. I brought them back with me. I thought we could make a fire in my room and have a little picnic. Only I'd like to have a hot bath first to get properly warm.'

He fetched his bags from the car and then showed her how to lay a fire while his bath ran and the steam from the hot water crept in and swirled round them like mist on a moor.

'You put the paper on first, then the kindling, and then a few lumps of coal or wood on top. You don't want to put on too much or you'll stifle it. It's got to have room to grow and breathe, like a plant.'

He lit a few corners of the rolled-up newspaper then went to have his bath, leaving her with instructions to add more coal once the fire got going properly. Alone, Claire walked around his room, drawing the curtains, studying the pictures, trying not to laugh out loud with joy. She found some plates in a cupboard, white, with a black and yellow criss-cross border, and put them on the coffee table in front of the fire. In front of them she arranged the cheese and biscuits and a pot of anchovy relish.

'How's it doing?' said Peter, coming out from the bathroom in a towelling dressing gown, his calves and feet bare.

'OK. I added some more twigs.'

Peter crouched in front of the fire and poked it vigorously until it flared into life.

'Oh good, you found the cheese. There's some fruit as well somewhere – grapes, pears, even some lychees. I think they got put in a box on their own so they didn't get bashed. Sandra insisted I took some with me. She said they'd never get through it all on their own.'

He brushed the coal dust off his hands and took her in his arms again. There were drops of water on his chest, she saw, trapped in the hairs like dew in a spider's web. She wanted to dance.

'Shall I put some music on?' he asked, as if reading her thoughts.

'Yes. Something jolly.'

He put on a tape and went into his bedroom to change, coming back in clothes she had never seen before and had not imagined him owning – purple cotton jersey pants and a long-sleeved T-shirt, clinging, pinkish red. The sound of a woman's voice, low and husky, floated round the room.

'You don't mind?'

'What?'

'Me wearing these. Only they're so comfortable.'

'Of course not. I don't mind what you wear.'

'Good. Now, what do we need? Candles, serviettes, glasses, knives, something to drink. That's all, I think.'

They ate Belgian chocolates after the oat cakes, and wedges of Christmas cake with slivers of cheese. Afterwards they sat on the sofa, side by side, and looked at pictures of rooms in a book on interior design. Peter liked stripes and checks, Claire discovered, bright geometrical patterns. She preferred plain, neutral walls with the colour in the furniture or ornaments – a patterned throw, a translucent glass vase, an unusual bowl.

At about eight, possibly later, she was not wearing her watch, the phone rang. It was Tom. Charlotte had given birth prematurely to a baby girl, he said. Both were fine and the baby not that small considering she was three weeks early – 6 lbs and 8 oz. They had called her Meg after Tom's mother.

'Do you mind?' asked Claire after he had sat down again and

told her the news, after he had explained the choice of Christian name. 'Do you mind that they've called her Meg?'

'No. Well, maybe a bit. Yes, probably I do.'

The tape ended abruptly, the woman's voice cut off in the middle of a song. Peter did not turn it over.

'He's right, of course,' he said eventually. 'I did make his mother unhappy. Not deliberately. Just because of what I wasn't. We should have left one another but we didn't. No one did. Not then. Not unless you were rich or strong. That's one of the things I admire about you. That you did leave, that you listened to what your heart was saying, that you didn't cover it up like I did, bank it down like a fire, knowing it was still there underneath the Sunday joint and the week at the seaside in August.'

'It wasn't as hard for me as it might have been,' said Claire. 'You have to remember that it was during the war. There were a lot of women living on their own at the time. People simply assumed I was a widow.'

'I don't think you realise how much I've changed, how much you've changed me,' said Peter as if he had not heard her. 'That's what I meant by that quote from Marvell. I used to be so negative, so cynical. I was always looking for the catch in things, the down side. If I wanted to do something, I would always think, "I'm too old. It's too late. I won't be able to do it." Now I think, "I can do it. I can paint. I can learn the names of the stars."'

'I've changed too,' said Claire. 'I no longer have bad dreams about my mother.'

Peter laughed.

'What do you mean?'

'Well, you know what I said once about how she still influenced me, how I would worry about what she would think of something I had said or done, and how I resented this – the hold she had on me even though she was dead? Well, I used to have bad dreams about it. I used to dream I was being suffocated, that someone was pushing handfuls of feathers down my throat until I was choking, gagging, gasping for air, and always in the background there was my mother's face, smiling, nodding. Now I don't. I don't have those dreams any more. I feel quite light – as though all the bad feelings that have been weighing me down for so long have suddenly gone.'

'Good,' he said. 'I'm glad. I'm glad they've gone.'

Outside, in the corridor, there was the sound of voices, then a door shutting. Peter looked at his watch.

'Half past eight,' he announced, getting up and putting more coal on the fire. 'What shall we do? I feel restless after so long cooped up in the car. I'd like to go for a walk only it's too cold and it's probably still snowing.'

He walked over to the window as he spoke and drew the curtains slightly so that he could see out.

'We could play a game, if you helped me move my pieces. Ludo or Scrabble or something.'

Peter wrinkled his nose.

'Or we could do some printing. Iris has given me a book on crafts called *Try Your Hand*. There are some super potato print designs.'

She said it as a joke, not thinking he would take her seriously, but he did and half an hour later, after Diane, the agency girl, had fetched potatoes from the kitchen and Peter had mixed paint and poured it into bowls, there they were, sitting at his table, covering sheets of white paper with splodges of red and green and blue.

'If anyone could see us now,' said Peter, showing her the palms of his hands which had turned a murky purplish brown.

'Or if the phone rang,' said Claire, holding up her hands as well.

'I want to go to Kenya to see Meg. Will you come with me?' he asked after a while.

'Yes.'

'I wish I'd met you fifty years earlier,' he said after another while.

'Me too,' she said.

48

'Do you like it?' asked Iris, holding her hand up so that the stones flashed.

'Yes,' said Claire doubtfully. 'Yes, it's very unusual.'

'He had it made specially. He chose the design himself. It's an iris, you see. The sapphire is the flower and the jade the leaves.'

'Yes, I can see that.'

It was Wednesday, the day after Boxing Day, the day before Claire and Peter were going to Newcastle to see *Peter Pan*.

'When's the wedding?'

'June,' said Iris, spraying cleaning lotion on the mirror behind Claire's wash basin. 'I wanted a June wedding. Mum suggested we should wait until August or September but I didn't want to. Everything's starting to go off then – to look brown and dusty and dried-up – whereas in June everything's still fresh and green. I want dog roses in the church. I know they drop as soon as you pick them but I still want them. I want the church to look like that poem by Hopkins you were learning before Christmas – all wildness and wet, weeds and wilderness.'

Claire smiled, amused and flattered to think her reading should influence the decoration of the church.

'What do your parents think?'

'Dad's a bit concerned that he hasn't got a job. He kept on telling Quintin how risky the music industry was, how once you were married and had responsibilities, you needed a regular income. I think he thinks Quintin should give up the singing and become a lawyer or accountant – something sensible.'

'Maybe he will.'

Iris laughed.

'I can't see it somehow.'

No, maybe not, thought Claire. But then one could not see lots of things. She, for example, she had not seen herself as a sales assistant in ladies' separates.

'What about your mother?'

'She's not worried about the job,' said Iris cautiously, polishing more slowly. 'But . . . well, you know what mothers are like. I don't think she'd be a hundred per cent enthusiastic, whoever I married.'

Claire, examining her jewellery box, deciding what earrings to wear to the theatre, reflected that this was probably not true.

'You're not . . . you're not pregnant, are you?'

'No. Why? Do I look as though I've put on weight?'

She looked at herself in the mirror, stepping back to see more of her body.

She had, in fact, put on some – not much, just a little on her face and hips – but Claire had not noticed this until now.

'No, no, I'm sorry, I just . . . well . . . I just wondered . . . I suppose it was the suddenness of it. I know you said once that he wanted to marry you, but you didn't say anything about it after that so I assumed that . . . well . . . that you'd talked him out of it or said no or something.'

Iris refolded her duster and began polishing the mirror again. Claire shut the lid of her jewellery box. She would choose some earrings later, she decided. She could not concentrate now.

'You will come and visit me, won't you?'

'When?'

'When you're married. You will still drop in occasionally?'

'What do you mean? I'll be here every day, working, the same as I am now.'

'So you're not going to give up your job?'

'No, at least not for the time being. I won't stay here for ever – Quintin still hasn't given up the idea of travelling round the world – but we haven't any immediate plans.'

Claire noticed the easy, confident use of the pronoun 'we' – the assumption that plans would be shared – and remembered the day a man knocked on her door to look round the house she didn't even know was for sale. Her home.

'There. All done,' said Iris, standing back to admire the results of her work.

She put the duster and cleaning lotion back in the red plastic bucket near her feet.

'I'd better not stay and talk or Matron will be on at me again.'

'Why? What's happened? What's she said?'

'No, nothing. I'm only joking. She knows we get on well. I think she likes it that we talk – even if it does mean I take twice as long cleaning your room as anyone else's.'

She picked the bucket up then put it down again and walked over to where Claire was sitting in front of her dressing table.

'I know you don't like him . . .'

'But I haven't said anything!' protested Claire.

'You don't need to,' said Iris and they both laughed.

'Well, I hope I'm wrong.'

'You will be,' said Iris, hugging her lightly. 'Honestly, he's totally different when he's on his own with me.'

She went out, leaving Claire feeling the finger where she too had once worn an engagement ring. The heat and pregnancy had swollen her fingers that summer and she had not been able to get it off. She had tried soap and water, oil, and force, but it had stuck firm. In the end, she had become so obsessed, so desperate to be rid of it, that Mrs Flowers had taken her to a jeweller's to have it cut off. She had felt so relieved afterwards, walking back to the house, as if the ring had been physically hurting her, nagging like a toothache.

It did not matter what Iris said. She could not feel happy for her.

49

Matron came out as Peter was putting their bags in the boot.

'Are you going already?' she asked. 'Only I wanted to have a word with you. With both of you, actually.'

Claire shivered, bunching her shoulders against the chill of the wind. It was from the north-east. That was what the weather forecaster had said on the radio earlier. Dry and sunny but cold with a wind from the north-east.

'Can it wait?' said Peter, standing back to look at the bags and then slamming the boot shut. 'Only I'd rather we were off now. We don't want to be late.'

Matron fiddled with the bow at the neck of her blouse.

'Well, yes, I suppose so. Yes, I suppose it can. It's a matinée, you're going to, is it?'

'Yes, one o'clock start. So we haven't got that much time, you see. Come on, Claire. The door's open.'

Claire climbed in obediently.

'Bye then. Have a good time,' cried Matron as Peter slammed his door.

Claire waved, turning round to check that her walking stick was on the back seat.

'It's not a matinée, is it?' she asked, once they were on the road, driving away, together, safe.

'No, I just said that to get rid of her,' said Peter and grinned.

'What do you think she wanted?'

'Oh, I don't know. Probably to ask what colour we'd like the dining room repainted or what we think Eric would like for his eightieth birthday.'

'You don't think . . .'

'No. Come on. Let's not think about her. Let's think about us, about what we're going to do today.'

He leant across and rubbed her knee.

'Isn't this nice? Just the two of us, out on the razz together.'

She nodded, smiling.

They left their bags in the hotel and drove straight to the restaurant Peter had chosen from the *Good Food Guide*.

'The hotel doesn't do food. Apart from breakfast, of course. I thought it was better that way. Hotel food is never very good – at least not in this country. I thought it would be nice to go out for lunch. I love eating out at lunchtime. Besides, we won't have time in the evening. The performance starts at half seven and we won't be out until at least ten. Is that OK?'

'Yes, of course. It's perfect,' said Claire. She felt soft and passive, a stroked cat, purring.

'Was the room OK? Did you like it?'

'Yes. It was beautiful.'

It was large and light with leafy green wallpaper and an antique cream, pink and green quilt on the bed. Opposite the bed, in the south-facing bay window, was a sofa with petit point cushions. Next to it, on a table covered with a linen cloth, white roses and green ivy spilled from an enormous glass vase, casting shadows on the wallpaper in the sunlight so that you could not see which leaves were real and which ones reflected. The bathroom was white and comfortable, with large, soft towels and an easy chair so that you could sit and talk to someone having a bath. It was all spotlessly clean.

Their table in the restaurant was by a window overlooking a small, tree-lined square and, in the distance, the River Tyne. It was the last to be taken.

'I asked for the best table,' said Peter proudly, nervously. 'I said it was a special occasion.'

Claire smiled.

'Well, it is! Our first proper meal out together. I don't know why we haven't gone out like this before.'

The waiter brought their drinks, a cranberry juice for Claire and a gin and tonic for Peter. Soup of the day was carrot and fennel, he said.

'What do you think then? Do you like it? It's nice, isn't it? Nice and lively. I wanted there to be a good atmosphere as well as for the food to be good. I didn't want it to be too stuffy – you know, where you feel you have to talk in a whisper so that the people at the next table don't hear you. I wanted to be somewhere where people were enjoying themselves – talking, laughing, waving their arms, the kind of place where you have to raise your voice sometimes to make yourself heard, where you have a proper conversation.'

'It's lovely,' Claire reassured him. 'Really lovely.'

She had salmon fish cakes in a herb butter sauce to start with, followed by the monkfish. Peter had skate's wing in a caper sauce, followed by loin of lamb with savoury bread and butter pudding. For desert, they had orange cheese cake in a bitter coffee sauce, one between them, sharing the same plate. They were the last to leave the restaurant.

On their way back to the car, they passed a childrenswear shop.

'Shall we buy something for Meg?' said Claire, catching sight of a velour babygro in the window, so small it looked like doll's clothes.

Inside, Peter held up a smocked tartan dress.

'This is pretty.'

'Yes, but not very practical. Dresses ride up and leave their legs bare. And tights aren't a good idea, not at that age. The nappies are so bulky, you see. It's better to have all-in-one suits or dungarees, at least until they can walk.'

'People think we're grandparents,' he said, putting the dress back on a rail, smiling at the assistant who had approached them a few minutes earlier to ask if they needed any help.

'Well you are.'

'Yes,' said Peter doubtfully. 'Yes, I suppose I am. But I didn't mean that. I meant they thought *we* were – that we were grandparents together.'

She chose two outfits, one for a baby aged up to three months, the other for a baby aged up to six months. They grew quickly, she remembered.

'Will it be hot? Will these be too warm?' she asked, showing them to Peter.

He felt the fabric.

'No, they should be OK. The material's not that thick, is it? I expect they need to be covered up anyway, even if it is hot, so they don't get sunburnt or bitten by mosquitoes.'

'Yes, I hadn't thought of that.'

'Look,' said Peter, holding out a soft toy shaped like an octopus. 'Isn't this good? They're all different textures, you see.'

She looked more closely and saw that the legs were made of different material – one from satin, another from velvet, a third from corduroy and so on.

'They make different sounds as well. Feel one.'

She grasped the red velvet leg and squeezed it gently until it squeaked. The satin one rattled. The corduroy jingled.

'This is my favourite,' said Peter, grabbing hold of a pink, bobbly leg. 'Listen. It's all rustly, like sweet papers in the cinema.'

'Is this for Meg or for you?'

'For Meg, of course, for Meg,' he said, shaking it so that the legs danced.

Back in the hotel, it was not awkward as she had feared. They lay on the bed at first, just lay there, enjoying the warmth and the quiet, the touch of each other's hands. After a while, Peter got up and half drew the curtains so that the light in the room was softer. She was glad of this because she had worried about how her skin would look – what he would think of the sad, shrunken flaps that were the remains of her breasts. He removed her clothes first, then his, slowly, not hurrying, kissing her in between buttons and zips. She closed her eyes and let her hands explore, running her fingertips along the ridge of his spine, feeling the line of his thighs. He was squeezing her buttocks, cupping them in both hands, pressing so hard she thought she would cry out, his nails digging into her flesh. His hands moved round, eased her legs apart, wider, wider, felt for the soft throbbing tip, touched it lightly, touched it again, and again and again, until she was melting, moaning, aching for the fill of his penis. He guided her hand down, pressed the fingers round, moved them up and down, slowly at first, then faster and faster, his tongue and fingers playing her mouth. Then he was on her and in her, holding her down, throwing her head up and back, kissing her throat, pushing, pushing, pushing until suddenly she tightened, pulling him into her, crying out, feeling him quicken inside her, push harder and faster until he came, exploding, arching back, his eyes shut, his face contorted, ugly, beautiful, both of them twitching, sagging, like paper bags blown up and out.

She lay on the bed in the dim half-light and he pulled the covers up so she would not get cold.

'Would you like some tea?'

'Yes,' she whispered.

He put on his dressing gown and went into the bathroom to fill the kettle, and she raised herself on one elbow and watched him, warm and drowsy, her heart singing. After they had drunk the tea, they lay down again, her head in the crook of his arm, his hand stroking her hair, their legs entwined. I would not mind dying now, thought Claire. If I had to die, I would like it to be at a moment like this.

'We'll have to leave in an hour,' he said, twisting round to look at his watch on the bedside table. 'Would you like a bath or something?'

'A bath would be nice. There are some sachets of bubble bath on the shelf above the basin. But you go first. I don't mind waiting.'

'No,' he said, getting out of bed quickly before she could stop him. 'I'll have a shower. I prefer showers anyway.'

She rolled over into the space he had left and pressed her face into the pillow, breathing in his smell, the fresh tang of his sweat.

'Moisturising or relaxing?' he called out from the bathroom, shouting to make himself heard above the noise of the water running.

'Both, please.'

'Come on then. Hurry up, or I'll tickle you out,' he said, coming back into the bedroom and stroking the exposed sole of her right foot.

She giggled and withdrew the foot sharply.

Lying in the bath, listening to him whistle softly as he dressed after his shower, she cried because she was so happy, the tears rolling down her cheeks and dropping into the foam.

'It's not far to walk – only about ten minutes, according to the girl at reception – but I thought it would be nice to arrive in style,' he said when they were in the taxi.

She nodded agreement. He had complimented her on the green dress and choice of earrings and said how nice her perfume smelt. He had helped her put on her tights and coat and held open the door of the taxi for her. But he had not said he loved her. Not then when they were making love or afterwards when they were lying together. She had not noticed it then but now she had and it bothered her. She wanted to hear him say those words, those tired, old wonderful words – 'I love you'.

Their seats were in the front row of the lower dress circle, right in the middle, the most expensive seats in the house. There was a young couple to their left and an older couple in their fifties or perhaps early sixties to their right. The latter stood up to let them pass and, once they had settled down and stowed their coats under the seats, offered them chocolates.

'It's our wedding anniversary,' said the woman to Claire, unwrapping a chocolate and popping it in her purple, lipsticked mouth. 'Forty years. Is your husband called Peter too?'

'No . . . I mean, yes, yes he is called Peter but . . .'

'I thought there'd be more children here,' interrupted the woman. 'But I suppose it's too late for them. I suppose they come to the matinée performance.'

Claire handed Peter the box of chocolates, glad that as she did so, the lights dimmed, preventing further attempts at conversation by the woman.

'I'd better cover this up,' whispered Peter, taking her left ringless hand in his.

'What? Oh, yes, of course. What would she think?'

'Nothing, I expect. She's probably been doing it herself all afternoon.'

Claire leant forward and glanced at the woman's husband, a small neat man in suit and tie, his legs crossed, white ankles showing.

'I doubt it somehow,' she whispered, suppressing a giggle. 'Separate beds years ago, I should think.'

It was an excellent production – dramatic, moving, funny, and quite frightening in parts, especially the scenes involving Captain Hook. The curtain fell for the interval just after his capture of

Wendy and the other children, with Peter Pan asleep at the edge of the stage, a bottle of poison lying where his medicine had been, substituted by the pirates.

'Come on,' said Peter, his hand still covering hers. 'I've ordered drinks. We can leave our coats here.'

She fell as they reached the top of the stairs leading to the bar. Peter, who was close behind, lunged forward and caught her.

'Are you OK? Claire? Claire!'

There was no answer. He lowered her gently to the floor, scrabbling for her wrist, trying to remember whether one felt a pulse with one's thumb or fingers. There was something odd about her face, something different, he could not say exactly what. Behind him, people pushed and jostled, trying to see what had happened.

'What is it?' 'Someone's fainted.' 'It's an old woman. She's hit her head.' 'I don't know. I can't see. I think someone's hurt themselves.' 'Is anyone a nurse or doctor?' 'Where are the first aid people?' 'Don't push . . . there's no point pushing. I can't move forward. Someone's fallen over.'

One voice was louder and more forceful than the others.

'I thought she looked pale. She was white as a sheet. I noticed it when she came in. She was sitting right next to me.'

Peter glanced up. It was the woman with the purple lipstick. She had pushed her way to the front, was coming forward, bending over.

'What happened? Did she trip?'

'I don't know . . . I don't think so . . . she just went . . .'

'She's probably just fainted. It's very hot in there. It always is in theatres. Someone's gone for the first aid person. I wouldn't worry. She'll come round in a few minutes.'

She moved back and began to tell another woman how Claire's hand had been clammy, how she had felt it when she had passed her a chocolate, how she had wondered if she was OK at the time.

There it was. Thank God! He had found it. Her heart was beating. She was still alive. Someone pushed against him, treading on his fingers.

'Could you keep back please. Please! Don't crowd her. Could you give her some air.'

A woman in navy-blue trousers and cardigan knelt beside him.

'I'm Pat. I'm from the British Red Cross,' she announced, opening Claire's mouth and peering in as she spoke. 'Can you tell me what happened?'

'She just collapsed.'

'Did she bang her head?'

'No. No, I caught her in time.'

The woman bent over and put her face close to Claire's. Then she put two fingers against her neck.

'Is she taking medication for anything? Do you know if she's got a heart condition or anything like that?'

'No, she's got nothing wrong with her heart. Not as far as I know. But she has had two strokes,' said Peter.

The woman frowned.

'You don't think . . . you mean . . . but . . . but . . . but she's been fine all day. There's been nothing wrong with her. Absolutely nothing.'

'I don't know,' said the woman gently, covering Claire with a blanket. 'It's a possibility. There aren't usually any warning signs.'

Another woman dressed identically came up, spoke briefly to the first woman, and went off again.

'I've asked her to send for an ambulance,' explained Pat. 'It shouldn't take long. We're not far from the hospital here.'

She leant over Claire again and began to talk to her in a low, reassuring voice, explaining what was happening, how someone had sent for an ambulance, how they would soon have help. Peter stared helplessly at Claire's body, at the hair he had stroked, the arms he had kissed, the lips he had pressed. In his hand lay the crumpled ticket for their interval drinks. Behind him, the woman with the purple lipstick told someone how hot Claire's hand had been. 'Burning, it was. Red-hot. I wondered then if there was something the matter.'

Let her open her eyes, he prayed. Please let her open her eyes. Let her open her eyes and look round and ask what is happening, why she is lying on the floor. Let her say it was just the heat. The heat and the queueing to get out of the auditorium. That she must have fainted. That she hadn't said so before but she did faint quite often. Please let her say that. Please.

50

He sat in the corridor waiting, waiting for her to come back, for someone to say something, to tell him what had happened.

They had taken her away, had wheeled her up the corridor, said they needed to do a brain scan. A brain scan. Scan. Brain. The words repeated in his head like the fall of an axe.

A nurse had brought him some coffee in a plastic cup. He had not drunk it and it lay untouched on the floor by his feet – cold and brown. From time to time, the doors at one end of the corridor swung open and someone walked by. Sometimes they glanced at him, sometimes not. They must be used to people waiting, he thought.

He glanced at his watch. Half past ten. The performance would have finished by now. The audience would have gone home, back to their beds and Ovaltine, to their cats waiting to be fed, to their normal lives. The woman with the purple lipstick was maybe putting on cold cream, sitting in a nightdress in front of a mirror, saying, 'I thought there was something wrong. As soon as I saw her, I knew she wasn't well. Like ice, her hands were. I almost jumped out of my skin when I passed her the chocolates. And you know how hot it was in there.'

He needed to go to the lavatory, to urinate, but he could not because if he did, they might bring her back, they might look for him, she might ask for him, they might say he had gone, she might think he did not love her.

The door swung open and Peter looked up. No. It was the man in overalls who had walked past a few minutes earlier. He was carrying a bag now. A black plastic bag – like a bin liner only smaller – scrunched up at the top. He walked quickly, the rubber soles of his shoes squeaking on the lino floor, and disappeared round the corner. Peter shivered and put his hands in his coat pockets. Beside him, lying on the bench was Claire's coat and handbag. It was not her usual handbag but a different one, one he had not seen before, a small black velvet evening bag with bead embroidery at the front.

The door opened again and the nurse appeared, the nurse who had given him the coffee. Peter stood up. He had to know. If she wouldn't tell him, he would ask someone else. He could not go on waiting like this, not knowing, wondering, imagining.

'They're bringing her back now,' she said before he could say anything. 'If you'd like to follow me.'

She led him back through the swing doors, down a corridor, through more swing doors and into a room with a sofa and two armchairs.

'If you'd like to wait in here.'

Peter stood in the doorway, staring dumbly at the sofa.

'But where . . . where . . . where is she? I thought . . . I thought you were taking me to her. She is . . . she's not . . . she . . . she . . . ?'

'The doctor will be along in a minute or so. He'll be able to answer your questions,' said the nurse soothingly, taking Claire's coat and bag and hanging them on a peg on the wall. After she had left, Peter took them off the peg and hugged them, rocking to and fro, squeezing them tight.

The doctor said Claire had had a stroke. The scan showed extensive brain damage. A clot had formed in a damaged blood vessel in her neck and blocked the flow of blood to part of her brain, paralysing the left side of her body. It was not possible to be accurate about her chances of recovery, he said. The stroke had been severe but people had had worse strokes and still recovered. If she were to recover, she would be unlikely to regain full use of the limbs on the left side of her body. Most of the recovery usually took place in the first few days. However, there were always exceptions.

There were four beds in the intensive care unit, all occupied. Claire was in the first one. Her nurse, Sally, a girl with straight blue-black hair suggesting a Chinese mother or father, told Peter what the various attachments to her body were for.

'Unfortunately, there's not a lot we can do for her in the way of treatment. Not at this stage. The main thing we're doing is monitoring her, controlling her blood pressure, making sure there are no complications. She can't swallow yet so we're having to feed her intravenously. That's what that's for,' she said, pointing at a tube.

He stood at the top of the bed, near her head, and looked down. The left side of her jaw was twisted slightly and her mouth lop-sided, one corner turned down, the other turned up, as if she was pulling a silly face. Her eyes were shut.

The nurse said he could stay the night if he wanted. There were rooms for relatives of patients in intensive care, she said. They would call him if there was a change in her condition, if that was what he wanted.

'I'd rather stay here if I can. Is that allowed?'

The nurse said it was.

'Can she hear me? Can she hear what I'm saying?'

'Your guess is as good as mine,' said the nurse, bluntly but not unkindly. 'It's impossible to say. She might do. You never know.'

She drew up a chair so that he could sit down and asked if he wanted a drink. She was going to make herself a cup of tea, she said. She had not had a drink since coming on at eight.

'Can I touch her? Can I hold her hand?'

'Yes. As long as you don't move her,' she said. 'It's important to keep the arm straight and the leg bent. That way, they won't stiffen up.'

She crossed to the other side of the room and Peter reached out, over the bar at the side of the bed, and touched her left hand. It was warm but soft and floppy, not like it had felt earlier when he had held it in the theatre. He stroked it gently. Was it his fault, he wondered? Had it all been too much for her – the meal, making love, going out to the theatre?

He glanced across at the nurse. She was talking to one of the other nurses, stirring something in a cup, taking no notice of him. He closed his eyes, took a deep breath and began to talk.

I can see my life. See it spread before me. Scraps of memory pasted together, overlapping, like a collage, like the one I made for Peter. The tea party in the garden when I was five. The hot prickly feel of the grass against my bare legs. That first night in Oxford after the honeymoon, leaning out of the window in the bedroom, discovering there were no clean sheets on the bed. My mother. My mother in the kitchen kneading dough for bread. The look of her arms with the sleeves rolled up to the elbow, the white of the flour showing up the brown, hard strength of her muscles. My mother in Coventry. That walk in the rain after lunch. My mother dead. Reading this in the telegram sent to the rented house in Bradford. Her things in front of me. The new coat. The black velvet evening bag. The photo of me with the wigwam.

Miss Flowers is there, and her orchard. The one her father planted for her. So is Iris. That day in the summer when we sat under the cherry tree and she told me how she wanted to change things, to help make people's lives better, to make a difference. So too is Peter. Meeting him for the first time. Worrying about the wrinkles in my tights at the ankle. Biting the coffee bean he left behind in the conservatory. The trip to Lindisfarne. The day we drove to St Margaret's and he told me about being a Japanese prisoner during the war. Kissing him. Drinking coffee in his room. Telling him about Harry.

How much joy he has given me! I wish I could tell him this. I wish I had told him. That I had made my feelings clearer. Told him I loved him. But I didn't and now I can't. He wants me to open my eyes, to show that I can hear him, to move something – anything – so that he will know he's not talking in vain. I have tried. I have told my fingers to move, my eyelids to lift, but nothing has happened. My brain and my body are no longer on speaking terms. He is quiet now. I can't hear anything. Maybe he has gone to lie down for a few hours as the nurse suggested. No, there he is. He is tired now. I can hear that. Hear the tiredness in his voice. He is telling me about the house again, the house he will buy so that we can live together, so that we can be open, so that we do not have to pretend. I want to tell him that it would not work, that we could not manage on our own. Not now. That he does not realise how much help I need on the days when my hands are bad. He would get bored. Bored and frustrated. I tell him that, I say it, but I know that the words do not come out, that he hears nothing. It would be better for us to find another home, I say. A home that takes couples. Unmarried ones, in particular. I laugh when I say this. I hear myself laughing like you can hear yourself laughing in a dream. No, still nothing. He does not laugh back. Clearly, my laugh was silent.

I am glad that this will not go on for long. That it cannot go on. That it will end soon. I hang on though so that I can hear him say he loves me. Surely, he will say it soon. Surely, he cannot not say it. Not if he loves me. I thought he was going to say it just now but then the nurse came up and he stopped.

I think she's gone now. Yes, she has. He's talking again. But the words sound different, strange, as if he's talking in a foreign language. They are fainter too. So am I. I am going. Peter, I am going and I do not know if you love me. Please say it. Quickly. Quickly. Before I go. Please. Please.

52 ∫

'What's happened? What's wrong? What are you doing?'

No one answered. The noise went on, the noise which had brought first one nurse, then two, then three running to her side. It was a warning noise. He could tell that. It was high-pitched and urgent – like the crying of a young baby.

A man came in – the doctor who had spoken to Peter earlier. The nurses made way for him. Then they closed behind him. He could no longer see her.

The doctor said something. He looked at the machine. Then he bent down. They were doing something to her. He could see that now. There was something on her chest. Something over her mouth as well. The doctor straightened up. He could no longer see. The noise went on and on. What was happening? Could she still hear? Would this be the last thing she heard – this awful, wailing screech? The doctor said something else and shook his head and pulled at something.

The noise stopped. They turned. One of the nurses began to draw a curtain round the bed. The doctor touched him lightly on the arm.

'I'm sorry,' he said. 'We did our best. We tried to save her.'

Peter brushed the arm away.

'No! No! No!'

He shook his head, buried it in his hands, rocked backwards and forwards.

'She can't go. She can't. No! No!'

He took her head. He cupped it gently in his hands and lifted it off the pillow. He kissed her forehead. Then her mouth. Then her neck. Slowly at first then faster and faster until he was sobbing, hugging her to him, the tears spilling down his cheeks.

'I love you, Claire. I loved you! I loved you! I loved you!'

The doctor turned and left. So did two of the nurses. The remaining nurse finishing drawing the curtain. Then she too left. Inside, behind the curtain, Peter said those tired, old wonderful words over and over again.

53

'So she never knew? She never knew that he loved her?' asked the young girl.

'No,' said the old woman.

'How awful! What a sad story!'

'Yes, I suppose it is.'

'And then? What happened next? Was that when you went back to Wales?' asked the young girl, brightening up.

'Yes. I left my job and my boyfriend and I went home to my parents, to your great-grandparents. I did nothing for a bit, just moped around, getting in my mother's way, and then one day she said there were some elections coming up for Euro MPs. Why didn't I stand as a candidate, she said. She meant it as a joke really but I took her seriously . . .'

'Yes and you won. You were the youngest Euro MP ever to be elected. And then later you became the first European president, didn't you? Didn't you, Gran?'

'Yes,' said the old woman, smiling at the young girl's enthusiasm to tell the story herself, to take it over, to make it her story.

'I think it was the languages which made them choose me,' she went on, more to herself than to the young girl.

'The other candidates spoke only English. They were all men as well. I remember that. I remember them looking at me and thinking, "Oh well, that's one less to worry about. She won't win. She can't win. She's too young. They won't choose her." That was the first thing I said at the interview. I asked them not to judge me either by my youth or my sex. And they didn't. To their credit, they didn't. I just wish she'd been there to see it, that she'd known. She wanted so much to matter, to contribute, to make a difference – and she did! I'd never have done it without her. But she never knew. She died without knowing. She died thinking her life had been wasted – that she had lived in vain.'

'But if she hadn't died, you wouldn't have done it, you wouldn't have left – that's what you said,' said the young girl, looking puzzled.

'Yes,' agreed the old woman.

'So she had to die,' said the girl with the ruthless logic of the young.

'Yes, I suppose so. For things to happen the way they have done, she had to, yes.'

'And Peter?' asked the young girl, anxious to tie up the loose ends, for the end to be a proper one. 'What happened to him?'

'He went to Kenya and painted pictures of the sea. He became quite well-known towards the end. Quite famous.'

'Is that one of his pictures, that one above the fireplace in your sitting room? That one where the sky is half dark and half light?'

'Yes, that's his. He painted that soon after she died. Before he left for Kenya.'

'And your boyfriend? Quintin? What did he do?' asked the young girl, hurrying her on, anxious to be off now, to be doing something different, something new.

'He met another girl soon after I left and they married and had children. Three, I think, or maybe four. I forget. Later, he went back to college and became a chartered surveyor and later still he went into politics, local politics. He became a district councillor. His mother used to write to me. That's how I know.'

The younger woman who had appeared earlier, came out and began calling again.

'Time for bed, darling. Go on. Don't keep your mother waiting,' said the old woman.

The young girl stood up and put her arms round the old woman's neck.

'Night night, Gran.'

'Night night, darling.'

'Gran, tomorrow, shall we go to the park? I'll show you how I can do the obstacle course, shall I? I can do it all now, you know, even the bit where you have to balance.'

'Yes, OK. Yes, we'll do that.'

The young girl began to walk up the garden through the apple trees towards her mother. The old woman closed her eyes. In her mind there was a picture of a young girl, younger than her granddaughter, about five perhaps, playing in a garden in the sun. She did not know who the girl was, she had never seen her before but the picture was so intense, so vivid, she must have seen her somewhere. She had black springy hair and she was playing with marbles, burying them under rose petals. The hot grass was prickly against her bare legs. Somewhere else, out of sight, there was the sound of women's voices, polite and tinkly.

The old woman leant back and sighed. Beyond her, at the top of the garden, her daughter continued to call.

'Claire! Claire! Claire!'